Welcome back to Memphis, where when the sun goes down, shit starts popping off. The three major female gangs ruling the gritty Mid-South are the **Queen Gs,** who keep it hood for the **Black Gangster Disciples;** the **Flowers,** who rule with the **Vice Lords;** and the **Crippettes,** mistresses of the **Grape Street Crips**.

Rules are: there are no damn rules. Survive the game the best way you know how. If you want to be a boss, show no mercy. Memphis's divas are as hard and ruthless as the men they hold down. Your biggest mistake is to get in their way.

Also by De'nesha Diamond

The Diva Series
Hustlin' Divas
Street Divas
Gangsta Divas

Anthologies
Heartbreaker (with Erick S. Gray and Nichelle Walker)
Heist (with Kiki Swinson)
A Gangster and a Gentleman (with Kiki Swinson)
Fistful of Benjamins (with Kiki Swinson)

Published by Kensington Publishing Corp.

Boss Divas

DE'NESHA
DIAMOND

KENSINGTON PUBLISHING CORP.

www.kensingtonbooks.com

The Memphis struggle continues . . .

Acknowledgments

Special thanks to our heavenly father, who blessed me long before I had the common sense to realize it. To Granny, my baby Alice, who inspires me, though it's from up above now. My sister, Channon "Chocolate Drop" Kennedy—you're still the best. My beautiful niece, Courtney—I love you.

To Selena James for having the patience of Job while I navigate through some turbulent times.

And of course the fans who have been loving the series from day one. You don't know how much your love and support have sustained me.

Best of Love,
De'nesha

Cast of Characters

Ta'Shara Murphy was once a straight-A student with dreams of getting the hell out of Memphis, but she took a detour on her dreams when she fell in love with Raymond "Profit" Lewis, the younger brother of Fat Ace. The war between the Vice Lords and her sister's set, the Gangster Disciples, puts her between a rock and a hard place. When she failed to take her sister LeShelle's warning to heart, she was unprepared for the consequences.

LeShelle Murphy is Queen G for the Memphis Gangster Disciples. Not only does she love her man, Python, but she also loves the power her position affords her and there is nothing that she won't do to ensure that she never loses any of it—that includes doing whatever it takes to keep her younger sister in line and handling the many chicken heads pecking at her heels.

Willow "Lucifer" Washington is Fat Ace's right hand and as deadly as they come. A true ride-or-die chick to her core. The latest explosion between the sets will have her true feelings bubbling to the top, and when she's forced to step up and lead, she proves that you don't need a set of balls to wash the streets with blood.

Maybelline "Momma Peaches" Carver, Python's beloved aunt, believes and acts as if she's still wildin' out in her twenties. With an arrest record a mile long, Peaches is right in the thick of things, but when old family secrets start coming home to roost, her partying days may be far behind her.

Shariffa Rodgers is the ex-wifey of Gangster Disciple Python. She was kicked off her throne and nearly beaten to death after getting caught creeping. Now married to Grape Street Crip leader Lynch, Shariffa not only wants payback, she wants her new crew to take over the entire street game.

Ja'nay "Trigger" Clark, Shariffa's right-hand chick, proves that there's nothing she won't do for her girl. But one hit in the Vice Lords' territory lands her in Lucifer's crosshairs—the last place anyone wants to be.

Captain Hydeya Hawkins is the new Memphis police captain unraveling the secrets and corruption of her predecessor. But the straight-arrow cop has a few secrets of her own.

Purgatory

1

Ta'Shara

"**S**TOP THE FUCKING CAR!"

Profit slams on the brakes while I bolt out of the passenger car door and race into the night toward my foster parents' burning house.

"TRACEE! REGGIE!" *They're not in there. Please, God. Don't let them be in there.* "TRACEE! REGGIE!"

"Ta'Shara, wait up," Profit yells. His long strides eat up the distance between us even as I shove my way through the city's emergency responders. I've never seen flames stretch so high or felt such intense heat. Still, none of that shit stops me. In my delusional mind, there is still time to get them out of there.

"Hey, lady. You can't go in there," someone shouts and makes a grab for me.

As I draw closer to the front porch, Profit is able to wrap one of his powerful arms around my waist and lift me off my feet. "Baby, stop. You can't go in there."

"Let me go!" My legs pedal in the air as I stretch uselessly for the door. "TRACEE! REGGIE!" My screams rake my throat raw.

Profit drags me away from the growing flames.

Men in uniform rush over to us. I don't know who they

are and I don't care. I just need to know one thing. "Where are my parents? Did they make it out?"

"Ma'am, calm down. Please tell me your name."

"WHERE ARE THEY?"

"Ma'am—"

"ANSWER ME, DAMMIT!"

"C'mon, man," Profit says. "Give my girl something."

The fireman draws a deep breath and then drops a bomb that changes my life forever.

"The neighbors reported the fire. Right now, I'm not aware of anyone making it out of the house. I'm sorry."

"NOOOOOOO!" I collapse in Profit's arms. He hauls me up against his six-three frame and I lay my head on his broad chest. Before, I found comfort in his strong embrace, but not tonight. I sob uncontrollably as pain overwhelms me, but then I make out a familiar car down the street.

"Oh. My. God."

Profit tenses. "What?"

My eyes aren't deceiving me. Sitting behind the wheel of her burgundy Crown Victoria is LeShelle with a slow smile creeping across her face. She forms a gun with her hand and pretends to fire at us.

We're next.

LeShelle tosses back her head and, despite the siren's wail, the roaring fire, and the chaos around me, that bitch's maniacal laugh rings in my ears.

How much more of this shit am I going to take? When will this fuckin' bullshit end?

BOOM!

The crowd gasps when windows explode from the top floor of the house, but my gaze never waivers from LeShelle. My tears dry up as anger grips me.

She did this shit. I don't need a jury to tell me that the bitch is guilty as hell. How long has she been threatening the Douglases' lives? Why in the hell didn't I believe that she would follow through?

LeShelle has proven her ruthlessness time after time. This fucking "Gangster Disciples versus the Vice Lords" shit ain't a game to her. It's a way of life. And she doesn't give a fuck who she hurts.

My blood boils and all at once everything burst out of me. I wrench away from Profit's protective arms and take off toward LeShelle in a rage.

"I'M GOING TO FUCKING KILL YOU!"

"Ta'Shara, no!" Profit shouts.

I ignore him as I race toward LeShelle's car. My hot tears burn tracks down my face.

LeShelle laughs in and then pulls off from the curb, but not before I'm able to pound my fist against the trunk.

Profit's arms wrap back around my waist, but I kick out and connect with LeShelle's taillight and shatter that mutherfucka. The small wave of satisfaction I get is quickly erased when her piece-of-shit car burps out a black cloud of exhaust.

"NO! Don't let her get away. No!"

"Ta'Shara, please. Not now. Let it go!"

Let it go? I round on Profit. "How the fuck can you say that shit?"

BOOM!

More windows explode, drawing my attention back to the only place that I've ever called home. My heart claws its way out of my chest as orange flames and black smoke lick the sky.

My legs give out and my knees kiss the concrete, and all the while Profit's arms remain locked around me. I can't hear what he's saying because my sobs drown him out.

"This is all my fault," tumbles over my tongue. I conjure up an image of Tracee and Reggie—the last time I saw them. It's a horrible memory. Everyone was angry and everyone said things that . . . can never be taken back.

Grief consumes me. I squeeze my eyes tight and cling to the ghosts inside of my head. "I'm sorry. I'm so sorry."

Profit's arms tighten. I melt in his arms even though I want to lash out. *Isn't it his fault my foster parents roasted in that house, too?* When the question crosses my mind, I crumble from the weight of my shame.

I'm to blame. No one else.

A heap in the center of the street, I lay my head against Profit's chest again and take in the horrific sight through a steady sheen of tears. The Douglases were good people. All they wanted was the best for me and for me to believe in myself. They would've done the same for LeShelle if she gave them the chance.

LeShelle fell in love with the streets and the make-believe power of being the head bitch of the Queen Gs. I didn't want anything to do with any of that bullshit, but it didn't matter. I'm viewed as GD property by blood, and the shit hit the fan when I fell in love with Profit—a Vice Lord by blood. Back then Profit wasn't a soldier yet. But our being together was taken as a sign of disrespect. LeShelle couldn't let it slide.

However, the harder I fight the streets' politics, the deeper I'm dragged into her bullshit world of gangs and violence.

"I should have killed her when I had the chance." If I had, Tracee and Reggie would still be alive. "She won't get away with this," I vow. "I'm going to kill her if it's the last thing I do."

2

LeShelle

"Rot in hell, bitch." I jam on the accelerator. My clit thumps at the sight of the bright, orange flames engulfing the Douglases' house, which is still in my rearview. Watching Ta'Shara's hysterics almost felt as good as when I ordered June Bug and Kane to strap Tracee and Reggie down to the bed so I could douse their asses with gasoline. The only thing that could've made the night more perfect would be to have my precious lil sister roasting right next to them.

The bitch doesn't know how much I wish I could pump the brakes and finish what I drove out here to do. That's all right. I'm going to get my chance. The GD initials are still carved on Ta'Shara's ass, which means I still own it. I won't stop coming for her until she's being lowered into the ground. I know that shit is cold, but whatever love or loyalty I had for her is long gone.

While the tall flames stretch to the sky, laughter rumbles from my chest. The number of games I'm about to play with this dumb bitch multiplies in my head.

I corner onto Poplar Avenue, and June Bug and Kane's Expedition falls in line behind me. The sight of them takes the edge off my revenge high and plunges me into a pool of irritation. I hate having babysitters.

My cell phone rings from the car's charger.

Unknown caller.

Bullshit. It's Python calling me from a burner. No doubt June Bug's blabbing ass has already called in and tattled. Well, fuck him—and fuck Python, too. I'm so through with his ass I don't know what to do.

Instead of sitting on our throne on Shotgun Row, our asses are hiding out from the police because his dumbass got too hot and snuffed one of his chicken-heads-slash-baby-mommas. Too bad her ass was also a fucking a cop. And not just *any cop.* She was the police captain's daughter. I mean, you got to have a certain talent to fuck up that bad. Granted, some of the heat has cooled off because people believe that Python is dead—supposedly killed in a fiery car crash off the Old Memphis Bridge a few months back.

But Python has nine lives—that or the devil keeps spitting his ass back out.

The phone stops ringing and the call rolls to voice mail. I know I'm gonna hear about the shit. Python always has a shit fit when I don't answer his calls, but I'll deal with his ass later. Reaching for the blunt I left in the ashtray, I quickly put fire to the tip and fill my lungs to the max. I hold that shit in until my brain fogs and my eyelids droop.

Despite feeling copasetic, I review the other shit I gotta deal with—like that grimy flower Qiana. Bitch double-crossed me. The deal was that I murk a snitch within my own ranks and in exchange she dusts off Python's latest pregnant side bitch, Yolanda. Simple. How in the fuck did this bitch fuck that shit up? I gotta see on the news that Qiana snatched the baby out of the corpse? Of course I wanted the little fucker dead, too. That shit should have been obvious. If Python even suspects that his baby is out there somewhere, he'll comb every street looking for it.

Shit. He's already chasing after one ghost—his long-lost brother, Mason. Somehow, someway, he's convinced himself that Fat Ace, the ex-leader of the Vice Lords, is his brother. All because of some birthmark.

I'm not going to be sucked into the land of make-believe with Python's ass. It don't matter anyway. Fat Ace—Mason—whatever the fuck his name is—is dead. End of story.

Python needs to get his mind right—and that don't mean putting his shady-ass cousin, Diesel, on the throne. I met him earlier tonight. He may be fine as fuck, a six-four, green-eyed brotha with his name tatted around his neck, but I don't trust his ass worth a damn. He'll rule these damn streets over my dead body. Bet that shit.

I puff out a thick cloud of smoke while my mind floats higher.

Riiiiinnnng! Riiiinnng!

Unknown caller.

I take another deep toke and let the call roll to voice mail again. The last few minutes, I coast the dark streets in silence. When I arrive at my and Python's temporary crib, I kill the engine and think about rolling another blunt. I ain't in the mood to deal with my husband's shit right now.

Husband. I'm still not used to the word.

I stare at the rock on my finger. I can't decide whether it's been worth it. *What's the point of being a queen if you don't have a throne?*

June Bug and Kane pull up at the curb and shut off their engine.

Python peeks through the venetian blinds.

Shit.

Abandoning the idea of rolling another fat one, I climb out of the car and head into the house. The front door is snatched open before I lay a hand on the knob. One of Python's thick, muscular arms jerks me into the house. I open my mouth, but my head rocks back before I actually hear the *SLAP!*

I crash into the wall behind me, and then slide down to the floor while blood fills my mouth.

"Where in the hell have you been? I've been calling you for hours."

Python growls, towering over me. His bulky chest flexes while he pumps his fists at his sides. "I got June Bug and Kane blowing me up, but you can't seem to answer my calls?"

I spit the blood from my mouth. "I must've had it on vibrate," I lie, peeling myself off the floor.

"You're a muthafuckin' lie." Python's face twists up.

"Whatever. Believe what you want." I press my fingers up to my lips to feel the damage. "What's the big deal? When I left here, you had your head so far up Diesel's ass, I didn't think you needed me."

His black gaze rakes me up and down. I stare back. Python has a face only a mother could love: a black gargoyle right down to the snake-forked tongue. Physically, his shit is on point; but the side bitches who drop their panties for this nigga are drawn to the power he represents—my ass included. I'm not cold and heartless. I do feel some kind of way about his ass. Shit. It might even be called love—but I love his power more.

"I ain't no chump nigga," Python says. "Unless you're dead or bleeding in the streets, you pick up the phone when I call."

"What's the fuckin' problem? Your lil babysitters reported my every damn move anyway." I test my luck by bumping his shoulder and marching around him.

"You're damn right they check-in—that's what your ass needs to be doing. These fuckin' streets are hot. I can't be up in this bitch tryna make moves *and* be worrying about you at the same damn time."

I smile in the middle of his barking. "You were worried?"

Python paces like he's tryna wear a hole in the carpet. "Shelle, I ain't got time for fuckin' games. Brothas around me dropping and disappearing into thin air: Momma Peaches, Melanie, Mason, Yolanda—the baby."

Aw shit. Here he comes whining about that damn jizz baby. When I get my hands on that damn Qiana . . .

"Melanie hardly counts since you offed the bitch yourself," I remind him and head into the living room.

"Don't start that shit."

"Start what?" I ask, innocently. I plop down in front of the coffee table that's stacked with bricks of cocaine, cash, guns, pill baggies, and vials of shit I ain't never seen before. I ignore that hard shit and go straight for the blueberry Mary Jane.

"What happened after you left Passions?" he asks.

I grab the package of cigars. "You already know what happened. Your boys told you."

"I want you to tell me."

I ignore him and continue making my shit.

He continues to interrogate. "How in the hell you end up burning down your sister's crib and leaving Kookie as part of the barbecue?"

"Why are you asking me about my business when you keep me out of yours?"

"What the fuck are you talking about?"

"Diesel! Are you seriously going to give him the keys to the throne? You're just going to give up? I mean, I'm a boss bitch. I make sure all these punk-ass muthafuckas out here know it. Kookie and her nigga McGriff had been playin' our asses, and making deals on the side—the situation needed to be addressed—and I handled that shit."

A doorknob rattles. I cock my head to the side to see Diesel's pretty ass exit the bathroom. I didn't know that his ass was still here.

"Damn, nigga. You dropping logs or eavesdroppin' back there?" I ask.

Diesel smirks, but his greenish-blue eyes signal that he's far from being amused. "I see you found your way back home. Cuz was worried."

"Speaking of home, why don't you carry your shady ass back to Atlanta?" I challenge, matching his smirk. I want it crystal damn clear that I don't like his honey-colored ass—I don't give a damn what his reputation is down in the A. All I know is he ain't taking what's mine.

"Damn, Shelle. What the fuck is up with you?" Python scolds. "D is fam. You need to treat him as such."

"Family, huh?" Diesel and I glare at each other. "Yeah. I can do that. I just *love* family."

"*Annnd* on that note, I think it's time that I head out." Diesel winks.

I toss him the middle finger.

Python hands over the joint and climbs back onto his feet. "A'ight, cuz. Sorry about that. She must be PMSing."

No, this nigga didn't.

"We gonna hook up tomorrow, right?" The men slap palms, and bump shoulders.

"Two o'clock sharp," Diesel confirms and then turns.

Python follows him, pounding Diesel's broad back while he escorts him to the door.

I put fire to the tip of my blunt, though my lips are still throbbing like a muthafucka. My gaze tracks the cousins across the small house. All kinds of alarms sound off inside my head. This muthafucka is too pretty, too smooth, and too fuckin' powerful to be trusted. What the hell is my man doing, handing over the keys to the throne without firing a single bullet?

This shit is fucked up.

At the door, Diesel turns one last time and smiles. "It was nice meeting you, LeShelle," he says.

"Uh-huh."

He laughs and then slips out.

Python closes and locks the door behind his cousin before strutting his ass back into the living room.

I shake my head. "Damn shame."

He huffs out a long breath. "What?"

"You're making a big mistake."

"I got this."

"Do you?" I challenge.

"Yeah." He reaches over and takes the blunt right out of my mouth so he can toke on it for a few puffs. "Shit on our end is sloppy as fuck—has been for a little while. My soldiers are wide open and protection is close to nonexistent. That bitch Lucifer and the Vice Lords are feasting on my fuckin' streets and tagging so many niggas hell can't keep up." He takes another hit, but it doesn't settle his nerves. "Nah. If I'm going to settle this shit, I'm gonna need a solid nigga I can trust."

I laugh. "And you think that you can trust a muthafucka from *Atlanta?* Since when? Those niggas ain't got no fuckin' home trainin'. We don't need him."

"*I* trust Diesel. That's all that matters. We're going to settle some scores and then he's going to hold shit down while we go to Mexico and chill out for a while—there's too much heat around here."

"Mexico?" My eyes bug. "You don't know a goddamn thing about Mexico—other than they chop off muthafuckas' heads when they step out of line. What the fuck are we going to do in Mexico?"

"Diesel has a connect with the Sinaloa Cartel. We'll work that shit and establish some new ties. Within two to three years we can have something jump off that's bigger than what Memphis has ever seen."

"The *Sinaloa Cartel?* Wait. There's like a billion people in that country. They don't need some confused, country nigga doin' shit for them—other than slinging their shit up here. No. We keep our asses right here and fight for what's ours."

"Squash it," Python warns, backing away. "Your mouth is reckless right now."

"Me?" I explode out of my seat. "This whole situation is reckless? You want to know why? Because of *you! You* are the reason that we are in this piece-of-shit house in the middle of no-goddamn-where. *You* couldn't keep your dick in your pants and so you let some fuckin' pig bitch play you. Then *you* got hot and murked her ass—not thinking her damn daddy was gonna chase us off our throne. Now we're stuck playing *Where's Waldo?* with the muthafuckin' police and FBI. And you wanna give me shit about my mouth being reckless. Get the fuck out of here with that." I stomp away, my high blown. Fuck. At this point it would take a horse tranquilizer to chill me out.

"Where the fuck are you going?" Python marches behind me.

"I'm going to take a shower to wash off all this shit you're shoveling around this bitch."

He snatches my arm and spins me around. "Damn it, Shelle, I'm not done talking. Don't fuckin' turn your back on me." His fist flies toward my head.

I brace myself.

He punches a hole into the wall inches from my face.

I stare dead in his eyes. "Are you done with your temper tantrum?"

"Goddamn it, Shelle. Is it too much for you to hold a nigga down? You wanna be queen and rule shit, but the crown has a price. We ain't always gonna be on top. You gotta be willing to get into the gutter and ride shit out some times."

"Don't talk to me like I'm brand new," I snap. "Just be fucking real with me. If you don't know what to do next, then say that shit. If you feel the walls are closing in on you, admit it. If you're feeling all kinds of ways because you lost so many people, then let's sit down and deal with it. But whatever the fuck you do, don't tell me you traded your dick in for a pussy and that you think the best thing for us to do is to run like slob bitches out of this muthafucka. Cuz I ain't down with that shit."

I chest-bump his ass, but it's like bumping steel and it doesn't give me any additional room. It doesn't matter. I'm heated and determined to get his ass to see reason. "We stay. We fight, god-damn it. That shit is real, that shit is life. You don't get your fuckin' feelings tripped up over nobody in this game. Fuck them dead niggas—and fuck you if you're afraid to ride this shit until the world blows."

Python's face purples. "I ain't afraid of shit."

"Ain't nobody gonna believe that shit if we turn tail and run to Mexico. Trust and believe."

"Why the fuck can't you understand?" he huffs.

"Oh, I understand. You just need to understand that I ain't going no-muthafuckin'-where. Adios."

Python wraps his large hand around my throat. "You will do exactly what I tell you to do," he growls.

"I'm not leaving Memphis," I rasp with what little oxygen I have.

He squeezes tighter. "You always gotta try me. You know how easy it would be for me to snap your goddamn neck right now?"

"Do what you gotta do."

BAM!

He slams my head against the wall—a signature move for him that makes stars dance around my head. "I tell you what's real. As long as you got my last name, I fuckin' own you. You got that shit?"

BAM!

More stars. But I'm still running on adrenaline. I hock up some spit and launch that shit in his face.

"Fuckin' bitch!" A right hook sends me crashing to the floor. My jaw feels like it's been unhinged and blood pools into my mouth. Before I can react, Python is back on me like white on rice. My fists are smaller, but they pack a powerful punch as I land one blow after another. But Python isn't interested in fighting me anymore, he's ducking and dodging as he yanks my clothes off.

"I fuckin' own you, bitch. I fuckin' own you," he growls.

I'm as bad as he is because somewhere along the way my anger has turned into lust. I'm on fire for his ass and I start wrestling his shit off, too. When his monster cock slams inside my pussy, I damn near come on the spot. There ain't no fuck-in' foreplay. He's murdering my shit and rattling my teeth.

"Say it, bitch. Tell me who this shit belongs to."

Our bodies pound so hard I revel in the pain and pleasure.

"Say it, goddamn it," Python demands, jacking my legs up over my head. At no point does his hand ease its grip on my neck. The lack of oxygen intensifies the nut building in my clit.

"SAY IT!"

"I—I—" My brain goes dead. I forgot what jumpstarted this shit. All I know is that I don't want it to end.

"Who's your nigga, Shelle? Whose pussy is this?"

When I still can't answer, he pulls his dick out until just the mushroomed head teases my pussy lips. "Whose is it, Shelle?"

"Yours." I grab his ass. "Don't stop."

"Nah. You're a bad bitch. Maybe I should leave you to fin-ish off by your damn self." He glides his cock over the top of my clit. "Would you like that?"

"Pythoooon," I whine.

He dips his dick in for one thrust and then backs off again. "Let me hear you say it."

Dip. Thrust. Stop.

Going out of my mind, I wrap my legs around his waist in an attempt to fuck *him* instead.

Python presses me back to the floor. "You don't want your man, baby? Huh?"

Dip. Thrust. Stop.

"Y-yes." I wiggle my ass and pound on his chest. "Give it to me."

"Then tell me."

Dip. Thrust. Stop.

If my mind was right and I wasn't horny as hell, I'd hold out longer, but at this point I'm one hundred percent his bitch. I tell him what he wants to hear. "It's yours. Yours," I admit.

Dip. Thrust. Stop.

"Mine? You sure?"

Dip. Thrust. Stop.

"Yes! Yes! Stop playing and fuck me," I shout.

"There you go again." His dick dives back in and then drills me into the floor. "I'm gonna get that fuckin' mouth under control," he says, sweating and pumping.

"AHHH. FUCK!" My clit explodes, my pussy come hoses his dick down while my body convulses like I'm in the middle of a grand mal seizure. I'm soaring so high I can't see Earth.

Two more strokes and Python loses his shit, roaring as he whips his dick out and hot, thick globs of come skeet all over my body. He collapses leaving a sweaty, funky mess on top of me. "I swear to God, Shelle, if you ever try to leave—or do me dirty . . . ," he whispers while nibbling on my neck. "I'll fuckin' kill you."

3

Momma Peaches

I wake up choking on rancid air and burning oil and then struggle to lift my head and open my eyes. I can't see shit and every bone in my old body hurts. Coughing makes my chest feel like it's on fire and my head feels like it's stuffed with bricks.

SQUUUUEEEEEKKK. A door's rusted hinges threaten to pop my eardrum as a whoosh of cool air eases the burn in my chest.

"Lady. Lady. Are you all right?" a frantic woman asks, shaking my shoulder.

"Aaaaagh!" I knock her hand off of me. "What are you tryna do, kill me?" I glare at her, but I'm confused as to why she looks like a blurry smudge. I blink, but it gets worse.

"I'm sorry, but do you know what you just did?" she asks. "You saved my life."

"I did? Well, who the hell are you?" I blink again. "Why in the hell can't I see shit?"

The smudge inches closer. "You were in a car accident," she says.

I was? I think for a moment and memories come rushing back to me. Darkness. Pain. Hunger. *Alice*—my sister. *The crazy bitch kidnapped me.* I remember now. Alice snatched me from my own house after she killed Cedric. I've been locked up for months. More memories race by until I'm nauseous and I start to dry heave. Every muscle in my body locks up. I haven't eaten in a long time.

"Are you sure you're all right?" the woman asks, sounding shaken up herself.

I nod and peel my eyes open. *I need to get to the hospital.* Everything remains a blur—but I'll live. Thank God. Pushing away the deflated air bag, I turn in my seat and attempt to climb out of the van. But I forget I only have one leg and I hit the ground.

Thump.

"Aw, shit!"

"Are you all right?" she asks.

"Yeah. Just help me up." I swing an arm around her shoulder. Despite my ass being thin as a rail, it takes some time and work to get me propped up. By the time I'm up on my good leg, I'm a sweaty mess—but at least my vision is clearing up.

The white woman in front of me has blond hair and large, frightened blue eyes. But she's fucked up with a busted lip and a purple bruise over her left temple.

Dribbles. I remember now. She stole my nephew Mason.

"Look. We gotta get out of here," Dribbles says. "We need to find help. Okay? Let's go!"

I ignore her hysterics and look around. "Where is Alice? I need to see her."

"Forget about her." Dribbles directs me back to the van. "She's dead. All right? We have to go."

"There she is." I swat Dribbles's hands away, brace myself against the van, and then hop toward the hood. By the time I make it, my vision is twenty-twenty and I take in the bloody scene in front of me.

The top half of Alice's body is folded over the hood of the van while the rest of her is pinned against the oak tree. But she's not dead.

Not yet.

She's trembling while small bubbles of blood form around her mouth.

"Alice," I gasp, shaking my head.

"Leave her," Dribbles begs, tugging my arm. "We have to go."

With my gaze locked on my baby sister, I fight off the woman's grabby hands again. "Child, go on and sit down and calm your nerves," I tell her. "We'll get out of here soon enough."

Dribbles sobs, but falls back to let me do what I gotta do.

I hobble up close and brush back globs of Alice's hair so that I can see her face better. Under the moonlight, Alice resembles the fragile twelve-year-old girl I remember nearly forty years ago—the same little girl who was raped by my former cokehead boyfriend, Leroy. He ripped her world apart and despite killing him, she was never the same.

Years later, Alice was a strung-out junkie who dumped her first kid on me and then bounced. When she popped up again, she was delivering a second baby, Mason. That time, she claimed she was going to take care of him. Convinced herself that she was going to be a good mother. That was until I showed up one day and found her strung out in her nasty apartment and Mason missing. There was a city-wide search, but everyone believed she'd sold the child for a few crack rocks—including me.

Guilt sinks like a jagged rock in the pit of my stomach as I look at my broken sister. Despite the hell she has put me through, I'm fucked up about the way this shit has gone down.

Alice convulses and more blood bubbles around her nose and mouth. Her body is shutting down. Whatever the fuck I need to say, I better say it now—but I'm speechless. This situation got my head and my heart fucked up.

"Please, let's go," Dribbles whines.

Ignoring her, I lean toward Alice so that I can be in her line of vision. When I'm close enough for her to hear me, I speak from the bottom of my heart. "I hope you rot in *hell*, bitch."

Like in a horror movie, Alice shoots out a bloody hand and grabs a patch of my hair.

Dribbles screams.

"Shit!" I jerk back, but she has a death grip on my shit and almost snatches it clean off.

With a force that belies her condition, Alice pulls me back down to her eye level.

She works her mouth for several seconds before her voice stutters, "I—I'll meet y-you in h-hell." She chokes, gurgles, and then, at last, goes still.

The light in her eyes fades under the moonlight. *It's over. She's dead.*

"Help me," I shout, struggling to pry myself loose.

Dribbles hesitates, but when she finally sees that Alice isn't moving, she rushes over. "Can we *please* go now?" Dribbles begs, pulling me along. "I'll drive," she announces and then shoves me into the passenger seat. Once she slams the door, my gaze returns to my sister through the cracked windshield. The scene is surreal, but I'm ready to put this shit behind me.

Dribbles climbs in behind the wheel and fights with the deflated air bag before turning the ignition. The engine plays like it doesn't want to start. "No. No. No. Please, don't do this, God," she begs. She tries it a couple more times and just when I think our asses are going to have to hitchhike, the engine roars to life.

Thank you, Jesus.

Dribbles shifts into reverse and jams the accelerator—but our asses don't move. The tires just spin in one spot.

"Shit. We're stuck," she states the obvious. "I don't fuckin' believe this."

"I do." It's the kind of luck I've been having lately.

She tries it again—but nothing. "One of us is going to have to get out and push."

I glance down at my leg and then back at her. "And which one of us do you suppose that should be, chile?"

"Fuck!" Dribbles shifts back into park and climbs out of the van.

I struggle and fight my way back over into the driver's seat.

At the front of the van, Dribbles's face twists in disgust as she gets next to Alice and places her hands on top of the hood. "Ready?" She shouts.

I shift into reverse. "Ready!"

The petite white woman shoves her entire weight against the van while I floor the accelerator. The tires spin and kick out dirt, but nothing happens.

Fuck. I take my foot off the accelerator while my mind scrambles for a solution. We need to place something underneath the tires. I glance back at my nana Maybelle's old, desolate house. *There's no fucking way I'm going back in there.*

"Let's try it again!" Dribbles shouts, after scooting even closer to Alice's dead body.

I floor the accelerator with a fevered prayer, "Please Lord, one more miracle."

The tires spin.

The van rocks.

I meant what I said, God. I'll go to church every Sunday. Please.

The van rockets backward.

Dribbles face-plants into the dirt while Alice's body remains pinned to the van. When I'm clear of the soft earth and hit gravel, I slam the brakes.

"Thank you, Lord. Thank you." Tears race down my face. They've been pent up for more years than I have time to count. *It's over. Thank you, Jesus.*

Dribbles picks herself off the ground and runs to the van. She stops for a few seconds to stare at Alice, then cautiously walks over to the body and pulls it off the hood by the shoulders.

Alice collapses with an audible thump. My stomach pitches acid up my throat, and I throw the van door open in time to empty it onto the ground. My abdominal muscles twist and cramp to the point that I can't straighten back up.

"Are you all right?"

I can't answer her. It hurts too much.

Dribbles shoves me over to the passenger side while she climbs behind the wheel again.

If I weren't so weak, I'd curse this bitch out, but right now I want to curl up and go to sleep for ten years. However, there's a voice in the back of my head that says to resist because I might have a concussion. Relying on my survivor skills, I force my eyes to stay open. It's hard to keep my shit together while the van jostles violently down the rocky gravel road. It feels like forever before Dribbles gets us on smooth asphalt and mounts distance between us and that house of horrors.

"Hang in there," Dribbles says. "I'll get you to the hospital."

Nodding, I force myself to relax. Headlights, street lamps, and niggas mobbin' ten and twenty deep all zoom by my window. I'm finally back among the living.

Minutes later, Baptist Memorial Hospital comes into view. Dribbles jumps out of the van under the EMERGENCY sign and hollers for help.

A team rushes toward the van. Even one of Memphis's boys in blue tag along. I can honestly say that I've never been more thrilled to see a cop in my life.

4

Shariffa

"Lucifer."

A shiver races down my spine and then I get the feeling that if I say the bitch's name out loud three times, hell will spit her up to slaughter the rest of us standing here in Crunk's Ink tattoo shop. I take another look around at the carnage inside. It's hard to process it all, especially with Crunk's head still spinning from the ceiling fan with his dick shoved into his mouth. Even more troubling are the names written in blood on the walls.

Brika. Shacardi. Jaqorya. Trigger. Shariffa.

Next to them a five-pointed star and single letter L.

The bitch is coming after us next.

"I told you that we fucked up," Trigger hisses in my right ear.

I turn towards her green half-moon eyes ready to spit fire, but at the last second I bite my tongue and push past her. I don't have time for her BlacAsian ass.

Trigger grabs my wrist to snatch me back.

"Don't walk away from me," she growls. Red heat splotches her delicate brown skin. "What the fuck are we going to do?"

I glance down at her hand on my wrist. When she refuses to remove it, I wrench it back and then do a quick scan of the mob of Grape Street Crips and Crippettes hovering near the shop's door before planting my face in front of hers. "You need to calm your twitchy ass down."

Trigger stands her ground. "How in the fuck am I going to calm down with that sick bitch out there somewhere ready to do this same shit to us? It was *your* idea to make that hit on Da Club. We should have kept our asses on our own fuckin' color line."

"Oh. Your ass tryna rewrite history now? You bitches were all down for jacking the Vice Lords. Shit wouldn't have gone south on the hit if you hadn't smashed that nigga Bishop. After he got his dick wet, his pride was on the line when he realized you set his ass up—and by the way, you're welcome for me saving your life. If I hadn't blasted a hole in that nigga's dome, he would've pumped you full of lead."

Trigger laughs. "Yeah. Thanks. Now all I have to do is sit back and wait for his murdering ass sister to come play chop-a-bitch with me." Her green gaze rakes me with disgust before she marches off.

Bitch.

I glare at her back even though I know she's right. Lucifer is the last bitch that anyone wants to fuck with—no matter what colors you're flagging. Her name puts fear in the heart of many niggas everywhere and her wet work is legendary. Given the number of body parts lying around this shop, Crunk learned that shit the hard way.

Turning, I work my way back to the front door. Brika, Shacardi, Jaqorya, and Trigger are huddled together, whispering and casting angry glares my way. *I swear, I can't stand gossiping bitches.*

I wasn't always a Crippette. Years ago I was the head bitch in charge of the Queen Gs. Python's old lady—before I got my panties twisted fucking around with a Crip thug by the name of King Loc. The shit seemed fair since Python was always too busy spreading his seed with every bitch that could stand still. But all these trifling niggas out here got double standards. Bitches aren't allowed to creep. For a long time, I kept my shit on the down low, but then I got too cocky and too slick and Python busted my ass. He rolled up on King Loc and unloaded a shitload of bullets. After that, he torched the car. The muthafucka made me watch and then turned his wrath on me.

I blacked out on the first punch. When I woke, I was laid up in the hospital and sucking on a tube, wishing that he'd killed me. I'd been stripped of my power and of the only family that I'd ever known.

The biggest insult was seeing Python waste no time replacing my ass with LeShelle. A bitch he pulled off the pole from his club, the Pink Monkey. A fucking bitch he married, if the rumors in the streets are true.

Despite it being five years and him nearly killing my ass, him marrying that bitch is fucking with me. I held that muthafucka down for *years*. I put up with all his baby-momma bullshit and the nigga never once said shit about marriage.

That's because he always had his nose shoved up Melanie Johnson's ass—that is, until he killed her.

Regardless, Python's *wife* has quite a rep. She's a mean, nasty bitch who don't take any shit from anybody. Hell, she even had her own sister raped and put in the crazy house for disrespecting the color lines. After watching her make moves, a lot of bitches have turned up on their game. Now Queen Gs, Flowers, and Crippettes put in more work than the average foot soldier.

For me, starting over in a new set wasn't easy—far from it. I was a castoff. Nobody trusted my ass. I suffered through a lot of fucked-up shit but still climbed my ass up the ranks. I did what I had to do to survive. My big break came when I got in on a bank robbery and deflated a security guard's gut when he tested my ass. It was a quick score and it changed my life.

Lynch, the chief enforcer, peeped me out and loved that I kept my shit tight with my fitness. He caught my eye, too. His gangsta was undeniable and his ass was fine as fuck: six feet, Hershey's-bar brown and built like a quarterback. One look and I was determined to make his ass mine.

Two years later, I birthed his twin boys and took his last name. My transformation was complete. I was back on top, this time as the head bitch of the Grape Street Crips—but am I ready to go up against Lucifer?

"Lock it down," Lynch shouts. "Clean this shit up and make sure that you don't leave a fuckin' toenail behind."

Niggas pull down shades and lock the doors. The cops won't be investigating this homicide—not with our names painted in blood on the walls. That shit would just lead them to our front door. Ain't nobody got time for that shit. This is a personal matter and it's going to stay that way.

Trigger and the girls remain hugged up in a corner. The second I make it over to their small huddle, the bitches break off their convo in midsentence.

"Oh. It's like that now?" I grind my back teeth together.

Instead of answering, their gazes dart among themselves.

These punk bitches here. "Fine. If you guys think that you're better off tryna fight Lucifer on your own, have at it." I toss two deuces and give these hos my back.

"Wait," Brika barks before I storm off.

Lynch looks up from his huddle of soldiers. He gives me a look, asking whether everything is cool with us.

Nodding, I let him know that I got this shit under control.

The girls surround me.

"Look, Shariffa," Jaqorya starts. "We don't mean no disrespect. We're a little freaked out. You understand that shit, right?"

I refuse to answer her ass.

They sneak looks at each other before Trigger gets to the point. "Look. You got a fuckin' plan or what? If not, then I say we bounce our asses south of the border for a little while. We wait for this shit to blow over."

"Blow over? What? You think that bitch is going to forget that we killed her brother? Does your dumb ass also believe in Santa Claus and the Tooth Fairy, too?"

Trigger glares like she wants to smack the shit out of me.

"Then what's the plan?" Brika asks. "I'm down for whatever as long as we get the shit poppin' soon. I ain't that bitch that likes sittin' around and waitin'. I say if that bitch wants to go at it then we bring the heat straight to her. I ain't scared of no bitch that pisses sittin' down, you feel me?"

"I agree," I say. "We get to the bitch before she comes at us."

"And how in the fuck are we going to do that?" Trigger asks.

I have no fuckin' idea. "Leave that shit to me," I say.

The girls' gazes shift around.

"What say you, Shacardi?" Trigger nudges her.

All eyes shift to her and her honey-blond pixie haircut. Most niggas sleep on her because she's petite and looks like she wouldn't harm a fly. It's how she beat a murder charge a few years back.

"We don't have a choice," she says. "It's her or us, right?"

We nod.

"Then it's settled," Jaqorya says.

Lynch joins our circle. "Y'all working or what?"

We peel apart to start scrubbing the place down. Lynch grabs my wrists. "I told you this shit was going to happen," he hisses. "You can never leave shit alone."

"I—"

"You better call my momma and tell her not to bring the boys until late tomorrow. We're going to be here all night." He storms off, not waiting to hear my bullshit.

Aw, shit. He's going to be hot for a while. He didn't want the set to get on the Vice Lords' radar—and now I've dragged our asses right into the center of that muthafucka.

I pat my pockets and then remember I left my phone out in the car. Bolting to the door, I unlock it and rush outside. I don't realize how bad the stench was inside the tattoo shop until I suck in the night's air. After I scramble to get my cell phone out of our Range Rover, the hairs on the back of my neck stand up.

Somebody is watching me.

I pop back out of vehicle and scan the area. I don't see shit, but I feel someone's eyes.

It's Lucifer. It's her. I know it. My gaze keeps darting around—until it lands on a black Escalade quite a distance down the road. I have to squint to make it out, but it's her. I know it.

"Shariffa!" Lynch snaps.

I jump.

"What's taking you so long?"

"I'm comin', I'm comin'." I head back into the shop, but before I close the door I twist to check for the Escalade again.

It's gone.

5

Lucifer

Silent as the grave, I'm nestled quietly in the back of the Escalade with my bloody Browning hunter's knife in my lap. These muthafuckas killed Bishop and now they have me to deal with. I watch Shariffa exit the tattoo shop while an ice floe circulates in my veins.

I know that bitch.

Not personally, but back in the day, she flagged for Gangster Disciples—another one of Python's ex-flames. There's so many, I don't know how the fuck he keeps up with them. Yet, I am surprised that Lynch would wife another nigga's leftovers—especially from another gang. That kind of shit don't happen every day—if ever. Whatever the bitch is putting down in the bedroom must be strong enough for muthafuckas to overlook rules and violations.

Not me.

Tombstone looks up into the rearview mirror. "What do you want to do?"

Stone-faced, I contemplate the question. I can tell him to hit the accelerator and power down the windows. We can take care of this old-school style, but that would be too easy. I'd rather get my hands wet. Slice her ass open and listen to her scream and beg for her miserable life . . .

Shariffa looks up and spots us.

My hands drift from the bloody Browning to the TEC-9 lying at my side. *It would be soooo fuckin' easy* . . .

"Lucifer?" Tombstone nudges me. "You want to do this?"

Sooo easy . . .

Lynch steps out of the tattoo shop and startles his wife.

The spell is broken.

I exhale a long breath and pull my hand back from the gun. "Let's get out of here. I'll take care of her later."

"Whatever you say, boss." Without hitting the headlights, Tombstone makes a U-turn from the curb and rolls back out the way we came. During the ride back to Ruby Cove, the Vice Lords' stronghold, the bloodlust in my heart grows. *Patience.* The word repeats like a mantra in my head. *I gotta have patience.*

Rolling through the streets of Murder City, my mind trips down memory lane. Big hits, large scores, tons of body bags; Bishop, Mason, and I have been a part of it all most of our lives.

Losing Bishop so soon after Mason's death is fucking with me in ways that I'm not ready to deal with yet. Ask any muthafucka and they'll tell you that I'm not the emotional type. My brother was the emotional one. Boo-hooing every time someone close to him dropped. Don't get me wrong, he was a strong soldier, but he was never ruthless. It wasn't in him.

But it's in me.

Exhaustion has settled into my bones by the time Tombstone coasts onto Ruby Cove. Like cocaine, murder has a way of taking you on an incredible high, but then it smashes your face into concrete, knocking you out. The way I feel now, I could sleep for a week—but no way that shit is going to go down. I have too much on my plate. As the de facto leader of the Vice Lords, I know that before the sun comes up I'm gonna have to deal with more street politics.

I have to reassure our drug connects that business will go

on as usual, build on our crew's relationship with our new gun runners, the Angels of Mercy biker club. Not to mention, I also have to hunt down Python and his crazy bitch, deal with Cousin Skeet, and plot how I'm going to take out Shariffa and the rest of her crew. Eventually, I'll have to go head-to-head with Lynch's shady ass, but fuck it. It's me against the world.

"Lucifer?" Tombstone cuts into my plotting thoughts.

"Yeah?"

He shrugs. "We're here."

I look up and see that we're parked in my driveway. Hell, I hadn't noticed that we'd arrived. Still, I don't reach for the door. Instead, I look at my crib like it's just a stack of bricks. Who the fuck likes an empty house?

Tombstone shuts off the engine and sits patiently behind the wheel. After a while, the silence gets to him. "I know it's not any of my business—"

"Then shut the fuck up."

He snaps his mouth shut.

I'm not interested in his two cents. My issues are *my* issues. People need to stay in their lane.

The peace shattered, I sheath my bloody knife, climb out of the vehicle, and trek up to my front door.

"Is it done?" My mother's voice floats out of the darkness the moment I walk through the door. She doesn't even flinch at the sight of my bloody clothes. "Is it done?" she asks again, pushing up from a chair. Back in the day, Lucille Washington was what the neighborhood called a brick house. My dad used to tell me stories about how niggas would line up for blocks tryna get her to notice them. Her once-fit frame is now ringed with love handles. Her legendary breasts have collapsed under the weight of gravity. Still, there's a beauty about her that will never go away.

Momma's hands remain clamped tight at her sides. Her eyes are bloodshot—probably from hours of crying.

"I got one of them—and the names of the others. It's just a matter of time," I tell her.

She thrusts up her trembling chin and nods. "Good." She doesn't seem to know what to say next. A long, awkward silence lapses before she creeps forward.

"You're such a good daughter," she says, throwing her arms around me.

My breath catches and unexpected tears burn the backs of my eyes. It's the praise that I've been waiting for all my life, but I didn't know it. Slowly, I lift my arms and wrap them around her thin frame and squeeze.

Like a number of women, I have mommy issues. My main grievance is how fast she jumped into Cousin Skeet's bed so soon after my father was gunned down in our front yard. Being a daddy's girl, I can't forgive her for it. Cousin Skeet isn't blood, but he's family through gang affiliation—only those clowns down at the police department don't know that their celebrated super cop, Captain Melvin Johnson, is deep into the game. He looked real official on paper, him and his dutiful wife, Victoria. His shady ass is an O.G. through and through, and my momma loves Cousin Skeet's dirty drawers. Right now, we're still grieving over Bishop and I'm gonna have to put all that shit aside.

Our connection feels odd, but good at the same time.

"Maybe you should go and tell your brother tomorrow," she says.

I'm confused for a moment and then understand that she wants me to visit his grave. "I will."

She nods and then shuffles out of the house toward her place a few doors down.

My exhaustion deepens as I make my way up the stairs. In the bathroom, I strip out of my bloody clothes and shove them into a bag. Once I'm in the shower, the water is near scorching, but I accept the pelting punishment readily.

First Mason. Now Bishop.

My head is caught up on too many woulda, coulda, and shouldas. The ground has been snatched from up under me and I feel like I'm falling. I don't like the feeling. I'm not even sure if I want to be the leader of the Vice Lords anymore. What's the point? I only got into the game because of my brother and Mason—and now they're gone.

Gliding my soapy hands over my body, I strain to recapture that magical feeling that Mason set off so easily. Desperately, I struggle to recall the heat of his mouth against my neck, the smoothness of his dick pressed against my ass and the nasty way he whispered in my ear. I brush my fingers across my breasts and squeeze my eyes tighter, but my memory and imagination fail to transport me. Sadness as wide as the ocean engulfs my soul while an ache that will never be satisfied throbs between my legs.

My hands drift to the sound mound of my pregnant belly. Pretty soon, I'm not going to be able to hide the truth—then what?

More challenges to the throne?

When the shower cools, I shut it off before I turn into a human pickle. After wrapping a towel around myself, I gather the bag of bloody clothes to take downstairs. There's a metal barrel out in the backyard. I'll toss them in and start a small fire. I might even grab a beer and watch the flickering flames destroy the evidence.

When I'm halfway down the stairs, a noise catches my ear and I freeze.

Silence.

But it's *too* damn quiet. In this life, it pays to be paranoid.

Crrreeeeakkkkk.

Someone is in the house.

The staircase is pitch dark and I don't have a weapon. I creep down the rest of the staircase, scanning the room slowly. I don't see anyone, but I feel the weight of someone's stare.

There's a burner in the table next to the bar—if I can just get to it. At last, I detect someone, and I drop the bag and dash for the table.

The second my hand closes around the gun, a voice cracks like a whip, "Willow, wait! It's me."

I freeze.

It can't be. Slowly, I turn around as a familiar physique steps in front of slices of moonlight from the venetian blinds.

Shocked, I try to take in the ugly black-and-red burns covering half of a bulbous face. My gut churns as I lock gazes with the man's eyes, one brown and one milky-white. My heart explodes with joy. "Oh my God. Mason!"

6

Shariffa

Lynch is still pissed as shit. He hasn't said a word since we spent the night scrubbing that tattoo shop. I don't know what the fuck they did with the body parts and I don't want to know. My mind is whirling over how we're going to play defense with a bitch that thinks her ass is the Terminator.

He storms into the house and marches straight to our bedroom. I follow, thinking the moment we're alone he's gonna really let me have it. Jaws clenched, he snatches sheets and pillows from the bed.

"C'mon, Lynch. You don't have to sleep out on the sofa. We can sit and talk about this."

"I'm not sleeping out there." He rams the shit into my arms. "*You* are."

"Me?" I blink.

"Damn right. You sleep out there until I don't feel like killing you anymore."

"But—but . . ."

Lynch grabs me by my shoulders and spins me toward the door. "Shar, you don't want to fuck with me right now. I'm trying real hard to remember that you're my babies' momma," he warns.

"But—but . . ."

With one shove, I fly out of the bedroom door. *What the fuck?* Pissed, I jerk back around, but he slams the door in my face.

Muthafucka!

I grab the doorknob. *Locked.* "Lynch. C'mon. Open the goddamn door!"

"Walk away, Shariffa. I mean it," he barks.

The last thing I need right now is for this nigga to be on his fuckin' period. Determined to settle this shit, I drop the sheets and pillows and pound on the door.

BANG! BANG! BANG!

"I'm not going anywhere until you open this door."

BANG! BANG! BANG!

"LYNCH, OPEN UP!"

BANG! BANG! BANG!

After a full minute, Lynch snatches the door open. "What the fuck is your goddamn problem?"

I ignore him and push my way into the room. "I fucked up! There! I said it. Now can we cut the drama and figure out what our next damn move is? In case you forgot, I'm at the top of some psycho bitch's hit list."

"What the fuck did you think was going to happen?" he roars, planting his face in front of mine. "You pushed and pushed to start a fuckin' war with those VL niggas and now you've got your goddamn wish. Congratu-fuckin-lations!" He chest bumps me and I stumble backwards.

"What the fuck?" I rush back at him and shove him, but all I end up doing is hurting my arms.

"I'll tell you what the fuck," Lynch says, going in. "None of my niggas want to tangle with that bitch and her crew over some bullshit that *you* started. They made that shit perfectly clear to me tonight."

I flinch. "What the fuck is that supposed to mean?"

"C'mon, Shar. You can't be that goddamn stupid. These niggas ain't buying that your ass is a true Crip. They only put up with you because I wifed your ass. All that swag you strutting around here can't buy your ass a McDonald's Happy Meal outside this crew. Everybody looks at you and all they see is a Queen G perpetrating. They view you as *my* muthafuckin' problem—not theirs—so don't be expecting for a Crip army to charge at those bumble-bee-wearing muthafuckas. Fuck. You got one of their favorite homies chopped up. They want to kill you more than that slob, black and gold bitch."

Lynch's words punch me and I'm left to stand here looking like I'm stuck on stupid. *Here I am, busting all these moves and making all these plans for a crew who despises me?* I plop down onto the edge of the bed.

"Look. That shit came out harsh." He brushes his hands over his low-cropped hair.

"But it's true?" I ask.

He hesitates.

"I don't give a fuck about it being harsh. I need to know whether the shit is true. I always want the fuckin' truth, Lynch. You know that shit."

Lynch huffs out a long breath, deflating the anger in his chest, but he doesn't attempt to answer my question.

"Is it true or are you just fuckin' with me because you're mad?"

"It's true. Maybe I should have told your girls to tell you—"

"Fuck them bitches! You're my man. You're the one who is supposed to always keep it one hundred with me."

Lynch explodes again. "What the fuck are you talking about? I *told* your ass plenty of times to have a muthafuckin' seat—several seats, in fact. Did you listen? No! You kept right on stirring the pot, pulling your bullshit trap-house robberies and pissing niggas off. The set isn't what it used to be, baby girl. Niggas are in this shit for self. Too many niggas have been bodied or locked down. The ones in the joint, we're struggling to put money on *they* books and to hold down *all* their wives *and* baby mommas. It's to the point we can only concentrate on feeding the niggas that are pulling their weight in the streets.

"The cartels don't want to hear about no fuckin' ghetto, hood, soap opera shit we got going on in Memphis. I'm tryna focus on moving product. Period. Now I gotta deal with this side shit because you're obsessed with invisible thrones? Nobody owns these streets but the goddamn devil. You're blind if you don't see that shit."

"I don't need a fuckin' lecture. I—"

"Fuck it. I'm tired of talking about this shit." He turns and storms out of the bedroom.

"Lynch!"

In the hallway, he snatches up the bedding. "*I'll* sleep out on the sofa."

Tossing up my hands, I watch him storm off. "Now what?"

7

Lucifer

"I don't understand." I take a step back and nearly trip over air. "This isn't happening. This can't be happening." I'm seeing things. I *have* to be seeing things.

Mason's ghost moves forward. "I know that you're in shock right now," he says.

Fuck. He even sounds like Mason. *But it can't be him.* I go for the gun again. In no time, I have it cocked and leveled at the intruder. "Don't you fuckin' move," I snap. For the first time in my life, I'm visibly shaking with my finger on the trigger.

Mason, or whoever the fuck he is, doesn't make any sudden moves. In fact, he slowly lifts his hands. "All right. Calm down."

"Don't fuckin' tell me to calm down!" *Shit.* I need to get it together so that I can think. "Who are you?"

"You know who I am," he says.

"But that can't be. You're . . . dead."

"I should be dead," he agrees. "But I could've died a lot of times before . . . and would have if you weren't around to save my ass."

"Python's car. The explosion," I insist. "I saw it flip off that bridge. Everyone saw it. It was all over the news. But you were dead *before* then. I know it. I know what I saw."

Mason sighs. "My memory is still spotty about that night. I remember our accident—chasing Python on the highway—the car flipping—the fight with Python. Then he must've knocked me out. After that, I remember fire and then suddenly being submerged underwater. The rest . . . like I said, is a blur."

"And what?" I ask. "You're going to tell me that you've been swimming around in the Mississippi for two months?"

"No," another voice barks out of the darkness. "Me and my grandson fished him out the river."

I jump and swing my weapon to three o'clock. "Who's there? Who are you?"

"Willow, it's okay," Mason says. "He's with me."

Footsteps pad across the carpet to the window, where stripes of moonlight splash onto an old, gray-haired black dude. "Name's Eddie," he says, flashing a remarkable set of white teeth. "Like I said, me and my grandson grabbed him up out of the water two months back. I have a small place out in the woods in Osceola—Arkansas. Small town—a river town about an hour out from Memphis." Nervous, Eddie glances over at Mason. "He was messed up pretty good when we found him, barely conscious—but alive."

My heart sinks. He was alive. How could I have gotten that so wrong? My mind flashes back to that night, but it's no longer reliable. It's playing tricks on me and adding things that I hadn't previously remembered. Did the rain obscure my vision? Could there have still been a light in his eyes?

Eddie rocks on the soles of his feet as he slips his hands out of his pockets and looks at Mason. "I guess these still had some healing in them. I used to do a whole lot of doctoring back in my army days," he boasts. "Now they mostly work on cattle and other farm animals."

"Why didn't you take him to a doctor?"

"We were gonna, but, uh, the patient here wouldn't hear of it." Eddie chuckles. "He might not have been able to say much, but he did make it clear that he didn't want to be taken to no hospital."

Mason laughs with him like they are sharing an inside joke.

"And the cops? The feds dragged that river for a while. Surely they checked your neck of the woods?"

"Yeah," Eddie says. "They came snooping around, but I don't care too much for police. Not since they killed one of my nephews ten years ago. He was unarmed and walking home from the store one night. Apparently that's an unwritten crime when you're black. They pumped thirty-six bullets in him. I guess they wanted to make sure that they got him. Of course they claimed that they mistook him for another random black man and gave the family their sincerest apologies. Kenny was a good boy, wanted to be a doctor someday—like his favorite uncle." Eddie lowers his head with a humble smile.

The story has taken us off course, but that's okay. I'm still struggling to wrap my brain around the fact that Mason is truly standing in my living room. I size him up and down. He's the right frame, but he's lost a lot of weight—a lot of muscle. His once-bald head now sports a nest of black, tightly coiled hair. He even has a thick beard and mustache. But it's the eyes that leave no doubt. One brown. One white.

Mason creeps toward me. "It's really me." He reaches over and removes the gun from my hands.

I don't protest. I can't stop staring at him. He's a walking, talking, *breathing* miracle.

He clicks the safety back on and places it down on the table. "I missed you, Willow." He pulls me into his embrace. Only when his muscular arms envelop me in a familiar cocoon do I accept that it's true.

I lift my arms and let them drift around his neck. His warmth sinks into my own and stills my trembling. Before I know it, I'm melting into him and thanking God for a miracle that I don't deserve. My shock gives way to joy and I can't help but laugh, and then cry at the same time. When our embrace loosens, it's only so that our lips can find one another.

He tastes like Hennessy and chocolate, a heady combination that is as delicious as it is addictive. Our tongues dance in an erotic rhythm. In no time at all, my nipples are rock-hard and my pussy is throbbing beneath this towel wrapped around me. We're seconds from giving Eddie the show of his life when he loudly clears his throat.

"AHEM!"

Mason chuckles as he pulls back. "I haven't forgotten you, my man. Sit tight." With that, he keeps his arm looped around my waist and pulls me towards the dining room. "You still got my emergency stash here?" he whispers.

I hear the words, but it takes me a while to understand what he's asking. *He's here. Mason is really here.* The world's burdens lift from my shoulders.

"The stash," Mason repeats. "I promised the old man that I would break him off after he got me through this rocky patch, nawhatImean?"

I nod.

"Okay. Then where is it?" Mason presses.

"Where is what?"

"The money." His brows crash together.

"Oh. The money," I blurt, snapping out of my trance. "It's in the basement."

Mason glances over his shoulder at Eddie. "Sit tight. We'll be right back."

Together we turn and head down into the cluttered basement. Plowing through the mountains of miscellaneous junk, I lead him to the back brick wall. From there, I feel around for the loose brick. Once found, I claw at it with my fingers. After I get the first one out, it's easy to get the other ten surrounding bricks to get at the steel safe. I punch in the passcode and pull it open.

Mason grabs a few stacks of bundled cash. "Lock the rest of that up," he instructs before turning and heading out.

I quickly do what he says, but leave the bricks down so that I can rush behind him. Now that he's here, I don't want him out of my sight.

In the living room Mason hands over the money to a stupefied Eddie. A second later, his white picket-fence smile returns to his face and erases ten years off of him. "Thank you—and don't you worry," Eddie says. "Me and mine know how to keep our mouths shut."

"You've already proved that." Mason slaps him hard on his back, and then escorts him to the door. "Now remember, if you need anything . . ."

"We'll give you a call," Eddie says.

"You got it, man. You're part of the family now. I'll never forget what you've done for me," Mason says. He opens the door and they exchange their final good-byes.

When he returns to the living room, he stops and flashes a smile. His burned skin crinkles at the edges—but it's still a smile that steals my heart—a smile that I've always loved.

For a long, silent minute, we stare at each other. Then, as if someone has fired a starter pistol, we rush toward each other, our arms wrapping and our lips locking together. I drown in both the taste and smell of him—and yet I need to get closer. I *need* him—inside of me. *Now.*

My towel falls to the floor with a soft *whoosh,* while I, suddenly possessing the strength of ten men, rip off his T-shirt and jeans. He's steel hard and rough like I love it.

Lamps, vases, picture frames all crash to the floor as we stumble over an end table. We don't give a fuck. Our minds are gone and our bodies have completely taken over. Neither of us have any time or patience for foreplay. He jams me up against a wall. My legs go east and west around his hips. A second later, his dick impales me with one long, smooth stroke. I gasp as stars explode behind my eyes.

He feels so fucking good.

"Willow, I missed you," Mason pants before shifting his hot mouth to vacuum-suck my titties.

I want to tell him, "me, too," but I'm dizzy as hell and I can't get the words out. His dick game goes into overdrive, hammering me into the wall until breathing is no longer possible.

Small explosions begin at my toes and then roll upward, taking over my body limb by limb. When he hits me with that perfect stroke at the perfect time, a scream rips from my soul and my nails dig deep into his shoulders.

Mason's lion-esque roar follows suit and this big brick building of a man trembles while his knees buckle. We cling to each other for dear life while slowly sinking down onto the carpet.

We remain locked together in each other's embrace, too afraid to let go. *I never want to let him go.* Never.

8

Hydeya

Thirty hours. I've been up for over thirty hours, working this new case. My hubby has long since crawled into bed, probably annoyed that *once again* I've brought my work home with me. Not because I want to make an impression with the new police chief, Yvette Brown, but because the horrific idea of someone cutting a baby out of a woman's body has pushed all of my buttons. I've been a cop a long time and I've never seen no shit like this before. I've heard of a few cases in other places, but I never had one hit my desk.

Sighing, I fish out the forensic photos of the two women discovered way off Peebles Road in south Memphis in advanced stages of decomposition—two months according to the coroner. The ex-pregnant woman's corpse still has a bag over her head and plastic cuffs locked around her wrists. There's very little skin left or biomass for insect colonization. It's mostly bones and connective tissues. Crows and other animals had their feast and destroyed most of the crime scene evidence.

I've lost track of the number of homicides I've worked, but this heinous crime will be forever burned into my memory. On the surface, this case looks like a hard nut to crack, but so far, the forensic team has been phenomenal in getting good tire-track molds, fingerprints, and footprints. The discarded silver Terrain is registered to a Yolanda Terry. There was also a cell phone with a strange text that read: Ticktock.

We traced the number the text came from back to one of those cheap disposable phones that could be purchased from any big-box store.

Yolanda Terry was no stranger to the Memphis Police Department. When I typed her name into the system, a lengthy arrest record scrolled onto my screen and ran for at least five minutes. Off the bat, one of her addresses was on Shotgun Row. That told me that she was gang affiliated: Gangster Disciples to be exact. Her previous arrests consisted of charges for trespassing, prostitution, and narcotics.

In her mug shots, she was an attractive girl, but in the end, she was a product of her environment. It takes a lot to overcome your station or circumstances in this world. When I talked to Yolanda's mother earlier, a Ms. Turner instead of Terry, I was stunned by her total lack of reaction. If in anything, she gave me the feeling that I was annoying her by interrupting *Family Feud*. I glanced around the room and noticed that there were no pictures of her only daughter. The place smelled like mothballs and Bengay. When I asked her whether her daughter had any enemies, Bettye claimed not to know anything about her daughter's business. She added that whatever trouble Yo-Yo, as she called her, got into, she probably brought it onto herself. "God don't like ugly," she kept preaching to me. Evidently Yolanda had chased off her mother's man a few decades back, and she'd never forgiven her for it.

I got lost in her conversation and logic, but I went ahead and nodded like she made all the sense in the world. Only when I was about to head out the door did the older woman ask, "What about the baby?"

I froze with my hand on the doorknob, a sudden sickening dread curdling up in my gut. Ms. Turner said that Yo-Yo had been nine-months pregnant. I got back on the phone with the forensic team and we took another look at the body and crime scene. Time and the environment had done away with a lot of evidence and we couldn't find a corpse of a baby anywhere.

The coroner called back and said that, upon another review of the body, they had discovered there were crude knife marks around the pelvis of the handcuffed corpse. The baby had been cut out. Was that the reason for the murder?

And what about the other body? Cause of death: a single bullet in the center of the skull. No ID. Time, environment, and scavengers had done a number to her body as well. For now, she'll be toe-tagged as Jane Doe until we get lucky. If I had to put money on this shit, I'd bet my pitiful salary that this whole mess was gang-related—like everything else in this city.

There's a lot of shuffling going on at the department. The accelerated crime rate and angry citizens demanded change. For the first time in more than twenty-five years, the polish on Captain Melvin Johnson's shield had tarnished and to the surprise of the whole department Mayor Wharton tossed his beloved super cop into early retirement.

If Captain Johnson can go down, then that means none of our jobs are safe. I came to Memphis from South Chicago, which is in worse condition than Memphis—that includes the gangs *and* the politicians. I review the reports over again. At some point I must've fallen asleep because the next thing I know, I jolt upright, disoriented.

Riiinnnggg.

My gaze falls to the smartphone lying on the paper-covered table. I rub the sleep from the corners of my eyes and try to remember how to answer my new fancy phone.

Riiinnnggg.

"You want me to answer that for you?" Drake asks, sounding irritated and amused at the same time.

"I got it," I tell him, swiping the screen to answer the call. "Hello." My voice is scratchy so I cough to clear it. "Yeah. This is Lieutenant Hawkins." I reach for my coffee cup, and then groan at finding it empty.

Drake, like the sweet angel I've always believed him to be, appears by my side, coffeepot in hand, and pours me a refill. *Thanks*, I mouth to him, while taking a moment to appreciate the black silk boxers hugging his V-cut hips. At six-one, my Italian husband is at an average height, but he definitely has that Harlequin cover model look with his shoulder-length, ink-black hair.

We pissed a lot people off when we got married. My black militant stepfather refused to walk me down the aisle and, to this day, my mother still has a bet going on with my aunts on how long our marriage will last. It's been five years and counting.

Silence hangs over the phone. I'm embarrassingly aware that my caller has stopped talking and I have no idea of what was just said. "I'm sorry. What was that again?" I sip my coffee for the caffeine kick.

"We need you to come in. We have a one-eight-seven out at 530 Frank Road," the officer repeats.

One-eight-seven—homicide. Of course there's a homicide. This is Memphis. "I, uh, where is—"

"It's been a busy night, Lieutenant. The chief knows that you've already worked a double shift, but she requested that you come in on this one."

"All right." I look around the table for a pen. "Give me the address again." When the officer repeats it, an odd feeling comes over me. "Why do I know this address?" I whisper, but the caller hears me.

"Because it's Captain Johnson's home. He and his wife have been murdered."

9

LeShelle

Python's dick game put a bitch to sleep—a deep sleep.

What's troubling about this shit is that I'm not dreaming about him, but about his shady-ass, honey-coated cousin with the *waaaay* too damn pretty eyes. In my fantasy, his ass gives Python a run for his money in knowing how to tear up my pussy. I'm clawing at this muthafucka's back like a panther in heat and growling nasty-ass shit in his ear. I don't even like this nigga so the dream doesn't make sense—but the shit feels so damn good that I'm coming in my sleep.

A phone trills somewhere in the background and then slowly sinks into my consciousness. "Somebody get that," I murmur between gasps of Diesel's deep strokes. The ringing persists and fucks up our flow. "Get the goddamn phone!"

"All right. Shit," Python snaps, stretching across my body.

Jarred, I pop my eyes open. *Holy shit. Was I talking in my sleep?*

"Yeah. What is it?" he moans into the phone.

Yawning, I roll over, hoping to get back to the exact spot I left off in the dream.

"Come again?" He sits up. "You gotta be fuckin' shittin' me," he barks.

I grab a pillow and stuff it over my head. *Diesel. Diesel. Come back, baby.*

Python snatches the sheets off our bodies and swings his legs over to perch on the edge of the bed.

What the fuck? I snatch off the pillow and hiss, "Who the fuck is that?"

Ignoring me, Python's face drains of color. *This can't be good news.*

"She's *alive*," Python croaks. "That's what you're telling me?"

"Who's alive?" I crawl across the bed to him.

"How is that possible? Where has she been?"

"Who?" I rock his shoulder to get his attention, but he swats me away.

"The cops are there with her?" He huffs out a long breath. "Shit."

Anxiety rolls around in my gut as my imagination takes flight.

"All right. All right. I'm coming, but . . . I need to figure a few things out first. Yeah. Call me back if her condition changes. A'ight. Bye." He disconnects the call.

I wait two seconds and then bark impatiently, "Well? Are you going to tell me what the fuck is going on?"

"Momma Peaches," he says. "She's alive."

Silence explodes between us while I try to process what he's saying. I know that no one ever found a body, but I wrote her old ass off. Charged whatever the fuck she was involved in to the game and was keeping it moving. "I don't understand. You said—"

"I know what I said! I don't understand it either, but Vicious's sister working at Baptist Memorial called him and said that Momma Peaches showed up at the emergency room tonight all banged up."

"What?"

"He said her and some white chick claimed that they'd been kidnapped. They're running all kinds of tests and even had to pump her stomach because she was filled with so many toxins."

"Is she going to be all right?" I ask, only mildly concerned.

Python brushes his hand over his low-cropped hair. "She doesn't know." He visibly struggles to keep his shit together.

Python and Momma P are as thick as thieves. Although she's his aunt, she raised him like he was her own when his mother bailed on him to feed her crack habit. Hell. Everybody loves Momma Peaches. She's an old-school gangsta and has taught most the bitches on Shotgun Row the real rules of the street game. Clearly, she's still a survivor. I just wish her ass liked me half as much as she liked that retarded bitch Yolanda.

"I gotta go see her," Python announces, grabbing clothes from the floor.

"Whoa." I hop off the bed and snatch his jeans from his hands. "What do you mean that *you gotta to go see her*? Is that smart right now?"

"Probably not—but she's my people." He jerks the jeans back.

"I get that, but the minute you stroll into that hospital every law enforcement officer in the tri-state area is going descend and lock your ass up!" I go for the jeans again and then get locked into a tug-of-war.

"Stop it, Shelle. I ain't got time for this shit right now."

"Make time because your ass is about to fuck up." *Again.* "I mean, how do you know this shit ain't a trap? Huh? Vicious called, so what? That nigga ain't nobody."

He pauses.

"Call the hospital yourself. Check it out, but don't do something this stupid. You're the most wanted muthafucka on the streets right now and you're going to just go stroll your ass up in the hospital where they got cameras and shit? What—are you gonna call a damn time-out with the damn cops because

your aunt may or may not be up in that bitch? C'mon. Think."
I let go of his jeans. "I don't know what the fuck happened to
your head after you drove off that bridge, but it must've
knocked a few screw loose cuz I swear your ass done lost it."

"Shell—"

"You asked him whether the police were there. Well, are
they?"

The muscle in his jaw twitches, which tells me all I need to
know. I suck in a deep breath and then approach this shit another way. "I know you love her," I say softening my voice.
"You're concerned—but if you go down there, everything is
going to go left. The FBI or the cops probably have her surrounded because of her association with you. They gotta be
hoping that you pop up down there." When I can't tell
whether I'm getting through to him, I reach up and mush him
in his thick head. "Wake the fuck up, Python. You're smarter
than this!"

"ARRRGH." He spins around and punches another hole
in the wall.

POW!

Then, as if realizing the pointlessness in him beating up the
wall, his shoulders deflate and he props his head against it instead.

Exhaling a long breath, I ease up behind him and slide my
arms around his waist. "I understand you're upset," I tell him.
"But isn't it good just to *know* that she's alive—that she's going
to survive whatever hell she's been through?"

No answer.

His back muscles flex and knot during his internal war.
Feeling for him, I pepper kisses across his broad shoulders.
"There's plenty of ways to get word to her, Python. She'll under-
stand why you can't go and see her. When she gets better and is
released from the hospital, *then* we can arrange a meet-up." Kiss.
"But you gotta be patient." Kiss.

Finally, he relaxes.

"It's going to be all right. You have her back now. That's all that matters."

Python nods. "I still need to get word to her though. The sooner the better." He turns around and faces me. "And you're right. I need to do it with someone I can trust—and someone Momma Peaches trusts, too. Family."

"Oh, shit." I drop my arms and step back. "Don't say it. Python—"

"I know you don't like him—but Diesel is the best man for the job."

Diesel. Diesel. Diesel. I see right now that I'm going to have to get rid of this muthafucka.

10

Hydeya

Captain Melvin Johnson is dead.

The words keep repeating in my head, but they refuse to sink in—not even when I turn onto Frank Road and see that it's lit up like a Christmas tree. It looks like the entire police department has responded. I park behind a line of emergency vehicles and exit my car with my heart enlarged in the center of my throat.

A stint in Afghanistan and years on the police force taught me to be prepared for anything. Still, every once in a while, life throws you a curve ball that knocks you on your ass. This is one of those times.

The neighbors have all poured out of their perfect suburban homes to catch a peek at what's happening. No one likes to see yellow crime scene tape go up in their neighborhood. It has a way of affecting property values.

I duck under the tape and shove my way through a cluster of police officers near the front door. "Excuse me. Pardon me."

The officers move an inch at a time, all in the wrong direction. As soon I cross the threshold, the chief barks from across the foyer, "HAWKINS!"

Police Chief Yvette Brown barely kisses five-feet, but her presence has a way of filling up a room. She makes eye contact and gestures me toward her, the deputy chief, and the lieutenant colonel.

I blink and then try to swallow my heart back into my chest, but it refuses to budge.

"Welcome to your new case," Chief Brown says in her usual no-nonsense tone. "I'm sure you know Deputy Chief Collins and Lieutenant Colonel Bertinelli?"

"Of course," I lie and shake their hands.

"Well, congratulations," the deputy chief says. "I wish it could've been under better circumstances."

I'm confused. "Congratulations?"

"Your promotion," Chief Brown answers, matter-of-factly. "You're now the new captain of police." She juts out a hand.

When I'm too slow to react, she grabs my hand and pumps it like she's jacking up a car to change a flat.

"Captain?" I blink, confused "But—"

"It's all been taken care of. The board and the mayor held an emergency meeting so that we can expedite a new chain of command before tomorrow morning's press conference."

She means before more shit hits the fan. "Press conference?" I sound like I'm stuck on stupid while giving them the deer-caught-in-headlights look. I *hate* public speaking. Any time I have to say more than two sentences in front of a camera or a crowd, I'm reduced to a blubbering idiot with overactive sweat glands.

"Don't worry about it," the chief continues. "We'll get you all caught up to speed."

I nod again and then remind myself to blink. However, three sets of eyes remain locked on me—that means I need to say something back. "Thank you," I cough up. "Thank you for the opportunity." Inwardly, I flinch at the way my tongue stumbles over the words. My delayed response must've been what they were waiting for because I'm suddenly flashed three sets of veneers and my hand is passed around for quick handshakes.

"Congratulations," Bertinelli says and then spins away on his heels.

Collins does the same thing, leaving me alone with the chief.

"You're on," Brown says, turning toward a room off to the right.

I follow close behind.

The next cluster of officers parts like the Red Sea when the chief starts barking, "All right, people. You know how this works. All who aren't on this case need to get out. I don't want a contaminated crime scene—so move it!"

They grumble, but peel out of the house. I look around Captain Johnson's home office, which is painted in blood.

One of the first questions we normally ask a victim's family is whether there is anyone who might've wanted to harm the victim, but in this case, I'd imagine that list will be a long one. The number of people the former captain put behind bars in the last two decades would be just the beginning.

My gaze sweeps around the room while a forensic team combs every inch, snaps pictures, and dusts for prints.

"Was there a sign of a break-in?" I ask no one in particular.

"No," the chief responds. "The killer was either known or was able to trick her way into the house."

"Her? How do you know it was a woman?"

"The grandson. He saw the whole thing and then ran to a neighbor's house. They are the ones who called this in."

Christopher. I know the name well because the department spent months looking for him after his mother, Officer Melanie Johnson, was murdered. The eight-year-old boy was abducted and held by Memphis's most wanted, Terrell "Python" Carver—a name that strikes close to home.

"But get this." Brown faces me. "The kid says our suspect identified herself as his grandmother."

"What?" I glance down at the floor, where Victoria Johnson lies covered up next to her husband. "From the father's side?"

"Must be."

"He has a name?"

"Actually, the kid says he's never seen her before."

"Okay. Who's the father?"

"He won't say." Brown folds her arms, takes another look at the mess and shakes her head. "You should put a call into county and get a copy of his birth certificate. Hopefully, his mother listed the father."

"Where's the kid now?"

"Upstairs. Packing." She sighs. "Children's Protective Services are on their way."

I huff out a long breath. "I'll go up and talk to him."

The chief says, "Good luck. The kid's been through a lot these past few months."

"Got it." I thread back out of the office and then head up the staircase. At the top, I spot an officer standing outside a bedroom door. "The kid in there?" I ask.

"Yep." The cop nods and then steps aside.

I knock once and wait, but when I don't get a response, I twist the knob. "Christopher?" I duck my head inside and then ease farther into the room. For a few seconds, I don't see him—but the window is open. "Shit." I rush across the room, but then I spot him quivering in the far corner.

My heart melts for the kid. He looks terrified, lost, and lonely. His large brown eyes swim with tears.

"Heeeeey," I greet, creeping forward. But the closer I get, the smaller he becomes. "Everything is fine. Everything is going to be all right," I reassure him and then squat down so that we're at eye level. "I'm Lieuten—I mean, I'm *Captain* Hydeya Hawkins. I'm going to be the one who's going to find out what happened to your grandparents. Do you think that you can help and tell me what you saw?"

"I . . . I already told them," Christopher says sullenly. "A crazy woman killed my grandparents."

"I know—but I want to hear the whole story from you. Do you mind? Do you think that you can tell it again?"

His tears finally splash over his long lashes and run down his chubby cheeks. He's quiet for so long that I wonder whether he has the fortitude to repeat his story.

"M-my family is dead," he says. "They are *all* dead."

My gut twists in anguish. "I know, sweetheart. I'm so sorry—but we're going to find who did this and lock them up. We're going to keep you safe, too. I promise."

"Y-you can't promise," he says, seeing right through me. "My mom was a cop . . . and my granddaddy was too, and they couldn't protect themselves."

"I know. I know." I place my hand on his knee and give it a gentle squeeze.

In response, Christopher burrows deeper into the corner. He can't make himself small enough.

I remove my hand, not wanting to frighten him further. "If we're going to find the woman who did this then, we're going to need some more information. Do you remember what she looked like?"

There's a long pause before Christopher nods. "S-she . . ." He licks his dry lips. "She said that she was my grandmother."

"Was she? Have you ever met her before?" I ask.

The little boy shakes his head.

"Okay. Let me ask you this: what's your father's name?"

Christopher's eyes grow as large as two silver dollars. "I'm not supposed to talk about him."

I frown. "What do you mean?"

"Mom said that I'm not supposed to tell anyone about him. Nobody—not even granny and grandpa. She said that they would get mad."

"Did she say why?"

He pauses and then shrugs. "She said that grandpa wouldn't like it."

"Oh." I let that rotate in my head. Was this whole thing a family drama on steroids? "It's okay now to tell me who he is—so we can call and talk to him. Maybe you can stay with him for a while—"

"NO!"

The outburst startles me.

"I don't want to go back there! They're mean and awful and . . ." He's trembling harder.

"And what?" I press, even though I just want to take him in my arms and wipe away his fears. Instead, I remain professional and keep my distance.

Christopher's war between what he should and shouldn't say plays on his face.

"It's okay. You can tell me."

He shakes his head.

"I can't fix anything if you don't share with me," I tell him.

Christopher swallows so hard that he actually makes a *gulp* sound—but he keeps his secrets.

Giving up, I back away. "You don't have to tell me now if you don't want to. I'm not going to force you."

"Don't make me go back there. I don't want to go back there. Please. Please. Don't do it," he cries.

Go back? "All right. All right. You won't have to go," I say, desperate to calm him down.

Knock. Knock.

I glance over my shoulder toward the bedroom door in time to see the chief enter.

"We have to go," she announces before tossing a casual glance at the kid in the corner. When her gaze swings back to me, I read the invisible question: *How's it going?*

I answer by shaking my head.

"We may have a lead," she says, changing the subject.

I stand as she motions for me to follow her. However, before I step away, I flutter an awkward smile at the kid. "I'll be right back." Walking to the door, I can feel his large eyes track my every move.

In the hallway, Chief Brown fills me in on the latest. "You need to get over to Baptist Memorial. Two women were admitted, telling the staff and security over there one hell of a story. One woman claims that she was abducted from here tonight."

"We have names?"

"Yeah. Barbara Lewis and Maybelline Carver."

Carver? There's a click in my head and a kick in my gut. "I'm on my way."

11

Ta'Shara

Fuck sleep.

The way I feel right now I'll probably never sleep again. In the meantime, I have to force myself to lie next to Profit in his king-size bed and stare up at the ceiling. He can't sleep either, I can tell by his breathing. Maybe he's waiting for me to have another breakdown. Hell. I'm not too sure that I won't.

What am I going to do now? What's going to become of me? I'm supposed to be smart. Why don't I have an answer? Why have I never developed a plan B or a C? I was supposed to go to college and then medical school. I was supposed to become *Dr. Ta'Shara Murphy*—now who am I going to be?

Profit squeezes my hand and I sneak a moment to study him. He's no longer the thin, cute hottie I met at the mall almost two years ago. He's packed on muscles since his release from the hospital and his boyish good looks are transitioning into a handsome man—my man.

I love him so much that I can hardly breathe—and yet, in the back of my head, a voice lays the blame for my pain at his feet. Tears sting my eyes because, despite it all, I still don't want to live without him. He is my heart. To deny him and what we have is to deny life itself. To blame him is to blame myself.

My gaze shifts back up to the ceiling and I will my tears to dry. There's only one person responsible for all this shit, and that's LeShelle. I'm tired of asking myself why things keep happening to me, why my own flesh and blood would torture me the way that she has. Because there's only one answer: she's evil. Plain and simple. And somehow, some way, I have to stop her. I gotta beat her at her own game.

BUZZZZZ! BUZZZZ!

Startled, I bolt straight up in the bed.

Profit sits up with me and presses a reassuring hand on my shoulder. "It's all right," he whispers, sweeping my hair back from my face. "It's my phone."

On the nightstand, his cell phone, set on vibrate, rattles around.

BUZZZZZ! BUZZZZ!

He reaches across me to grab it.

I feel foolish. LeShelle has turned me into some pathetic creature who's scared of her own shadow.

"Yeah. Talk to me," Profit greets his caller. There's a long pause. "Momma?" he asks. He listens again and then hops out of bed. "All right. Calm down. Now *what* happened?"

Shock blankets Profit's face.

Concerned, I go to him. "What is it, baby?"

He holds up a finger and concentrates on the call. Whatever is being said, it's not good news. *What in the hell could be happening now?*

"All right," Profit says. "Which hospital are you at?" He looks around the floor and snatches up clothes. "Sit tight. We're on our way." He disconnects the call and barks out one order: "Get dressed."

"What's going on?" I grab my jeans.

"My mother was kidnapped by some crazy bitch and almost killed tonight," he says with disbelief.

My mind zooms to LeShelle. "Fuck."

"Let's go!"

"I'm going. I'm going."

We dress in record time and we race out of the door. Even as we're jumping into the car, I can't get my mind to think straight.

Profit is a wreck.

"Do you need me to drive?"

"Nah. I got this." He turns over the ignition, and then zooms out of the driveway. "Do you think that LeShelle has anything to do with this?"

"I don't know what to think." He's rattled.

I squeeze his hand to give him moral support, the same way he did me a few hours ago, but it's not enough. "It's going to be okay," I ramble. "She called so that means she's all right."

He doesn't respond. Hell, I don't even know if he heard me. He's so focused on the road.

At the hospital, we jet out of the car as fast as we can. The emergency room is choked with people, most looking like they've been camped here all night.

Profit races to the registration desk, tugging me along. "I'm looking for my mother. She called and said that she was here. The name is Barbara Lewis."

The chick behind the counter with a phone tucked under her chin remains unfazed and lazily lifts a slender finger, telling us to wait.

With no time for bullshit, Profit reaches over the counter, snatches the phone out of her hand, and then hangs the bitch up. "The name is Barbara Lewis," he growls.

The nurse's face twists like she's about to get turned up, but Profit's look dares her to do it. Her attitude melts away and whatever shit she was about to spit is put on pause. Turning to her computer, she asks, "What's the name again?"

"Barbara. Lewis."

We wait through her two-finger typing on the keyboard. "Yes. She's been admitted. She's in room 712."

"Admitted," Profit repeats. "What's wrong with her?"

"You'll have to talk to her doctor about that. I don't have that information."

"This is fuckin' ridiculous." He slams a fist down on the counter.

The nurse jumps in her seat. "I'm sorry, but that's all I know."

"Profit, baby." I touch his shoulder in hopes he'll calm down.

"C'mon." He grabs my arm again and pulls me toward the elevators.

I don't have the heart to tell him that he's pulling my arm out of its socket so I roll with the pain.

He jabs the up button a dozen times in two seconds while the glowing green numbers above the door descend at a snail's pace.

"C'mon. C'mon," he grumbles.

"Profit, don't get yourself so worked up."

He ignores me and keeps pacing. I drop my hands to my sides and let him roam around in a circle.

By the time the elevator doors slide open, I'm about to crawl out of my skin, too. We rush into the small box, press the button for the seventh floor, and then suffer through another excruciating wait as it climbs at the same slow-ass pace.

On the seventh floor, we spring out and immediately notice a cluster of police officers in the center of the hallway—a major clue as to which room a kidnapping victim is lying in. Dread creeps up my spine. Bad news is the only news we know lately.

"Mom?" Profit inquires, rushing into the room. He drops my hand when he sees her lying in the bed. She's banged up pretty good: one black eye and a busted lip and nose.

I hang back, awkward, like a third wheel.

"Raymond," his mother exclaims, opening her arms.

Profit leans into her embrace and they hold each other and

rock together for a moment before he begins his interrogation. "Momma, what happened?"

KNOCK. KNOCK.

I turn around to see a woman with a police badge draped around her neck enter.

"Hello, I'm Captain Hawkins," she says, jutting out a hand. "I'll be investigating your mother's case. I came to get a statement."

"Oh, no. She's not my mother," I correct her.

"She's mine," Profit says, eyeballing the cop suspiciously.

"Sorry about that." The captain smiles and then walks over to Profit to shake his hand. "And your name is?"

Profit ignores her question and leaves her hand hanging in the air. "Who did this shit to her?"

"Raymond, baby." Barbara says, patting a spot next to her on the bed. "Please, sit down."

He shakes his head. He can't sit right now—not when he's ready to punch someone.

"That's exactly what I came here to find out." Captain Hawkins lowers her hand and then turns her attention to his mother. "Okay, Mrs. Lewis, if you could start from the beginning . . ."

12

Lucifer

He's alive.

I'm scared to go to sleep, afraid that I'll wake up to an empty bed, like this is all a crazy dream. I can take a lot of shit, but I won't be able to take that. I lost him once—I can't do that shit again.

Mason must feel the same way because after a long session of lovemaking he's lying beside me and staring into my eyes. Only Mason knows how to transform me from a stone-cold killer to a passionate woman.

I'm his bitch.

I'm his woman.

I'm his everything.

I wouldn't have it any other way.

Dawn comes too soon. At any moment, the real world outside my window will intrude. There's so much to tell him—so much has happened since his "death" that I don't know where to start. The wars, the infighting—the deaths.

"Whassup, Willow?" He brushes a kiss against my lips. "What's got you thinking so hard?"

"Bishop," I whisper, my voice shaky as fuck. "He's dead."

Mason stiffens. He waits as if expecting a punch line; but

after reading the truth in my face, he bounces out of the bed with an explosive, "FUUUCCCKKKK!" When that isn't enough, he grabs my lamp from the nightstand and launches it toward the wall.

CRASH!

He looks around for something else to break, but then forces himself to stop. He stands next to the bed, huffing out his rage and pain. He and Bishop were like brothers. I know the news of his death is ripping a hole in his heart.

"WHO?"

"The Grape Street Crips."

He twists around, his face incredulous. "Those crooked-walking muthafuckas came hard at us like that? Where the fuck did they get the balls?"

"The shit took us by surprise."

"Nah. Nah. Those niggas were on the come-up 'cause they thought the king had fallen. They tested your skirts—"

"And they're all gonna feel my blade for that shit," I shout back. He's making it sound like I couldn't handle the job. "Bishop fucked up and let the wrong bitches get too close to him at Da Club. It was a setup to jack him and his boys' poker game, and the shit must have went to the left."

"A couple of bitches took my man out?"

"The hardest lesson for y'all niggas to learn is to trust no bitch," I tell him. "There were six muthafuckas involved. Five Crippettes and a getaway nigga that I sliced up last night."

Mason cocks a brow. "You put in work last night, Willow?"

"And I will every night until I cut the head off their leader—that fuckin' double-flaggin' snake, Shariffa."

"Why do I know that name?"

"She's one of Python's ex-wifeys."

"So she's a Queen G?"

"No. She was kicked off her throne a while back so she slithered over to the Grapes and locked down their chief."

"That takes talent. I didn't know Lynch's ass was into recycling." Mason sneers, shaking his head. "The whole damn world has gone crazy."

"Crazy or not, I'm gutting every one of those bitches—nice and slow." My anger has me simmering again. "That Crunk nigga I sliced up sang like a bird. Lynch's chick got the wrong understanding on who runs these streets. I'm fuckin' duty bound to formally introduce myself. You feel me?"

Mason bobs his head, though I can tell that the news is still eating away at him. "A'ight. I'll let you handle that." He climbs back in bed.

My body instantly welcomes his warmth.

"How are you holding up?" he asks, softly. He knows better than anyone that despite all the sibling bullshit, the love between me and my brother ran deep.

"I'm all right—better now that you're here."

He takes my chin between his fingertips and tilts up my head. "You're always the strong one."

"I don't know how to be any other way," I confess.

"I wouldn't want you any other way."

We kiss. It's one of those slow, mouth-exploring kisses and it makes me melt into his arms all over again. His hands drift down my body, caress my belly, and then encircle my waist. He pulls back with a soft chuckle.

"My lady has gotten a little thick around the middle while I was gone."

The baby. I still haven't told him about the baby.

"Hey. Don't worry." He pulls me closer. "I love a woman with a little meat on her bones." He nibbles on my bottom lip.

"Is that right?"

"Um, hmm. More cushion for the pushin." He slaps me on the ass and then squeezes it.

"I don't know. Maybe we need to ease up on all that pushing," I say.

"What? Don't tell me that I've already wore your ass out."

"Ha! Check your ego at the door. I'm giving your ass a break since you've been rehabbing out in the woods like a black Grizzly Adams." I roll him onto his back and then climb up to straddle his monster cock. No words can describe how good it feels to ride his smooth, satiny dick. His shit stretches and fills me up.

Golden morning sunlight slices through my venetian blinds and gives me a better view of my king—in the streets *and* in my bed. Gently, I run my fingers over his burned skin. His gaze locks onto my mine and I know that he's tryna see whether I find him repulsive, but the opposite is true. He's the most beautiful thing that I've ever seen.

Squeezing my pussy muscles as I ride, I watch him squirm and writhe beneath me.

"Aw, shit," he pants.

"You like that?" I pick up the pace until our bodies slap together, giving me a nice sting against my ass.

"That's right, Willow. Fuck me. Fuck your nigga. Show me how much you missed this fuckin' dick."

My grip on his dick tightens. His breathing becomes choppy as he grabs my waist so that he can control our rhythm.

I knock his hands off, but then pin them down on opposite sides of his head. "I got this."

Mason chuckles and moans at the same time. I can see in his face that he wants to shoot off, but he's fighting it.

"You wanna fuckin' come, baby?" I tease him.

He growls while sweat beads across his brow.

"Answer me, baby," I lean forward and lick the side of his face. "Don't you want to come in my sweet pussy?"

"Grrrrr."

"Ain't this the best pussy you ever had?"

"Fuck yeah."

I find the strength to grip him tighter. "Then come for me. Show me how much you love this pussy." I love him for submitting to me. Some niggas don't know how to let a woman be in control. A smile creeps across my face when his bottom lip quivers. He's about to nut.

"That's it, baby. C'mon. Come for momma."

"AHHHHHHHHH!" His arms break free from my grasp as he sits up and wraps his meaty arms around my waist.

Within seconds, my body explodes and honey gushes between my legs, sticking us together.

Exhausted, I curl up against his chest.

Mason keeps his arms wrapped around me and peppers the top of my head with kisses. "I love you, Willow," he whispers.

My eyes fly back open.

"I had to get back here so I could tell you that. I have always loved you."

Lifting my head, I look up into his eyes. "I love you, too."

My cell phone rings, but I don't have the strength to answer it.

"Don't you think that you should get that?" Mason asks.

"Nah. There is such a thing as voice mail." As soon as the ringing stops it starts up again. "Shit."

"It may be important," he says.

"It's always important. These soldiers need constant babysitting. But right now, all I want to do is sleep, fuck, and sleep some more."

"Yeah?"

"Um-hmm. We can work out the other shit later."

"What other shit?"

"Like, how are we going to handle your whole return-from-the-dead situation?" I say, resting my chin in the center of his chest. "Everyone is going to freak out."

"First, we'll call a meeting with all our top people, and then we put the word out to all the foot soldiers and corner boys. They'll spread the shit far and wide in the streets that I'm back."

I smile. "Just like that, huh?"

"Just like that. I'll be a legend."

"You *and* Python."

He flinches and diverts his gaze from mine.

"I don't know if you know, but he survived that crash, too." I watch him, trying to catch a flicker of emotion. He doesn't know that I found out about his family's dark secret— that he and Python are brothers. His mother spilled the beans. How and why he kept something like that from me for all these years, I don't know.

"No. I didn't know that."

"Yeah. Profit and I sniffed him out after his wedding, if you can believe it. He married that crazy bitch, LeShelle. We drove by to pay our respects, replaced the confetti with bullets."

"Let me guess. He survived that shit, too?"

"What can I say? You two have a lot in common."

He stares at me.

"You both have nine lives," I answer, intending the double meaning.

"Humph. So the war continues," he grumbles under his breath. "I'll catch up with that muthafucka sooner or later."

I nod, but get nowhere trying to read him. Gangster Disciples and Vice Lords were beefing long before there were eight-tracks. I've always thought, Mason's main drive to defeat the GD's head nigga was about the shoot-out that cost him an eye, but now I'm wondering if it has more to do with Python killing Melanie. Not because she was Cousin Skeets's daughter, but because he was in love with her.

My heart drops into the pit of my stomach. After all, he didn't crawl into my bed until after she was out of the picture. "Well," I break in to change the subject. "I think the first person we need to talk to is Profit. He isn't too happy with me nowadays and he ain't shy about lettin' my ass know it."

A goofy smile breaks out across Mason's face. "Is that right? Lil man missed his big bro?"

"Fuck yeah. He was tore up over the shit. I can't wait to see his face when he sees you."

He sits up. "I can't wait to see his ass either. Maybe we should do that shit first thing. Call him over for breakfast."

"*If* he takes my call."

Mason frowns. "It's *that* serious? What went down?"

My cell phone goes off again. "Fuck."

"Answer it." He slaps my butt. "Clearly, whoever it is is going to keep calling until you pick it up."

Annoyed, I stretched over and grab the phone. "Yeah. What is it?"

"HE'S DEAD. HE'S DEAD. HE'S DEAD!"

I almost didn't recognize my momma's wailing. "Momma, calm down."

"HE'S DEAD. HE'S DEAD. HE'S DEAD."

"I know, Momma. I know." I climb off of Mason and swing my legs over the bed. "But Bishop wouldn't want you to be crying like this," I say soothingly, though I have no idea if that shit is true or not.

"No. Not Bishop. It's *Melvin*. He's dead. It's all over the news," she screeches.

"What?" Did I hear her right? "Cousin Skeet?"

"OH, GOD. WHHHHYYYYY?"

"Holy shit!" I bounce out of bed and hit the television from across the room.

"Whassup?" Mason asks.

"*. . . the police are stumped as to why this escaped mental patient, Alice Carver, murdered the city's twenty-year police captain and his wife in their home. Authorities have offered little information about* *the case, but stated that they are currently interviewing two women who were kidnapped by the same woman: Barbara Lewis and Maybelline Carver—an older sister of the alleged killer . . ."*

"Barbara Lewis," Mason responds, catching his mother's name. "What the fuck? Has the whole damn world gone crazy since I've been gone?"

13

Momma Peaches

"Maybelline, can you wake up for me?" a man's voice floats somewhere above me. I wish that he would go away. This sleep is feeling too good. In fact, I wouldn't mind lying here forever. "Maybelline?" he persists—to the point that I don't think that he's ever going away. "Maybelline?"

"Whaaaat?" My small grunt irritates my dry throat and I erupt into a coughing frenzy—which makes it worse.

"That's it. That's it. Here. Drink some water."

Someone helps tip my head up and I lean and take a sip from the cup. Sweet Jesus, it's the best water that I've ever tasted.

The spasm disappears and I collapse back against a hard bed and a flat pillow.

"Feel better?" the voice asks.

I nod and start to drift back to sleep.

"Maybelline, do you think that you can wake up and answer a few questions for me?" the voice asks

Now?

"C'mon, Maybelline. I need you to wake up," he insists. "C'mon."

Since he's working my last nerve, I go ahead and fight to open my eyes, but they fuckin' weigh a goddamn ton.

"Thata girl." A blurry face is now attached to the voice. It's an old white man with cotton-white hair and beard. "How are you feeling?"

"Like shit," I croak and then remember my vow to turn over a new leaf. "I don't feel well," I amend.

"I'm afraid that you're going to be feeling like that for a while," he says, flashing a small light into each of my eyes. "I'm Dr. Berg and I'm going to be your primary doctor during your stay here at the hospital. Do you remember how you came to be here?"

I hesitate. I haven't had time to come up with a story or at the bare minimum sync my shit up with that crazy, baby-stealing bitch, Dribbles. Should I play dumb and say Alice was plum crazy and I don't know why the fuck she did what she did, or confess the truth and let the chips fall where they may? I should send that white bitch to jail.

What would Jesus do?

That's a dangerous question because I don't like the answer. The truth would draw *waaaay* too many secrets out of the closet and have them play out on the evening news—and what's the point in that?

Alice is dead.

Python is dead.

Mason is dead.

"It's okay if you can't answer right now," Dr. Berg reassures me. "Judging by the trauma you've sustained, it's not unusual to suffer some memory loss."

A lie of omission—I can roll with that for now.

"Rest. I'm gonna do all I can to take real good care of you." He opens a folder. "If you're feeling sore, it's because we had to pump an awful lot of nasty toxins out of your system. Somebody upstairs must be looking out for you. It's a miracle you're still with us."

I smile. *You have no idea.*

"*But* . . . you have sustained some kidney damage, though

I don't think you'll need dialysis. We can probably fix it with medication. You also have two broken ribs and a dislocated shoulder.

"The good news is that you'll survive. We're going to work hard to get you through this," he reassures. "Now is there anything else that I can do for you? Are you comfortable?"

Didn't I tell him that I felt like shit?

"All right. Save your energy." He presses a hand against my good shoulder. "I'll be back to check on you later." He steps away from the bed only to be replaced by a female cop. She's not in a uniform, but I know a cop when I see one. My mood goes from bad to worse.

The chick stares at me, to the point that I think that she's waiting for my ass to say something first.

"Uh, hello," I say.

She snaps out of her trance. "Hello, Mrs. Goodson. I'm Captain Hydeya Hawkins with the Memphis Police Department. I was hoping that I could take a few minutes of your time and ask you some questions—I need a statement from you about exactly what happened between you and your sister over the last few months?"

"I . . . I . . ." My throat spasms out and I start coughing again.

A nurse appears out of nowhere and helps me get down some more water.

"Captain, maybe this can wait for another time," Dr. Berg interjects, saving my ass.

She hesitates, and then gives me a stiff smile. "All right." She reaches inside her jacket, removes a card, and places it on the table beside my bed. "I'll be back later—but if you want to talk sooner, give me a call." She flashes me another fake smile that doesn't reach her eyes.

As she turns and heads for the door, it hits me that she reminds me of someone, but I can't put my finger on who.

The captain opens the door and allows the doctor to walk

ahead of her. She pauses and we exchange a long stare before she finally walks out.

What the fuck was that about?

I stare at the closed door and review what just happened. "Mrs. Goodson?" No one ever calls me by my married name—not even my no-good husband who's currently serving a bid in the federal pen. *Maybe she's already done her homework on me. Lord knows I have a lifetime of arrests to keep her entertained.*

Tired, I dismiss the incident and close my eyes for a second. When I open them again, it's three hours later and there's a bouquet of flowers sitting on the table. Curious, I reach for the small, white envelope nestled in the center of the arrangement.

> *Get well. I'll see you soon.*
> *D.*

D—Dribbles. I roll my eyes. It's gonna take more than flowers to make up for what she's done to my family.

"Knock, knock," a voice singsongs.

I look up and see Dribbles, walking in with another bundle of flowers. Her face is banged up, but it doesn't stop her from spreading a smile across her busted lip.

"Oh good. You're up." She enters, waving in people behind her.

In comes a tall, good-looking young man who has me lifting an interested brow. Behind him, a young fresh-faced little girl with sad, troubled eyes.

"I hope you don't mind," Dribbles says. "But Ms. Maybelline Carver, I'd like to introduce you to my son, Raymond, and his girlfriend—ah, I'm sorry, what is your name again?"

"Ta'Shara," the girl answers. "Ta'Shara Murphy."

I choke.

"Oh, goodness." Dribbles rushes to the bed and quickly prepares me another cup of water.

Now I'm coughing and drowning at the same time. Tilting me forward, Dribbles gets the bright idea to whack me on the back.

"Mom," Raymond says, coming forward, hopefully to save my ass. "You're hurtin' her."

"Oh." She stops. "I'm sorry. Are you all right?"

"Fine." I croak, holding out my hands and signaling for her not to touch my ass again. I glance back at LeShelle's sister, confused. *Wasn't she locked up in a mental hospital?*

"Anyway," Dribbles says, "we didn't get a chance to formally meet and . . . after you saved my life like that I . . . wait. Where's my head? I'm Barbara Lewis." Unable to keep her hands to herself, she grabs my hand and squeezes it tight. "I thank God that you were there last night. I mean, I hate that you went through all that you went through with Alice and everything, but—"

"Mom. She gets it," Raymond cuts her off with a smile.

Nice dimples. The old cougar in me sits up and takes notice. If I didn't look a hot mess, I'd give his young girl a run for her money.

The ceiling lights flicker. Remembering God can hear my thoughts, I wipe the smile off my face and mentally apologize for my impure thoughts. *Oh God. This shit might be harder than I thought.*

Raymond takes my hand from his mother's and instantly my body is infused with lust.

Yeah. This is going to be reeeaaal hard.

"Thank you for saving my mom's life." He glances at Dribbles and sighs. "I'd be lost without her. We've already suffered an incredible loss in the family and—"

"Mason." My eyes wet up.

Raymond blinks. "You knew my brother?"

My gaze shoots to Dribbles.

She places a hand on my good shoulder, while panic enlarges her blue eyes. *Fuck* this bitch. *I don't owe her damn thing.* "Mason was my nephew. Your mother stole—"

"Raymond, honey, can you give us a few minutes alone please?"

"—him from us. Your momma should be in jail."

Raymond drops my hand like a hot poker.

"Raymond, please?" Dribbles insists, her voice squeaking.

Silence fills the room as Raymond backpedals. He looks stunned, but not surprised. Suddenly, he turns, grabs his girlfriend's hand, and bolts out of the room.

"You didn't have to do that."

"Fuck you." I look her up and down. "I don't understand how you could just take Mason like that. The whole city was looking for him. We thought he was dead. *I* thought he was dead. You didn't hear all the names I called my sister—or how I turned my back on her."

Dribbles sighs and lowers her head. "Let me explain."

"You ain't got to explain shit. Your ass needs to be locked up."

Dribbles shakes her head. "You don't understand. You weren't there. Alice was fuckin' out of her mind. Doped up and knocked out. We found Mason screaming his head off inside the fuckin' *oven*. Who does that shit? I mean . . . I'm no fuckin' angel and I had the same monkey on my back and I wouldn't have never done no shit like that."

"The oven?" I flash back to that day when I'd showed up at Alice's apartment. She was knocked out with her crack rocks lying everywhere and Mason nowhere to be found.

"Me and my man kept thinking: what if she'd turned it on?" Dribbles asks. "What if we didn't show up when we did?"

Her question gut checks me, but I still can't let go of my anger. "You didn't have the fuckin' right to keep him. He had a family. I was his family. I would've taken care of him."

"I get that you're upset, but, at the time, with all the media attention, it would've brought a lot of heat on us and our situation."

"You mean you didn't want to go to jail."

"For doing the right thing?" Dribble snaps back.

I can't fuckin' believe this bitch. "You don't get it. You stole my sister's baby. You stole her life. You stole her sanity—what was left of it. I turned my back on her over this shit. *That's* why my ass was in that fuckin' basement. *That's* why she beat and poisoned my ass, because of *you*."

Lord, please help me to not jump out of this bed. I don't wanna have to beat this white woman's ass.

"You need to bounce out of here," I tell her. "I made a mistake in saving your ass because the way I see it right now, you deserve to be in that fuckin' grave Alice was about to put you in. What you did is unforgiveable."

Dribbles's eyes fill with tears, but the fuckin' waterworks ain't gonna work on my ass. "Are you going to tell the police?"

I let the question hang in the air for a long time. "What's the point? They're all dead now. Every last fuckin' one of them."

Dribbles reaches for my hand, but I jerk it away.

"Get the fuck out of here before I finish what Alice started."

14

Ta'Shara

"**W**hat in the hell just happened back there?" I ask Profit as he drags me out of that old lady's hospital room. "What did she mean that she's Mason's aunt? Are you guys related? Why did your mother tell the cops that she's never met her before tonight?"

Profit shakes his head and shrugs at the same time, but something is off. There's something that he's not telling me.

"What did she mean by your mother stole—?"

"Shhh." Profit jerks me up against him, cutting me off. He glances over his shoulder to make sure that no one is listening in on our conversation.

"Just tell me. What the hell is going on?" I feel as if I'm caught up in some kind of matrix.

Profit releases my arm. We're standing in a small waiting area with one old guy huddled up and snoring in a corner. Even then, Profit doesn't seem to be in any rush to spit the truth.

"Well?" I press him.

"All right, look," he starts under his breath. "There's a lot of shit in the family closet that I'm not supposed to know, but . . . one of the obvious things is that Mason and I weren't really truly brothers—not by blood. I mean, at heart, we accepted each other as brothers. We were brought up together and everything."

He's rambling. To calm him down, I take his hand and smile. "So? Mason was adopted." I shrug. "I figured that much. No offense. It's not like you two look anything alike." I laugh to soften the mood.

It doesn't work. In fact, he gets more worked up. "Mason wasn't adopted," he says, running a hand over his head and looking back over his shoulder again. "He was kidnapped."

"What?" I blink, and then run his words through my head again. "I don't . . . What do you mean?"

Profit huffs out a long breath, hesitating to spill his family's secrets. "I don't know. Mason only told me the one time . . . and he was pretty fucked up that night that . . . shit. I thought his ass was trippin'."

"You're jumping all over the place. I don't understand. What happened?"

He takes another deep breath and starts over. "There's this one time, years ago, at Mason's eighteenth birthday party. My mom and I flew up from Atlanta. We had this huge block party. No expense was spared. We had the best La, the best girls, the best food and music—you name it. Mason was officially a man—*The Man*—and he wanted everyone to fuckin' know it. Of course, we all knew that Mason was already boss. He'd been head nigga in our set since Smokes got locked up.

"Vice Lords all up and down the East Coast rolled through and dropped off gifts. Mason basked in that shit, took me under his wing and told me that one day niggas were gonna be bowing down to me, too, if I followed his lead. At that time, Momma wasn't tryna hear about my ass moving back here. Memphis had too many bad memories for her. Anyway, some time during the party, Mason disappeared so I went looking for him.

"When I found him, he was . . . upset, but he wouldn't tell

me why. He went back to the party, but from that moment on, it was clear that he wasn't feeling it. Momma was acting funny too that night, but I couldn't get anything out of her either. For hours I watched them, knowing something was up. Hell, I thought that they were fighting over me—on whether I could move back to Memphis and stay with him.

"Hours later, when niggas were falling out and hooking up for the night, I found him again. This time he was angry. I pressed him on what was up. He shook me off for a little while, but then the Hennessey kicked in and loosened his tongue. . . ."

"She snatched me. Can you fuckin' believe that shit, dawg?" he said.

I didn't understand what the fuck he was talking about. "Who snatched you?" I asked him.

"Moms. Straight snatched me from my people and . . . nah." He shook his head. "Doesn't matter. Doesn't matter. This is my real family—not those grimy . . ." He worked his mouth like he couldn't even say the words. "The oven . . . the bitch put my ass in the damn oven like I was fuckin' dinner."

I was still lost.

"Don't you think that shit is fucked up?"

I shrugged even though I wasn't sure what to make of his drunk rambling.

"My blood . . . runs black and gold—there's no coming back from that. . . . What the fuck am I supposed to do with that information now? After all this time? I mean, why tell my ass now?" Mason jumped up from his armchair and paced around like a caged animal. "Nah. Nah. We squash this shit. Right here. Right now. We're never gonna talk about this shit again. You feel me?"

I hesitated only because I wasn't too sure of what the hell I was agreeing to squash.

"YOU FEEL ME?" he demanded.

I jumped, but quickly agreed. "A'ight. Yeah. Cool."

"Cool. Cool." Mason turned up his bottle of Henney.

I side-eyed him, tryna gauge his mood. Hell, I was young. I didn't know what to make of the shit. Couple of seconds later, he changed up. He plastered on a smile, grabbed my head like it was a football—that shit used to always bug the fuck out of me—and then refused to let me go until I cried uncle.

When he let me go, he had this strange look on his face. "Tell you what, Ray. No matter what nobody says, I'm always gonna be your big brother. You got that?"

"Yeah. I got it."

Mason's smile wobbled. "Good. Now forget all that other shit. Get the fuck out of here and let your big brother go find something soft and gushy to get up in—before this fucked-up birthday really goes to shit."

When Profit's story drifts off, I wait a second to see if he's going to finish it, but then he doesn't say anything else. "That's it?"

His eyes snap back to me. "That's enough, don't you think?"

I pause a minute so that I can digest that story. "So that woman back there *really* was Mason's aunt?"

"I don't know." Profit shrugs. "She could be." His cell phone rings and he quickly scoops it out of his pocket.

"Who is it?"

"Lucifer." He shakes his head and then stuffs the phone back into his pocket. "I'll call her back later."

I glance back down the crowded hallway at the closed hospital room. "So the woman who kidnapped them was—?"

"I said I don't know. Fuck. Enough with all the damn questions."

"All right." I toss up my hands. "Forget I said anything."

Profit's mom races out of the room with her face in her hands, running blindly.

"Mom." Profit takes off after her.

I toss another look at the guarded hospital door. Maybelline Carver. *Carver. Isn't that Python's last name?*

15

Lucifer

Uncle Skeet is dead.

That shit is another shock to the system—even though I never liked his crooked, monkey ass. The main reason is still wailing in my ear. For years, my mom has been content to be Skeet's sideline chick—happy to take any piece of him that he would give her. I never got it and I'll never understand it—especially since she wasted no time opening her legs to him within weeks my father was gunned down right in front of us in the front yard.

"What am I going to do? I don't have anybody left."

Jeez. Thanks. "Mom, let me call you back after I find out what the hell is going on."

"NOOOOOOOOOO," she cries, pathetically. "He can't leave me like this. He can't." Her devastation pulls at me, but for my own sanity I have to throw up a brick wall on this shit.

"Momma, I'll call you back."

"What am I gonna do? How am I going to live without him?"

Click.

Sorry, but I don't have time for this shit.

"Call Profit." Mason's eyes are still glued to the news report.

"Already on it." *I just hope that he takes my call.*

Of course he doesn't.

My irritation climbs a few more notches. The level of disrespect from Profit is straining the fuck out of my patience. The line rolls to voice mail and I disconnect the call and rush over to the bedroom window. "His car isn't parked in his drive," I tell Mason. "Maybe he already knows."

"Kidnapped." Mason is visibly shaken. Dribbles has always had her problems but there is no doubt that Mason loves her. "Alice Carver."

I glance back at hearing him say his mother's name. He's struggling to keep his emotions in check.

"Let's roll," Mason orders.

We take thirty minutes to shit, shower, and change before scrambling out. I'm aware that the second we walk out the door that all hell is gonna break loose. Fat Ace's miraculous rise from the dead will be official.

We take two steps out the door and see Profit's ride blaze down Ruby Cove toward his crib.

"Wait. There he goes."

I spot his girl Ta'Shara in the back seat and Dribbles riding shotgun. The anxiety rolling around in my gut relaxes a bit even as Mason and I break out into a slow trot toward Mason's old place.

When the car is parked, Dribbles climbs out and the first thing I see is the battery of bruises on her face.

"What the fuck?" Mason takes off.

As we're rushing toward the house, niggas around us stop dead in their tracks. Next comes the finger pointing—and then the whispers.

"PROFIT—MOM," Mason barks when he's inches from the driveway.

Profit climbs out of the car and freezes.

Mason quickens his pace.

Dribbles removes her shades. "Oh my God." Her mouth

falls open and then, in the next second, she slaps a hand across it in stunned disbelief. "Mason."

Profit is still unable to move as his mother takes off running.

Mason grins from ear to ear as he sweeps his mother up into his arms and swings her around.

"My baby! My baby!" Dribbles shouts. She doesn't give a damn about the crowd they drew. She keeps peppering Mason's burned face with kisses. "You're alive! You're alive!"

Profit moves away from his car door like a rusted robot, his eyes dilated with shock. He takes in the afro, the beard—and the eyes. "How in the fuck?" At last, he accepts that his eyes aren't playing tricks on him and the biggest smile I've ever seen monopolizes his face.

Mason sets his mom back down in time to receive a quick one-armed hug and a shoulder bump from his little brother.

"I don't understand? How in the fuck are you alive? Where the fuck have you been?" Profit fires off.

"Well, I fuckin' missed you, too." Mason sweeps both his momma and his brother into his mountainous arms.

"Oh, shit. It *is* that muthafucka!"

A lone voice shouts from behind us. A thick mob, about fifty deep, creeps toward us like the zombies on *Walking Dead*. Their eyes are wide. Their mouths open.

"Yo, Fat Ace is alive," another voice shouts.

"Fat Ace! Fat Ace!," they chant at the top of their voices until his name rings out from every inch of Ruby Cove.

Sixty deep.

Seventy deep.

Eighty deep.

This Lewis family Kodak moment transforms into a city-block celebration. Shots are fired in the air and somebody cranks up the music. It's official. Memphis's chief Vice Lord is back.

The streets will never be the same.

Skeletons

16

Qiana

"**Y**ou need to get rid of that damn baby," Li'l Bit says, shaking her head. "It was all over the news last night that they found that bitch and Tyneshia's bodies last night."

"I know. I know." I sit across from her at my kitchen table, tryna spoon-feed Jayson this yucky oatmeal stuff, but he's more interested in playing in the shit and splashing it everywhere.

"You know?" Li'l Bit asks. "Then what's the plan? You're just gonna raise some other bitch's kid? Have him running around and calling you mommy? Is that the game plan? If so, that shit ain't gangsta, bitch. It's fuckin' crazy."

My eyes nearly roll out the back of my head. "Girl, you're slicing up my last nerve with this shit. I done told you that I got it."

"Do you?"

"How many fuckin' times do I have to tell you that the kid is insurance?"

"Insurance against what?" she explodes. "LeShelle isn't interested in that baby. She wanted it dead—like his momma. And if her crazy ass is watching the news, she gonna know that you snatched that bastard and she's gonna want to know why—which means that she's gonna be looking for your ass."

"She ain't gonna do shit, not if she don't want her man to know her ass was behind the hit on that yellow bitch."

"Okay. What shit have you been smokin'? That ugly reptile ain't going to take your word over his woman's. He's fuckin' that bitch. Who are you?"

I stop feeding Jayson to look up and smirk. "I'm the one that's going to throw LeShelle off her throne."

"How?" Li'l Bit asks, rocking her neck.

"It's about time your slow ass catches up." I wink at her.

Jayson chooses that moment to grab a fistful of oatmeal and launch it at my hair.

Li'l Bit cracks up.

"You little fucker." I jump up from the table and snatch paper towels down from the counter.

Jayson takes a cue from Li'l Bit and bursts out laughing. He's adorable with his big head and big dimples. It's kind of hard to stay mad at him. At four months, he's turning out to be quite the comedian. Everything is funny to him.

Li'l Bit stops laughing and gawks at me. "Oh. My. God!"

I wipe the smile off my face. "What?"

"You've gotten attached to this big-headed baby."

"I have not . . . and his head isn't *that* big," I lie. Jayson has a big muthafuckin' head.

"Aww, sheiiit. You got my ass twisted in some bullshit," Li'l Bit snipes.

"Don't start." I wipe the oatmeal out of my hair and return to the table.

Li'l Bit keeps grumbling. "This shit ain't right. I still got a baaaad feeling about all of this." She stares at Jayson. "And what about that damn birthmark on his neck, huh? What are the damn chances that this baby and your new man, Diesel, have the same muthafuckin' birthmark in the same fuckin' place?"

"It's gotta be a coincidence," I reason. "Plenty of people have birthmarks. I have a black beauty mark on my left shoulder."

Li'l Bit ain't tryna hear it. "Tyneshia was right. We're caught up in some demonic curse for cutting him out of that bitch. You shouldn't have shot her ass for spitting out the truth."

Heat rushes up my neck. I grab Jayson's bowl and toss the rest of the oatmeal dead in her face.

Li'l Bit jumps up, gasping. "What the fuck?"

Jayson cracks up.

"Don't fuckin' say that bitch's name." I glance around the kitchen to make sure my brother or nosey-ass daddy ain't ear-hustling. "What are you tryin' to do—blab it to everybody? If they find out we bodied one of our own—"

"We?" My girl swipes gobs of oatmeal from her face. "What the fuck is this *we* shit?"

"*We*—as in, if *I* go down then I'm taking you and Adaryl *with* my ass. Got it?"

Li'l Bit shakes her head in disgust. "I knew that you were going to pull this shit."

"Then stop actin' surprised and keep your damn mouth shut."

"Qiana, niggas 'round here may be crazy, but they ain't *that* fuckin' crazy. Sooner or later the police are going to ID Tyneshia *and* that boy's momma. When they do, they're going to come around here and start asking questions. And everybody knows your ass didn't birth no fuckin' baby. One and one is always gonna be fuckin' two. These bitches are going to look upside our heads and know that our asses are dirty. *We* need to be getting a story together *or we* need to get rid of this bastard."

"She got a point," another voice floats into the kitchen.

Li'l Bit and I jump. GG, my brother's girlfriend, has snuck in and propped against refrigerator.

"Fuck. Don't you knock anymore?"

GG dangles a key. "Your brother thought it was time that we took things to the next level."

"The next level is for his ass to get his own place," I snipe.

GG flashes me a smile and then swishes her big hips over to the baby and kisses his forehead. "How's my sweet boy doing today?"

While she coos with the baby, I can't help but wonder how much of our conversation she overheard. The way Li'l Bit's eyes are shifting around, I know that she's wondering too.

"Don't mind me," GG says. "Y'all can go ahead and finish y'all conversation."

Li'l Bit opens her mouth, but I cut her off. "We're done."

GG smirks. "Really? So what did you decide to do?"

"I'm going to keep on minding my own business, set an example for other muthafuckas to follow."

Her neck swivels back. "Oh. So I'm a muthafucka now?"

"If the shoe fits, lace that bitch up."

"Ding, ding, ding." Li'l Bit jumps in the mix to play referee. "Back to your corners, bitches. It ain't even that serious."

GG struggles to back down. "A'ight. You know what?" she says. "I'm gonna let you have that shit 'cause it looks like you have enough rope to hang yourself."

Bang! Bang! Bang!

Someone is pounding on the door.

"Who the fuck is that?" I go peep who it is. The second I snatch open the door, Adaryl blows in like a fuckin' tornado.

"Ohmigod, bitch. Have you seen the news?" Adaryl doesn't wait for an answer; she blows straight through the door and into the living room.

I follow, hissing behind her, "I know they found the bodies—"

"You do?" She turns to blink at me.

"Yeah, but we can't talk about it right now. GG is—"

"What about the fire?" she asks.

"What fire?"

"The one that's all over the news." Adaryl grabs the remote from the coffee table and turns on the TV. She flips through the channels until she comes to a clip of a house burning on channel five.

"So?" I shrug. "Whose house is it?"

"Watch," Adaryl says.

The news camera pans away from the on the scene journalist to a girl screaming. "Is that . . . ?" Profit rushes up behind the chick, grabs and holds on to her. "What the hell is this?"

"Ta'Shara Murphy's foster parents were killed last night in that blaze."

The scars slashed across my face throb, reminding me that I still have a score to settle up with that bitch. Ta'Shara slithered her stank-pussy ass onto Profit's arm and got his nose so wide open that if he walked outside on a rainy night, he'd drown. He should've been my man. I suck in a deep breath while plotting in my head.

"Look right there!" Adaryl points to the corner of the screen,

My heart skips a beat. Ta'Shara bolts from Python's arms and races to kick the taillight of a car: a burgundy Crown Victoria.

"LeShelle," I whisper.

Li'l Bit and GG join us in the living room.

"What's going on?" Li'l Bit asks.

The pieces snap together. "That psycho bitch murdered her sister's foster parents."

Li'l Bit gasps. "We need to get rid of this damn baby before that psycho bitch comes looking for him."

I nod. *The sooner, the better.*

17

LeShelle

It's been all over the news for two days. Python's momma—
who, for some damn reason, I thought was long dead—escaped
a mental hospital and went all Freddy Krueger on everybody. I
don't know what the hell is going on. Suddenly, Python has
family members coming out of the woodwork.

Python has calmed down, but he's still not thinking clearly.
He still wants some grand family reunion. I don't know what
the fuck I'm going to do about him. I've worked too hard to
get where I am to lose this shit now, but I swear to God I can
feel it all slipping through my fingers like the hot water in this
shower. What trips me out is that Python is acting like he
doesn't care. I ain't never had to ride his ass to fight for the
throne before. Hell, I don't understand him *at all* anymore—
and I married his ass.

There has to be a way for us to get back on the same page.
I need for him to get his head back into the game before he
hands control of the Gangster Disciples to some pussy-ass fuck
nigga from the A. Sheeeiit. I lower my head under the shower
spray and wait for the hot water to do something about the
tension coiling my muscles. The only thing that happens is the
fuckin' water turns ice cold on me.

Some fuckin' honeymoon this shit has turned out to be.

Bam! Bam! Bam!

The bathroom door jumps around on its hinges.

"C'mon, Shelle. We gotta roll," Python barks.

Annoyed, I huff out a breath and shut off the water. But while rushing to dry off, my gaze snags on my reflection in the mirror. Fuck. I lean in squinting. Same petite frame, same sick curves, yet still at certain angles, I don't look like myself.

This is what happens when you sell your soul for a crown—or a man. My gaze sweeps across the dozens of keloids spread across my chest. Stab wounds courtesy of my lil sis—same for my chewed-up right earlobe, but at least I can hide it with my hair. "Bitch." As I touch each wound, I can't help but feel pride. I underestimated her. If shit had gone down differently and I could've taken Ta'Shara under my wing—made her a real *boss* bitch with the Queen Gs. She has heart and an underlying ruthlessness inside of her that's dying to get out.

Bam! Bam! Bam!

"Fuck, girl. Let's go!"

Bam! Bam! Bam!

"All right. All right! I'm comin'. Shit." Rolling my eyes, I turn from the mirror and rush to get dressed. Black jeans, white tee—I pull my wet hair into a low ponytail and then jet out of the bathroom to strap up with two burners.

"It's about time," Python grumbles, eyeballing me like I'm the reason his ass is in a bad mood.

I'm not biting today. I'm tired of dealing with his confused ass. "I'm ready."

Python's face twists, but he pumps his brakes on fuckin' with me as we head out the door. The first thing I see when I step out is June Bug and Kane jacking my Crown Vic on a tow truck.

"Yo, yo. What the fuck are they doin'?" I take off after them. "Yo, hey! Put my shit down."

Python grabs me and pulls me back. "They're doing what the fuck I told them, to get rid of the car that was splashed all over the news in front of that fire project you were involved in last night." Our eyes lock. "Sloppy."

He's baiting me, but again I let the shit slide.

A sweet silver GL Class Mercedes rolls up to us—I have to step back and admire the ride.

"Now this shit is what I'm talkin' about."

"You like it?"

"Hell yeah. I fucks with this."

Python's face softens as he opens the back door. I hop inside, feeling for the first time since I married his ass like the queen he promised I'd be. I sink into the soft, white leather seats and glance up at the dashboard, which looks like a slick-ass spaceship. Hell. It still has that fresh brand new car smell.

"Please, please tell me this shit is my wedding gift," I tell Python.

"Humph." He looks around, unimpressed. "Too fuckin' flashy."

I know he means that shit. Memphis street niggas don't bling. Shit brings way too much attention from the local and the federal agents. Since most country niggas don't pull W-2s, the last thing you want to do is roll around in a seventy-thousand-dollar car with the cops pulling you over every five minutes as a suspected thief. But a bitch like me could definitely get used to this.

My pissy-ass mood is long forgotten during the forty-minute ride back to Memphis. Python slides on his reflective shades and sinks back in his seat as if the dark-tinted windows aren't enough to shield him from possible prying eyes. When we reach the heart of downtown, I finally ask, "Where the fuck are we going?

"Sit tight."

I roll my eyes and wait out the ride. A few minutes later, the driver rolls us around the back of Club Diesel and stops. "This it?"

"Apparently."

The driver hops out and opens our door so we can make our exit. We enter the back of the club and are led toward a narrow hallway and a set of steep stairs. Off in the distance, I can hear the club's morning crew busting their asses to get the club ready.

I don't know what the fuck is going on and it's clear that Python isn't in the mood for twenty fuckin' questions so I shut my mouth and play follow-the-leader. At the top of the stairs there's a landing and an option to enter two different doors. Our escort takes us to the one on the far right, where he gives two quick knocks and waits for the barked order, "Come in!"

Fuck. It's Diesel.

The fact that I even recognize this slick muthafucka's voice is a sign that shit is too much of a problem. Gritting my teeth, I enter an office so immaculate and sick I look upside Python's head. *How in the hell is he rolling like this?* My eyes sweep around the office while I choke back my jealousy.

Meanwhile, Python and Diesel do a one-shoulder hug.

"You like what you see, ma?" Diesel asks, grinning at me.

Those sexy-ass dimples send a tingle up my spine and my clit churns up a good batch of honey. "It's a'ight." I downplay my reaction, but Diesel gives me the impression that he reads right through me.

"Well. I do what I can. Got a good deal on the place." He glances at Python. "Better watch out, cuz. Your chick is hard to impress."

Python's dark gaze shifts to me. "I'm not interested in impressing her as much as I am in taming her off-the-hook ass."

Diesel laughs. "I know what you mean. Bitches nowadays ain't got no home training."

I buck. "Excuse you?"

Python chuckles. "I know what you mean, cuz. This one has never worked a stove in her life. Thank God the pussy is good though."

"Damn, niggas. I'm standing right here!"

"So what can I do for you, cuz?" Diesel asks Python, changing the subject "*Mi casa es su casa.*"

"Momma Peaches is alive."

Diesel's smile melts off his face. "What?"

"There's been a change in plans."

"Whoa. Whoa. Roll that shit back. What's this about Aunt Peaches?" Genuine concern washes over Diesel's face.

"She turned up at the hospital last night. I'm tryna find out what the fuck is going on. The news is blasting her and my mom's name all over the place."

"Aunt Alice?" Diesel blinks. "I thought she was locked up at the cra—I mean, the mental hospital?"

"So did I. Apparently she broke out—and get this: she killed Captain Johnson."

"Get the fuck out of here."

"I know. At least that is one small silver lining. I don't have to worry about his bloodhound ass tracking me anymore. But this shit about my mom murking him and his wife and kidnapping Aunt Peaches—and then Aunt Peaches killing her—it's just crazy. I was wondering if I can hit you up for a favor and see if you can ride over to Baptist Memorial. Represent and hold her down. Also let her know what's up and that we're gonna arrange something so that we can hook up after she's released."

"Done and done." Diesel and Python exchange daps and shoulder bumps again. "Don't even worry about it. I got you."

Python cast a look my way. "Yeah. That early retirement plan we discussed?"

Diesel's brows dip. "Yeah?"

"I'm gonna pump the breaks on that shit for a little while."

Diesel shifts around on his feet while his eyes darken to a stormy green, but somehow he keeps a smile on his face. "Oh yeah?"

"Yeah." Python looks over at me. "My ol' lady and I decided we're gonna ride this shit out until the world blows. NahwhatImean?"

Diesel nods, but it looks like he's chewing a mouthful of nails.

I slap on the biggest smile I make, thrilled to have snatched the throne from under him before he sat his country ass down.

"That don't mean that there isn't a place for you at the table," Python tells him.

"Look, cuz," Diesel says, smiling. "I'm here for you. Whatever you need, I got you."

"Good. I'm gone need some niggas I can trust. You feel me? I lost a lot of good soldiers in the past year. If I'm gonna rebuild this shit, I'ma do it right. You got the extra muscle to whip my crew into shape so we can take it to the Vice Lords and lock our shit back down."

"Done."

Python nods. "After you roll over to check on Momma Peaches, I'ma need you and a few boys to find someone for me."

"Oh?"

"Yeah. A bitch that goes by the name Lucifer."

18

Lucifer

The Angels of Mercy are not my favorite muthafuckas in the world—but they serve a purpose: to keep my soldiers armed through our two wars spreading throughout the streets. For decades, Cousin Skeet filled that role, and when Mason was presumed dead, I went around his shady ass and established a new connect. It's clear that these rednecks can't stand my black ass, but like every area of my in life, cash moves everything around me. When I informed Mason about the relationship, he wasn't happy. But now with Cousin Skeet gone, the connect is more important than ever.

We load up two SUVs. Me and Mason in one, and Profit and Tombstone in the other. The second I climb into the passenger seat, I'm reminded of the last time I rode shotgun with him—and how it ended in disaster.

"You're sure that these muthafuckas are cool?" Mason asks.

"We'll never be invited to their family barbecue if that's what you're asking. But as long as our money stays green, our transactions will always be as smooth as butter."

Mason grunts his doubts while keeping his eyes on the road. He's in a strange mood today—all business. I spent the morning updating him on the set's business activities. I kept waiting to see if he was proud, but instead he appeared to be annoyed. Maybe I ran shit a little too well. I get it. No one likes the idea that life goes on without them.

The baby. I need to tell him about the baby.

I look at him, but the words get stuck in my throat. I love him—and I believe he loves me—but I need to get some resolution about Melanie. I don't like the possibility of being the rebound chick. We fall into a weird silence during the rest of the ride to the Royal Knights motorcycle club. The large wooden shack is located off the beaten path and nestled in the middle of no-damn-where.

When we pull into the gravel lot before a sea of Harley-Davidsons, Mason mumbles under his breath, "I can't believe that I'm about to deal with this Aryan Nation bullshit."

"They're not Aryans—just racist hicks," I correct him.

"Same fuckin' thing." He shuts off the engine and stares up at the large wood shack. "I don't have a good feeling about this shit."

"Money over everything." I open my door, but Mason grabs my arm before I hop out. "Are you telling me that you actually trust these fools?"

"Don't be ridiculous. I don't trust no damn body." I turn and hop out of the vehicle. Mason's gaze remains trained on me as I head toward the front door. Loud metal rock blares out of the Royal Knights, giving me an instant headache.

Mason climbs out of the SUV and signals for Profit and Tombstone to follow suit. This shit is on me and, truthfully, it can go sideways real quick. We gather on the wooden plank before the door and give each that look that says, *Prepare for anything.*

I take the lead. "Let's get this shit over with." I push open the door and in two seconds everything grinds to a stop.

Hundreds of leather-clad bikers with a wide variety of facial hair and beer bellies glare at us with a combination of rage and shock.

"Y'all lost?" Even though the word *nigger* wasn't said, it hangs like a noose in the middle of the room.

"Nope. We're just making ourselves at home." I push up a half smile and stroll into the place as if I own it. I've been in here several times, but not with a three-man entourage—and certainly not with someone as large as Mason, Tombstone, or even Profit. The sight of three virile men tends to itch these Confederate boys' trigger fingers.

Ignoring their outrage, we make a beeline through the place to the back door, where I knock and wait. Behind us, bikers turn away from their pool games with their cue sticks still in hand, and some climb off their bar stools and abandon their longneck beer bottles to follow us.

"I don't think your new friends like us," Mason jokes.

I remain calm as my hand drifts to my gat—in case we *do* have to shoot our way out of here.

Finally, the locks disengage and the back door swings open and Stony, a middle-aged mountain boy who looks like his moniker, pops out his salt-and-pepper head and grins at us. "Ah! If it isn't the devil herself," he shouts. "You're early. I thought you people were always on CP time?" He tilts down his shades and scans my entourage. He stops at Mason. "And *you* must be the new boss man." He makes another sweep of him. "You're a big, *ugly* buck."

Mason's patience thins. "You good ol' boys want to do business or talk shit?"

The muscles twitch around Stony's eyes, but he still flashes us his butter-colored teeth.

I sweat this shit for a second because if Stony closes this door in our faces we'll definitely have to shoot our way out of this muthafucka.

"LET THEM IN," a voice booms behind Stony.

Disappointed, Stony grumbles as he pushes up his shades and then steps back from the door to let us enter.

Mason's not happy, but he strolls into the back office first, ready to meet whatever the fuck is waiting for us on the other side.

I fall in line behind him into a dark room filled with thick, pungent cigar smoke. Six burly white men clad in leather coats and dark shades sit in a semicircle behind a long wooden table. We stop in front of them and engage in a staring contest. It's difficult not to feel uncomfortable. The whole setup has an auction-block feel to it.

"So we finally meet the big man," thunders Thor Steele, the leader of this Memphis charter. He shoves a fat cigar into his mouth and then gestures for Mason to take the only empty chair.

"Let me be one of the first to welcome you back from the dead," Thor says. "Very impressive."

"What can I say? I'm an impressive muthafucka."

The six-man panel exchange looks, but I can't read what they are thinking. Relationships in this business are built on trust, and if these men can't get along we'll have to go back on the open market for another arms dealer.

"Your old lady over there has been a very good customer. I have to admit that we were all surprised when she came to us a couple of months ago. I always thought you *blacks* had your own supplier in the city."

Silence.

"We took her business, even though she goes through a lot of trouble to hide she has a nice ass and good rack. Worked out like a dream. Payments and deliveries go down without a hitch. We like that. Our supplier likes that. As long as *you people* keep your hood drama from *darkening* our door, I don't see why we can't continue to do business."

Mason doesn't respond. Instead he stares at them until *they* start squirming in their chairs. "No deal." He stands. "But it was nice meeting *you boys*. Good day." He heads toward the door.

We follow.

"Whoa. Whoa. What's the rush? I thought you guys came here to make a deal?"

"I don't deal with racist muthafuckas who disrespect me and *my lady*—especially when we came here in the spirit of friendship. It's only because my momma raised me with manners that I'm not jumping across that table and ramming my fist down your throats and ripping out your spinal cords."

Big Bubba, sitting next to Thor, unwinds his pink, meaty arms, but I doubt that he can get his fat ass out of that chair fast enough without a crane. The other four men climb to their feet while cracking their knuckles.

Fuck. Looks like we might have to fight our way out of here after all.

For a solid minute, Thor allows the tension to build. Then unexpectedly, he cracks open a smile and fills the room with a big belly laugh. His boys look at him as if he's lost his mind before adding their spatter of awkward chuckles.

We don't relax for shit. In the South, there is nothing more dangerous than a crazy cracker.

"You know what?" Thor says. "I like you."

"I can't say the feeling is mutual," Mason says.

Thor laughs again and then turns to his boys. "All right. Everybody sit down. Let's see if we can start over and handle some business."

The good ol' boys return to their seats.

Thor gestures Mason back to the chair. "My apologies if I have offended you and your ol' lady. You have my word that it won't happen again. Please. Have a seat."

Mason tosses me a look to evaluate what I thought. Hell. I just want this shit to be over. After I give him a nod, he returns to the chair, the chip on his shoulder larger than ever.

Thor ignores this. "All right then, Mr. Fat Ace. Let's play *Let's Make a Deal.*"

19

LeShelle

"Lucifer?" I ask, turning toward Python. I ain't gonna lie, the bitch's name has a way of making a heart skip a beat. After all, she and Profit popped up out of nowhere and mowed down half our wedding party. "What the fuck do you want with that bitch?"

Python drops into the leather chair across from Diesel's desk. "You can ask that shit after she and your sister's lil boyfriend turned our nuptials into a red wedding?"

My smile twitches. "You're thinking about extracting a payback?"

"Fuck yeah. I don't have patience for bitches who think they have bigger balls than I do. It's past time to check that bitch and her crew of cockroaches. They destroyed the Pink Monkey, the construction company, and even cost the set our Colombian connect with that massacre on that last delivery."

"That shit ain't on us," I argue, outraged. "McGriff cut that deal tryna sneak a come-up. For all we know they were in it to-gether. Sheeiit. If you ask me, those muthafuckas got what they deserved. That's why I capped McGriff's sneaky-ass bitch, too."

Python shakes his head. "The shit is still on me. McGriff was my representative and I'm supposed to be in charge of protection. As far as the cartel is concerned, McGriff was operating under my authority. To heal any hurt feelings is gonna take a whole lot more cash than I have on hand. That's why I figure that we should go with Diesel's supplier so we can get some more candy on the streets quick and bring back our loyal customers."

"I know that you're not suggesting that crackheads have loyalty."

"No, but they value quality product. And Diesel here only fucks with that top-echelon shit that has never been stomped on. We're talking pure as fresh-driven snow. Muthafuckas down in the A can't get enough of it."

"Uh-huh." My gaze slices back to Diesel as he eases back in his chair with a cool, confident smile.

I know what he's doing and he knows that I know.

My clit thumps again. It takes everything I have not to jump over the table and rape his fine ass. *Fuck.* I look away when I realize the thoughts I'm having inside my head right in front of my man. But I don't do it fast enough because when I look at Python, he's staring dead at my ass.

"Like I said, cuz," Diesel continues like he doesn't notice shit. "Whatever you need, I got you. I'll call up a few of my top niggas from the A until we get everything set up here. We'll have our shit up and running in no time."

"*Our* shit," I correct him, not liking how he included him-self.

Diesel cocks his head. "Yeah. That's what I said."

Slick muthafucka.

"Are you two finished?" Python interrupts, irritated. "If we're going to move, then we're going to need to do it soon. With that dirty-ass Captain Johnson finally off to suck on the devil's nut sack, the Vice Lords' weapons supply is going to dry up. They're going to be on the hunt for a new connect. There are only a couple of muthafuckas arms dealing in the tri-state area. You," he says, looking at Diesel, "and those crazy-ass, racist, Hell's Angels–wannabe muthafuckas who want to help us speed up the city's genocide." He shrugs. "Maybe there's one or two others I don't know about—but they would be the main ones."

I know exactly who he's talking about. "The Angels of Mercy? They would never go to them. Who would want to deal with those racist fuckers?"

"Business is business," Python says. "Everybody's money is green."

"That it is." Diesel laughs, reaching for the phone. "Let's call them up."

My ass does a double take. "You *know* those assholes?"

His laughter deepens. "How in the hell do you think they get *their* shit?"

Holy shit. This nigga is deeper in the game than I thought. What makes this shit even slicker is that he has them on speed dial. I'm looking at him with brand-new eyes. Why doesn't Python have that kind of reach? Diesel hits the speaker and we listen in.

"Yell-o?"

"Thor! How's my white nigga doin'?" Diesel greets heartily.

A deep-baritone laugh rumbles over the line. "Not so good if your ass is calling."

They exchange brief chuckles.

"Look, my man. I need a solid from you."

"Yeah? There's a first time for everything," Thor says. "What can I do for you?"

"I'm looking to stake a mean bitch by the name of Lucifer. Heard of her?"

A long pause hangs over the line.

Everyone's brows go up as we exchange looks and then lean closer to the phone.

"She's on your radar?" Thor finally asks.

"Got her in my crosshairs. Has she come to you yet?"

"Been doin' business with her for a few months."

I'm stunned. What in the fuck did that shit mean? The Vice Lords and Captain Johnson split off *before* his death?

"If you'd called a couple hours ago, I could've handed the phone over to her," Thor says.

"She placed an order?" Diesel asks.

"Yeah. Her and her crew—big niggers, about your size."

Diesel's hand shoots out to pick up a pen. "When and where are you supposed to deliver?"

"We got a warehouse off of Rivergate. It's a large order. We arranged delivery for next Friday night. Ten o'clock."

Big smiles break across our faces as we hover over the phone.

"Tell you what, Thor. My cuz and I are gonna take that order off your hands and handle it personally."

"It's all yours, my black brother."

20

Hydeya

"**F**uck the police." I toss up my hands in front of the bathroom mirror while bitching to my husband. I know that he gets tired of me bringing my work home, but I can't help it. I'm so frustrated, overworked, and flat-out tired. "You know, I'd respect people more if they would come on out and just say that shit. Instead I have to put up with people always lying to my face and thinking my ass is stupid. Take this Barbara Lewis chick. Her story doesn't make a lick of sense—or there's a whole lot of shit she's not telling me."

"The woman that was kidnapped?" Drake asks, focusing most of his attention on shaving.

"Yeah. One of them."

"What do you think she's hiding?" he asks.

"I don't know. I'm supposed to believe that this crazed mental patient escapes, kidnaps her sister, kills the sister's boyfriend and some bystander in the neighborhood off Shotgun Row, takes the sister to their childhood home—I don't even know how the extra body, Arzell Carter, fits in. Maybe he was Alice's accomplice. Anyway, some time later, Alice goes to Captain Johnson's place, kills him and his wife, tells the kid, Christopher, that she's his grandmother and then, on her way out the door, kidnaps Barbara Lewis. But *nobody* knows why any of this happened? C'mon."

Drake shrugs. "Sometimes you can't explain crazy."

"I'm not buying it," I say. These people are insulting my intelligence. "Mrs. Lewis's story doesn't pass the smell test."

"Well." He leans over the vanity sink. "If anyone is going to figure it out, it's you, babe." He kisses my cheek, leaving a dab of shaving cream on my face.

"Hey. Watch it." I swipe my face and toss it back at him. However, my mind goes back to the Johnson case. "I don't know. Maybe Ms. Lewis really was at the wrong place at the wrong time, but it still has my Spidey senses going off."

"Oh. I married a superhero?"

"Oh. I got all kinds of powers," I brag, reaching over and grabbing him by his cock. He may not be a brotha, but he must have some black genes somewhere because my man is hung like a horse.

Drake laughs. "All right now. Don't start nothing you can't finish, *Captain*."

I glance at my watch and moan. "Maybe a rain check?"

"Uh-huh. That's what I thought." He slaps me on the ass and then goes back to his shave.

Once again, my mind goes back the case. "Why didn't Alice kill Barbara Lewis at the captain's home? Why take her with her?"

"You're like a dog with a bone."

I slap him with my towel. "I'm serious. Why?"

"Maybe she planned on torturing her."

"*Exactly*," I agree. "The shit was personal. The two knew each other. Why not admit it? Why hide it?"

"Did you ask her?"

"Of course I did. She denied it, and then threw up a brick wall so fast, I nearly broke my face on it."

"What about the other one?"

"Maybelline—Carver."

Drake stops and meets my gaze in the mirror. "Momma Peaches?"

I shrug, but Drake knows that Momma Peaches has been a source of fascination for me since long before I joined the Memphis Police Department. The old woman is practically a legend, with a rap sheet that takes up a few gigabytes in the system. I've never had any direct dealings with the infamous lady gangsta until yesterday—but it has always been a matter of time before we met.

"So what do *you* think is going on?" he asks.

"I don't know—but you can bet your ass that I'm going to find out."

Drake cocks his head at me. "Did you get any sleep last night?"

"I'll sleep in my next life," I tell him. "I better go. I have a full schedule today—which includes another press conference."

"Oooh. My baby is going to be on *teeveee*." He slides behind me and loops his arms around my waist. "Since I can't have sex this morning, maybe I can get your autograph?"

"Quit it." Smiling, I try to wiggle out of his arms. "I'm going be late."

He nuzzles my ear and squeezes my ass. "Well. If you're already late."

"You're incorrigible, you know that?"

"You might have mentioned it once or a million times. I can't remember." Laughing, I push him off and head to our adjoining bedroom.

Drake grabs my arm and pulls me back. "Aren't you forgetting something?"

I frown as he reaches for the flesh-colored bandages on the

vanity counter. "Oh." I roll my eyes for being so absent-minded.

"Turn around," he says.

I follow his order and sweep my hair out of the way so that my husband can cover the large, six-pointed star of the Gangster Disciple tattooed on my neck.

21

Momma Peaches

I feel like death warmed over. Make no mistake about it, I'm happy to be alive, but all this poking, prodding, and pricking me is riding my last nerve. I'm ready to get the hell up out of here. Two days of hospital food and old bitches—*pardon my language, Lord*—sponge-bathing and wiping my ass is driving me up the wall.

Why did Alice come after me? Why did she kill Cedric Robinson? Who helped her escape the mental hospital? Who was Arzell Carter's backstabbing ass? What about Rufus Jones, who was found dead in the backyard? What is my relationship with Barbara Lewis? Have I ever met her before? Was I sure? Why did Alice kill Captain Johnson? On and on the questions went until my head felt like it would explode.

I should've gone with the truth. I'm too old and tired to try to keep up with a lie, plus I promised the man upstairs that if he got me through Alice's crazy, bat-shit meltdown I'd turn over a new leaf.

What can I say? Changing is harder than I thought.

Between interrogations and catnaps, I sneak glimpses of the local news from the television mounted on the wall. The constant up-to-the minute updates on the death of the city's beloved Captain Johnson have the city reeling.

"Hello?" A new nurse sticks her head into the room. "Time for another blood draw."

"I'm not going to have any blood left by the time y'all get through."

She laughs, but I'm not joking. The nurse sets up by the bed and glances up at the television. "Damn shame." She pricks my arm without warning. "This city is going to hell. You'd think we live in a third-world country or something."

"Humph." This nosey bitch knows that I'm tied to the case. She and the others have been creeping in here every chance they can, trying to get my ass to talk so they can have something to gossip about around the nurse's station. I don't have time for messy bitches—*Excuse me, Lord.* Yet, the old me wants to say, "That grimy, punk-ass bitch nigga with a badge finally got what the fuck he had coming to him." He made most of his career-making busts off the backs of the Gangster Disciples. He even put my husband, Isaac, in the clink ten years back. Hell, Captain Johnson was gunning for Isaac since he rolled in from Chicago. Yet, at the end of the day, Captain Melvin Johnson lived by the streets and he died by the streets.

End of story.

Now, knowing the role he played in Mason's disappearance, I hope his ass is roasting in hell with a fucking apple in his mouth.

On the screen, the news replays this morning's press conference. Captain Hawkins stands in front of the cameras looking like a deer caught in headlights. It's almost funny since she's more competent and on her game in person than she comes across on TV. Still, I keep staring and thinking that I know her ass from some place. I don't usually forget faces—but then again, I'm stacking some years on this old body and maybe one or two names have slipped between the cracks.

The Memphis Police Department is going out of its way, trying to convince the public that they're united in getting the city's growing violence under control. They ain't fooling nobody. The city is broke, and niggas here outnumber the police by a wide margin.

"All right. That's it," the nurse says after filling the last vial. "I'll see you in a few hours." She grabs everything up and then swishes her thick hips toward the door.

"Afternoon!" Captain Hawkins says, strolling into my room with a forced smile. "You're looking good today."

Oh, damn. Not again.

Instead of answering, I swing my gaze to the tall, lanky cop waltzing in behind her. *Who in the hell is this?*

"I'm sorry. This is Lieutenant John Fowler. He will be the lead investigator on your case. Of course, I'll be working with him and overseeing everything while transitioning into my new position."

"It's nice to meet you," Lieutenant Fowler says, extending his hand.

Reluctantly, I accept the handshake, only to wince when his grip is too tight and aggravates the butterfly needle that's controlling my IV.

"Sorry about that," he apologizes.

"It's okay," I mutter before returning my attention back to Hawkins. "Look. I've already told you everything I remember."

She nods with that tight smile of hers. Clearly, she doesn't believe a word I've told her. "Well, I guess we may never know what really caused Alice to snap like she did."

"She was mentally ill," I say, dropping my gaze.

"Apparently." Hawkins clasps her hands behind her back, and then stares at me.

Normally, I like to think of myself as being too old of a cat to be scratched by a kitten—but there's something about this woman's laser-like stare that has me squirming in this bed.

"I was wondering if you'd heard from your nephew Terrell," Hawkins bombs me nonchalantly.

My eyes snap back up. "What the hell kind of question is that? He's dead."

"Missing," she corrects. "We never found his body."

Hope is a young woman's game, but here I am grasping at this news with a mustard seed of hope, while cursing myself at the same time. "He's alive?"

"Anything is possible. Just like . . . it's possible that Terrell may be Christopher Johnson's father."

This bitch is dropping missiles all over the place. I'm not sure how to play this or how to figure out her game plan. "I always tried to stay out of my nephew's personal business. He was a grown man."

Hawkins bobs her head—again, not believing me. "Well, I'd hoped to get answers when I got hold of Christopher's birth certificate. But it turns out his mother didn't list the father's name—so, dead end." She shrugs, but I see the trap door that she's aiming to push me through. "Unless, you wouldn't mind submitting to a blood test to see if you're related."

"I mind."

Her fake smile turns slick. "I thought you might. Guess we'll just have to test him using Alice's DNA. At least she's not in any position to protest."

Bitch.

"Well. I guess we should let you get some rest." She taps her partner on the shoulder, signaling that it's time to go.

He gives me his own tight smile. He knows that his new boss just handed me my ass.

Before she is able to take a step toward the door, an image on the news catches her attention. "Do you mind if I turn this up?"

Like I have a choice. "Knock yourself out."

Hawkins walks over to the television and turns up the volume.

"Authorities have released the identities of the two bodies discovered a few feet away from where I'm standing: twenty-two-year-old Yolanda Terry and seventeen-year-old Tyneshia Gibson. The police are seeking tips or any information as to

who may be behind these heinous murders. We have learned that the body of Ms. Terry was discovered with a bag over her head and her hands bound with plastic cuffs. The medical examiner's report also states that Ms. Terry was pregnant at the time of her death. However, no fetal corpse has been found at the scene. Sources within the department believe the baby was forcibly taken from Ms. Terry.

The cause of death for Ms. Tyneshia Gibson was a single bullet to the head. Anyone with information pertaining to this case is asked to contact the department's office of detectives . . ."

Yolanda. That poor child . . . and my great nephew!

I chew on my bottom lip while I digest all the crazy bullshit that has gone on while I was trapped down in that damn basement. Maybe my family has some biblical curse on us. I don't know how else to explain it. Bad things keep on happening. I want to put my trust in the Lord, but it's hard.

A part of me also wants to put this on Python. He dragged Yolanda into his mess. I loved him, but he plopped out more shit than a barn full of horses. He knew better than anybody what kind of life Yolanda had been through and he knew her light bulb wasn't screwed in too tight.

I liked the girl. I don't know why. There was just something about her that tugged on my old heartstrings. Back in the day, Yolanda's momma cared more about keeping a man in her bed than she did about her child. That is an epidemic in this city. I mean, damn. I like a good dick like the next chick—*excuse me, Lord*—but there's no way I'd ever sacrifice a child.

Twelve-year-old Alice flashes in my head.

That was different. Wasn't it?

Shoving my guilt aside, I return my thoughts to Yo-Yo. Did anyone mourn her death? The girl had so many strikes against her when all she wanted was to fit in—but she never could. It wasn't until she grew up and filled out her Coke-bottle curves that she caught people's attention. Next thing anyone knew, she spit out three kids by three different niggas. Python's would have been the fourth. What will happen to Malcolm, Amin, and Vivian now? Damn. I don't even know how in the hell I remember their names.

The state took Yo-Yo's kids when her momma reported her as an unfit mother. Maybe she was, but her heart was always in the right place. The last time I spoke with Yolanda, she talked about getting herself together and getting her babies back. The problem was that she was depending on Python to make that happen and her head got too big. She openly flaunted her jump-off status in front of Python's wifey, LeShelle.

Big mistake.

LeShelle cornered and pistol-whipped her in the middle of Fabdivas Hair Salon in front of everyone. The situation got so dire that Python had to move her ass off Shotgun Row and stash her some place safe. Now her picture is flashing all over the news. I don't have to be a detective to figure this one out.

LeShelle killed that girl. I'm willing to bet everything I own.

Hawkins sighs as she turns away from the new report. "Another one of the cases lying on my desk." She shakes her head and then stops. "Yolanda Terry was your neighbor, wasn't she?"

Here we go. "Yes. She was a sweet child."

The captain's hawkish eyes narrow on me. "Any idea who'd want her dead?"

"No." *I'm going to hell.*

Hawkins's expression calls me a liar. "Well. Just thought I'd ask. Get yourself some rest. Let's go, Lieutenant."

The confident captain heads out with strong, powerful strides. Clearly, she is not the bitch to be fucked with. Hell. Who knows? Maybe she will be able to turn this damn city around.

When Hawkins reaches for the door handle, it suddenly flies open and a huge figure fills up the doorway.

My heart stops on a dime. I haven't seen that face in years.

"Oh, excuse me," Captain Hawkins says, pausing briefly to take in the large man.

"No. Excuse me," the man volleys.

"Diesel?" I blink, thinking my eyes are playing tricks on me. "What are you doing here?"

"Aunt Peaches!" His full lips stretch while dimples wink at me. "Are you kidding me?" he asks, strolling farther into the room with a bundle of flowers in one hand. "My favorite aunt is laid up in the hospital and you think I wouldn't come running?"

Captain Hawkins freezes by the door, looking *waaay* too interested in my new visitor.

I'm still blinking as Diesel strolls toward me, stretching his arms out wide. "You have no idea how happy I am to see you." When he leans over the bed and envelops my old, frail, body, I feel only one thing . . . fear.

22

Hydeya

Good Lord Almighty. I'm staring at the finest brotha that I've ever seen: a six-four, honey-coated, muscular god with cool pastel-colored eyes. His voice is a smooth, sexy baritone that flows over the ear like a lover's whisper. One minute in the room with him and I already feel like I'm cheating on my husband.

Once that treacherous thought crosses my mind, I shake out of my trance in time to catch Maybelline's horror-stricken face before she slides it behind a fake smile. *What the hell is that about?*

"Hello." I move away from the door and approach the bed to interrupt their mini-family reunion.

Mr. Fine releases his aunt to swing his baby blues on me—*wait. I thought they were green when he entered the room.*

"Captain," he greets, giving me a smile that gets my heart hammering like a teenager, but has my head ringing alarm bells.

Danger, Hydeya Hawkins. Danger. "You know who I am?"

"Well, you have been all over the news the last couple of days. Looks like the city is keeping you busy."

"I'll sleep when I'm dead."

His shoulders shake with his low, rumbled laugh. "Won't we all?"

No doubts that this man's Colgate smile alone has broken plenty of hearts. "You have me at a disadvantage, Mister . . . ?"

"Carver." He extends his hand. "Diesel Carver."

We shake, and I force myself not to react to the electrical current radiating from his touch. The man exudes a strange power that fascinates me. "Nice to meet you." A brief silence hangs in the air until Lieutenant Fowler clears his throat and jolts me out of my trance again. "Oh. Uhm. Are you from around here?"

"No. Actually, my branch of the family tree is in Atlanta." His smile widens as he crosses his arms. "You know, I'm glad that you're here. I can ask you directly—how's the investigation is going?"

"For Terrell?"

"Terrell?" Diesel's eyebrows jump—more out of amusement than surprise or curiosity. "Isn't he dead?" he asks.

I take two seconds to try and read his sincerity, but fail. "The jury is still out on that."

"Captain," Maybelline interrupts. Her impatience with me is etched in the small lines in her face. "I'd like some time alone with my nephew, if you don't mind."

Our eyes lock, but I don't have grounds to push the issue so I pin on a stiff smile and promise myself that we'll take up our mental battle at another time. Soon. "Of course not." I back away from the bed. "If anything else comes up, I'll keep you informed."

"I'd appreciate that," Maybelline says, her smile flat.

My gaze shifts to Diesel Carver. "It was nice to have met you."

"I promise you that the pleasure was all mine."

Fowler and I exit the hospital room.

"That was interesting," Fowler quips, struggling to keep up with my quick, angry strides.

"Interesting or bullshit?" I punch the down button for the elevator and then start pacing. I can't dismiss the feeling that I'm being played somehow.

Confusion twists across Fowler's face. "I was referring to your reaction to Mr. Playa back there."

"What?" I roll my eyes in a bad attempt to convince him that he didn't see what he saw. "Don't be ridiculous. I was putting him through my bullshit meter."

"Uh-huh." Fowler smirks. "And?"

"And—he's full of shit—or, at the very least, hiding something."

"Humph. And here I thought he was just a nice guy checking in on his aunt—who, by the way, has been through one hell of an ordeal. I don't get why it felt like you were putting the woman on trial for something."

"Don't be glib."

"What's with all that stuff about Terrell Carver—and he may or may not be dead? Did I miss a memo or something?

DING!

The elevator doors slide open and I jump inside, shaking my head. "Give me a break."

"What?" He follows me. "You know sometimes things *are* what they seem."

"Not in my world."

Fowler laughs and then preaches to me about my trust issues all the way back to the precinct. It all goes in one ear and out of the other. I know what I know. The second I return to my office, I shoot over to my computer and type in the name Diesel Carver.

23

Momma Peaches

Diesel Carver came into the world a murderer.

The way he clawed out his mother's insides in the prison hospital set tongues wagging for years afterwards. Don't get it twisted—not too many people mourned his momma's passing. Rumor was that Zaire killed her momma the same way, and then took out her daddy and uncle with a double-barrel shotgun after they doped her up and ran a train on her on her thirteenth birthday. By fourteen, she was a full-blown coke addict and hit the corners and became a ghetto-superstar in Atlanta's infamous red-light district. There, she met and fell in love with her favorite john, my brother, Ty Carver.

The Carver family is a large one. I done said before, my momma spit us out like her pussy was on an assembly line. Majority of us were sent to Nana Maybelle to raise, but Momma kept a few close to her. Ty's father, Titus, was one of them—until he came of age and then headed down to Atlanta because it was supposed to be the next black mecca. The city's promises turned to shit. The results were the same as they were here in Memphis: more niggas in concrete plantations than the good ol' boys ever had picking cotton.

Ty, Alice's fraternal twin, died in a hail of bullets from the Atlanta Police Department during a routine traffic stop. With her nigga and her main coke connect murked, Zaire turned tricks for drugs instead of money. When her looks went to hell, and her pregnant pussy wasn't putting her on like it used to, she robbed and stole—which led to someone being killed: an undercover cop.

If Diesel hadn't killed his momma, those Georgia boys would have. To make shit even more fucked up, the state sent Zaire's murderous baby to Ty's wife, Daniella, to raise.

She didn't want the child, at first, but I did play a part in convincing her to do the right thing. Hell, I was raising Terrell at the time and the system had way too many little black boys that no one wanted. I even took Terrell down south every year for his birthday so he could establish a relationship with all his cousins in that neck of the woods.

Diesel was about eight when I suspected that something was a little . . . *off.* Don't get it twisted. Whenever I came around, Diesel always said and did the right things, but it always struck me as being a well-rehearsed act. But like my Nana Maybelle always said, you can't out-slick a can of oil. I watched him closer, knowing that sooner or later, his perfectly constructed mask would crack.

One day, Daniella called, begging me to take Diesel off of her hands. The scandal was that a lot of the neighborhood pets were going missing. People suspected and then pointed fingers at Diesel. Turned out they were right. Neighbors reported to the police that their garage stunk up the whole neighborhood. When they opened it up, they found more than fifty cats and dogs in there—not only with their necks twisted, but each with their heads scalped and their organs gutted out.

The whole thing frightened Daniella and I had to race to Atlanta to calm her down. . . .

It was April of '94. The heat and humidity in Atlanta was unbearable and to top things off it was college spring break and the annual Freaknik with the historically black col-

leges was in full swing. Loud rap and hip-hop music boomed from every car speaker while barely legal college girls lost their minds and most of their clothes in the city streets.

Terrell watched the whole scene with wide eyes and a sagging jaw even though we were baking in the car during the drive from the airport, which should've taken twenty minutes instead of three hours. When we reached Daniella's place, she met us at the door with a glum face.

"I can't do this. The little bastard has to go."

"All right. All right. Calm down, chile." I pushed my way through the screen door, my arms loaded with suitcases. "Terrell, go find Diesel so y'all can go on outside and play."

"Okay." He took off running. "DIESEL!"

"Boy, stop all that hollering. I could've done that." I shook my head and dropped the bags. "Daniella, girl, you gone have to get me something cool to drink before we sit down and talk."

She huffed out a long breath and then turned toward the kitchen. I followed, fanning myself and wondering if the woman's air conditioner was on the fritz. If so, we were going to take our asses to a hotel or something. I was too delicate to be melting like a candle up in there.

"Don't try to talk me out of this," Daniella said, pulling out a pitcher of iced tea. "I've made up my mind. There is something wrong with that boy."

"Now that may be, but he's still Ty's boy and he wouldn't want you to toss him out on the street."

"Fuck Ty and his community dick. Why in the hell should I give a fuck what the hell he wants when he's the one that laid down with that deranged hooker in the first place?"

"Oh? So now you're gonna act like he didn't pull you off the street corner, too? Just because you got a job down at the phone company now, don't try to act like you're brand new." She handed me a drink.

"That's not fair, Peaches. I don't know too many women out here willing to raise their dead husband's bastards. As far as I'm concerned, the muthafucka could've rotted in the bitch's pussy right along with her."

Movement from the corner of my eye stops me from going ham on Daniella. When I look over, Diesel and Terrell are staring wide-eyed at us.

Daniella gasped.

"What the hell are you two doing there, listening in on grown folks' business? Didn't I tell y'all to go outside?"

"Yes, ma'am," Terrell said, backing away from our door. "W-we came to ask if we could go down to the pool."

"I don't care! Go on!"

A smile exploded across Terrell's face. "Thanks, Aunt Peaches! C'mon, D!" He popped Diesel on the back and took off running.

Diesel didn't budge. He remained rooted in front of the door, glaring at his stepmother with his eyes changing into funny colors. That shit made my skin crawl—and I don't scare easily, by any means. The whole thing made me think of a movie about a demon boy terrorizing everyone.

"Diesel, go and play," I said, but in a softer tone. Even then, he waited a few long seconds before Terrell hollered again.

"DIESEL! C'MON!"

Calmly, Diesel turned and walked away.

"You see what I mean?" Daniella whispered, panicked. "That boy ain't right."

The bitch was right as rain on that.

Daniella pulled out a pack of cigarettes from her titties. "One of the parents at the school told me that torturing animals is a clear sign of a future psychopath. I mean, damn, what if the little shit is planning to murder me and my real kids? Shit like that is in the news all the time."

"Whoa. Whoa. Slow down. You're letting your mind run away from you."

"Goddamn!" Daniella pounded her fist on the table. "Don't treat me like I'm fuckin' crazy. I'm not crazy!" Terror rippled across her face.

I leaned over and wrapped my arms around her to comfort her. That was all it took for her to break down sobbing. "I don't know what to do. He's been expelled from three schools. Parents complain to me all the time that he's terrorizing their kids."

"Expelled? Again? What for this time?"

"He took a loaded gun to school."

"Oh, Lord." I shook my head. Raising boys is hard. Thank God I had Isaac helping me out with Terrell. I'm convinced that there are just some things that a woman can't do for her boys, no matter how hard she tries. That didn't mean that my ass was in the clear. Each day, Terrell was learning a new bad habit from knuckleheaded children who live up and down Shotgun Row and whose parents are M.I.A. Not to mention, my crib was well stocked with illegal guns—and the idea of him taking one to school? Heartburn.

Daniella's sobs ratcheted up.

"It's okay. Everything is gonna be all right. Y'all are gonna get through this and I don't want to hear any more talk about you putting that boy out in the streets. You have raised him now for eight years. You're the only mother that he knows."

Daniella's body shook through her tears.

I sympathized for the girl. After all, like she said, she had her two real kids, Tyrese and Shannon, to look after. One thing for damn sure, after peeping that creepy shit for myself, Diesel's ass wasn't coming back to Memphis with me and Terrell.

When we left Atlanta a week later, Daniella had enrolled Diesel in a new school, and the state was getting him psychiatric help.

I thought I'd done a good job playing Captain Save-A-Ho.

However, one month later, Daniella, Tyrese, and Shannon were all dead. They'd all been killed in a ghoulish house invasion—according to the news. Miraculously, they said, Diesel survived because he'd hidden himself under the bed when he heard the mayhem.

I knew better. . . .

"What are you doing here, Diesel?" I ask.

He cocks his head and fixes his soulless eyes on me. "I told you. When I heard what had happened to you, I rushed right over."

"All the way from Atlanta?"

"Well, no. Actually, I was already in town." He places his bullshit grocery-store-bought flowers down next to the numerous flower arrangements that had been delivered earlier from family and friends. "You're a popular woman," he notes. "It's nice to have people who care about you, huh?"

"You can say that."

Diesel gives me another one of his creepy grins as he makes himself comfortable on the edge of my bed.

Reflexively, I scoot over, not wanting him to touch me again. After surviving one crazy-ass family member, I'm not too eager to deal with another one.

"It really is good to see you again, Auntie. Who knows? Maybe now that I've moved to Memphis, we'll get a chance to spend more time together. Wouldn't that be nice?"

My heart sinks. "I thought you were living the life in Atlanta. You're a very powerful man, I heard."

"So you *have* been keeping tabs on me? I'm touched." His eyes say otherwise. "In the past, I've always felt like, uh, I don't know—that maybe you felt a little . . . uncomfortable around me."

I don't respond.

"Well. It was probably just me." Diesel shrugs. "I do tend to have a wild imagination."

"Why are you here?" I ask again. "The truth. I'm too tired for games."

"I told you the truth. I was concerned—Python was too. He's practically climbing the walls, worrying about you."

"What?" I sit up straight, temporarily forgetting about my fear to inch closer. "What are you talking about? Python's dead."

"Missing," he corrected. "You heard Captain Hawkins."

Gobsmacked, I stare at him. "If this is some kind of sick joke, it's not funny."

"C'mon, Aunt Peaches. You know that I wouldn't joke about something like this." He reaches into his pocket and scoops out a cell phone. "Would you like to talk to him?"

My heart rockets back into my chest. "Y-yes. Of course I wanna talk to my baby."

Diesel dials.

He's not bullshitting.

"Yo, cuz. I'm here," Diesel says. "Hold on." He hands over the phone. "For you."

I snatch the phone. "H-hello? Terrell?"

"The one and only." He chuckles. "How are you holding up over there? Are they taking good care of you?"

"Oh, praise Jesus! Terrell, baby. I thought you were dead. Where are you?" My heart pounds. This is a miracle.

"Well. I can't get into that right now," he says. "You never know who's listening, nawhatImean?"

"Yeah. Okay." I lower my voice to a whisper. "I don't understand. What—?"

"Don't worry about it. Just know that I'm alive and well,

and when the time is right, we'll hook it up so that we can see each other. Until then, sit tight. A'ight?"

I nod, sucking in a deep breath. "All right." Tears spill over my lashes.

"A'ight. I'm gonna let you go."

"But—"

"Don't worry. You'll hear from me again."

"But—"

"I promise," he chuckles. "You know that you can't keep a Carver down."

24

Ta'Shara

I'm happy for Profit.

I really am—at least that's what I keep telling myself. Maybe if I say it a million more times, I'll believe it.

It's been three days since life on Ruby Cove changed forever. The once long, war-weary faces have been rejuvenated with Fat Ace's return. Now everyone talks about taking the streets back block by block. The Gangster Disciples and the Grape Street Crips are officially on notice. I try my best to blend into the celebration, and play my position as a new petal with the Vice Lord Flowers. So far these evil bitches won't give me the time of day. I have history with a few of them from Morris High School—particularly with Qiana Barrett's ratchet-ass. If that bitch ain't raping Profit with her eyes every time I turn around, she's busy staring a hole into the side of my head.

Only one chick has even bothered to say more than a few words to me and that's one of Qiana's besties, who gave me a warning: *Watch your back.*

If she thought I was scared, I set the confused girl straight. "Step to me again and I'll give you and Qiana matching profiles."

Adaryl reflexively touched her scar-less her face. "You're

never gonna be a *real* Flower. I don't give a fuck whose arm you're hanging off," she said, scrambling back to her side of the road.

"Don't let them get to you," Profit whispered. "Give it some time."

He means well, but I don't think he gets it. It's all right. I'm not interested in him fighting my battles. I can take care of myself. I'll have to earn my own reputation. At the same time, I don't know if I want to be a part of these bitter bitches' family, but what else is left? I can't go back to the safe life in suburbia.

That road, that avenue—that's over now.

Every day since the fire, I've picked up the phone to call Tracee or Reggie's parents. What are the police saying? Have they claimed their bodies? Will there be a funeral? Will I be welcome?

That last question is what's fucking with me. I didn't torch the house, but there's no doubt in my mind that I am responsible for the Douglases' death. I unleashed LeShelle on them. There are no words to make up for that.

Finally, this morning, Tracee and Reggie Douglas are listed in the obituaries. Funeral services will be at Forest Hill Funeral Home.

"Are you going to go?" Profit asks.

"I don't know." I set down his smartphone, on which I was reading *The Commercial Appeal* online.

Profit glides into the empty seat across from me at the kitchen table. Shirtless, he's still wearing an easy smile that he's had on since his brother rose from the dead.

I reach for my bowl of cereal, but I have no interest in eating it.

"You should go."

My eager gaze jumps to meet his eyes. "Yeah?"

He nods. "I can go with you. You know—for support." He takes my hand.

"But . . . what if they hate me?"

He laughs. "C'mon, baby. Nobody hates you."

My brows arch high for a you-can't-be-serious look.

"Okay. Nobody but that evil-ass sister of yours—but she doesn't count. I'm going to take care of her ass soon enough. The bitch can only be so lucky for so long."

"I don't know. There's been a lot of street miracles lately."

Profit leans back and pats his legs. "C'mere."

I stare at him, but then get up and sit in his lap with my head bowed. "Look at me." He tilts my chin up. "Have faith in your man and trust me."

"I do—with my life."

Doubt flickers across his face.

"You don't believe me?"

He hesitates. "I want to believe you, but given what happened—"

"Profit"—I ease my arms around his neck—"you did everything you could that night. You fought for me."

His gaze bounces around the room. I cup the sides of his face and force him to look at me. "I love you so much for fighting that night. It means the world to me. Truly."

After he searches my eyes for the truth, his large smile spreads back across his face. "I love you, baby."

"I love you, too." I press a kiss against his lips and enjoy the flutter of my heart. The past is the past. This man is all I have left in this world and I'll do anything to protect and keep our love alive.

The next morning, a short, black Chanel dress hangs on the back of our bedroom door. "I figured that you'd need something to wear to the funeral," Profit says, smiling.

Of course, I tear up again. "Thank you. That's so thoughtful of you." We kiss and then fall into a sober silence.

Not to be outdone, Profit also purchased a black Brooks Brothers suit. My mouth falls open when he transforms from a gangster to a gentleman right in front of my eyes.

"How do I look?" he asks, striking a few male-model poses before the bedroom mirror.

"You look like the man of my dreams," I tell him, rewarding him with a kiss. We look good together—attractive. I just wish that we weren't going to a double funeral.

We skip breakfast because my stomach is twisted in knots, and when we roll into the funeral home's parking lot, my hands are slick with sweat. The place is packed. Undoubtedly the guests are from Tracee and Reggie's jobs, church, and charity organizations. They spent their whole lives giving back to their community. They touched so many and did so much. Their deaths will leave a hole in the universe.

Disbelief and tears flow down everyone's faces as they head into the building.

"This is a bad idea," I tell Profit, stopping him from climbing out of the vehicle. "Let's go back home. I don't want to do this. I—"

"Shh. All right. Calm down." He loops an arm around my shoulders. "You're scared and upset. I get it, but it's gonna be all right."

"No. No. I can't go in there and face those people. Don't make me do it. I'm not ready." I unleash a torrent of tears onto his new suit.

"Now. I'm not going to force you to go in there if you really don't want to—*but* if you don't go, there's a strong chance that you'll regret it for the rest of your life."

My heart lurches.

"You gotta close this chapter, baby. It's the only way that you can move on."

I know that he's speaking the truth, but this shit hurts so fuckin' bad that it's hard to breathe.

"You can do this," Profit whispers until I find a kernel of strength to do what I have to do.

"All right," I say. "Let's go."

"That's my girl."

Forcing a smile, I ease out of his arms and mop up my tears.

"You ready?" he asks.

I nod.

"Then let's do this." He brushes a kiss against my forehead and then climbs out of the vehicle. By the time he reaches my door, I've powdered away my tear tracks and put on a brave face.

Arm in arm, we enter the funeral home. At the door of the ceremonial room, a twenty-by-thirty smiling wedding photo of Tracee and Reggie greets the guests. It's another double punch to the gut. They were so young and so in love.

I destroyed that.

Profit squeezes my hand and I force one foot in front of the other. Like the parking lot, the place is packed to capacity. However, when everyone sees me, they part as if I were Moses. As we make our way down the aisle, a steady buzz of whispers builds behind us. Focused on the two closed caskets in the front of the room, I block out what people are saying. Those are my parents up there. The only ones that I've ever known.

In the first pew, Tracee's mother, Olivia Sullivan, stands and smiles. "Ta'Shara, we're so happy that you came," she says through her tears.

My stomach twists into knots.

"We were so worried about you. We've been looking everywhere."

I sob. "I can't believe that they're gone." Before I know it, I'm wrapped in Olivia's arms.

"I know, baby. I'll miss them, too."

We hold each other for a while, and when she finally releases me, I'm passed to Tracee's sisters, Joan and Donna. From there, Reginald Douglas Senior sweeps me into a bear hug. *My family.*

Afterwards, I introduce them to Profit, who was met with a few stiff handshakes. I can only imagine the things Reggie told his father about Profit. He made it perfectly clear to me how much he hated Profit and blamed him for what happened on that prom night.

At exactly two o'clock, the service begins with the song "His Eye Is on the Sparrow." The lyrics wring every ounce of water from my tear ducts. Through the prayers, scripture readings, and more songs, somehow I manage to keep it together. During the friends' and families' expression portion of the service, Olivia's eyes remain on me, begging that I'll say a few words. I pretend that I don't notice, but finally give in and walk to the lectern on legs that feel like Jell-O. As I stand before the grim-faced crowd, my mind draws a blank. I've never had to do something like this before.

"Umm, Reggie and Tracee changed my life," I begin. "I'd never met anyone like them before. They accepted me—wholeheartedly—and loved me as though I was their flesh and blood and I loved them the same way . . ."

I want to say more but can't. My throat closes and chokes off my windpipe. Embarrassed, I scramble back to my seat and tuck my head onto Profit's shoulder.

He loops his arm around me and presses a kiss on top of my head. "You did good, baby."

Twenty minutes later, the service ends and a crush of visitors pushes to surround us. I'm subjected to so many hugs, kisses, and well wishes that I feel guilty for thinking these people hated me.

We start to leave for the cemetery for the burial.

"Excuse us, Ms. Murphy?" a voice booms. I turn toward two large police officers. "Are you two Ta'Shara Murphy and Raymond Lewis?" the biggest of the two cops asks.

Confused, I blink. "Yes."

"Why do you want to know?" Profit challenges.

Two sets of handcuffs are slapped onto our wrists.

"You are under arrest for the murders of Markeisha Edwards and Tracee and Reggie Douglas."

"What?"

"You have the right to remain silent. Anything you say can and will be used against you in a court of law."

"Wait. Wait. There must be some mistake," I protest.

They shove us out of the funeral home.

"You have the right to an . . ."

Their words transform into white noise as the guests' mournful faces turn into shock. This time when the crowd parts, it isn't because I'm Moses—but because they think that I am a killer.

Outside, as I'm being shoved into the back of a patrol car, a face across the parking lot catches my attention and freezes my heart.

LeShelle.

25

LeShelle

Blue and white strobe lights line the front door of the Forest Hill Funeral Home. It's hard to see what's going on with so many people crowded around. The idea of my coming all the way out here for nothing raises my blood pressure. After reading about Tracee and Reggie's funeral services in the paper, I lay in bed all night unable to sleep.

I don't like loose ends.

An eighteen-wheeler zooms past me, where I'm parked on the side of the road across from the funeral home. For a brief moment, my line of vision is obstructed and the Escalade rocks in its wake.

When I'm able to see again, the crowd is parting and Ta'Shara and Profit are being shoved through with their hands behind their backs.

"Well, I'll be damned." I watch in shock. What in the hell did my bougie-ass sister do to get arrested?

A cop places his hand on top of Ta'Shara's head and crams her into the back of the police car. As soon as she is tucked in, she glances my way.

Laughing, I lift the gat from my lap and salute her. Her eyes widen. Our dance with death will have to wait.

When the squad car pulls off, I tuck the gun underneath

my seat and wait to follow three cars behind them. This turn of events keeps me chuckling the whole ride to the precinct. There, I'm unable to follow behind the gated area where the cops escorts their suspects into the building—but I am able to drive down the road a ways and park in a KFC parking lot.

I need to think.

Who knows when I'll be able to get at Ta'Shara again? Even if she's able to get out of whatever this situation is, I have no doubt that Profit will tuck her back onto Ruby Cove, where she'll be surrounded by Vice Lords and stank-ass Flowers. It'll be impossible to get at her. Today was to be my best shot. I'm hardly in the position to play hide-and-seek. I'm already playing that game with the police my damn self.

Maybe you should just let this shit go.

My jaw clenches at that annoying voice in the back of my head. A part of me still wants to go back to playing the protective big sister to that backstabbing bitch. "I won't do it," I vow, staring into my eyes through the rearview mirror. I spent my entire life looking after that girl, got locked up, raped, and tossed in the streets while she lived the life of a princess in suburbia, dreaming of becoming a doctor.

Where I was hard and jaded, Ta'Shara believed that her shit didn't stink, with her straight A's and her track star status. I told her to wake her ass up, but she looked down on me and heard nothing I said. Things went south when I set out to prove to her that Reggie Douglas was no different from any other nigga that had taken us in over the years.

I'll admit it: I overplayed my hand and got tossed out in the street after my attempt to seduce him.

I didn't care. I was ready to go anyway. However, Ta'Shara plunged the first knife into my back and refused to leave with me. That shit hurt, but I bounced and got myself a job down at the Pink Monkey strip club. I worked the pole, learned how to use my pussy, and clawed my ass out of the gutter. All the while, I still looked after her. My name gave her protection in the streets—and in that shitty high school. And what did she do in return?

Showed me her ass—and laid down with my enemies. Who the fuck does that shit? Ta'Shara picked that nigga over me so now she has to deal with the consequences. The way I see it, her taking a couple of bullets is the least her ass could do.

A rogue idea strikes. I scramble for the cell phone that I'd tossed over into the passenger seat. I scroll through my mental phone book and call a junior Queen G.

"Yo, Avonte. I got a job for you."

"Sure, my queen. I got you."

"I'm over here by the police station off of Third. Who do we have in holding over here right now? Anybody?"

"I'm not sure, but I can find out."

"Good. The sooner, the better. There's someone there that I want to make sure doesn't come out alive."

26

Ta'Shara

"**Y**ou're making a big mistake! I didn't kill my parents!"

The expressionless cop then ignores my pleas and jerks me toward a small, isolated room. The humiliation of being arrested at the funeral home extends to being fingerprinted and shoved in front of a camera for my first mug shot. Last year, I was hauled in for questioning over a Gangster Disciple and Vice Lords shootout at The Med, but I was never arrested.

An arrest is a permanent record—proof that I'm headed down the wrong road fast. Now I'm a statistic. *This can't be happening.* I'm trying to be strong, but I'm overwhelmed with a sense of helplessness and that things happening to and around me are constantly out my control—and I'm sick of it.

"I'm innocent," I shout.

"That's what they all say," the cop says, giving me a final shove into the room. "Take a seat."

I whip around and then suppress the instinct to lash out and knee this asshole's balls up to his throat.

"Take. A. Seat," he repeats, gritting his teeth.

Defiant, I glare at him with my chest heaving.

Unimpressed, the cop shoves me into the chair. "Thank you," he sneers and then walks behind me to unlock my cuffs. "Now. Can I get you some water? Soda?"

"No."

He shrugs a *suit yourself* and walks out. There's a loud *click* when the door closes behind him, letting me know that it's useless for me to make a run for it.

My gaze sweeps around the small room. A nervous twitch thumps against my temple. I rub my hands and wrists to massage the pain from the last few hours—and to give me something to do with my hands. All this room is missing is an iron bed and a straitjacket for me to feel like I'm back in the mental hospital.

I sit still as the minutes tick by. They're probably watching me behind the glass. That's how they do it in the movies—let your guilt eat at you until you're ready to confess everything you've ever done your entire life.

The thing is, guilt eats at the innocent, too. If I'd never entered the Douglases' lives. If I'd never hooked up with Profit. If we'd never gone to the prom. If Profit and I had never had that fight with them the night I left.

If.

If.

If.

Damn. Why didn't I ask for that glass of water? I lick my lips, but my mouth remains as dry as the Sahara desert.

The door bolts open and that walrus-looking lieutenant, Andrew Blalock, waddles in, looking cranky as fuck. "Ah, Ms. Murphy. Glad to see that you could make it, seeing as how you missed your appointment the other day."

I frown and then vaguely remember the lieutenant talking and handing me his business card the night my world burned to the ground.

My guilt reverses itself and my anger roars back. "You have no right to fuckin' arrest me. I didn't kill anyone."

"Like you didn't try to kill your sister, LeShelle, a few months ago?" He slaps a thick folder onto the table. "It took four orderlies and two nurses to pull you off of her and take the bloody knitting needles from your hands."

My hands ball on the table as I remember the feel of those needles. Instant recall has LeShelle's body fighting and struggling between my legs. Before my homicidal lust completely takes over me, I snap out of it and remember where I am. "That was different."

His bushy eyebrows jump comically. "Different how?"

I grind my teeth. I'm tempted to snitch all the horrors my *wonderful* sister has put me through—but that war is between me and LeShelle.

"That's what I thought," Lieutenant Blalock pulls up a chair, and when he squats to sit, his knees crack in protest. "Tell me what happened. To your parents."

"Nothing. I had nothing to do with that fire."

"All right. Tell me about the fight between you, your boyfriend, Raymond, and your parents a few days before the fire."

That catches me off guard.

"Didn't think we'd find out about that?" His brows lift again—this time with amusement. "You young people think that y'all are the smartest one in the room."

I hold my tongue while he flips through the folder. "The neighbors reported shots fired at that address that night. When the police questioned your parents, Tracee admitted to firing the gun to break up a fight between her husband and your boyfriend. Does that jog your memory?"

Shame pricks my armor. I lower my hardened gaze for no more than half a second before stiffening my spine. "It was a misunderstanding."

"Really?" he echoes. "That must have been one hell of a misunderstanding. They kicked you out over it, right?"

I tense. "I *moved* out—temporarily."

"Hmmm." Lieutenant Blalock shakes his head as he rereads

the file. "That's not what I have here. Reggie Douglas stated clearly that you were not welcome back at their home. *Ever.*"

His words slam into me like a punch to the gut. I know that Reggie was angry, but I don't want to believe that he meant those words. I want to believe that when I returned they would've welcomed me with open arms.

Now I have doubts.

"So. What was the disagreement about it?" Blalock inquires.

I sniff and wipe my face dry. "You tell me since you know so much."

Blalock closes the folder. "I'd say that fight was a little bit more than a misunderstanding. Since things got physical between Raymond and your father, I'd say you two went back there to either try and settle it or go for round two. I'd say it's the latter—and given the amount of accelerant you two doused throughout the house, you came well prepared to end the war for once and for all."

"That's ridiculous."

"I've seen crazier shit out here in these streets."

"And that other chick?" I ask him. "I've never even heard of her. Why would I kill her?"

"Markeisha 'Kookie' Edwards." He switches to another folder and pulls out a photo—a mug shot—of a face that I've definitely seen before. *Kookie. LeShelle's friend who was there the night I was raped.*

Oh shit.

"Judging by your expression, I take it that you *did* know her?" Blalock asks.

I ease back in my chair, thrilled to know that the bitch was dead. "Like I said: I didn't kill anyone," I tell him. "And you can't prove that I did!"

"Oh. You'd be amazed what we can do around here." His smile sickens me. "How did you hear about the fire?" he continues.

"What?"

"The news cameras were there, but given the hour, the first time the breaking news footage aired was five o'clock that morning. You were there within a half hour of the emergency responders. How was that?"

I shouldn't answer his smart ass. "Because I was returning home."

He levels a flat look.

"Believe what you want to believe," I say. "There's no way you can prove this bullshit story you're spinning. A fight? Name a kid who hasn't had a fight with their parents."

"True. But the list gets smaller when you add gunplay into the mix."

"Whatever. You wanna lock me up, lock me up. I don't give a fuck."

"Well, let me assure you that I don't give a fuck either."

"I didn't kill them."

Blalock's careful mask slips and anger twists his walrus face. He slams his folders closed and jumps from his chair. Something tells me that he'd bet the house on getting a confession.

Smug, I ask, "You think I can get that water now?"

He storms out.

I never get that water, but minutes later I'm led to a crowded holding cell. One glance at this circus clown show and anxiety knots my stomach. When the guard orders for the door to be opened, all heads swivel to check out the fresh meat.

The iron bars slide open.

"In you go, Miss Murphy."

A few more heads swivel to give me closer scrutiny. Drawing a deep breath, I stiffen my spine and thrust my chin higher. I don't bother looking for a seat because I know that shit will spark off a fight.

As soon as the jailer's footsteps fade, a tall, shapeless bitch with matted dreadlocks strolls up to me. "Murphy? You LeShelle's lil sister?"

I meet her jaundiced eyes with the same attitude as she's giving. "How is that your business?"

Two more ugly bitches flank Ms. Rasta's side. "Answer the fuckin' question."

My nose twists at their sour and funky breath. "What the fuck? Y'all been eating ass all night?"

Laughter ripples around me.

"Oh. You're a fuckin' comedian, huh?" Rasta flips my hair off my shoulder. "Let's see how many jokes you tell after I break my foot off in your ass."

I steel myself for anything. If it's going to pop off, I'm ready.

"The word on Shotgun Row is that you're open game in the middle of hunting season."

"I don't know what the fuck you said—was that shit even English?"

"Fuck you, bitch!"

Rasta shoves my shoulder—hard. I jerk back, but I waste no time spitting the blade from my mouth. My hand comes up in one beautiful golf swing, but this seasoned street veteran knows better than to keep her ass standing still, and pulls a *Matrix* back bend. I only manage to slice off half of a crusty-ass dreadlock. When she pulls her upper body back up, she and her two girlfriends charge forward. To my surprise, five girls rush up to flank my sides, pumping the Queen Gs' brakes.

"A'ight. Y'all done had your fuckin' fun," says a six-foot redbone sister with a Vice Lord *Playboy* bunny tattooed on her neck. "You know the drill. You come for one of ours, you come for *all* of us."

More girls in the cell stand up.

Rasta and her two crackhead zombie twins back down. "Oh. So it is true," she growls. "You flaggin' black and gold."

My hard glare is my only answer. Hell. I'm as shocked as she is that the Vice Lord Flowers have my back, but I'm not about to show that shit. Lucky for me, the Flowers outnumber the Queen Gs in the holding cell today.

"All right. 'Til next time." Rasta backs up to her previous spot on a hard bench, careful not to give the Flowers her back.

The redbone turns and winks. "It looks like Profit pulled a bitch with some fuckin' heart." She tosses a sly grin. "Name's Mackenzie. People call me Mack."

"Ta'Shara," I say, keeping my brave act intact.

"Welcome to the fam, Ta'Shara. As Profit's girl, you're officially one of us."

27

Hydeya

"**N**othing." I toss up my hands and then collapse back into my chair.

Lieutenant Fowler shrugs and then moves from hovering over my shoulder. "Well, what's a couple of more hours wasted in the grand scheme of things?"

"I don't know why you're laughing. You know that when I get a feeling about someone, I'm never wrong," I gloat.

"Never? Never ever?"

"Whoa! I was right about that asshole!"

Fowler gives me a look.

"Okay. So maybe he wasn't *technically* a murderer."

"Which was the whole point since we were investigating a murder." Fowler drops into the chair across from my desk, snickering. "You nearly blasted an innocent man's head off because you thought that he killed his son."

"You're right. He didn't kill him. He only molested and prostituted him and his other children to feed his lifestyle and drug habit. My bad. He was still a bad guy—and that's the same vibe I'm getting from Mr. Diesel Carver."

Fowler sighs and shakes his head.

"You shouldn't patronize me. I'm your boss now, remember?"

"I have a feeling that you're never going to let me forget it."

"Damn right." I smirk.

As far as colleagues go, Fowler is all right with me. He has this weird ability to come off easygoing and aloof when in fact nothing is further from the truth. He's tenacious and as dedicated as they come. He takes his job seriously and he doesn't kowtow to the hard blue line that often pits cops against the very people that they're sworn to protect. The us-against-them mentality that's prevalent in most urban cities' police departments.

"So now what? Crazy lady went ballistic and went on a kidnapping and killing spree? Case closed?"

I shift in my chair, uncomfortable putting the case in a neat box.

"I'll take that as a no," Fowler says.

"I didn't say anything."

"Didn't have to. I know that look—it resembles the one my wife gives me when I ask for sex on my birthday."

"It might have something to do with the fact that you're divorced."

"See? You're even starting to sound like her."

Laughing, I shake my head while reviewing things in my mind. "We need to take another tour through Captain Johnson's residence. There's gotta be something there that better explains all of this. We don't have that much time. I'm already getting hints that the mayor wants this case to go away as fast as possible."

Knock. Knock.

"I was told to deliver these forensic tire and shoeprint reports to you."

"Great." I wave her in and take the report. "Thanks, Detective."

She flashes a smile and leaves.

"Which case is that?" Fowler inquires, while I prop open the folder.

"The Terry-Gibson case."

He shakes his head. "Another seriously fucked up case."

"Are there any other kind?" I ask, not tearing my eyes from the report. "At least we got a brand from the molds. Firestone Destination ST."

"So we're looking for an SUV?"

"That should narrow things down to about a million." I hand over the top report and pictures in the folder. "Get on the phone with Firestone and find out what car shop or dealership where this DOT number was shipped to. Maybe we'll catch a break and find whose car those tires belong to."

"Unless they were stolen."

I cut him a sharp look. "Are you going to be Debbie Downer all day?"

"Sorry. It's hard to control my pessimist side sometimes."

"Try a little harder. Look at this." I hand him the next report and set of photographs. "Shoeprints. Five different sets— two belong to our victims."

"Three killers. Definitely gang activity." He shrugs. "We already knew that."

"Yolanda Terry was from Shotgun Row. Given her arrest record, I'd bet my house that she was a Queen G."

"And Tyneshia Gibson? She lived closer to the Ruby Cove area."

"Vice Lord Flowers. Oil and water." I lean back in my chair. "Shoeprints are small, suggesting they're females."

"Or very dainty men?" Fowler jokes.

I rub my pulsing temples. "We're looking for either a group of Flowers or a group of Queen Gs—or a collection of both."

"We can't rule out that it could be another group that doesn't like either those gangs. The Crippettes or the Blood-ettes or—"

"Get out of my office," I snap. "I don't need you popping my bubble every time I think I'm on a roll."

Fowler laughs and then tosses the reports and photographs back onto my desk. "I thought that we were brainstorming."

Knock. Knock.

Sighing, I look up again to a different detective, hovering. "Yes?"

"Captain Hawkins, there is a James and Theresa Gibson here to see you."

The names don't set off any bells.

"The Terry-Gibson case," Fowler jogs my memory.

"Oh. Of course. Send them in."

Fowler heads for the door.

"Wait. Stick around. You're going to be lead on this."

He nods as the Gibsons are escorted to my door.

I climb to my feet and extend my hand. "Mr. and Mrs. Gibson, please come in. Have a seat."

Fowler vacates his chair in order for the victim's parents to sit down.

"We've been calling to talk to you, but they kept telling us that you were out of the office," Mrs. Gibson begins.

"Yes, ma'am. I'm sorry about that. How may I help you?"

She hesitates and then glances over at her husband.

"We want to know how the investigation into our daughter's case is going. The news stations aren't saying much of anything and we'd hope that you would've called us back by now."

"Yes, ma'am. Let me reassure you that we are working diligently on Tyneshia's case. We have a few leads, but I got to warn you that this is going to be a very long process. We're not going to be able to solve this case overnight."

The couple glances at each other, and I get the distinct feeling that they want to tell me something. "What is it?"

Theresa grabs hold of her husband's hand for strength. "We'd like for you to talk to Tyneshia's friends."

"Oh?" My gaze slices to Fowler as I retrieve a pen and pad. "And what are their names?"

They hesitate again.

With my hand poised over the paper, I resist rolling my eyes and snapping at them. It doesn't matter how old people are, the rules in the streets remain the same: no snitching.

"Mr. and Mrs. Gibson, do you want us to find your daughter's killers or not?"

James Gibson's chin lifts with renewed resolve. "Shamara Moore, Adaryl Grant, and Qiana Barrett."

28

Cleo

I miss Essence. The whole family does. The once loud and rowdy house is now a permanent wake. Everyone's faces stretch while their accusatory gazes ping-pong. I don't look any further than my reflection in the mirror. It's my fault that Essence is dead. The blame is on me. I knew that when Kookie and Pit Bull stepped to Essence in Fabdivas Hair Salon to do LeShelle's bidding that shit was going to go south and what did I do? I let it happen anyway.

I. Let. It. Happen.

Being the older sister, I always gave Essence grief, but I loved her. I hope she knew that. I love my family. We're a tight unit—something rare out here in these streets. I've seen too many sisters and brothers turn on one another to know that what we have, despite playful banter, is unique. My only hope is that this tragedy won't tear us apart.

LeShelle led everyone to believe that Lucifer was somehow behind Essence's murder, and I ranted and raved that I'd get that bitch back for that shit. But then my path crossed with the infamous Vice Lord in the middle of a cemetery. The chick snuck up on me while I was at Essence's grave. By the time I heard and thought to go for my weapon, Lucifer made it clear that such a move was suicide. I've been out here a long time and I've never come across anyone like Lucifer.

Powerful. Graceful. Even while I was standing there, hating her, I couldn't help but admire as well. She wears her danger and power well. It rolls off of her like heat waves. She's the last bitch that anyone wants to tangle with. At the same time she was dropping information bombs around me that completely rocked my world. She said unequivocally that she'd had nothing to do with Essence's death and I read nothing but truth in her dark eyes. She had no reason to lie. I hardly posed a threat to her that night. But LeShelle? Everybody knows that there isn't an honest bone in the bitch's body.

The dilemma now is whether to tell the rest of my family. My brothers, Kobe and Freddy, will wild the fuck out. But our allegiance to the Gangster Disciples and the Queen Gs will put the whole family in between a rock and a hard place. We'd all buck and that shit might get our asses slaughtered.

So do I tell or not tell?

Hell, I'd hoped that when I dropped dime to Lucifer that LeShelle and Python were about to get hitched, and even gave her the address, that the problem would've been handled. But bullets don't seem to have an effect on that bitch and her man.

I could take the bitch out myself—but how? I'm no fuckin' killer. Never have been. The most I've ever done is pull bullshit robberies and burglaries in my teen years. I've never been about that life. The other Queen Gs can have all that shit. Selling pussy or slinging dope ain't for me. I have bigger dreams.

Music is supposed to be my ticket out of the streets. All my life, people have told me that I am talented and that I'm going places. I'm supposed to be the lethal combination of Whitney Houston, Mary J. Blige, and Rihanna. But I get that mostly from niggas tryna gas me up and use me.

The bathroom doorknob rattles. "OCCUPIED!"

"Well, goddamn. Did you fall into the toilet? You've been in there for over twenty minutes," Percy, one of the Studio B audio engineers and an all-around pain in the ass, pounds on the door.

"I'll be out in a minute," I bark, wanting to take his head off, but holding back. Lately, that's about par for the course. I go from wanting to fight every damn body who crosses my path to flipping the script and curling up in bed and crying all day. I'm an emotional wreck because I want my sister back.

In the midst of that shit, I got my fiancé, Kalief, buzzing in my ear about how this is the perfect time for us to roll up in the studio and record tracks. He insists that all the famous recording artists produced their best shit when they were at their lowest. If that's true, my ass is going straight to the top of the chart.

Kalief and I go all the way back to high school. He was *that* nigga. He was fine and knew how to stack his paper, and we shared a love for music. We spent hours at his crib, listening to the oldie but goodies: Billie Holiday, Etta James, Sarah Vaughan, all the Motown greats, and then there was Aretha Franklin, Tina Turner—the list went on and on.

Those were some good times.

If I can't do nothing else in this world, I know that my ass can sing. When I was a kid, my grandma would always gather her girls together and I would put on my best dress and perform in the center of the living room. My brothers and sister would ham up, but in the end, I know they have all been rooting for me. Kalief has always held me down and believed in my talent. In the beginning, it was easy to love him. He was kind, warm, and funny. He could even hold a note or two if I got the right ratio of weed and liquor in him. After high school, Kalief proposed *and* pressed me to make him my manager. My singing was supposed to save him from the streets too.

I said yes to both.

Big mistake.

Six years later, Kalief and I are exactly where we started: still engaged and still hustling in this fucked-up industry. Only now he has a coke problem, a drinking problem, a gambling problem, a lying problem, and a cheating problem.

But I *still* fuckin' love him: hood girl problems.

I hang my head as another wave of tears threaten to fuck up my makeup. I gotta pull it together. This studio is costing me money and since I'm the only one locking down three jobs to pay the bills, I need to get out there and lay these damn tracks or . . . I toss in the towel. Black female singers who can blow are a dime a dozen. What the industry wants are white girls who *sound* black. And the few black girls who get through . . . they have to be the right shade to upgrade.

I'm a tall, chocolate sister with a nice frame. The minute I walk into a room full of executives, their eyes glaze over. In their view, I'm another ghetto black girl who belongs in front of her local church choir instead of selling out at Madison Square Garden.

No matter how many failures or setbacks, Kalief never loses faith. My big break is around the corner, he always says. *Hang in there, baby. Trust me, baby.* Lately, he wants this shit more than I do. For now, we're independent, throwing up music on iTunes and YouTube and praying that God still performs miracles. In other words, we're going nowhere fast.

Bang! Bang! Bang!

The bathroom door rattles again. "Damn, girl. Pinch that shit off and call it a day. Damn!"

Heated, I swipe away my tears and jerk away from the mirror. Ready to give Percy a piece of my mind, I snatch open the door. "Nigga—"

Percy grabs my hand, jerks me out of the small bathroom, races inside, and slams the door in my face.

"Damn, Percy! I . . . uuuugh." I twist up my face and cover my nose. Bubble-guts sounds seep through the door.

"Aaaaahhhh," Percy moans.

"Damn, Percy. Your ass is nasty!" I turn and head back into the booth. I need to concentrate. All day I've been missing notes and sounding like I smoked a carton of cigarettes and downed a bottle of Jack Daniels before rolling up in there.

"You good, ma?" Joe, the senior audio engineer, asks.

Sighing, I put on a brave face and give him thumbs-up.

He shakes his head at my pathetic acting performance. We've worked together long enough for him to know what time it is.

Kalief leans forward in his producer chair to grin at me. "Shake all the bullshit off, baby. You can do this." Big thumbs-up and a wink.

I smile, but it doesn't reach my eyes.

"All right. Let's take it where we left off." He punches a button and the riffs of Billie Holiday's remix of "Gloomy Sunday" pour into my headphones. The slow, haunting melody is fucking with my heartstrings before I even open my mouth.

"Sorrow has taken you . . ."

My voice croaks as an image of Essence floats to mind and Joe has to kill the music . . . again. "Sorry. I can't." I drop my head into my hand as another wave of tears crests my eyes.

Joe sighs. "Maybe you're not up for this today," he concludes, taking pity on me.

"Nah. Nah. She's all right," Kalief interjects, bolting up from his producer chair, sniffing. "Aren't you, baby girl?"

I roll my eyes. I don't need a cheerleader right now. I want to go home.

Kalief rushes into the booth with me. "C'mon. C'mon,

baby girl. You gotta pull it together. You can do this. I *know* that you can do this."

The fact that he's talking a mile a minute tells me that he's coked up again. "I'm not feeling it, baby. I'm tired."

"Tired? You don't get to be tired. Do you know how much this studio time is costing us right now?"

"Of course I know how much it's costing. I'm the one that's paying for it," I remind him. "Hell, I'm the one that pays for *everything*."

"What the fuck is that supposed to mean?" His jovial mood evaporates. "Are you tryna say that I'm not pulling my weight? Is that it? It's not enough that I wake up every day and bust my ass tryna make *you* a star? I make the moves, I make the connects—*I* make shit happen. That shit means nothing now?"

He's so close that he's spitting in my face. Instinctively, my hands ball at my sides while my back teeth grind together. I weigh whether I want us to have an Ike and Anna Mae moment in the middle of the studio. It's dangerously close to happening, but I'll be damned if I'll be Anna Mae. He realizes it, too, and takes a step back with his smile returning bigger and brighter than before.

"All right. You're right," he says. "You're too tired to do this right now. So let's call it a day and you go on home and get some rest. We got that audition at Club Diesel coming up." He sniffs and rubs at his red nose.

I'm shaking my head the whole time he's talking. "I don't know if I'm going to be up to that. I need time off."

Kalief grabs my shoulders and shakes me one good time. "What the fuck? Do you know what I had to do to get this dude to come and hear you sing? He's up here from Atlanta and the nigga knows *all* the right people. He can put you *on*. I'm telling you. *This* is it. This is your time. If you don't do another muthafuckin' thing for me, you gotta to do this."

I stare into his wide eyes and feel myself giving into his ass once again. Sighing, I remove his hands from my shoulders. "Fine, Kalief. I'll do it."

"That's my girl." After a quick peck on the cheek, he turns to leave.

I remove my headphones, but I have one last question for him. "So who is this big shot from Atlanta?"

Kalief stops before slipping out of the booth. "The new top dog in Memphis, Diesel Carver."

29

Hydeya

Ruby Cove.

Rolling through Vice Lords' hostile territory, I'm still prepared for anything to go left. Acting on the Gibsons' tip, I don't know what to make of their suspicions of Tyneshia's girlfriends—especially since when we first interviewed them a few days ago, they swore that their daughter wasn't part of a gang and that she didn't have any enemies. Now, apparently, they've had a come-to-Jesus moment and forced themselves to face a few facts about their daughter. For example, that she had been having problems at school and had been hanging out with a set of friends that her mother referred to as "tramps." None of Tyneshia's new friends bothered to call or show up to their daughter's funeral yesterday.

After a little digging, I discovered that whenever Tyneshia was arrested, the same three girls the Gibsons named were hauled off to jail with her: Adaryl Grant, Shamara "Li'l Bit" Moore and Qiana Barrett. Lieutenant Fowler and I visit Adaryl Grant's place first, but despite a car being in the driveway, no one bothers to open the door. Next stop: Shamara Moore. Here, her grandmother opens the door and says she has no idea where her grandchild is and then grills us for twenty minutes about what the child has done now.

"We just want to talk to her."

The old lady doesn't buy it.

I hope we have more luck with Qiana Barrett.

When we park in front of the Barretts' address, I'm convinced that we must've tripped an invisible alarm wire because large crowds of people spill out of their houses to peep us out.

"This should be fun," Lieutenant John Fowler says, removing his mirrored shades and shoving them in his front pocket.

"I don't know about you, but I live for excitement." I sweep my gaze around our growing crowd. If they're trying to intimidate, they got me confused. I grew up in the streets and I can get gutter with the best of them.

"Then you're certainly in the right place." He opens his car door and climbs out.

Laughing, I follow his lead, snapping open my holster for easy access.

When we reach the front door, I knock and then we wait.

The seconds tick by like hours while the number of bodies surrounding us increases.

KNOCK! KNOCK! KNOCK!

Fowler leans over my shoulder. "I'm not too sure that we won't have to shoot our way out of here."

"Chill," I hiss, certain that did nothing to alleviate his anxiety.

The curtains on the side window shift, but when I look over, they drop back into place. However, the door doesn't open.

"C'mon," I mutter, irritated. "Open the damn door."

"Y'all pigs need to get the fuck on," an angry male voice yells behind us. "Y'all are stinking up the whole damn street!"

Laughter spreads among the crowd. Fowler casts me a look that tells me he'd rather be playing Russian roulette in his momma's basement right now.

"I think you're mistaking us for your bottom lip." I level him with my best Dirty Harry look.

The young gangster looks me up and down, trying to decide how much he wants to show off in front of his friends.

"Hey, ain't you the new captain of police?" a female asks. "Yeah. Yeah. I seen you all over the news."

That got everyone's attention. They look me over again and then back the hell up.

Fowler chuckles. "Damn. I need to carry you around in my back pocket. Maybe I'll finally get some respect."

KNOCK! KNOCK! KNOCK!

A female voice shouts, "Who is it?"

"Police! We'd like to ask a few questions."

Silence. And the door remains closed.

What the fuck?

"If you like, I can call in for a warrant."

A series of locks disengages. I pass another look to Fowler. The door creeps open enough and a young lady with two large flesh-colored bandages on her face appears.

"Yeah. What do you want?" she demands.

"Hello. I'm Captain Hydeya Hawkins." I flash my badge. "And this is Lieutenant Fowler. We need to talk to Qiana Barrett. Is that you?"

"You know I am," she sasses back.

She's right. I do. I have a copy of her last mug shot in my file. "May we come in?"

The girl looks to the crowd a few feet away. Every single one of them is trying to ear hustle in on our conversation. "What do y'all want?"

"We want to ask you a few questions about your friend Tyneshia Gibson. In case you've been under a rock, her body was discovered off Peebles Road in south Memphis. Mind if we come in?"

She hesitates and I can tell that she wants to tell our ass to go to hell, but I'm sure she knows that's not a smart idea. "Two minutes," she says and then steps back from the door so we can enter.

Lieutenant Fowler and I exchange here-we-go looks before entering. Out of habit, I look around, taking in as much as I can. The house isn't a pigsty, but it isn't going to win any housekeeping awards either. The dining room and living room are filled with oversized and mismatched furniture.

"All right. What do you want?" she asks, settling her hands on her hips.

"Don't you want to know the details of your friend's death?"

"I already know. It's been all over the news." Qiana switches her weight from one leg to the other.

"And you don't know anything other than what's been reported?"

"Should I?"

I shrug and play dumb, too. "You tell me."

We engage in a staring contest.

"Why didn't you attend Tyneshia's funeral yesterday?"

She shrugs. "I didn't want to see her like that."

"There wasn't much to see," Fowlers says. "The animals did quite a number on her body." He heads down the hallway.

"Hey! Where are you going?"

"Are you here alone?" he asks while continuing his walk-through.

"I don't see how that's any of your business." She chases after him, looking like an angry tornado.

Fowler opens one door, peeks inside, and then moves to another.

"Hey, muthafuckas, you can't do that! I know my rights!"

"What's the problem?" I ask, pretending to be mystified by her indignation.

"Y'all pig-muthafuckas ain't got no warrant. Y'all can't just barge through my house like you're paying the fuckin' bills up in this bitch."

Yeah. I have no problem picturing this Tasmanian devil slicing one chick and blowing a hole in another's skull. Her face is purple with rage. However, Fowler continues searching.

"Ms. Barrett, you did invite us in—and I could've sworn that I heard you say that we could search the house. Didn't you, Lieutenant Fowler?"

"That's what I heard."

"Nah. Y'all dirty fuckers got to get out of my house!"

"We'll leave as soon as you answer our questions," I tell her, while I wait for Fowler to find something 'cause I'm getting one of my vibes about this chick.

"What damn questions? What the fuck you wanna know?"

"For starters," Fowler says after checking the last door, "what took you so long to answer the door? We were out there what—five minutes?"

"At least," I agree.

"Shit. I don't know you muthafuckas. I don't answer the door for any damn body. Shit. This ain't the damn suburbs."

"The place is clear," Fowler says.

"Great. Now that y'all are finished illegally searching my shit—y'all can get the fuck out."

We ignore her. "Did you know Yolanda Terry?"

"Who?"

"The pregnant woman that was found with Tyneshia—only she was missing a baby," I add. "What do you know about that?"

"Nothing," she says. "Why in the hell would I?"

Bullshit. "Now why don't I believe that?"

"I don't give a fuck what you believe."

Calmly, I meet the girl's eyes. "That would be a mistake. You don't want to be on my shit list. I'll make your life a living hell just for shits and giggles."

Qiana clamps her mouth shut and glares at me.

"You don't have to like me, but you will answer my questions—either here or down at the station. Your choice."

"Whatever. I still don't know anything."

Fowler jumps back into the mix. "When was the last time you saw Tyneshia?"

She shrugs. "Don't remember."

I step forward. "Days? Weeks? Months?"

"Months," I suppose."

"And you never wondered where she was?"

"No. I'm not nosey like that. If people want me to know their business they'll tell me. If not . . ." She shrugs.

"So you have no idea why a Vice Lord Flower and a Gangster Disciple Queen G were just hanging out, huh?"

"Not a clue. Maybe they were secret lovers or something," she suggests.

"Humph. We were told that you, Adaryl, Shamara, and Tyneshia were as thick as thieves."

"Who told you that?"

"We're the ones asking the questions, Ms. Barrett. And I have to tell you that I find your behavior right now highly irregular—suspicious even. One of your best friends was murdered and you're not even mildly curious to what had happened to her."

"She wasn't my best friend."

"Did you two fall out or something?"

The girl wants to fire off another sharp reply when she clearly realizes that she needs to watch her mouth. "No. I'm just saying we weren't best friends. We just hung out every now and then. That's all."

"Hung out every now and again, huh? Not enough times for you to give a damn about what happened to her?"

Exasperated, Qiana tosses up her hands. "Look. What do you want from me?"

"The truth might be nice," I say.

"At the very least, refreshing," Fowler agrees.

"I told you the truth. Now, y'all can stand here and harass me or drag my ass down to the station. I don't give a fuck. My statement is going to stay the same. I don't know shit, I didn't hear shit, and I certainly didn't see shit."

"What about the baby?"

Qiana's face drains of color. "What baby?"

"The baby James and Theresa Gibson say that you've been keeping here."

She forces out a hard laugh. "Do you see a baby around here?"

Fowler and I laugh.

"Whatever. Muthafuckas around here—"

The door bolts open and a tall brick building of a man storms in and growls menacingly at us, "What the fuck is going on in here?"

"And you are?" I ask.

"I ain't gotta tell you shit! You're standing in my house. Where y'all's warrant?"

"We don't have a warrant, we just—"

"Then y'all need to bounce! Qiana is underage anyhow. You guys aren't supposed to be up in here asking her about shit without parental permission." He opens the door. "Have a nice a day."

"We'll be back," Fowler says, removing his shades from his shirt pocket and slipping them over his eyes.

Qiana's champion smiles. "Make sure that you bring that warrant when you do."

I offer them my business card. "If you hear or think of anything that might help solve your friend's murder, give us a call."

Qiana takes the card, holds it up, and then rips it in two. "Leave."

"Sure thing." I swing my gaze between Qiana and her angry giant one last time before making my exit.

The door slams behind me.

"That went well," Fowler says as we march back to our patrol car.

"Swimmingly." I glance over at the driveway and then whip out my notepad.

"What?"

"Two SUVs. We should get the VIN numbers and license plates. Who knows? Maybe we'll get lucky."

30

Qiana

I stare out of the door's peephole with my heart hammering in my chest until the police car pulls out of our driveway.

"Qiana, I know that you fuckin' hear me," Tombstone barks behind my back. "You want to tell me why those fuckin' pigs were up in this bitch?"

The coast is clear. I expel a long breath, giving relief to my burning lungs.

'Qiana!"

"Fuck, Tombstone, get out of my ear with all of that hollering. I done told you to stay out of my business. The shit don't concern you."

"Don't concern me? I know you like to play like you done lost your mind, but I know muthafuckin' better. I can't have the goddamn cops up in here—especially with the whole damn street seeing and buzzing about it. It just takes one muthafucka thinking our asses is snitching about some bullshit to set shit off and change all of our breathing habits. I sure as shit can't roll out of here not knowing what the fuck is going on."

KNOCK! KNOCK! KNOCK!

"Now who in the fuck is that?" Tombstone explodes.

I whip around to peek out of the peephole. "It's Li'l Bit." I snatch open the door, grab her arm, and pull her inside. "Get in here."

"Shit, girl. They went to my house, too. My grandma is pissed as shit. What did they say?"

I take her by the arm and attempt to drag her to my bedroom. But Tombstone blocks our path.

"Qiana, I swear to God. If you—"

"Tell me what happened over there at that tattoo shop," I challenge him.

"Wh-what?"

"You know, that tattoo artist you and your secret dream girl chopped up a few days ago."

He makes a threatening step forward. "You keep your mouth shut about that shit. It doesn't concern you."

"How about you take your own fuckin' advice when it comes to my shit?" I shoulder my way past him, dragging Li'l Bit with me.

"Sorry," she squeaks when she moves around him. We make it to my room and I quickly close my busted door and then collapse behind it. "Shit. Shit. Shit. I think I fucked up."

Li'l Bit's eyes widen with alarm. "You didn't confess to anything, did you?"

"Don't you think that they would've hauled my ass to jail if I had?" Sometimes my girl isn't operating with a full deck.

"Oh." Her body deflates with relief. "Then what did you do?"

"I fuckin' lost my temper—because they were snooping around here like they owned the damn place."

"Oookay," she says, not understanding.

"I didn't confess, but they *knew* that I was lying." I toss up my hands. "Shit. I haven't lied that bad since finger-painting all over the walls when I was six years old."

"Oh. Fuck. Me," Li'l Bit whispers.

"Yeah. Exactly. They even asked me about the baby."

"They did?" Eyes doubling in size, Li'l Bit drops onto the edge of my bed looking like she's about to hyperventilate. "What *did* you say—exactly?"

"Nothing." I shrug. "I mean. I don't know. I just played dumb and thank God my pain-in-the-ass brother showed up when he did or that bitch cop would've pulled me all the way out of my character."

Li'l Bit stares at me.

"Look. It's okay," I reassure her. "Next time, I have to be on my p's and q's with them."

"Next time? You think that they're coming back?"

I guarantee it. "I don't know. Maybe I'm just freaking out for nothing. I wasn't expecting them to just pop up like they did."

Li'l Bit looks like she's going from bad to worse.

"All I'm saying is *if* she comes back, I'll play it cooler. That's all."

"But your temper," she says, shaking her head.

"I'll be fine. *You* got to remember to play it cool, too."

"Me?" If her eyes get any wider, they'll pop out of her head.

"You said they went by your house, too, right?"

"Yeah."

"Well. Then, they are going to want to interview you, too."

"Aw, shit. Aw, shit." Li'l Bit bounces on the bed. "I don't know about this, Qiana. I'm not a good liar either. And if *you* couldn't handle her, then—"

"You'll be fine," I tell her. "I was just taken off guard. Now that I know that they don't have shit, I can handle it better."

"But why did they even show up here?"

"They're fishing because Tyneshia's parents got pissy and suspicious because we didn't go to her funeral yesterday."

"That was yesterday?" She looks horrified. "I thought it was tomorrow."

"Don't sweat it. The point is that they got nothing. As long as we keep our mouths shut, nothing is going to happen."

"But what about Adaryl? Have they gone and talked to her yet?"

My heart drops. "I don't know—but I'm sure that Adaryl is gonna keep her mouth shut, too. The bitch doesn't want to go to jail any more than we do."

"But she's been acting funny the last few days—real funny. She won't take any of my calls or respond to my texts."

Damn. I'm getting a bad feeling about this. "It's going to be okay," I say, forcing on a smile. "Adaryl may be feeling some type of way, but she's not stupid. All right?" *And if she becomes a problem, I'll take care of her.*

Li'l Bit looks like she wants to keep arguing, but she's run out of words.

"All right?" I press.

She nods, but her doubts are written all over her face. "By the way"—she glances around the room—"where *is* Jayson?"

31

Lucifer

Jaqorya Hampton has one hell of a right hook. That's abundantly clear after watching her spar with one bitch after another in Tony's Gym for a couple of hours.

"C'mon, baby. Keep your chin up. You got her on the run now," Jaqorya's coach shouted from the sidelines.

The girls' boxing gloves pound against each other, coupled up with a few wild swings.

The third time Jaqorya's sparring partner misses her chin by a mile, Jaqorya leans in and goes to work on the girl's ribs.

The amateur backs away only to find her ass is trapped in a corner.

"Ooooh." Everyone around the ring winces collectively as their faces twist with pity and fascination.

Jaqorya shows no mercy. By the time the sorry-ass referee steps forward to untangle the ladies, the woman's opponent pitches forward head first onto the mat.

Jaqorya throws up her hands in victory as her small team rushes to surround and pump her head with praise.

I'm no more impressed than I would be watching a pit bull maul a teacup Yorkie. Exiting the gym, I head straight to the ladies' locker room. As I go in, one chick is coming out. She is so absorbed with wrapping up her hand that she doesn't even notice me. I walk past the lockers and then two bathrooms stalls, and a double sink vanity with a wall-length mirror. Around the corner, there are three shower stalls separated by tiled walls.

The locker room door swishes open and I reflexively withdraw my Browning knife and slip behind one of the stalls.

"Fuck, girl. You're gonna be unstoppable at the fight Monday night," an excited woman exclaims.

"We'll see," Jaqorya replies, cryptically.

I can barely hear them.

"Damn, bitch. Why aren't you juiced up about this shit? We're talking about an easy fifty K to whoop on some knock-kneed bitch with a glass jaw. Yo! You know that shit beats slinging candy any damn day of the week."

"Yeah. Well, there might not be a fight Monday." Locker doors are being opened and slammed closed, and I have to lean my head out of the stall in order to hear them better.

"What do you mean, there might not be a fight? You know something that I don't know?"

"I might have to go out of town for a little while. Lay low."

"Lay low? Are you shitting me? After all this training?"

"Look. It can't be helped. The girls got ourselves in a little situation and we might have to bounce. No big deal."

"What kind of situation?"

"You don't want to know."

There's a long silence before Jaqorya's friend goes in again. "Please tell me this isn't any of that gang bullshit. I told you not to go down that fuckin' road."

"Nikki, don't start."

"At least tell me that it doesn't have anything to do with what happened to Crunk."

More silence.

I step from behind the tiled wall.

"That—and some other shit."

"Damn, girl. You *were* a part of that? I heard Lynch and them found his ass chopped up like horsemeat. What the fuck happened?"

"Some bullshit." Jaqorya sighs. "Shariffa got the girls into hitting Da Club a couple of weeks back."

Nikki gasps. "That was y'all too? Have y'all lost your minds?"

"Look. Shit didn't go down the way we'd planned. We were supposed to be in and out. We were just going to jack a high-stakes poker game going on in the back room. Brika and Shariffa went around the back, murked the nigga guarding the door, while me and Shacardi closed in from the front. Shots were fired and we went in. Fuck. I can't even tell you who shot who. The shit went down so fast."

While the locker room goes silent again, I picture Nikki with her mouth wide open.

Jaqorya's voice lowers with worry. "We didn't plan to kill that nigga Bishop. At least *I* didn't, but the shit happened and now we got his crazy-ass sister pissed the fuck off. What she did to Crunk . . . girl, I ain't never seen no shit like that. What kind of bitch beheads and dismembers muthafuckas? Shit. She even painted the walls with his blood."

"*Fuuuuccckk*," Nikki whispers. "What are y'all going to do?"

"I don't know about those bitches, but I'm bouncing."

"To where?"

"I don't know. Maybe Cali or Vegas. They got a good women's boxing circuit. Maybe I can go and get something started out there."

I shake my head at her pathetic dream. The bitch killed that shit the night she and her road dawgs murked my brother.

"Well . . . I'll hate to see you go," Nikki says. "Have you told coach yet?"

"No. I have to do what I have to do. But, hey, don't say nothing. I haven't made up my mind yet when I'm leaving. I have to see where the other girls' heads are at."

"My lips are sealed. Are you gonna be all right?"

"Yeah. I just hate I ever got involved with that fake bitch Shariffa."

"Shit. If it's anybody's fault, it's Lynch's. His wife is bad news."

"Well. Now she done started a war with the wrong bitch. Fuck. Now that I think about it, maybe I shouldn't say shit and just jet. Memphis is played out anyway."

"All right. Keep your head up. I hope I see you Thursday, but if not, I'll understand."

"Thanks, girl. I'm gonna knock off some of this funk and head out."

"Cool. See ya." The locker room door opens and closes. When I hear Jaqorya's rustling around, I move back behind one of the tiled walls and wait.

A minute later, a naked Jaqorya heads toward the showers.

I don't have much time to do this and it's incredibly risky since someone could walk in at any moment. Jaqorya selects the stall to my left. The shower cuts on while my knife twitches at my side.

Seconds later, she sings while she lathers up.

Quietly, I move from my stall and creep to the other side.

"THIS GIRL IS ON FIRE," she belts at the top of her lungs—off key. "THIS GIRL—"

I round the corner and a startled Jaqorya jumps.

"Hi, champ." My blade slices across her throat before she remembers to scream. Her hand clamps over her open throat as if that will be enough to keep her head attached.

It's not.

Blood shoots from her neck, mixing with the water, swirling down the drain. And I'm just getting started.

32

Ta'Shara

I spent a night behind bars, getting to know the Flowers in lockup. They don't care about LeShelle's position with the Queen Gs. In fact, many of them claim to have members within their families split among different gangs.

"Honey, you can't help who your family is," Mackenzie laughs and high-fives her girl Romil. "I got four brothers. Two Vice Lords, one Crip, and one Blood. Trust me. It makes the holidays a fuckin' trip."

"All that matters now is that you're one of us," Romil cosigns. "You put in work, prove your loyalty to the Flowers, and your ass is set. Fuck. You've already locked down the chief's lil brother. In a lot of ways, you're already royalty, you feel me? You ain't got shit to worry about—especially *this* bullshit that punk-bitch Blalock is tryna lay on you."

That catches my attention. "What do you mean?"

Mack laughs. "They keep coming back here for you every couple of hours tryna run some guilt trip on you, hoping you'll confess. That fat fuck thinks that because you're young and green to the game that all he has to do is put some pressure on you and your ass will sing like a bird. He ain't got shit. If anything, he's probably tryna impress the department's new captain. Your lawyer will pop you out of here in no time. Trust."

"Lawyer? I don't have a lawyer," I tell her.

Mack and Romil laugh.

"Yeah, you do. You just ain't met them yet," Romil says.

Mack nods. "They'll be here before arraignment starts. You can bet on that shit."

Hope flutters in my chest, but it dies when I remember the run of bad luck that I've been having. What's the point of praying or dreaming? No matter what happens, I can never show my face to the Douglases and Sullivans again. I've been completely humiliated.

Do they believe the charges? Will they sit in court and root for my incarceration—my death? My eyes burn with tears. This shit is not fair.

Mackenzie tugs on her cigarette like it's her third lung. "You know what? I like you," she says. "When we get out of here, you should kick it with us. We'll get you up to speed and introduce you to all the right bitches. It'll be fun."

"Yeah. That'll be cool." Romil grins. "You do know how to party, don't you? I mean, you kind of look like a square."

"Sure." I shrug, not believing I'll be sprung any time soon. "That sounds cool."

Friends. It's been a minute since I've made new friends—not since Essence. I miss my girl. I can only imagine what she'd say about this shit I got myself into—but I doubt her being here would've changed anything, other than her sitting right next to me. Then again, that would be enough.

Minutes later, three jailers appear at the cell door. We line up to be shackled. They bind my wrist to a chain wrapped around my waist, and then I'm off to see the judge. *So much for my lawyer riding to my rescue.*

Another hour passes before my name comes up on the docket. Four burly officers lead me into court.

An assistant district attorney moves to a podium and starts rattling off my information. "Ta'Shara Murphy is charged with three counts of murder—two of which were her foster parents: Tracee and Reggie Douglas and a Markeisha Edwards. It is believed that Ms. Murphy and her boyfriend, Raymond Lewis, murdered the Douglases after an escalated argument that took place between them a couple weeks prior. At that time, gunshots had been reported by the neighbors."

I roll my eyes.

The judge doesn't bother to look up from shuffling paperwork around her bench. "How do you plead?"

I open my mouth, but another voice booms from behind me.

"Not guilty, your honor!"

I turn around and see a curvy African American woman with thick, black-rimmed glasses rush into the courtroom. "I'm Hillary Owens of Owens & Owens Attorneys. I'll be representing Ms. Murphy in this case."

Dumbfounded, I say, "You will?"

"I will." She flashes a smile, while her dark eyes tell me to shut up and go with the flow.

The assistant district attorney interrupts our mental conversation to address the judge. "Your honor, the state requests that bail be denied, given the horrendous nature of this crime."

Ms. Owens laughs. "Your honor, that is ridiculous. My client has no previous record—and up until a tragic incident that landed her in the hospital—"

"Where she had a violent outburst and tried to kill her sister," the district attorney argues.

"No charges were filed—"

"That's because—"

"Save it for trial," the judge interrupts, bored.

"As I was saying, Judge," Owens continues, "Ta'Shara Murphy

was a straight-A, honor-roll student. We fully intend to expose that this is a farce of a case in which the state has absolutely no evidence of my client's guilt."

"Sounds fascinating." The judge shuffles more paper before announcing, "Bail is set at five-hundred thousand."

Five hundred thousand?

The judge flips some more paper. "Trial can begin on . . ." She flips more pages. "How's June eighteenth for everyone?"

Owens scrolls through her Google calendar on her smartphone. "That date works for me, even though I doubt that this case will come to that. Thank you, your honor," Owens says confidently.

The assistant DA shakes his head but agrees to the date.

My mind reels over the bail amount. *Where in the hell am I going to get my hands on that kind of money?*

As if she heard my thoughts, Ms. Owens leans over and whispers, "Don't worry. Your bail has been handled. You'll be out of here in no time."

"What?" My burly escorts latch onto my elbows and drag me back out of the courtroom before I get a chance to get her to clarify what she meant.

"How did it go?" Mackenzie asks once I'm back in holding.

"I have a lawyer," I say, stunned.

"Court appointed?" Romil asks.

"No. I don't think so. Her name is Hillary Owens. Anyone ever heard of her?"

Mack and Romil laughs.

"Shit, girl. Don't you know nothing? Hillary Owens is a miracle worker around here. The big man got you covered like Allstate. I told you that you didn't have shit to worry about."

Hope flutters again.

True to Hillary's word, forty-five minutes later, the jailers return.

"Ta'Shara Murphy, you got your walking papers!"

I jump off the bench, wanting to get out of here before they claim there's a mistake.

"Catch you later, girl!" Mack shouts

"Yeah. See you on the flip side," Romil adds.

Happy for the connection, I smile and wave. However, my release process takes another thirty minutes before I'm given back my belongings.

"Do you know if Raymond Lewis has posted bail?" I ask an officer.

"Ta'Shara!"

I spin around at my man's voice.

"Profit!" I race across the precinct and then melt in his arms. "Thank God. Thank God."

"Are you all right, baby?" he asks.

"Yes. Please. Get me out of here."

"You got it. C'mon." He turns and leads me toward the front door.

"Ta'Shara?" a woman calls.

Who could be calling my name?

"Ta'Shara Murphy?"

We stop and turn to meet the next wave of bad news.

A tall, skinny black woman with an unblended lace-front rushes toward us with a no-nonsense expression and her arms loaded down with files. "Hello. I'm Roz Wagner. I'm your new caseworker with Family Children Services."

"You're a caseworker?"

"We've been trying to contact you since the death of your foster parents. My condolences," she says, looking uneasy. "I've been assigned to get you placed and settled into a new residence."

"What?" I step back. "I'm not going anywhere with you."

Ms. Wagner takes a deep breath. "Look. You're seventeen. I know I can't force you to come with me, but I do have to inform you that if you don't, the state will cut off all financial assistance for your living expenses."

"Whatever." I wave her off and tug on Profit. "Let's go."
"But, Ms. Murphy—"

We turn and rush out of the door as fast as we can. A shining black Escalade pulls up to the curb. My heart squeezes and my grip on Profit's hands tightens.

LeShelle.

33

LeShelle

"**W**hat the fuck do you mean that she's still alive?" I hiss, clutching this cheap-ass, pre-paid phone while pacing in the bathroom. "How hard is it to shank a bitch in hold-up?"

"You didn't tell me about her friends," Avonte says. "Our girl in the inside said that there was about a dozen Flowers in the tank with her that rose up like an army to defend her. Your sister is well-connected."

"Aaagh!" I throw the damn phone against the mirror. It breaks instead of the damn glass. "FUUUCCCK!"

BAM! BAM! BAM!

"What the hell is going on in there, Shelle?" Python barks.

Go away! "I'm fine. I'll be out in a minute."

There's a long silence before I hear him turn and walk away from the bathroom's door. Huffing out an angry breath, I brace myself against the sink and then count to ten. I should've known better than to trust somebody else with this shit. After all, look what happened with that scarred-up Flower Qiana. What the fuck did that shit get me? That dirty-dealing trick is still on my shit list.

I look up into the mirror and glare back at my own reflection. "This shit ain't over. Not by a long shot."

"DIE, BITCH! DIE!"

Ta'Shara and those damn knitting needles flash inside my head and my grip on the sink tightens. Still hot, I turn on the sink and splash cold water over my face. When I exit the bathroom, I'm blotting my face dry with a towel while Python is opening the front door.

"Everything is a go," Diesel announces, breezing in with five big-shouldered men behind him.

I stop in my tracks and take a moment to appreciate the sheer size and power these men exude by their very presence. *Now these are some real soldiers.*

"Python, cuz. Let me introduce you to a few of my homies," Diesel says. "This is Madd, Beast, Bullet, Matrix, and last but not least Chrome."

Python shakes each man's hand as he's introduced to him. "Yo, man. Y'all c'mon in and have a seat so we can talk some business." Python turns to me. "Shelle, grab us some beers."

I turn with a roll of my eyes. I resent it when I'm reduced to waiting on him. I should be a part of this business meeting. I'm a boss, not a maid. But I march into the kitchen and return with their beers as fast as I can.

"Before we get started, I wanna thank you, cuz, for running interception with Momma Peaches like you did."

"Aww, man. We're family. I was happy to do it."

"Any word on when she's going to be released?" Python asks.

"Don't know. She looks like she's been through hell, man. I ain't gonna lie. Your momma worked her over good."

Pain twists Python's face. "I don't know what the fuck that shit was about. Then again, maybe if we'd reached out to her more while she was locked up. Hell, she sent me a birthday card every fucking year . . . and I pitched that shit in the garbage. Whatever demons she was dealing with can't touch her no more." His thoughts drift for a moment before he realizes his guests are growing uncomfortable. "I guess we all just gonna have to be thankful that it's over." He downs the rest of his Henney and then pours himself another glass.

What the fuck?

Diesel studies Python with open calculation. "Don't worry about it, cuz. Aunt Peaches is as tough as they come. I'm sure that she'll open up when y'all get a chance to talk one-on-one."

"For sure. For sure." Python nods, but it's clear to everyone in the room that the shit is fucking with him.

"We're all set for tonight," Diesel says, changing the subject. "Thor called with the time and place for the delivery. With my men here, we now have the organization and the firepower. The way I see it, this should be a quick hit-and-run. You feel me?"

"Humph."

Everyone's eyes shift to me. "What?"

"Shelle, ain't you got something else to do?"

"No." I roll my neck back to Diesel. "If you're going up against Lucifer, there's no such thing as a 'quick hit-and-run.' Trust and believe."

Diesel laughs, but anger flashes in his eyes.

"Chuckle it up, pretty boy. I'm for real. I'm don't know what kind of bitches you're used to fucking with, but Lucifer is on a whole 'nother level."

Slowly, his smile melts. "Yeah. I've heard plenty of stories about how this she-devil got most of these niggas out here shook. I'm not worried. That bitch ain't never ran across a nigga like me and I haven't ran across a bitch yet that I can't put down."

Our eyes lock, causing my body to wilt beneath an intense heat wave.

"Humph. Then you won't mind if I play tag—so that I can see these skills for myself?"

Python twitches with irritation. "Shelle, you're gonna keep your ass right here."

"Nah. Nah." Diesel leans back in his chair while he finally pops open his beer. "Let her come. Hell, she might learn a few things."

This nigga is really feeling himself. I don't know how this is really going to go down, but I do know that his shit better be on point if he's planning to fuck with Lucifer.

"Fine. Whatever," Python snaps, eyeballing me like I've done something wrong.

"What?"

Instead of answering, Python grinds his jaw and then cuts his eyes back to his cousin. I better do a better job at hiding my *small* attraction to Diesel. The last thing I want or need is to fuck up and become another Shariffa.

34

Lucifer

Tombstone and I roll up to the precinct as Profit and his girl, Ta'Shara, are bolting out of the door. I power the window down and order them to get in.

The color in Ta'Shara's face drains. For a girl who is always neck-deep in some real shit you'd think her ass wouldn't be so damn scared.

"NOW!" That puts a fire under their asses as both rush toward the back door and climb inside.

"A triple murder charge?" I ask, removing my shades and sizing them up. "Impressive."

"Not funny," Profit huffs, slamming the door behind him.

Tombstone immediately peels off from the curb.

No surprise that Profit is in one of his moods again. Irritated, I push my shades back up and try to hold on to my temper. "You're needed for a job tonight."

Profit eyeballs me. "What sort of job?"

"Gun run. Are you're ready to earn your stripes?"

"Are you asking or is Mason?" he challenges.

My eyes narrow. "Answer the fucking question." I may not be able to kill him, but I can do anything just short of that for the disrespect.

"I was born ready," he says, pumping out his chest, probably to show off in front of his little girlfriend. Until he gets a few more hairs on that muthafucka, he ain't doing a damn thing for me. I make sure that shit is reflected in my face. "We'll see."

My gaze shifts to Ta'Shara. She's looking at me like she can't decide whether to smile or jump out of the vehicle screaming. Frankly, I'm not sure how to take her ass either. Her crazy sister has put her through the fire more than a few times and her ass is still standing. I can respect that shit—but she's going to have to do something about that wide-eyed innocent look she has about her.

After a twenty-second staring contest, I've had enough. "Look, petal. Either punch me or kiss me, but stop staring."

Ta'Shara turns five shades of red before jerking her gaze out the back window.

I roll my eyes and then catch Profit glaring. "What?"

He clamps his mouth shut until his jaw becomes a hard, straight line. I have to clamp my mouth shut in order for this shit not to escalate into a full-blown situation. I hoped with Mason being back that whatever issue Profit has with me would be squashed. Guess I was wrong.

What the fuck ever. "Pickup is at nine so we're going to roll out no later than eight-fifteen. Be ready."

"Where is this pickup?" Profit asks.

"See. You're worried about the wrong damn thing," I say. "You just make sure that you're ready. Got it?"

"Yeah. A'ight. Whatever."

When we arrive at the Forest Hill Funeral Home, Profit springs out the door but then is very gentle when he turns to offer Ta'Shara a hand in exiting the vehicle. Once he slams the door, I'm left sitting in the backseat, wondering what the fuck is his problem. The young couple returns to the car that they left at the funeral and then we follow them to Ruby Cove.

We're halfway home when it occurs to me that Tombstone

is being awfully quiet today. In fact, he looks troubled about something. "Is everything all right?"

He doesn't answer.

"Tombstone?"

"Huh?" His gaze shoots up to meet mine in the rearview mirror. "I'm sorry. What did you say?"

"I was asking if everything is cool with you. Your mind seems to be elsewhere."

"Ah. It's nothing." He shrugs. "Family shit."

I nod, waiting to see if he'll say more, but when he doesn't, I let it go. I'm not trying to be in everybody's business. When I return to the house, Mason is coming down the stairs. His head and face are freshly shaven and he looks like his old self—except for his skin. The red and purple burns make him appear like he's in constant pain. I push up a smile. It feels so good and natural for him to be back.

"Hey, baby. Is everything set?"

"He's in."

"Good." Mason wraps his arms around me, but when I feel my growing belly brush against him, I step back.

"Whoa. Where are you going?" He tightens his arms and cocks his head.

"Nowhere I . . . just want to go upstairs take a shower and maybe lay down. I'm tired."

The worry lines in his forehead deepen. "You take naps in the middle of the day now?"

It's an innocent question, but it feels like an interrogation. "Is that a problem?"

His arms fall from my waist and I pretend that I don't notice the hurt that flashes across his face. "Nah, ma. Do you."

Apologize. "Got it." I move past him and stomp my way upstairs. I don't know why I can't bring myself to just ask him about the whole Melanie situation. The shit is probably all in my head anyway. Besides, it's not like he's mentioned her or anything since he's been back. And he loves me. I know he does.

I feel like shit. My damn hormones are all over the place. I'm cool one minute and then pissed off the next. Is it going to be like this for the next five months?

True to my word, after a hot shower, I dive into bed, exhausted. But sleep teases me. I have a bad feeling about tonight's delivery. I don't know why, but I can't shake it.

Hours later, we're locked and loaded and ready to mob twelve deep. Despite my doing business with Thor for months, I'm still feeling some kind of way about tonight's job. But what will I look like if I say something to Mason? I'm the one who arranged this shit.

I shift around in my seat, uncomfortable in the bulletproof vest strapped over my sensitive breasts and my expanding belly. Soon I'm going to have to tell Mason what time it is. The moment I do, he's going to shut my ass down before I deal with those other evil, purple bitches on my shit list to gut and slice up. I'm not going to outsource my revenge for Bishop's murder.

No way!

"Are you all right?" Mason asks, cutting looks at me from behind the wheel. "You seem . . . off lately."

Tell him. "I'm cool," I lie. "Keeping my mind on the job at hand."

Mason nods, but knows I'm bullshitting. "A'ight. I'm gonna let you have that. When you're ready to talk, I'm here."

We're silent during the rest of the ride out to Rivergate Industrial Park, and that bad feeling grows as our SUVs gets waved through the gate.

I don't recognize the guards. Automatically, I slap a thirty-bullet magazine into tonight's weapon of choice: a Bushmaster AR-15.

"Talk to me," Mason says, taking my cue and going for his AK-47.

"The guards were black." My gaze skitters around the rooftops and into dark corners.

He parks and the other two SUVs flank our sides. "What do you want to do?"

I don't know. My gaze does another sweep of the area.

Tombstone and Profit climb out of their vehicle and toss us questioning looks.

"Willow?"

Maybe my ass is bugging. Exhaling slowly, I reach for my door handle. "I'm cool. Let's go." As I exit the vehicle, I keep my finger poised above the trigger.

When Mason climbs out, our cluster of six creeps toward the warehouse's metal doors. My gaze swings from left to right, looking for something solid to validate my paranoia.

A shadow passes by a light source above us and I shout, "IT'S A TRAP!"

Our gats come up as men with blue flags draped around their mouths open fire. *The Gangster Disciples?*

RAT-A-TAT-TAT-TAT.

RAT-A-TAT-TAT-TAT.

Bullets rain down like a firestorm. We spray back as much heat as we take in. Wrestling with the Bushmaster's kickback has the muscles in my arm feeling like they're on fire. In the distance, tires squeal as our backup team plows into the iron gate, bringing their own assault on the guards.

RAT-A-TAT-TAT-TAT.

RAT-A-TAT-TAT-TAT.

"AAAAAGGGHHH," Mason's Rambo-esque roar rises above the gunfire.

I move to flank his side as we inch back, one step at time toward our vehicles. Luckily, we were closer to them than the building. We would've all been dead if the opposite was true. *You're losing your edge.*

Out of the corner of my eye, I see Profit take a hit and fly back a few feet.

"Shit!"

"BRO, YOU A'IGHT?" Mason shouts.

Profit grunts.

I ease off the trigger and rush over to him. Bullets whiz by my head as I grab the back of his collar and drag him behind an SUV.

PING! PING! PING!

Bullets slam into the vehicle and even take out one of the headlights.

"Where are you hit?" I shout.

"I'm good. I'm good," Profit pants, sitting up. "Took the hit to the vest."

"GRIMY MUTHAFUCKAS. COME SUCK ON DADDY'S DICK," Mason shouts. He's a fucking live wire, mowing muthafuckas down.

RAT-A-TAT-TAT-TAT.

RAT-A-TAT-TAT-TAT/

"HOLD YOUR FIRE," a voice yells from somewhere above.

"PEEL OUT." I race to Mason and pull him to the vehicle. He's enjoying this shit too much.

RAT-A-TAT-TAT-TAT.

RAT-A-TAT-TAT-TAT.

The gunfire is now coming more from our end as the Gangster Disciples heed whoever is hollering for a cease-fire.

"Let's go!" I smack Mason on the shoulder to get his attention.

He eases off the trigger and hops back into our ride.

"MASON!"

I jerk a look over my shoulder and make out Python's unmistakable outline on the roof. Now I know why he called a cease-fire. He's reaching out to his brother.

"Get in the car," Mason barks.

"MASON!"

"GET IN!"

Removing the molasses out of my ass, I hop in as the engine roars back to life and Mason floors the accelerator. Even through the thunder of the SUV's horsepower, I can still hear Python roaring, "MASON!"

35

LeShelle

"How in the fuck is that nigga still breathing?" I snap at Python with my M4 holstered up in the air. He's looking like he's stuck on stupid while we watch this muthafucka and his boss bitch peel out.

"MASON!"

I clench my jaw and roll my eyes toward Diesel, mentally telling him to get his cousin before I knock the shit out of his ass.

Diesel steps forward and places a hand on Python's shoulder. "Let it go, cuz. We got to roll out."

Python stands, huffing and puffing as if he'd raced a marathon. When Diesel touches his shoulder again, Python jerks away from him.

"Goddamn it," I hiss, pacing around in circles. I gotta calm down before I approach Python. I'm not in the mood for another episode of *As The Hood Turns*.

Clearly, his ass is back to tripping on that brother shit. I got his ass to bury that bullshit since the nigga was dead any goddamn way, but now here his ass is back among the fuckin' living. These damn Carvers are immortals or some crazy shit.

"If they'd made it into that warehouse, we would have killed him," I catch Python muttering to himself.

"Good," I shout. "His ass deserves to be six feet under."

Python spins and roars, "He's my fucking brother!"

Without thinking, I backhand his ass. *SLAP!*

"Snap out of it!"

BAM!

I reel backwards, hitting the building's concrete roof and dropping my M4.

RAT-A-TAT-TAT-TAT

Niggas duck and run.

Python ignores all that as he grabs the front of my shirt and pulls me up against his growling face. "If you ever disrespect me like that in front of my men again, it'll be the last fuckin' thing you do. You got that shit?"

The left side of my face swells and throbs like he hit me with a two-by-four. I turn my head and spit out the pool of blood in my mouth. It's getting harder to respect this gangsta when he's pussying out over this brother shit all the time.

"You got it?" he yells.

"Got it." I flash my bloody smile and then snatch myself out of his grasp.

Python towers over me like he's thinking about stomping my ass.

Diesel approaches up behind him. "We got to head out, cuz."

"Fine. Round these niggas up and let's go."

Python rakes me up and down and then storms past me like my ass ain't shit.

Muthafucka.

Diesel lingers and then offers me his hand.

Knowing what will happen if I touch him, I ignore it and pull myself up on my own.

"Pride before the fall," Diesel says, chuckling.

"Get the fuck out of my face," I tell him, slurring my words since my lips are also swollen. "I told you that you wouldn't bag that bitch."

The amusement dies in his eyes. "Blame your man. We had them surrounded," he says and marches off.

Our army was reduced by five—one of them was Diesel's homeboy, Chrome. We quickly stack the bodies, pack up our shit, and roll out as the sound of police sirens fills the air behind us.

During the flight back to the safe house, I stare a hole into the side of Python's head. What I wouldn't give to wail out on his ass right now. Why am I the only muthafucka thinking straight? Fat Ace needs to be eliminated. Full stop—period.

Two cars return to the safe house. Ours with Python, Diesel, and myself and security guards Kane and June Bug. After a bottle of Henney and a few bumps of cocaine kickers, Python barks out orders. "I want to know everything. Put ears everywhere. How did Fat Ace survive that crash? Where has he been? When did he return? Everything."

Kane and June Bug nod. "We're on it, boss." When they don't make a move for the door, Python yells, "NOW!"

They jump like toasted Pop-Tarts and scramble for the door.

Diesel speaks calmly, "I'll get you some more security out here."

"I don't give a shit about that."

"No. You're on that brother shit again," I mumble.

Python jerks toward me. "And you. Shut the fuck up! I don't want to hear another goddamn word out of your slick-ass mouth. This is my shit and I'll handle it!"

"Handle it how? Handle it like you told me to *handle* Ta'Shara—or are you too much of a pussy for that shit?"

Python lunges for me.

I smash a beer bottle on the coffee table and lift the neck and its jagged-shard edges up, ready to rumble. "What the fuck you gonna do?"

Diesel jumps in between us. "Whoa. Whoa. Slow down."

He holds his cousin back. "LeShelle, maybe you should give us a few minutes?"

"Fine. See if you can screw his head back on right. I'm tired of trying." I turn with a flourish and storm back in to the bedroom with my broken beer bottle. How the fuck am I going rule the streets with a mad king on the throne?

36

Lucifer

"Shit! Shit! Shit!" I pound my fist onto the dashboard. "I knew it! I knew it! Why didn't I listen to myself?"

Mason scowls. "Wait! We were making this deal on your fuckin' word. You said those crazy-ass crackers were good for this shit. *Now* you're gonna tell me you weren't feeling it?"

"Back off!" The last thing I need is for his ass to ride my nerves. "We gotta deal with that lying, double-crossing, redneck muthafucka."

"What do you want to do?" he asks.

"What the fuck you think?" I snap. "Go at his ass. Hard!"

"You want to turn up on the good ol' boys?"

"You damn right! No muthafucka plays me. They got me twisted." I'm so heated, I can't think straight.

Mason lets that shit hang in the air for a second and then reaches for his phone. "Tombstone, change of plans."

I nod with my trigger finger itchy as hell. No way these muthafuckas think we have the balls to jump off some racial shit, but I'm about to show them how low my steel balls sag.

We rumble back off that beaten path, locked and loaded. That god-awful country twang assaults the night. Our four Escalades don't even ease off the accelerator when we approach a line of Harley-Davidsons parked outside.

Mason mows over that shit with no remorse.

The front door of the club explodes open, but when the first wave of angry rednecks spill out, I slap in another magazine into the Bushmaster and hop onto the ledge of my open window to mow those wiggas down.

RAT-A-TAT-TAT-TAT.

RAT-A-TAT-TAT-TAT.

The second wave of stupid hillbillies comes running with handguns and a couple twelve-gauges, but they're unable to even fire off a shot before Tombstone plows straight into the club, busting through the front door and a panel of windows.

RAT-A-TAT-TAT-TAT.

RAT-A-TAT-TAT-TAT.

I spring out of the vehicle and hold tight to my weapon during recoil after recoil.

Half-naked bitches are screaming everywhere while we aim at everything with leather jackets. Shit gets nastier when more rednecks pour from the back room, most of them rocking with twelve gauges and fucking up the grills and front hoods of our cars. But my ass ain't playing tonight. I pick their drunk asses off one by one.

RAT-A-TAT-TAT-TAT

RAT-A-TAT-TAT-TAT

Exchanging cartridges, I look for Thor's ass among the dead and wounded. When I don't find him, I grab's Stony by the back of the head and jerk his mat of bloody hair up off the floor. "Where is he?"

"Fuck you, you black bitch!"

BAM!

I slam the butt of my gun against the back of his head and then lifted that fucker back up. "I'm the wrong black bitch to fuck with, you cousin-fuckin' half breed. Now, where the fuck is he?"

I'm listening to his ass choke on his own blood when I hear Thor's ominous voice speak above me.

"I'm right here, bitch."

I glance up into the barrel of a twelve-gauge.

RAT-A-TAT-TAT-TAT-TAT.

RAT-A-TAT-TAT-TAT-TAT.

Thor drops his weapon as he's lifted into the air and blown back a good five feet. When he finally hits the floor, his body is riddled with bullets.

Rising up, I glare at the dead redneck while Mason walks over broken glass behind me.

"Are you all right?" he asks, panting with fear reflecting in his eyes. Had he not taken Thor out, I wouldn't be standing here right now.

Stony grunts at my feet. I look down, aim my weapon at the back of his head, and tap the trigger.

RAT-A-TAT.

Stony's head explodes open, drenching my new black Timberlands.

"Yeah. I feel much better now."

37

Ta'Shara

I can't sleep.

I can't eat.

Hell. I can't even think straight. All that runs through my head are all the different scenarios of how Profit can get hurt tonight on this secret gun run. Shit goes left out here on these streets every day of the week. The morgues and the prison cells are like fucking factories in this city.

I jump up off the sofa and pace a hole in the carpet. *Shouldn't they be back by now?* I rush to the window and peek out. *Where are they?*

The knots in my stomach tighten. I have a bad feeling about all of this. Pulling from the window and fighting a new wave of anxiety, I go to the bedroom and retrieve my bottles of Xanax, Inderal, and Tofranil that were prescribed to me from the hospital. The bottles are more than halfway empty. *What am I going to do when I run out?* Tossing common sense out the window, I wash the pills down with a glass of Pinot Grigio. Five minutes later, I have an incredible buzz that smoothes my rattled nerves.

Thump!

At the sound of a car door, the wineglass slips out of my hand and smashes onto the kitchen floor. Ignoring it, I race into the living room just as Profit opens the front door. "Profit! Oh thank God!"

I launch into his arms, and my hands and legs wrap around him like a hungry octopus while I pepper his face with a thousand kisses. "I'm so happy you're home. You have no idea how worried I was." I smother him with even more kisses before I hear his painful grunts.

"What's the matter? Are you hurt?" I spring back out of his arms and flip on the light switch. "Let me see."

"Turn it off," he barks, the second the light hits him.

"Why? What's wrong? Something happened, didn't it? You can tell me. I can handle it."

"T!"

"I want to see for myself." I pat him down and spin him around, looking for bullet holes or blood—something to confirm my worst fears.

Profit hisses and then jumps away from my touch when my hand lands on his padded rib cage.

"You *are* hurt," I gasp. "Where? Do we need to get you to a doctor?"

"Calm down, T." He groans and chuckles at the same time. "I'm fine. I just need to sit down for a minute." Wincing and limping, he heads toward the sofa.

"Let me help you." I drape his arm around my shoulder. "Just lean on me."

He wants to argue, but he relents and lets me help him. Once on the sofa, he unstraps his bulletproof vest and pulls it off.

"Are you going to tell me what happened or are you going to let me imagine the worst?"

"It was a setup. We were ambushed."

"What?" I drop next to him, my heart hammering.

"It's okay. It's all right. By some fuckin' miracle our asses got out of there without losing a man. But I swear, Lucifer's ass is slipping all over the place. It's been one fuck-up after another with her lately. Thank God Mason is back. Who knows what the hell would've happened under her so-called leadership."

Shocked, I'm caught off guard by his venom.

"What?" Profit snaps, defensively.

"Nothing." I shrug. "I just never heard you talk about Lucifer like that before. I thought y'all were cool."

"She's a'ight. I mean—shit. She's Mason's problem. I've never understood why he's always put so much trust in her."

"Because she scares the shit out of everybody, I'm guessing." My answer seems to irritate him.

"Can I get a beer or something?"

"Oh, uh. Yeah." I pop off the sofa and jet into the kitchen. When I return, he has peeled out of his shirt, displaying his broad, muscled chest with a purpling bruise against his rib cage, beneath the spray of bullet-sized keloids that he received from LeShelle.

"Here you go." I hand over his beer. "Do you want something else—something to eat?"

"Nah, I'm cool." Profit pats the empty spot next to him.

Smiling and curling up against him, I search for the right words. "Do you want to talk about what happened?"

Profit huffs out a long breath. "There's not much too say. Lucifer vouched for some redneck Confederate boys on tonight's pickup and when we got there those grimy Gangster Disciples scrambled out like cockroaches."

"I don't understand. Why would *they* be there?"

"Clearly those biker muthafuckas got some fuckin' allegiances."

"Was . . . LeShelle there?"

"Shit. I don't know. I was too busy trying to take out as many of those muthafuckas as I could."

She was there.

Profit looks over into my spooked face. "Hey, don't worry about it. You see I made it home okay."

This time, I glance back at his purpling bruise. "But you were hit."

"And I was protected." He gestures to his vest. "I can take care of myself, despite what anyone else thinks."

I'm confused. "What?"

Profit chugs from his beer bottle. "I'm just saying that I don't need anyone treating me like a kid. I'm a grown man and I don't need a fucking babysitter. When Lucifer dragged me back, the other dudes looked at me like . . ." He sucks in a deep breath and calms down. "Never mind."

I'm stunned to see him so upset—especially at someone like Lucifer. She's always been so hardcore and everyone in the set respects or fears her. "So what happens next?"

He tightens his arm around me. "Well, after we got out of there, Lucifer tried to make up for the fact that she screwed up and took us out to that bikers' club out in the middle of no-damn-where and we just . . . mowed down everything that moved. It was a fuckin' massacre."

His words hang in the air between us while he drains the rest of the beer.

"They had it coming," I conclude, nodding.

Profit's gaze finds me again.

"If they double-crossed her, she couldn't let it slide. Muthafuckas will keep coming at you until they break you. I don't blame Lucifer. She did the right thing."

"Oh. You're her cheerleader now?"

I shrug. "Well, just because she doesn't like me doesn't mean that I don't like her. In fact, I kind of admire her."

"You do?"

"Yeah. She's a boss bitch." Another shrug. "I wish I was more like her."

Profit laughs, hurting my feelings.

"What's so funny?"

"Oh. You were serious?" He sets his beer down.

"Of course I'm serious. If I was more like her, I would be

hunting LeShelle's ass down instead of being walled up here on Ruby Cove afraid that she's going to pop out of nowhere all the time."

Profit leans over and brushes a chaste kiss against my lips. "Baby, I don't want you worrying about that crazy bitch anymore. You're safe here."

"I don't want to just be safe. I want to fucking take her out—beat her at her own fucking game."

He looks at me strange again.

"What?"

"N-nothing. It's just . . ."

"It's just what?" I demand, pulling away and glaring.

"It's just that, no offense, you're a good girl." He pulls me back, but I try to resist. "You're *my* good girl."

At the touch of his lips against mine, I sigh and melt. He has always been able to do that to me. His tongue glides deeper and dances erotically with my own.

"Mmmmm."

He tugs up my T-shirt and then tosses it across the room. "You'll always be my girl," Profit mumbles, abandoning my lips to dive his head down between my breasts.

Every cell and atom in my body come alive under his touch. By the time his mouth closes over my right nipple and my panties slide off my hips, fireworks are exploding inside my head. He knows how to work my body. His kisses continue to trail down the center of my body until he reaches the soft hairs shielding my pussy.

"Open up," he commands.

I spread my legs east and west while he settles in for a late-night snack. When his slippery tongue dives in, my hips lift off of the sofa and I grab and squeeze my own titties in total bliss.

Profit takes his time taking me to the edge. Hot, dizzy, and tingling all over, I scream out when my first orgasm hits—and still he refuses to stop. Panting, I try to inch away from his swirling tongue, but it's beating my clit mercilessly. Before I know it, another orgasm steals my breath.

He doesn't stop.

I'm practically up on the arm of sofa, when he locks onto my hips and drags me back down to the center.

"AHHHHHHHHHHH!" I can't breathe. "P-Profit, please." I push on his head, but he refuses to bulge. "AHHHHHH-HHH!"

I'm floating. Where? I don't know. But at long last, Profit takes mercy on me and releases my honey-filled pussy. Between more kisses and caresses, I have trouble remembering exactly how or when he removed the rest of his clothes. I just know that when his thick cock enters me, my body welcomes him with warm honey.

"Damn, baby. You feel so good."

Our bodies entangle as love and lust take over. I lose track of time and the number of orgasms. For this one brief moment in time, I'm content and happy.

38

Hydeya

The Royal Knights motorcycle club . . .

This damn city is going to hell fast and dragging my ass down right along with it.

Forty-three muthafuckin' dead bodies. I can't even wrap my head around this shit right now. I haven't even been captain a full week and now I have a damn massacre on my hands.

Black folks have gone crazy.

The white folks have gone crazy.

What in the hell is going on?

"Here you go," Fowler says, coming up from behind me and handing me a cup of coffee. "You look like you could use this."

"Only if you spiked it with a little sumpthin' sumpthin'," I say accepting the cup.

"I would if I could, but word is that the chief is coming down."

"Of course she is. Why miss an opportunity to put her other foot into my ass and then drag me in front of the cameras?" I glance up to where the Royal Knights' windows are supposed to be to see a train of news vans and reporters clicking and filming away. *It's going to be another one of those days.*

Huffing out a long sigh, I chug half a cup of coffee in one gulp. Since I'm operating on less than two hours of sleep, I'll likely need a caffeine IV drip before the end of the day.

"Well, I guess you can look on the bright side," Fowler says in between his own sips of coffee. "At least there are bodies to match up to the blood everywhere. Last night, the department responded to reports of gunfire out at the Rivergate Industries parking lot only to find a hell of a lot of blood stains and spent cartridges—but no bodies. Whatever the hell went on, the shooters were kind enough to clean up after themselves."

"Humph. No bodies equals no homicides, which equals no paperwork, which equals nothing to jack up my sky-high murder rate even higher. You need to learn to stop looking a gift horse in the mouth, Fowler."

"*Your* murder rate?" He chuckles. "Look at you. You're already talking like a seasoned captain."

"Do me a favor and start acting like a detective and find me some clues to who's behind this bloodshed so I can limit the number of times I look like Boo Boo the Fool on the evening news. Can you do that?"

He busts a smile and gives me a two-finger salute. "Aye, aye, Captain."

Watching his wise-cracking-ass march off, I chug down the rest of my coffee. After I spend another ten minutes supervising detectives and the forensic team, a commotion stirs up outside and the herd of reporters swarms around the chief.

"Chief Brown! Chief Brown! Chief Brown," they chant in unison before competing to outshout individual questions at her.

"I have no comment at this time," the chief keeps repeating while trying to push her way behind the crime scene tape. Once she's inside the bullet-riddled motor club, she snatches off her cheap sunglasses and zeroes in on me like there's a hidden tracking device on my ass.

"Hawkins," she barks, and then goes on the march.

In my sleep-deprived head, I envision myself turning into the Road Runner, giving her ass a few *beep-beeps,* and then jetting out of here.

"This is the last damn thing the department needs right now."

And the award for stating the most obvious shit goes to . . .

"Do you hear me, Captain Hawkins?" Brown snaps.

"Yes, ma'am. We're all on top of it."

"I don't need you to just be on top of it. I need results—on *something!* The mayor is riding my ass so hard my hemorrhoids got fuckin' hemorrhoids, you understand me?"

"Yes, Chief." *Talk about a visual that I could've done without.*

She sucks up a sharp breath and then glances around. "Now. Do we have *any* idea what the hell went on out here?"

I take in a deep breath, prepared to deliver the bad news, when Fowler's shout cuts me off. "WE GOT A LIVE ONE HERE!"

Everyone's heads whip around to a back door. Chief Brown and I race to the sound of Fowler's voice like a pair of competing Olympians. By the time we reach the entryway, Fowler has a white woman scooped into his arms and is carrying her up the stairs. She's wearing a tiny jean skirt and a bikini top and is covered in blood except for the tears running from her powder-blue eyes.

"Oh God, please tell me that she saw who did this," Chief Brown prays openly.

At the woman's nod, I'm flooded with relief as well and wait for her to speak with bated breath.

"They were niggers."

39

Lucifer

The pungent scent of strawberries and pussy assaults my senses the second I creep into the basement of a two-story brick home a few blocks off Orange Mound. I follow the unmistakable sighs and moans of women mounting toward climax. My senses heighten; I concentrate on keeping my movements graceful and silent.

As I ease my way from the basement to the main floor, the sex mewing grows louder along with the steady pounding of skin against skin. Despite this shit clearly being two bitches getting it on, my clit thumps along with their nasty rhythm.

I slide my Browning from its sheath.

Brika and Shacardi are in the middle of the living room, lost in their own world. Shacardi is on her hands and knees, her head snatched back by the bondage leash that Brika is fisting while drilling a strap-on dildo into her thick, ghetto booty.

"You fuckin' love this shit, don't you?" Brika asks.

"YEEESSSSS! Oh, fuck! I'm about to come."

Brika grips her shit tighter. "Then come on, *puta!*"

For a bitch, I'm quite impressed with Brika's stroke game. She's working that cock like she was born with it. I admit that for a second, I'm torn on whether to let these bitches catch this last nut before I send them straight to hell or not.

In the end, I wait. Hell, even I can show mercy.

Slap! Slap! Slap!

The harder Brika goes in, the redder Shacardi's caramel-colored ass gets. This girl is squirting so hard, pearls of pussy juice are rolling down her inner thighs.

"AHHHHHHHHHHH," Shacardi screams, trembling like a leaf.

That was it. In a one-two motion, I grab Brika by the back of the head and swipe the Browning hard across her throat. Bone and muscle melt away like butter. Blood sprays across Shacardi's back.

Brika releases the grip on Shacardi's leash to claw at her own throat.

"Wh—what the fuck?" Shacardi's fresh nut is crushed as she whips a look over her shoulder.

I toss Shacardi a smile and a wink before she scrambles off Brika's fake dick and races across the floor like a squirrelly rat, trying to get away. In case she's going for a weapon, I stroll behind her bloody and baby-oiled ass before reaching down and grabbing hold of her leash.

"And where in the fuck do you think you're going?" I ask, yanking her back.

Choking, Shacardi does the same clawing at her throat.

I yank harder, flipping her onto her back.

"No! No! No!" She goes into a kicking fit, where her legs fly in every direction.

Unluckily for her, she'd allowed her lover to put those in chains as well. I easily gain control of that shit by reaching for the iron bar that had been discarded on the sofa and snapping it onto the chains.

"There. That's better." I give her another wink and then glance back over my shoulder at Brika. The dead bitch is now face down in a pool of her own blood. "Shit. I didn't really get a chance to have any fun with your friend." I turn my attention back to Shacardi. "I guess that means it's all up to you to entertain me."

"Please. Please," she begs. "It wasn't me. I had nothing to do with what happened to your brother. I swear."

"Oh. Well." I pretend to think that shit over. "I guess that means that I fucked up here, huh?"

Tears flow down her face.

"Only . . . the security cameras in Da Club got some bitch that *looks* like you all up in the mix. Not to mention when I had a little chat with that nigga Crunk, he spit your name before I laid a blade on him."

She whimpers.

"That's some shit, ain't it?" I squat down next to her and run the tip of my bloody knife along the side of her face. "You gotta be pissed about a mix-up like this—an innocent bitch like you—at the top of *my* shit list?" My anger transforms my sneering face into stone. "You must think I'm stupid. Don't you, bitch?"

"N-no."

"Yes, you do. Let me tell you, the second y'all killed my brother, you should've put the gun inside your mouths. Now I'm gonna do this shit nice and slow."

"Please. Please," she begs. "I don't want to die. Please."

"Shhh." I press my finger against her lips. "Save your energy. You're gonna need it." I slide the blade over her chin, down her throat and circle around her titties. "Tell you what? Since you like ridin' so much, why don't we see how you can handle these ten-inches, huh?"

Her eyes nearly pop out of her head.

"I bet a hot box like yours can handle this shit." I bring the blade down the center of her belly and then shave a few pubic hairs before positioning the weapon at her open pussy.

"Scream for me," I order and then jam the knife hilt-deep.

"AHHHHHHHHHHHHHHHHHH!"

This shit is sweet music to my ears.

40

Shariffa

The streets are blazing with the news of Fat Ace's miraculous rise from the dead. First Python and *now* this nigga? Where the fuck do they make they asses at—and can somebody sell whatever zombie shit they smoking so I don't have to worry about Lucifer's terminator-ass stalking me?

My world is spinning out of control. The set ain't whispering no more. They're open with their disrespect. Hell. Even my girls are tripping. It's Saturday and we usually hit the hair and nail salons. I've done called, texted, tweeted, and Facebooked for their asses to call me, and I ain't heard from none of them. I knew this shit would happen after Jaqorya's body was found at Tony's Gym sliced the fuck up. There's no need to guess who the hell did the shit. But we're stronger together than apart. I'm trying to get that shit to sink in, but Lucifer got everybody shook.

"Fuck them bitches!" I toss my phone aside and then give my hand back to the nosey Korean bitch doing my nails.

"Your friends no come?" Her short, square-shaped ass asks after staring in my face.

"You tell me since you're all up in my business," I snap.

She gives me a nasty look, and then turns toward her friend and spits that fast-funky Korean shit.

"English, goddamnit."

Their eyes snap up.

"You bitches rude as fuck," I say, not in the mood to put up with more disrespect from these no-label broads.

This bitch wanna say something, but she knows who my ass is and how my set gets down. Wisely, she sticks a cork in it and gets back on her job.

Simmering in my chair, I glance around and catch a few eyeballs darting away. It's no joke how quick niggas change up out here.

Nails done, I toss a few bills on the counter and roll out. I need some fucking shop-therapy so I head out to Wolfchase Mall for shoes, bags—whatever else that'll make me feel like a boss bitch again. Fuck Lucifer. I ain't running scared.

A knot of cash later, my feelings are on the mend and my mind is scrolling through some options to get my ass back on the come-up—with my man and my set. A nigga ain't shit out here without a street family. I'm going to need more than this platinum ring on my finger to cement my place with the Grape Street Crips. Not only do I need to put in some work, it needs to be some shit that removes all doubt of where my loyalties lie.

Crip up or grip up.

I mean that shit. I need to flip the spin on my dropping that grimy Vice Lord Bishop into something positive. If I were a dude and I caught that nigga slipping like that, my name would be ringing out in the street as the next king. Who gives a fuck whether we got the numbers to take on both the Gangster Disciples and the Vice Lords? The point is to prove that we ain't never scared to shake shit up.

If I can take that bitch out, it would really put me on. That shit floats around in my mind for a while. When I roll back over to Orange Mound, niggas' sour looks cause some old feelings to rise to the surface and I don't know what to do about it.

At the crib, I climb out of my sleek silver Range Rover with my arms loaded down with shopping bags and stroll through the front door and set everything on the dining room table, then head on back to my bedroom to change before getting started on dinner. When I approach the bedroom door, I hear voices—and one of them is definitely a female. *What the fuck?*

Creeping forward, I discover the door is cracked open. I lean in close and peek inside. My mouth and heart drop at the sight of Trigger straddling my husband in the middle of our bed.

"Face it, Lynch. You're going to have to cut her loose. The soldiers are bugging and talking fat shit. It's a matter of time before someone rise up and challenges your authority."

"I brought you back here for some pussy—not a lecture," Lynch says irritably.

Trigger rolls her hips, but she ain't finished spitting in his ear. "Look, I know that she's your baby momma and you got feelings, but your responsibilities to the Crips come first. You don't want this set turning into one of those undisciplined, riffraff gangs all in for self. We're better than that shit and, once upon a time, we knew better than to turn on both the GD and VL. We can't handle them tag-teaming our asses. We might as well all march out to the cemetery and pick out our own plots."

Lynch slaps her on the ass. "Get off. My fuckin' dick ain't feeling this shit no more."

Trigger climbs off, but then eases up behind Lynch when he sits up on the edge of the bed, to give him a shoulder rub. "I'm not trying to upset you, but something gotta be done—before Lucifer relieves me of *my* head."

"Calm down. I got you. I put word out in the street that I wanted a meeting with Fat Ace."

I'm stunned.

"You did? When? How? Have you heard back from him?" Trigger asks, wide-eyed and filled with hope.

"As soon as I heard that his ass had returned from the dead," Lynch says. "I got a meeting with him in an hour."

"Shit. For real? And you're just now telling me?"

Hell. He didn't tell my ass either. I grit my teeth and continue to listen in on their conversation.

Lynch continues, "Maybe now that the big man is back in charge we can reason with him. A full-fledged war ain't gonna do nobody any good but fuck up everybody's Benjamins."

"You think he'll agree to back off? What about Lucifer? Surely, she ain't gonna charge our murking her brother to the game."

Lynch shrugs. "I don't know what's gonna happen, but right now this is the only card we got. I say we pay back that bullshit money y'all jacked from their trap houses and the poker game *plus* interest and see what he says. Fuck. It's money over everything out here. You know that shit."

"Yeah," she says, thinking. "I just hope it works."

"If not, I say you girls pack your shit up and we just gotta figure out a place to stash you until the heat dies down. It's either that or figure out a way to take Lucifer out."

"That's like trying to take out the President of the United States."

"Look. I'm keeping it real with you. This is what the fuck we got to work with."

"It's okay, baby," Trigger coos, peppering kisses across his face. "I know that you're trying. I appreciate that."

Lynch turns to her and they share a deep, soulful kiss during which he leans forward and dips his fingers in between her legs to play with her pussy.

She purrs against his lips before saying, "You know when we broke up back in the day, I thought you plucked this bitch out of the gutter as a way to get back at me. I never thought you'd be crazy enough to pump her full of babies and then marry her ass."

Lynch grunts. "If I remember correctly, you said no when I asked your ass."

Trigger stops rubbing and then wraps her arms around him. "I wasn't ready."

"You mean that you made a mistake," he corrects.

She shrugs. "Maybe."

"Nah. Nah. I wanna hear you say it." He turns around and then pulls her into his lap. Laughing like a fucking teenager, Trigger plays coy for a minute.

"Admit it," Lynch keeps saying, tickling her sides.

"All right. All right. I admit it." She stops giggling to become breathless. "I made a mistake. I should have said yes."

Hurt, I slap a hand over my mouth and then back away from the door. *This is not happening. This is not happening.*

But it is happening. I allowed this bitch in my bed and all along these two had a history together—and probably have been laughing at me behind my fucking back. My hand moves to the Glock that I have strapped at the small of back, but then I don't remove it. I can't. If I go in there shooting and take them out, what the fuck will I have left? Fuck. Where would I even go?

Then again . . . it would be so fucking easy to bust in there with bullets flying.

Do it. Do it. Do it.

I'm all in my feelings. Drowning as things start clicking in my head.

I hate his lying, two-timing ass.

I hate that lying, conniving man-stealing bitch even more.

A sob gets stuck in my throat and I choke on that muthafucka. Shit. I stare at the cracked door for another full minute, before quietly retreating with my damn tail and pride tucked between my legs. Needing a drink, I go to the bar in the living room. I find the bottle of Henney, bypass looking for a glass, and guzzle the shit straight from the bottle until my anger fades. Even then, my stomach twists into knots. I need to talk this over with my other girls before I body muthafuckas up in here.

I grab my Glock and purse and then storm out of the house, jump back into my Range Rover, and then ride out, tipsy as hell.

Three blocks over, I whip up into Shacardi's drive and spot Brika's car. The two have been besties since high school. I'll let them not answering my calls slide, but they better open the front door.

I bolt out of the car—but when my fist hits the front door, I'm stunned that it bangs open. Instantly, I'm sober.

"Hello?"

No answer.

My hand goes for the Glock before I step inside. "Yo. Are y'all bitches up in here?"

Silence.

"Hello?" I inch past the foyer when a metallic stench singes my noses. The hairs on the back of my head stand as I move toward the living room. My breath leaves me as I stand in the middle of a slaughterhouse that looks eerily like the chop job at Crunk's Ink.

"Oh my God."

Blood paints the ceiling and floor while Shacardi and Brika's heads spin from the ceiling fan. On the walls, the Vice Lords' five-pointed star and the letter L are painted with blood.

"Lucifer."

41

Lucifer

"Hold up," I order Tombstone from the backseat of the Escalade. I roll down the window and tilt my shades when a silver Range Rover whips around the corner and zooms up into the driveway. *Shariffa.* A smile spreads across my face at the sight of this bitch hopping out of the car and rushing up to the door.

Go on in. I got a nice surprise for you.

We wait.

A minute later, Shariffa races back out of the house, scared as shit.

"You want to follow her?" Tombstone asks while we watch this messy chick stumble back to her car and peel out, nearly taking out the mailbox.

Tempting.

"Nah. I want to save that bitch for last." Crunk confessed with his dying breath that Shariffa had been the head bitch in charge on that hit on Da Club. I'm going to have fun stalking and torturing her. "Let's go," I say, powering up the window.

Right about now, Mason should be meeting with Shariffa's nigga, Lynch. Ever since the buzz of Mason's return hit the streets, this nigga sent every bird that he could find to Ruby

Cove, talking that fat shit that he wants to arrange some kind of peace talk.

Ain't happening. He should've been about the business of putting his bitch in check long before now. I'm going straight biblical in these streets. An eye for an eye. A life for a life—or in this case, *six* lives for my brother.

Four down—two to go.

At J.D. Lewis & Sons Funeral Home, I enter through the back door. The soldiers posted outside nod and then step aside. I move through the prep room and the sub-zero freezer to the large storage room filled with coffins and embalming fluids.

"Glad to see that you could finally make it," Mason says, looking up from the room's crowded table.

Our soldiers, Monk, Droopy, Spider, and Profit, turn their eyes toward me. Spotting the wooden crates stacked behind him, I surmise our coke shipment arrived with no problems.

"You don't have anything to say?" Mason presses as I pull out one of the metal chairs from the table and drop down.

"What would you like for me to say?"

His brows bunch together as if to ask, *Are you shitting me right now?* "Y'all niggas step out for a few minutes."

Everyone hops up and files out. When we're finally alone, the tension in the warehouse is like a bundle of dynamite burning on both ends.

"You wanna tell me what's up—or am I supposed to play another round of 'Read My Fucking Mind'?"

"Everything is cool," I lie.

"C'mon, Willow. It's me you're talking to. Remember? I know you better than you know yourself."

"Ha!"

His face twists up. "What—"

"Mason," Profit calls out, poking his head back into the room. "He's here."

I jump to my feet, relieved for the interruption.

"This isn't over," Mason warns me before returning his attention to his brother. "Send him in."

Lynch struts in with an attitude and a three-man entourage. They're trying to play it cool, but I smell their fear and catch a few nervous twitches as they near our table. I move to stand behind Mason, who doesn't even bother to stand or acknowledge them in any way.

"Fat Ace, my man. For once, the rumors are true. It's good to see you back on the throne."

Silence.

Lynch stops before the table and remove his shades. "I appreciate you taking this meeting. I know that you didn't have to do that."

Silence.

He tosses a few glances at his wingmen and then clears his throat. "I want to talk to you about a truce."

Silence.

Lynch re-doubles his efforts. "Look, some people in my crew stepped way over the line. Shit went down that shouldn't have. I admit that—and it's up to me to try to make it right between the Grape Street Crips and the Vice Lords. We're not interested in engaging in an all-out war with you." He takes a moment to look directly at me. "Tell me. What's it gonna take to make peace?"

After another long silence, Mason draws a deep breath and then passes the torch. "Lucifer, he's all yours."

I flash Lynch a sinister smile, withdraw the .45 tucked at my back, and shoot this muthafucka in his leg.

POW!

"Owwww. What the fuck?!" Lynch drops to the floor like a stone. His boys jump back with their hands in the air. They had no other choice since our crew relieved them of their weapons before they were escorted back here.

I lower my weapon and then take my time walking from behind Mason. "I have to hand it to you," I growl. "You got a lot of fucking nerves showing your face here." My hand itches for my Browning. "Fuck your peace offering. I have no use for you or your kindergarten crew." I lift my gun again and aim at his head.

"Hey, hey. Whoa. Whoa. Don't shoot! This is supposed to be a truce, remember?" He holds up his hands and cowers behind them.

"Maybe my memory ain't so good," I say.

Pearls of sweat roll from his hairline. He shifts his attention to Fat Ace. "I thought we had an understanding?"

Mason gives him a careless shrug. "Your bitch mowed down her brother *and* my best friend. You show up here to offer us . . . what in exchange? Drugs? Guns? Money?" Mason rocks with laughter. "Nigga, we ain't starving. We're feasting. There's not a goddamn thing you got we want."

"Not exactly," I contradict Mason, my aim steady on this Kool-Aid gangsta. "I want your wife *and* your bottom bitch, Trigger—more specifically—I want their heads separated from their necks."

Lynch's face turns to stone as he lowers his hands and attempts to put more bass in his voice. "That's not going to happen."

"Oh. It's going to happen—one way or the other."

Seeing the seriousness in my face, Lynch stands on his injured leg and faces Fat Ace again. "I'm tryna make a deal here. We're talking about the mother of my children!"

Mason shrugs. "Lucifer's offer sounds reasonable to me. A life for a life. Rules of the street—or we can go for a whole blackout. That shit is up to you. You got two kids, right? What are they? Four? Five?"

I sneer. "It would be a shame for them to be the end of your bloodline."

Mason nods. "I know if it were me, there wouldn't be *any-thing* I wouldn't do to save my kids—my flesh and blood."

My gaze slices over to Mason just as I feel a kick in my abdomen. *Shit.*

"What the fuck?" Lynch roars, incredulous "You're threatening my *whole* fam like that—to my face?"

Fat Ace's charred face crinkles with a menacing grin as he spreads out his hand in generosity. "Abso-fuckin-lutely." In a snap, his features turn hard again. "Those bitches crossed a very bright line. Let me guess, they thought my ass fell off and, since Lucifer was battling the Gangster Disciples full-time, they thought the set was weak and they could go for the crown. Tell me I'm wrong."

I grind my jaw when Mason spits that *weak* shit again. This is the third time he's alluded that somehow my ass wasn't up for the job.

Lynch bumps his gums, but words fail his ass.

"What's the big deal?" I ask, shifting back into character and walking up to him until we're an inch apart. "It's not like she's a *real* Crip. Her flag changes colors depending on the nigga that's between her legs—there's a lot of bitches like that floating around." I cut another look to Mason.

He frowns, catching my meaning about him and that dead bitch Melanie.

"That's the deal." I return my attention to Lynch. "The only deal. Those last two bitches for Bishop."

"The last two?" Lynch asks, blinking.

I smile. "I've been very busy today."

Lynch puffs up his large chest. I know that he's not going to tuck his balls back for no bitch, including me. In fact, I'm counting on it. Our eyes lock. "You'll have to go through me," he threatens.

My smile spreads as wide as The Joker's. "Oh, goodie, goodie."

42

Cleo

Club Diesel looks like it's gonna be the shit. Set in an ideal lo-
cation in the heart of Beale Street, the multi-level club has
décor that's a combination of class, funk, hip-hop, and techno.
There are numerous cocktail bars throughout the club as well
as numerous dance floors. The owner has clearly dropped a
mint into the place. Everything screams money.

"Don't be nervous," Kalief reminds me for the millionth
time while the band sets up for sound check. Frankly, he's the
one who looks nervous.

"I'm good."

"Good. We really got to knock this audition out of the park.
I mean *really* nail it 'cause we need to make this money bad."

I frown. "Why? What's the problem?"

"Uh? Oh. Nothing. I'm just saying." He shrugs.

"You're not saying much of anything. Don't tell me that
your ass has been—"

"Whoa. Shhh. Shhh." Kalief looks around to make sure
that no one is listening to our conversation. "Will you calm
down? You're letting your imagination get the best of you again.
Ain't nobody been doing nothing. I'm just saying that we
gotta pay the band and catch up on our studio bill. That's all."

"How much is the job paying?"

Kalief's left eye twitches. "Don't know yet. Everything is still negotiable."

"Uh-huh." I roll my eyes and tell myself that it's not worth getting into a fight. I'm tired of arguing. He steps up and tries to get me to look into his lying eyes. The thing is, he thinks that when he makes eye contact, he looks earnest.

He doesn't.

"You trust me, don't you?"

"Kalief, go on with that. You've forgotten who you're talking to and I got to get ready."

Of course, he won't let it go. He always takes it as a personal insult when he can't convince me that his lies are honest. "I'm serious," he says, looping his arms around my hips and dragging me closer. "C'mon, baby. You know that I got your back. Everything I do is for you—for us. Just have a little faith in me."

I wish that were true. I'm so broken inside with so much bullshit that I can't even fake this shit no more.

"C'mon. Give me that smile," he presses.

"Kalief." I look around and see the band in position, tinkering with their instruments and waiting. "They're ready."

"I'm not moving until you give me that smile," he insists.

I cut him with a look, but he keeps grinning like a fool until those damn dimples hit my weak spot and melt my resolve. I smile.

"There it is." He grins and kisses the tip of my nose.

"All right now. G'on." I squirm and push out of his arms. I'm already hating myself for giving in—again.

"A'ight. I'm going." He smacks my ass and then shuffles off the stage. "She's ready, y'all. Let's get this show on the road."

Jase, my keyboardist, shouts, " One . . . two . . . three!"

The band plays the opening of Sade's "Soldier of Love." I close my eyes, block out the world, and let the music take over.

I've lost the use of my heart . . .

Instantly I'm connected to the music and lyrics. The song reflects every bit of my love for Kalief, even though in my heart of hearts, I know that this love is doomed. As the music's tempo accelerates, I open my eyes and find Kalief's steady gaze on me while he sits in a U-shaped leather booth with four other men. I wish, like countless times before, that he truly heard what I was trying to say to him.

It's a lot to hope for.

I've been torn up inside

A man leans over and whispers something into Kalief's ear. He smiles and then gives me the thumbs-up. Two minutes later, we end the song and I step away from the microphone with tears in my eyes and a lump in my throat.

"Thanks, guys," Kalief tells the band as he practically leaps onto the stage, clapping.

"Baaaabeeee," he coos, arms outstretched. "You did it. I knew you would."

Nodding, I fold my arms. "How much?"

He ignores the question and my body language and pulls me into his arms for a sloppy kiss between my chin and cheek. "I knew that they'd love you. We got the opening-night gig! Who's your daddy now?"

I glance back out to the table. The four men whom Kalief was huddled with have climbed out of the booth and are walking away. "Which one of them is Diesel?"

"Uh, he couldn't make it today."

"What? But I thought you said—"

"He had some pressing matters to attend to, but his man Beast said—"

"Beast? What the fuck kind of name is that?"

"What difference does it make? The man has the authority to green-light the entertainment for opening night and you're *it*, baby."

"And the money? What's the pay?"

"Let me worry about all of that. Okay?"

"But I thought you said that this Diesel had all these music connections?"

"He does—and don't worry. He will be at the club opening night. And when he sees you, you're gonna knock his socks off."

"Uh-huh. I don't know why I keep listening to this bullshit."

"No bullshit. Trust me. Everything is going to be *perfect.*"

43

Lucifer

It plucks my last nerve to watch Lynch limp his ass out of J.D. Lewis & Sons Funeral Home. I came close to putting his ass in one of our damn caskets and burying it. At least we made our position clear. This was his one and only "peace" meeting. The only way to head off a full-scale war against his weak-ass crew is to hand over Trigger and his multi-flagging bitch, Shariffa—something no *real* nigga would ever do. His balls are in a vise.

He knows it.

We know it.

The storage room's heavy door slams shut behind Lynch and his crew.

"You were very busy?" Mason asks. "You didn't tell me that you were going after those girls today."

"I didn't know I had to clear shit with you. It was a personal errand. I took care of it."

"I don't know what's gotten into you lately," he says. "Did I do something wrong? Did I piss you off? Tell me because I'm starting to think my coming back has thrown a monkey wrench into your plans."

"Whatever. Do what you want to do." Rolling my eyes, I turn to march off, but Mason grabs me by my arm. My emotions are a tinderbox and I erupt and flail punches at his head. "Don't you fucking touch me, you bastard!"

Profit and our crew creep out of the room.

"What in the hell?" He wrestles to get control of my hands. "What has gotten into you, goddamn it?"

"You and that pig-bitch's picture that's in your fucking pocket," I shout. "You're still in love with that bitch and yet you crawl into *my* bed, lying about how much you fucking love me! How stupid do you think I am? I'm not going to be your rebound bitch!"

"What? Calm down! Have you lost your damn mind? I'm not in love with that lying piece of dead shit. What the fuck?"

"Liar!" I free one hand and land a punch against the side of his head. "I saw the picture! You've been carrying it around the whole time while you were gone. Probably dreaming for months about her stretched-out pussy that you and that snake-loving bastard were sharing. Well, fuck you!"

"A picture?" He ducks my next swing and then grabs hold of my hand again. "*This* is over a goddamn picture? You gotta be shittin' me. That picture has been in my wallet for years. I never look at the damn thing. I just didn't take it out." He shoves me away from him. "Here. If it'll make you feel better." Mason reaches into his back pocket and removes his wallet. "I'll tear it up," he shouts.

I glare at him, my chest heaving like I've gone a ten-round bout with Floyd Mayweather.

Mason pulls out Melanie's picture, rips it into tiny pieces, and then tosses them over his shoulder. "There. Are you happy now? The bitch means nothing to me. I love your crazy, homicidal ass."

I struggle to hang onto my anger, but it's quickly slipping into embarrassment. Mason sucks in a deep breath and crosses his arms. "You ain't got nothing to say?"

I'm caught flat-footed with no way to get out of this.

"Do you love me, Willow?" he asks, softly.

My eyes well up. I don't like being vulnerable.

Mason unfolds his arms and moves toward me.

The closer he gets, the stronger I fight the urge to throw my arms around him and asks for his forgiveness. I've been a raging, jealous hormonal bitch lately and I have little experience in apologizing to people.

He draws me into his arms. "Look at me," he orders.

I hesitate because my eyes are burning. *Don't cry.*

"Willow," he says gently.

Reluctantly, I look up.

"I'm going to tell you this—and I want you to believe me because I mean it with all of my heart. I love you. I've loved you for so long that I can't remember a time when I didn't love you. The only reason that I never acted on it when we were younger was out of respect for my friendship with your brother. And I regret that. I can't tell you how much. You're not now, nor will you *ever* be, the rebound chick. Melanie was."

Tears race down my face as he leans over and captures my lips into the sweetest kiss I've ever tasted. I hate to be the kind of bitch who melts like a romance heroine—but that's exactly what I'm doing as his tongue dives into my mouth. My arms drift up his chest and then steal around his neck to draw him closer.

We remain lip-locked until my lungs beg for oxygen. Even then, his lips glide over to nuzzle my neck and pepper my collarbone.

"I love you," he whispers. "Do you love me?"

"I more than love you," I confess. "I'm *in* love with you." *Tell him.* "And I'm going to have your baby."

Mason's body goes still.

I freeze as well and hold my breath.

Finally, he leans back and looks down at me. "What did you say?"

My heart pounds against my rib cage, but I keep my eyes level with his. "I'm pregnant."

Shock is too mild to describe his expression. "Baby, are you sure?"

I nod. "I'm almost five months."

His eyes zoom to my belly and a new understanding emerges. "I'm about to be . . . You're pregnant! Holy shit!" He sweeps me up and spins me around. "Fuck yeah! I'm gonna be a damn daddy!"

44

LeShelle

"It's all over the streets," Kane confirms. "Fat Ace is alive. Niggas are saying his ass crawled out of the grave all burnt up—straight zombie shit. They're also bragging that he and Lucifer wiped out the Angels of Mercy charter for double-crossing them. Muthafuckas done kicked off some racial shit now."

Python grunts. It's nine o'clock in the morning and his ass is already drunk as hell.

My head zooms. Lucifer's gangsta gets nothing but mad respect from my ass.

"And that's not all," June Bug pipes in, frowning. "Fat Ace and Lucifer are now a couple. Rumor is she's carrying his seed."

"Good God," I say. "I can't imagine the kind of demon those two will shit out."

"At least her ass can have a damn baby," Python grunts.

I drop into the chair behind me as if he sucker-punched me.

"I want a meeting," Python says, changing the subject. "Mason and I need to talk."

"Python, don't do this," I warn.

"And where in the fuck is Diesel?" Python adds in his own fuckin' zone again. "I've been calling him all morning."

"He's probably at the club. You know he's got that opening coming up."

"Bring his ass here. Shit. Do I have to do everything my-self? His ass is supposed to be on top of this shit."

"You got it, boss," June Bug says, popping his sidekick on the shoulder and then leading him out the front door.

Once we're alone, I turn toward Python with open disgust. "This is a mistake—a *big* mistake."

Python blows me off to reach for another drink. "I don't know why you can't get it through your head that this is something that I gotta do."

"Why? For closure?" I jump back to my feet. "You can't seriously think Fat Ace is gonna welcome you into his life with open arms. *The chief of the Vice Lords?*"

"You don't understand," he mumbles. "I can't get you to understand."

"No. You can't—because the shit doesn't make sense. And even if I crack my fuckin' head and begin to live in this altered reality that you're in, what do you seriously think that's gonna happen? You two are gonna squash a lifetime of beef and the Gangster Disciples and the Vice Lords are gonna join hands and hum old negro spirituals because y'all share the same blood? You ain't Martin Luther King and that dream ain't ever gonna happen."

Silence.

I'm not getting through to him. "Fuck. Now I need a damn drink." I grab the bottle of Henney and pour myself a glass. As I toss back my liquid breakfast, I can't help but notice that Python looks guiltier than a muthafucka.

"What the fuck are you not telling me?"

This nigga glances away and mumbles something under his breath.

"All right, I'll bite. What the fuck do you think that nigga is gonna say after surviving your ass tryna kill him? Not once,

not twice—but too many times to count. You do remember
that was what you were doing before your hallucination of
him being your long-lost brother kicked, right? Even if what
you say is true—and I do mean *if*—what the fuck does that
change? Cain killed Abel. Fuck. *You* killed your cousin Dat-
won. I don't remember you getting all emotional over that
shit."

"It's not the same!"

"Are you shittin' me? Your Aunt Peaches killed your
mother—because she was tryna kill her! *My* sister stabbed me
thirty-six times. And let's not talk about the shit that *I* did to
her to prove my loyalty to your waffling ass."

"Don't put that shit on me. I told you to handle the situation. I didn't tell you to take the shit as far as you did. That's on
you, ma."

"The fuck it is." I jab my finger into his chest. "Go mind
fuck some other bitch. We both know what you meant." I'm in
his face, barely able to keep my fists from swinging. "And so
that we're clear: at the end of the day, I don't have any goddamn sympathy for this whiny bullshit you're on—and neither
does anybody else. The Gangster Disciples' war with the Vice
Lords is set in stone until the world blows up. Remember?"

Python takes another sip of his drink.

"There's still the possibility that Fat Ace already knows
who you are and doesn't give a shit," I remind him. "You and
Mason—*if* it's him—were dealt a bad hand—I get that. Everybody out here got a sad ghetto story—my ass included—but
there comes a day when you got to charge that bullshit and
pain to the game. There's too many niggas depending on our
asses holding shit down—winning our streets back and moving the fuck on. If you don't do it—another nigga will—including your shifty-eyed cousin, Diesel."

"Damn, LeShelle. Get off that shit." He shoulders me out
of the way.

"Don't sleep on that nigga. I don't give a fuck if he's family or not. His shit is suspect with me. He's always right there to lend a fuckin' hand. He's our new drug connect, he supplying our arms, he calls up his homeboys to help run your fuckin' crew, and now he buying up property all over Memphis? And I'm supposed to believe that his high-yellow ass don't want a damn thing in return? C'mon!" I stomp my foot. "You're not that fuckin' stupid. You've *never* been this stupid."

"Enough!" Python hurls his glass.

CRASH!

"I'm tired of your goddamn bitching about shit you don't understand! I'm the nigga running this shit. You don't like how the fuck I get down, then take off that goddamn ring and bounce your ass up out of here."

"Python—"

"I mean it, Shelle. Your job is to jump when I say jump and fuck when I say fuck. Anything other than that then you're thinking too damn much!" He turns to storm out the living room, but I ain't having it. I rush around him and block his path to the bedroom.

"Get the fuck out of my way, Shelle. I ain't playing with you right now."

"Tell me what you're not saying!" I fold my arms.

His voice drops to a menacing warning. "LeShelle."

I don't move.

"Don't make me bounce you off every goddamn wall in this bitch."

"That's fine. When you get through, you're still going to tell me what the fuck you're hiding."

His fists tighten at his sides as we eyeball each other in a heated combat.

"The full truth," I press.

Once he sees that I'm not backing down, Python retreats a few feet and then spins toward the living room, looking like he's ready to throw something else. "Fine," he roars. "You want to know the damn truth. I'll give you the truth." He takes a deep breath. "It's my fucking fault what happened to Mason. The shit is all on me."

"What?"

He heaves out a long breath. "When I was six-years old. I placed my baby brother in an oven."

45

Hydeya

"**S**leep is for pussies," I tell myself over and over. The Terry/ Gibson case, the Captain Johnson case, and now the Angels of Mercy massacre have me in contention for the "department conducting the most press conferences in a single month" award—and there's no end in sight.

" 'They were niggers,' " Fowler quotes every twenty minutes and follows up with a spatter of chuckles.

"It's disturbing how a mass shooting tickles you so much," I snap.

"I laugh to keep from crying," he says, hanging on to his goofy smile.

"Uh-huh."

We enter our war room, carrying a DVD that has been discovered at Captain Johnson's home. The forensic team marked it as urgent, and Fowler and I quickly huddle around a twenty-seven-inch television screen.

POP! POP! POP!

On the television screen, Detective Keegan O'Malley approaches what appears to be a large, muscular suspect in a dark alley somewhere. O'Malley glances over at a body that's lying on the ground but keeps his weapon trained on his suspect.

The detective says something. It's too low for the security cameras to pick up, but I don't think it's the man's Miranda rights. If fact, O'Malley doesn't appear to be interested in arresting this guy. If anything, he's trying to provoke a fight.

Another cop comes into view of the camera.

"It's Officer Melanie Johnson," I whisper.

Officer Johnson moves behind him to check on the body on the ground.

A deep, demonic laugh rumbles loud enough for the audio to pick up. The suspect isn't scared of the police.

Who is this guy? I lean in closer, wishing the suspect would move back a few inches so I can get a better look.

O'Malley taunts his suspect, never once going for the handcuffs on his hip. My gaze swings back to his partner. She's watching what's going on and reaching for something. *A gun?*

Hyped, O'Malley appears ready to shoot in cold blood. *Oh God. Don't let this tape be what I think it is. I can't handle any more surprises.*

Behind O'Malley, Johnson lifts the dead man's .45.

POP! POP! POP!

The back of O'Malley's head explodes as his body pitches forward and then collapses in a dead heap on the concrete.

"Holy shit," Lieutenant Fowler thunders, jumping out of his chair.

"Holy shit is right," I mumble, wishing I could have a strong drink.

The video keeps playing as the suspect lowers his hands, turns around, and finally reveals his face to the camera.

"FUCK ME," Fowler exclaims. "Please tell me that isn't who I think it is."

"Terrell Carver," I confirm. Dread curdles in the pit of my gut.

There's more. Carver inches up to Melanie, lifts her head, and lays a kiss on her that's worthy of the silver screen.

"Enough." I power off the video and collapse back in my chair while my brain absorbs what it witnessed. "The bitch killed her partner."

"Well, a whole lot of shit is starting to make sense," Fowler says, pacing. "This is our confirmation. Alice Carver told that kid the truth. She was his grandmother."

"A kiss doesn't prove that," I say.

He levels me with a look.

"I agree with you. Fuck. I figured that shit out weeks ago. And as soon as the lab report comes in, I'm sure Christopher and Alice's DNA are going to match." I reach for a folder in the center of the table and pull out pictures of Christopher Johnson and Terrell Carver. The truth stares me in the face. "So he kidnapped his own kid."

"After murdering the baby momma," Fowler injects.

"Oh, it's definitely his kid," a voice interrupts us.

We look up to Detective Wendi Hendrix at the door.

"How long have you been standing there?" I ask.

"Long enough." She walks in and tosses down another folder.

"What's this?" I grab the folder.

"The blood results from Detective Melanie Johnson's homicide. I remembered that Captain Johnson asked me to have the lab run a comprehensive DNA test as a favor. I owed him one so I did it and gave him the results without looking at it. Under the new circumstances, I requested a copy."

I'm listening and reading at the same time. It takes me a minute to understand the results. "This can't be right."

"That's what I said," Detective Hendrix says. "But Captain Johnson gave a sample and he's one of the primaries used for testing. Melanie was the other. He was a paternal match to two of the blood samples: Officer Johnson and Terrell Carver."

Fowler sits up. "What?"

"But there were three different blood types discovered at Melanie Johnson's crime scene," I say.

"Check out the mitochondrial analysis," Hendrix presses.

I flip to another page and read. "I think I'm going to be sick."

"What? What?" Fowler asks, sounding like a broken clock.

"Mitochondrial DNA is maternally inherited. And according to this, Terrell Carver's mtdna matches the third person in the room, but not Melanie Johnson. So . . . all three people that were in that bedroom were . . . *related?*"

Hendrix nods. "*And*"—she tosses down more reports— "the DNA testing on Christopher Johnson."

Hell. I'm too scared to even look at this one, but I snatch it up. "Oh shit."

Tired of waiting, Fowler leans over my shoulder to read for himself.

Disgusted, I hand over the reports to do a double face palm while a migraine hammers my temples.

Fowlers struggles with the truth. "The boy's mother and father?"

"Are brother and sister"—I fill in for him—"through the father: Captain Johnson."

"And the third sample . . ." He picks up the other reports.

"Are brothers—through the mother: Alice Carver." I shake my head. "This is some ratchet-ass, ghetto bullshit to the tenth power."

"You expect anything less out of Memphis?" Hendrix asks, shaking her head.

I glance over at Fowler.

"She got a point," he says. "But hey. Who's the third marker?"

Hendrix answers, "The prints lifted from the scene were Melanie Johnson and Terrell Carver. We couldn't get a clean print on the third set."

"Of course not," he complains. "That would make our jobs too easy."

I lift my head. "We need to find out how many children

Alice Carver had." I glance back over at detective Hendrix. "Pull everything we have on the Melanie Johnson case."

"Can't."

"What the fuck do you mean? Why not?"

"It's missing."

"*Missing?* How does an whole case file go missing?"

"Think about it."

Captain Johnson. "UUUAAGH." I drop my head onto the table. This shit is the last thing I need.

"Don't worry. We're good with puzzles. We'll figure everything out," Fowler says, confidently.

"You're just trying to make me feel better."

"Fuck you. I'm trying to make myself feel better."

That wrangles a laugh out of me. Sitting back up, I glance at all the paperwork on the table. "Captain Johnson wanted to put a lid on all this shit. The blood work. His daughter murdering her police partner. Her having a son with her brother."

"You think she knew Terrell was her brother?" Fowler asks.

"Who the fuck knows? Add this shit to the freezer chest full of frozen money in Johnson's basement, the ten pipe safes buried in the backyard, money in the walls, attics, garden—and even in the dog house. The asshole didn't even have a damn dog. And let's not forget about the crates of illegal weapons hidden in a panic room. We don't have a clue who these people are."

"Wait until the newspapers get a load of this," Fowler says. "We're about to go head long into one hell of a shit storm that will probably land us on national news."

Tell me about it. "I'll worry about CNN *after* Chief Brown reads the report I sent over this morning."

Fowler whistles low. "You already sent over a report?"

"It's my job."

"Damn. Every day I'm happy they promoted you instead of me."

"Asshole."

"Sticks and stones . . ."

Knock! Knock! Knock!

Expelling a breath, I look up at Detective Hendrix again. "What is it now?"

"Police chief wants to see you," she says gravely.

"Speak of the devil." My gut churns.

"Fair warning: she's with the deputy chief, the lieutenant colonel—*and* the mayor."

Fowler groans. "Fuck. That doesn't sound good."

"I haven't had good news since my promotion." Scrambling out of my chair, I cram paperwork back into the folders. The trip down the long hallway to the chief's office has every head in the building turning my way. *Damn. Does everybody know something I don't?*

"Chief, you want to see me?" I ask.

None of the bigwigs bother to stand or smile when I enter Chief Brown's office.

"Close the door and have a seat," she orders and gestures to the only vacant chair left in the room.

The tension thickens by the second as I follow orders. The second my ass hits the chair, Chief Brown cuts straight to the point.

"You need to wrap up the Captain Johnson case."

"Yes, Chief. My team and I are working day and night on this. As I've indicated in the report I sent over this morning, I believe that we've barely scratched the surface on this. Captain Johnson was clearly involved in a lot of—"

"It's a murder case," Mayor Wharton interrupts, agitated. "His killer was Alice Carver. She's dead. Case closed. I fail to see the problem."

After that announcement, everyone eyeballs me. I fight squirming in my chair and hold on to a degree of professionalism. "There's more here. The money—"

"You're changing the subject," the mayor complains.

"I'm not—I'm simply saying that there's more to this investigation than the murders allegedly committed by Alice Carver."

"Allegedly? What, are you a lawyer now?" Mayor Wharton snaps.

I'm stunned by his aggressiveness.

"Of course not, sir. We've recently uncovered evidence that Captain Johnson's *daughter*, Detective Melanie Johnson, gunned down her partner, Detective Keegan O'Malley. It's on video. Captain Johnson must've confiscated it from one of the proprietors in the area. It shows the murder as well as evidence that Detective Johnson also had a personal relationship with Terrell Carver."

Eyes dart around the room. I can't tell whether this new information surprises, angers, or shocks them. My attention zooms back to the chief. "What am I missing here?"

Chief Brown braids her fingers together across her desk and then looks me dead in my eyes. "It doesn't change anything. We're not interested in the money, the weapons . . . O'Malley's murder—or anything else you've stumbled upon. The public wants to know that we've solved the murder of their local hero. Period."

The mayor nods and takes over. "The last thing the city needs or wants is for us to fall down a rabbit hole to God knows where, especially if we don't know what we're going to find. The potential blowback is too high and could splatter over everybody. This is an election year, for Christ's sake. I'm getting my ass kicked every night on the evening news because people think that this city is turning into another Detroit. Forty-three killed at a biker club, fifteen killed at a nightclub—a strip club blown up like we're in Iraq or something. Kidnapping, high-speed gunfights—and now you want headlines broadcasting to the whole world that the city's most decorated police officer was running illegal weapons right under our noses—do I have that right?"

Speechless, I shift around in my chair. I can't believe what I'm hearing.

Chief Brown stands up from her desk, her authority wrapped around her like a cape. "All right," she continues when I don't respond. "Let me bottom-line it for you: the case is closed—and anything related to the case is closed. This department is not prepared to handle any surprise skeletons falling out of the closet of a civil servant who this city has been calling a super cop for more than twenty years. Captain Johnson's career is linked with too many others. They're already getting a whiff of what you've dug up and they're not liking what they're hearing one single bit."

"But the O'Malley case—"

"Will lead to reporters investigating Detective Melanie Johnson's background—which will lead to her father," the mayor cuts in. "No. Too risky. We're not going to bring down perhaps half the city's political players over one rogue . . . *crime* family in the system. Whatever Captain Johnson was involved in dies with him."

"And justice?" I ask.

"Everybody's dead," the mayor laughs with incredulity. "God has already divvied out all the justice that was needed in this case. What do you want to do, dig up the bodies and put them on trial?" Another laugh. "I'm going to go out on a limb and say that's definitely a waste of taxpayers' money." His laughter accelerates at his own joke.

I glance back at the chief to see whether she's serious. *She is.*

"Shut. It. Down," the chief orders. Her hard gaze sears into mine.

The office falls silent as I look at their grave faces. If I don't play ball, it'll cost my career.

"Are we clear, *Captain?*" Chief Brown leans against her desk.

Deputy Chief Collins and Lieutenant Colonel Bertinelli hold their breaths.

Mayor Wharton's eyes narrow, waiting for my response.

"Crystal clear." I stand up. "Are we through here?"

Chief Brown sizes me up. "Your discretion about what was discussed here today is needed and appreciated."

"And it'll be rewarded," the mayor adds, grinning

Unable to trust that when I open my mouth I won't curse this circle of co-conspirators the fuck out, I nod instead. At the same time, how am I ever going to look myself in the mirror again?

"Are those also part of the Johnson investigation?" Chief Brown refers to the folders in my hand.

I hesitate.

"You can leave them here with us. You need to prepare for your next press conference, announcing the Johnson case *closed*."

My tight smile withers. *You gotta be shitting me.*

"Problem?" she asks.

"No." I swallow my dignity and self-respect. "No problem at all."

"Good. You can go now."

I march out of the office. *This fucking city.* It's getting harder to tell which gang does more damage. The ones flagging in the streets or the ones with badges pinned to their chests.

46

LeShelle

"**W**hat the fuck are you talking about?" I ask. This conversation has jumped the shark. "You put your brother in an oven? What oven? I don't understand."

Python huffs and then plops onto the couch, where he buries his head into his hands. "Fuck, Shelle. This shit has been wearing on me for such a long muthafuckin' time. You just don't understand."

I remain standing in the center of the room with my arms folded across my chest, waiting for him to continue.

"I was a fucking kid. I didn't really know what I was doing," he confesses to the floor. "I hurt him. It was an accident. I didn't know what else to do." He pauses for a long time.

When a fuckin' tear splats onto the hardwood floor, I move to the La-Z-Boy across from him. "Start from the beginning."

I was young and I guess I adjusted to being raised by my aunt Peaches. It was all I knew, really. I came up believing that I was the man of the house and then suddenly my aunt moved this nigga Isaac into the crib and shit changed. Some for the better and some for the worse.

I didn't like it at first. I didn't like him. He was a big, bald dude that strutted through the house like he owned the place. Aunt Peaches was in love. She was happy so I tried to be happy, too.

But I didn't like him.

I didn't trust him. Not in the beginning.

I don't remember the exact day when I knew that Isaac was seeing other chicks. I only remember them always floating in and out of the house when Aunt Peaches wasn't around. A lot of times, he'd pay me a dollar, tell me to go out and play, and then take those girls into bedroom and lock the door. I'd listened to all the "oohs" and "ahs" and "oh my gods" filling the house while the bed's headboard banged against the wall. I don't think I knew what it meant. Aunt Peaches usually made the same noise whenever she was in there with him.

When my old childhood buddy KyJuan stole a few of his daddy's porno tapes, I got schooled real quick on what the hell was going on in that bedroom. That shit changed my life— 'cause KyJuan's father had some real freaky shit on those tapes. It made my lil dick hard.

From then on, I emulated everything Isaac did. I wanted all the girls in the neighborhood. Me and KyJuan would drag them behind houses and show them our dicks if they showed us their pussies. A few more boys in the neighborhood found out what we were doing and joined us. One lil nigga, Jimmy Gaines, went so far as to get Yolanda Terry to let him put his dick in her mouth for a box of Lemonheads.

It was funny as hell. Them fools never let her ass forget that shit.

Then one day, out of the blue, my mom called. She wanted to see us. Aunt Peaches snatched me up and we raced down to the hospital. I didn't know what to expect. The way Peaches acted, I expected bad news.

We got there and then was led to a room where a baby screamed its head off.

"Heeey," my momma greeted us, struggling to sit up.

I scrambled behind Aunt Peaches's prosthetic leg and then

peeked around. Momma looked horrible—like a dried-up zombie. Her hair was all over her head and there were these horrible purple and black tracks all over her arms.

"Wow. He's so big now." She flashed me a butter-colored smile.

"Yeah. Children have the tendency to grow," Aunt Peaches said, and then approached the bed.

The baby kept screaming.

"Hey, Terrell. You want to come over here and say hello to Mommy?" She opened her thin arms and pleaded with her sad, watery eyes.

I didn't want to touch her. She scared me.

Aunt Peaches pushed me forward, but I pushed back until she leaned down and whispered, "Remember what Isaac told you about fear?"

I nodded. Isaac said that a real man learned to embrace and conquer his fears—whatever they may be. I blinked up at my mom. My heart slammed inside my chest until it hurt.

The baby's screams had worked its way under my skin. I glanced at him, wondered why he wouldn't stop. Was he scared too?

"Go ahead. Go on." Aunt Peaches gave me another push and I walked over to the bed.

My mom's face lit up. I suspected that if she washed and brushed her hair she might actually be pretty. All at once, she leaned over and wrapped her arms around me and then smothered me with kisses that smelled like stale tobacco. It was weird—like I'd been missing her my whole life and didn't even know it.

"Mommy has missed you sooo much." She squeezed me tighter. "Have you been good for your aunt Maybelline? Huh? Have you been a good boy?"

"Y-yes, ma'am."

"What's wrong with this little fella?" Aunt Peaches asked, hovering over the screaming baby. "He hasn't stopped crying since we walked into the room." She picked him up. "Awww. What's the matter?"

The baby kicked and screamed as if he were being tortured. I wanted to cover my ears.

"Who knows what the hell is wrong with him?" Alice said grumpily. "I don't think that he's shut up since the doctor smacked him on the ass," she sniped, but then beamed a smile at me.

I smiled back.

"Awww, lil man," Peaches said. "It's gonna be all right." She kissed and rocked him in her arms. "Screaming and hollering is no way to spend a birthday. Is your diaper wet?"

"No. And he's ain't hungry either," Momma groaned. "He's been here six hours and he's already pissed at the world. Not that I blame him—I've been pissed about being here a long time myself." She pressed another kiss against my head. It was like she couldn't stop touching me now. "You never cried like that when you were a baby," she confided. "You were a good boy."

I turned to look at Aunt Peaches. "Can I hold him?"

Peaches smiled. "Of course you can, honey." She walked the baby over to me. "Now you have to be careful with him," she warned. "Hold out your arms."

I did like she said.

"Okay. Here we go." She transferred the baby to me. "Careful."

"I got him." I looked down at my baby brother.

He looked up at me, and then stopped crying.

Aunt Peaches and Momma gasped.

Smiling, I asked, "What's his name?"

"Mason," Momma said.

"Mason," I repeated, and then felt the urge to kiss his forehead. "Hello, Mason. I'm your big brother."

Mason cooed.

That was a good day—probably the last good one we had

together. When we drove home, Aunt Peaches fussed about how Momma was gonna take care of Mason. She was stressed, thinking and suspecting that Momma was gonna show up one day on Shotgun Row and leave Mason with us. I didn't think that would be so bad. I could teach him a lot of things. But months went by and nothing happened. Thing was, I think Aunt Peaches was disappointed.

Things went back to normal. Aunt Peaches ran her boosting ring of girls while Isaac worked at his auto shop and moved "packages" on the side. His side job was the most dangerous; he never left the house without a gun to do it. And, of course, Isaac continued juggling a lot of girls. Then one evening, I overheard him talking on his cell phone in the backyard. I hadn't meant to put my nose in grown folks' business, but it was my momma's name that caught my ear.

"Alice, what the fuck are you doing calling me on this line?" Isaac swore, looking around, but not catching me by the back window listening.

"You know Peaches checks my fuckin' phone." He listened and then clucked under his tongue. "Nah. Nah. I can't come out there and see you right now. What? Nah. She's not here right now, but . . ." He listened some more and then glanced down at his watch. "Nah. Nah. You can't be doing that shit with my seed over there. You're supposed to be getting your shit together, remember?" There was a long pause where he starts pacing faster. "Alice, quit crying. Al—nah, I can't—fuck if—shit!" He looked at his watch. "All right. Fine. I'll swing by for a few minutes—just for a few minutes. You got that?" He huffed out a long breath. "A'ight, bye."

Isaac disconnected the call, looked around, and then swore under his breath. When he headed to the back door, I raced into the living room in my Spider-Man footie pajamas and plopped down on the floor and pretended like I'd been watching TV the whole time.

"Hey, yo, lil man," Isaac said, coming into the living

room. "I gotta run an errand. You think you'd be cool chilling out here by yourself for a few minutes until I get back?"

I frowned and then reminded him, "I'm six."

"Yeah, but you're almost seven." He shrugged.

I couldn't believe that he'd said that.

"Yeah. You're right. Your aunt will probably kill me." He huffed, glanced down at his gold Rolex, cursed, looked at the watch again. "All right. Let's go."

I popped up off the floor and raced to my bedroom. "I'll go change!"

"Nah. No time for that shit. Just grab your jacket and let's roll," he ordered.

He got no argument from me. I was excited to be going to see my mom—and Mason—again. Who would've thought?

Isaac drove out to my mom's apartment with his gun on his lap. Every time we passed by boys grouped up together, he'd rest one hand on it like he was ready to shoot. Turning into LeMoyne Gardens, a tribe of teenagers threw up signs. I start to toss up the Gangster Disciples' like Isaac had taught me, but he stopped me.

"Don't do that shit," he warned. "We're in hostile territory over here. Don't start nothing, won't be nothing. You got that?"

I nodded.

Isaac parked the car and then killed the engine.

"We need to go over a few rules, lil man," Isaac said, pocketing his keys and turning in his seat. "Your auntie doesn't need to know we came out here. This is going to be our little secret, all right?"

He stared at me so hard I didn't think I had any other choice but to nod.

"Good. Rule number one: Real niggas don't snitch on each other. Got it?"

I nodded.

He tucked his gun beneath his jacket. "Now. We're going

in here to check on your momma. I need you to go in, sit down, and behave while we talk for a minute. Can you handle that?"

I nodded again, but he kept eyeballing me like he didn't know whether he could trust me. *"I'll keep my mouth shut. I promise."*

"A'ight," he finally said. *"Let's go."*

We climbed out of the car and made our way up the steep staircase to Momma's place. Isaac constantly checked over his shoulder with his hand on his gun. From outside the door, we heard Mason screaming his head off.

KNOCK! KNOCK! KNOCK!

We waited.

The baby's cries grew louder.

KNOCK! KNOCK! KNOCK!

We waited some more.

Mason wailed at the top of his lungs.

"Goddamn it," Isaac swore.

POUND! POUND! POUND! He used his fist.

I was getting cold.

POUND! POUND! POUND!

"Who is it?" a voice inquired.

"Alice, you know who the fuck this is! Open the goddamn door!"

It took her forever to undo the locks and crack open the door to peek out.

Isaac's patience snapped as he shoved his way through the door. *"Stop fuckin' around."*

"Shit. I didn't know it was you." Momma stumbled backwards. *"Oh, heeey, Terrell."* She closed her robe with one hand and scratched her bruised arm with the other. *"I didn't know you were comin' over, too. Did you miss your momma?"*

I stared at her. She looked worse than the last time I'd seen her.

Mason went on wailing.

Isaac kicked the door shut behind us. "You got company?" he asked.

"Nah. Nah. I've been waiting on you, baby." She wobbled toward him. "You remember to bring my medicine? I need it real bad."

She was sick. Suddenly it all made sense. I glanced at Mason, who cried relentlessly on the sofa. I walked over and wondered whether he'd stop crying if I picked him up—again.

Momma hugged Isaac and grabbed his dick. "C'mon, baby. I'll suck it reeeal good, if you just hook me up."

My eyes bugged out of my skull, but then I jerked my head away and pretended like I couldn't hear them over Mason.

"Please, Isaac. C'mon, now. You know that's why you drove over here. Stop playing." She opened her robe and then rubbed her titties against him.

Isaac stared at her body like he was in a trance. "A'ight," he said. "But this is the last fuckin' time. You hear me?"

"That's what you always say." She laughed and unzipped his pants.

"Whoa. Whoa." He jerked her hand away. "Not in front of the kids. Damn." He looked at me. "Lil man. Me and your momma need to settle some business. You stay out here and watch your brother."

Again, I didn't say shit. I watched Momma lead him to the back of the apartment. A few seconds later, a door slammed. A minute later, a bed was bumping against the wall.

I stood there left alone with a crying baby, not sure how I felt about this whole situation. One thing for sure, Mason's crying was working my damn nerves. I picked him up. He was heavier than the last time. I had him okay, but he didn't stop crying.

I sat on the sofa and rocked him. That wasn't enough. I don't know how long I was left there tryna calm him down.

Forever, it seemed. Toward the end, I was ready to pull my hair out. Eventually, I spotted a bottle out of the corner of my eye. A light bulb went off in my head.

He was hungry.

I grabbed the bottle, but it was thick with moldy-looking stuff inside of it. I tossed it aside and went into the kitchen. "C'mon. Let's get you something to eat." I walked and bounced him in my arms all the way.

Mason did more than scream. He kicked and wiggled in my arms. It got harder to hold him. "Calm down, lil man. Calm down." I opened the refrigerator and was hit with a horrible stench. I reeled back just when Mason wiggled and kicked too hard. He was in my arms one second—and then falling out of it the next.

Everything happened in slow motion. His fall. His head hitting the corner of the refrigerator, the loud THUMP when his body hit the floor.

Finally, he was silent.

No cries.

No kicking.

No wiggling.

I froze—stunned at what'd happened—and scared that I was about to be in trouble. Big trouble. "Mason?" I bent my knees and roll him over. There was a gash on his head and he was bleeding.

Momma's bed stopped bumping the wall.

Panicked, I picked Mason up, looked around until my eyes settled onto that ugly green stove. I don't know what the fuck I was thinking—if I was thinking.

I wanted to hide him and not get into trouble. So I jerked open the oven and crammed him in before racing back into the living room and sitting down.

A second later Isaac came out of the back room, tucking in his shirt and zipping up his pants. "Let's head out," he said, going straight to the door.

I jumped to my feet, expecting him to ask about the baby, but he didn't. Before following, I glanced back toward the kitchen.

Isaac misunderstood why I hesitated.

"Look, I gave your momma her medicine and she's sleeping right now. You'll have to see her another time. Now c'mon." He opened the door—and I raced out.

That was the last time I saw Mason.

The next day when Aunt Peaches and I showed up, my momma didn't even remember that Isaac and I had even been there. And when my aunt searched the house, I ran to the kitchen, but Mason wasn't in the oven. He was gone. Just . . . gone.

47

Qiana

"Just tell us what the hell you did with the baby," Adaryl hisses. "We have the right to know."

I shake my head, tired of going around in circles with them over this shit. "The less y'all know the better," I keep telling them, which is the truth. I can't trust these bitches worth a damn and now that I got this cop sniffing around my panties, I gotta play shit smart. I'm not about to fuck up and get locked down over this bullshit.

"Whatever is whatever," Li'l Bit pipes up. "I say we put that night out of our minds and just act like the shit never happened."

"I'm down with that," I say and then look to Adaryl. Clearly, she is feeling some kind of way because she can't even fix her face. "Whassup?" I explode.

"What? I didn't say shit," she retreats, defensive.

"You don't have to. My ass ain't blind. What I don't get is why do you give a shit? You've been on my ass for months to handle the situation. Now it's done and you still have a long face?"

"No. I don't," she lies. "I just don't understand why you're so secretive all of a sudden."

"Maybe because you've been acting so shady. Now you're

over here tryna play inch-high private eye. You still ain't told us what the hell you told the po-po when they came poking around *your* place."

"I didn't tell them shit," Adaryl barks.

"You had to have said something. That new captain don't take silence for an answer—and you're as prickly as I am so I know she had to get under your skin."

"No. She wasn't like that."

"Bullshit."

Even Li'l Bit cocked her head at Adaryl. Neither one of us are buying her story—which makes her twenty damn questions even more suspicious.

"I don't give a fuck what you two think." She waves us off and then hops up from our table.

"Where in hell do you think that you're going?" I demand.

"We're done here, right? There's nothing else to discuss. We can all go our separate ways and pretend this shit never happened." Without waiting for a response, Adaryl turns and skates off.

"Oookay." Li'l Bit shakes her head.

"I don't trust that bitch," I say. "Not at all."

Li'l Bit dismisses it. "She's always been a little funny. Don't let her get to you."

"Uh-huh." I stare a hole into the back of Adaryl's head, unable to settle this weird feeling I'm getting.

"Let it go," Li'l Bit insists. "She's not going to talk."

I shift my gaze to meet my girl's straight-on. "Are you sure? Are you willing to bet your freedom?"

Li'l Bit's confidence wavers as she casts a look over her shoulder at Adaryl joining the skaters rolling around the rink. "She won't talk. She better not."

"If she does, you know what we'll have to do."

My cell buzzes against my leg. I lower my slice of pizza and scoop it out of jean pocket. The name on the caller ID surprises the hell out of me.

"What is it now?" Li'l Bit asks.

I hold up the phone and flash it.

Adaryl's face goes from dread to shock—just like mine. "Where in the hell has he been?"

"No idea." My heart leaps into the center of my throat. *What do I say? What if I sound too anxious? Desperate?*

"Well? Are you going to answer it?"

I swipe my finger across the screen before the call is sent to voice mail. "H-hello." It's so loud in this joint that I have to cork my other ear in order to hear.

"Hello. I guess this means that you're still alive," Diesel says.

I pause, not sure how to respond.

"Hello," he says. "Are you still there?"

"Hey. Yeah. I'm here." I glance up as Li'l Bit moves from her chair to sit closer to me.

"Oh. It's like that now? You haven't been missing a brotha?"

I shrug, torn between admitting the truth and playing it cool. "I figured that you were busy and you'd call when you were ready."

Li'l Bit gives me the thumbs-up.

"Hmm. Well—you were right," Diesel says with a chuckle. "It's nice to hear that you have matured some since the last time we saw each other. I like it."

"What can I say? I like to keep people guessing." I wink at Li'l Bit, who is giggling into her hands.

"People—or men?" He comes direct.

"People."

"Uh-huh. You've been seeing anyone since you last saw me?"

Again, I hesitate.

"Don't lie," he warns before his voice drops even lower. "Have you given my pussy to someone else?"

"Your pussy?" Embarrassment, my face blazes. "I wasn't aware of you staking a claim."

"What? You just shoot up every nigga's house that you

smash? C'mon, Scar. Quit playing games. You know that you want me to be your man."

"I do, huh?" I squirm in my chair, remembering just how good this nigga is at straightening out a bitch's back.

"You gonna lie and tell me I'm wrong?"

Another pause.

"Well?"

"I haven't said either way."

"Humph. Then maybe I'm wrong and you *have* given my pussy out to some random nigga over there flagging those damn cartoon colors. Maybe I need to move on to the next bitch that knows something about loyalty and how to treat her man."

"So you're my man now?" I ask, liking the sound of that.

"I could be—if you do me right."

"I'll do you all right. The next damn time I see your fine ass."

"Is that a promise?" His voice keeps dropping into an incredible baritone that has my pussy creaming.

"Absolutely."

"Then how about you be my date for opening night at my club downtown. I want to make sure that I have the baddest bitch in Memphis on my arm. You with it?"

"A club, huh?" I clutch Li'l Bit's arm and bounce in my seat. "That sounds cool."

"Then it's a date?"

"Yeah. It's a date."

"Cool. I'll pick you up at eight next Friday. Tell your brother not to shoot when I show up at the door."

"You got it. I'll see you then. Bye." I disconnect the call, look at my girl, and then sing, "I'm gonna get laid. I'm gonna get laid."

48

LeShelle

"Is that it?" I ask Python when he finishes his long-ass story. "That's why you've been walking around here with your damn bottom lip sweeping the floor?" I hop up from the La-Z-Boy and mush him dead in his head. "Get the fuck out of here with that shit. You should've turned the muthafuckin' oven on and roasted his ass. Maybe then we wouldn't be going through this shit right now. Have you ever thought of *that* shit?

Python springs up out of his chair. "Fuck! I don't know why I bother telling you shit. You ain't got it in you to understand."

"You damn right I don't. You made sure of that shit the second you ordered me to handle *my* sister. You can play dumb now all you fuckin' want. But we both know what the fuck you meant—so *no!* I don't understand. I'll never understand. The past is the past. Leave that shit there and deal with the present—which is: *your muthafuckin' brother doesn't give a shit about you!* He will waste your fuckin' brains all up and down Memphis if given the chance. THIS IS WAR. This shit is bigger than you and Fat Ace."

Python throws up his hand, brick-walling this whole discussion before marching off toward the bedroom.

"Yeah. That's it. Walk away when you know that I'm right!"

He flips me off, storms into the bedroom, and slams the door.

Frustrated, I look around, wanting to throw or slam something, too. Babysitting a gangster is fuckin' insane. To calm my nerves, I roll my ass a fatty and blaze up. I need to anticipate what the fuck Python is going to do next. I don't trust him in this state of mind.

A car pulls up into the driveway. I climb back onto my feet and peek out of the blinds. Diesel eases out from behind the wheel looking more like a male super model than a ruthless gangster. His swag is out of control and has my knees knocking.

I move away from the window and over to the front door like a good wife, but I make sure I throw nothing but shade when he enters. However, the shit bounces off his ass as he hits me with one of his panty-melting smiles. *I hate this muthafucka.*

"What's up, Shelle?" He winks.

"Fuck you."

He meets my gaze and reads me like a book. "You'd like that, wouldn't you?"

"Not even if you were the last negro standing," I lie.

He laughs at my bullshit and strolls past me. "Where's big man at?"

"In the bedroom." *Crying like a bitch,* I want to add. "You look like you're handling shit well—considering. Word is that the Vice Lords took out your good ol' boy network. That's gotta hurt the bottom line."

A visible muscle twitches along the side of Diesel's face. "I'm handling it."

"Are you? Kind of how you handled Lucifer the other night? What was it you said? You haven't come across a bitch yet you couldn't put down?"

Another twitch.

"I told you not to underestimate that evil bitch."

"A minor setback," he says.

"Uh-huh." I rake my gaze over him and then I spit the only question that has been spinning inside my head since I met his ass. "What the hell do you get out of all of this?"

Diesel's slick smile grows wider. "The satisfaction of helping my family."

"Bullshit."

He makes a play of covering his heart with his hand. "I'm hurt that you don't trust me. *Truly.*"

"I don't trust nobody and I'm watching your ass. Trust and believe I'm going to do everything I can to protect my man and his crown. He's going through a few things right now, but if you step a toe out of line, I'll be too happy to shoot that muthafucka off."

His lips twitch. "You ain't the only nigga packing heat in this equation. You come gunning for me, you better make damn sure your ass don't miss. I don't show mercy for no muthafucka—with balls or tits." He stuns me by pinching my nipples so hard that I jump, despite the pleasure.

Diesel laughs as he leans in close. "If I were you, I'd check that temper, shawty. I ain't too crazy about bitches that don't know their places."

"My only place is on the throne. The rest of you bitch-niggas need to bow down."

He pinches my shit again. "Admit it. You've been dying for me to touch you since you laid eyes on me."

I step back. "Oh my. What a big muthafuckin' head you got."

"Yeah?" His fast hands grab mine and place it on the anaconda snaking down his leg. "I'm big all over, shawty."

He ain't fucking lying. I blame the weed for my ass not realizing that he had removed his hand and I remain clutching his dick like it's the last life vest on *The Titanic.*

"You can let go now," he says, laughing.

I snatch my shit back and suffer through the humiliation of him laughing in my face.

Python exits the bedroom. "Shelle, you got my ph—oh, D." He pulls up. "When the fuck did you get here?" His gaze swings back and forth between us.

"Just got here," Diesel says. "Is there somewhere we can go talk—in private?"

"Yeah, sure. Let's go out back."

"Are you for real?" I ask, hurt at the blatant diss.

Python doesn't respond as he leads Diesel out into the backyard.

Steaming, I follow close behind—but when Python sees me, he motions for Diesel to close the door.

That tickles the shit out of Diesel, who's only too happy to close that bitch right in my face.

Bitch-ass, pussy-punk muthafuck . . . I cut myself off and suck in a deep breath. After I get myself together, I lean forward and place my ear against the door and strain to hear what's being said on the other side. Python has walked out to the center of the yard where I can't hear shit.

This is ridiculous. I don't know how Python expects Diesel to help get more info on the Vice Lords than our street soldiers can.

"Qiana." The name rushes to the front of my mind. *Shit.* That fucking loose string I've left dangling in the wind. Fuck. I want to kick my own ass. Why, with all the fuckin' Flowers cluttering this shitty city, did Diesel have to cross paths with that sliced-up bitch? I try to calm down, but I can't. Bitches don't know how to keep their mouths shut—let alone some grimy Vice Lord. Hell. Had I not wound up in the hospital over Ta'Shara's bullshit, I would've taken care of her ass a long time ago.

"Don't worry," Diesel is saying, walking back toward the house with his arm wrapped around his cousin's shoulder. "I have my ways of getting muthafuckas to talk. I'll keep you posted."

They exchange fist pounds and a shoulder hug.

"I catch you later," Python says.

I roll my eyes.

Diesel chuckles as his cousin heads back to the bedroom.

I open the front door to show Diesel out.

He tosses up his hands. "I'm going. I'm going." At the door, he winks. "Have a good evening."

Instead of closing the door behind him, I step outside so that we can have our own private conversation. "So are you about to contact that VL jailbait you've been fuckin' with?"

"Why? Do you want to join us?"

"Hardly." I laugh, but it sounds like it sputtered out of a broken tailpipe.

Diesel's perfect brows lift with growing interest.

I trudge on like my act is Oscar-worthy. "Well, you're new to this city and you don't know how those withered-up Flowers are. You can't trust anything they fuckin' say. I wouldn't get my hopes up that you're going to get any real info from them."

He shrugs. "I disagree. It's not like Qiana is a nobody. From my understanding, her brother, Tombstone, is pretty high up on the food chain over there. He's Lucifer's right hand."

I stagger back. "What?"

Diesel studies me. "What's up? You know this chick or something?"

"What? No!" Again with that fucking tailpipe. "Why in the hell would I know that scarred-up bitch, Qiana?"

His gaze hardens on me. "How in the fuck do you know about her scars?"

49

Momma Peaches

Home sweet home.

After hospitals and rehabilitation centers, I have way too many feelings tripping inside my chest. It's not my first time returning after a long stint from the block. In the past, it involved my ass being locked behind iron bars. However, that's not the only thing different this time. I'm different.

That doesn't mean that I don't have a few things to work on. I do. But I see things differently now.

"I know that you'd rather Python brought you home," Diesel says, cutting through the car's awkward silence. "Believe me. He wanted to be here."

"When can I see him?"

"Soon. I promise." He glances at his watch.

"Why do you keep doing that? You got some place to be?"

"Nah. Nah. I got you." He glances at his watch and then smiles when he realizes he's done it again. "I got this joint opening up downtown next week. I got a lot of last-minute shit I gotta get done, but it'll keep."

"What kind of joint?"

"A club. You know, some music, girls, dancing. You should come party it up. Celebrate your return home. I'll even reserve you a table and everything."

"So you really are sticking around Memphis?"

He shrugs. "For a little while. You don't have a problem with that, do you?"

I suck in a long breath, but when he cuts his cool, calculating eyes my way, my protests die on my tongue. I've had all I can stand with psycho relatives. I gotta start letting shit slide. "Nah. It's a free country."

Diesel nods and then turns onto Shotgun Row. A whoop goes up and the entire block breaks out into cheers as if the First Lady of the United States were rolling through.

"Welcome back, Momma Peaches!" people shout.

A few kids run up and tap on the window. "Heeeeey, Momma Peaches!"

"Hey." I wave back with my eyes welling up.

More people crowd into the street and Diesel slows to a creep.

"Looks like you've been missed."

I want to say something smart, but the words get stuck. At this moment, I'm overwhelmed at the idea of returning home. For months, I thought I'd never see this place again. I lost count of the number of nights I prayed to die in that basement or the number of mornings I cried when I opened my eyes. Forget what you heard, God can be cruel. It's good to be back.

Damn good.

Diesel pulls up to my curb and kills the engine.

"Welcome home, Momma Peaches," my neighbor, Chantal, gushes as she grabs me by the shoulders and throws her arms around me. "We sure have missed you around here."

"Thanks. It feels so good to be home." I backhand a few tears and the crowd erupt into *aws* and *ohs* before I'm passed around for hugs. Overcome with emotion, I'm exhausted after a good ten minutes.

Music booms out into the streets and within seconds it's a full-fledged block party underway.

I glance at Diesel. "Who needs a club when they live on Shotgun Row?"

He bobs his head, smiling. "I see that."

A few young bucks swarm around. Nothing like the feel of muscles and the scent of Axe body spray to get the ol' kitty kat purring. It's been a hot minute since this body has had a good tune-up. As most know, I've never bought into the notion that at a certain age a bitch is supposed to put her pussy out to pasture. *The Lord is testing me.*

"Humph. Humph. Humph." My gaze lands on one chocolate buck with chiseled prison muscles and a shoe size I'm guessing to be a sixteen. "Lord, lead me not into temptation, but deliver me from evil."

Surprise colors Diesel's face. "You Bible thumping now?"

"*You* got a problem with that?"

He laughs.

It may be February, but it feels like spring. The smell of grilled burgers, chicken, and ribs is wafting up and down the neighborhood. I'm not even up the stairs on my new prosthetic leg when a fat joint is passed to me. It's halfway to my lips before the Lord taps me on the shoulder.

"Uh, I'm gonna pass."

Chantal's eyes bug out as she takes the blunt back. "Are you all right?"

"Yeah, girl. I'm fine. Tired is all." I flash a smile, knowing that niggas don't trust square muthafuckas worth a damn. I don't blame them.

She nods, but she looks at me like I've sprouted a second head.

My gaze slips past her to the porch two doors down. Bettye Turner is staring a hole in my head—as usual. That bitch don't let shit go. Unable to resist pushing her buttons, I wave. "Afternoon, Ms. Turner!"

Stunned at my audacity, Bettye's face purples before she turns in a huff and storms her wide ass back into the house.

Chantal laughs. "That woman ain't never gonna change."

"It's never too late to change," I say, thinking about myself. "Or to at least try."

"Here you go, Momma Peaches," another neighbor, Jia, race up my steps to hand me a beer.

I look at it and then at the joint settled between Chantal lips and decide to accept the beer. "Baby steps," I tell myself before pulling in a deep swig from the bottle. The second that smooth brew slides down my throat, I'm coasting through heaven. A bitch needed that. For real.

"Welcome back, Momma P," Jia says. "Sorry I didn't get a chance to come visit you in the hospital, but chile, you know how hard it is getting a sitter around here."

"Uh-huh." I wash her bullshit down with another swig.

"But damn, it's good to have you back. Shit has been crazy 'round here since you and Python left. Hell, I even miss that psycho bitch he married."

"Married?"

She blinks. "You didn't know?"

I whip my head around to Diesel, who shrugs. "What? I didn't get an invite either."

Chantal was in full gossip mode. "Gurl, it was like one of those Taliban weddings you hear about on the news, there were so many bullets."

"Bullets?"

"Yeah. The Vice Lords found out about the wedding and came out to pay their respect. Pit Bull was one of the first to fall."

"No shit?"

"Yeah, girl. A lot of shit has popped off. You know Le-Shelle's ass was like in a coma for a hot minute at the hospital before Python wifed her. I guess her sister finally grew a set of balls or came off her meds while she was in the crazy house because she wet LeShelle's ass up good with like thirty-something stab wounds."

"I don't blame her," Jia hops back into the convo. "I would've taken a chunk out of her ass, too, if she had my ass jumped, raped, and then emptied a full clip into my nigga right in front of me."

Chantal picks back up. "But you know how LeShelle rolls. She paid the bitch back and burned down her sister's foster parents' crib. They died in the fire."

One of the news reports I saw in the hospital flashes in my head. "You're fucking with me."

"Wish I was. LeShelle took her girl Kookie with her, but she didn't make it out of that bitch either. Thing is the news media is saying she took a bullet to the chest. Now my ass wasn't there, but I'm willing to bet my rent money that LeShelle was behind that shit as well. You know Kookie and her man was dealing dirty behind Python's back."

"Damn. I really have missed out on a lot."

"Python and LeShelle are the real Bonnie and Clyde out in these streets." She pauses for a second. "Then again, I wouldn't sleep on Lucifer and Fat Ace either. They say his ass rose from the dead, too."

"WHAT?" Again, I whip around to Diesel, but his poker face is like granite. *What the fuck? Fat Ace—Mason—is alive?* It can't be. My mind zooms back to Dribbles. Did she lie to me? Does she know? *Somebody got to tell me something—and soon.*

Jia accepts Chantal's joint, tokes on it, and then passes it to me.

I wave it off a second time.

Jia frowns. "You don't wanna hit this?"

"Nah. I'm giving that shit up," I announce. "I told the Lord if he got me out that damn basement, that I'd change my ways. No more drugs, no more"—my gaze shoots over to an attentive Diesel—"foolishness. I'm a born-again Christian. No more sex outside of my marriage either. I think the big man still frowns on that. I ain't too sure, but I'll check—trust and believe, I'm gonna check."

The girls stare in stunned silence and then burst out laughing.

"Momma Peaches, you're crazy," Chantal adds, doubling over.

"Yeah," Jia chimes. "You giving up dick is like . . . a muthafucka giving up oxygen. It can't be done."

"So much for you bitches supporting my ass."

"That's a nice Christian thing to say," Chantal says, cracking them the hell up.

"Fuck y'all." I cough and clear my throat. "Forgive me, Lord."

Their laughter spreads.

"You're going to be saying *that* a lot," Chantal laughs.

I let them have their laugh as I glance around. The streets are dirtier than I remember. The grass is dead. People don't give a fuck about taking care of their shit no more. Then, I spot the next tornado twisting toward my crib: Josephine Holmes.

Aw shit. Here we go.

"You got some nerve showing your face back around here," she charges.

Chantal and Jia step back.

Calmly, I meet Josie's anger. "I'm going to warn your ass right now, don't bring your bullshit over here. I'm tryna forgive and forget."

"Fuck that shit. I *told* you to stay the hell away from Arzell. Now look what done happened. He's dead!"

"I like your nerve." I get up in her face, ready to punch the Holy Ghost into her ass. "That dead muthafucka got exactly what his ass had coming. Lil kidnapper hooked up with my crazy-ass sister, killed my parole officer and Rufus before tossing me down in that basement. I ain't shedding no tears over that nigga."

"None of that shit would've ever happened if you hadn't infected him into your geriatric pussy, you evil woman!"

"What the fuck are you complaining for? I cut his ass loose. It's not my fault he inherited your crazy genes." I catch myself from going completely off. "Diesel, get this trash off my porch," I shout. "I ain't been saved that damn long and I ain't too sure that the shit took yet."

Diesel steps in between us. "All right. That's enough. You done said what you needed to say." He hustles Josie off my porch.

I should've dusted her ass off when I caught her riding my husband's dick *in* my muthafucking bed all those years ago. Instead I put a bullet hole in that ass and let her live. *Big mistake.*

"This shit ain't over, Maybelline," Josie threatens, wagging her finger as Diesel escorts her out of the yard. "This shit ain't over by a *loooong* fuckin' shot!"

Chantal leans over and whispers, "Momma Peaches, is that your new man?"

"Nah, girl. That's my nephew Diesel, from Atlanta."

"Humph." Jia checks him out from head to toe. "I didn't know that you had a nephew that looks like *that!*"

"I know that's right," Chantal cosigns. "He got a girl?"

Turning, I give both of them a stern look. "Listen up and take this shit to heart: keep those Hot Pockets of y'all in your panties. He ain't for you."

Their faces sour.

"Damn, Momma P. I thought we were friends."

I glance back at Diesel as he looks up and flashes me a smile. "We are."

WHOOP! WHOOP!

All heads turn at the familiar sound of two police cars rolling down Shotgun Row.

"Well, that didn't take long," I mumble.

Once again, niggas part out of the way. This time there's no shouts of jubilation, but there's an awful lot of mean-mugging at the cops inside the cars. They stop at my curb behind Diesel's SUV and hop out. Captain Hydeya Hawkins.

Aww, shit.

As she approaches, her face keeps nagging at me. *Where in the hell do I know this bitch from?*

50

Hydeya

"Mrs. Goodson." I tilt my head forward.

"Captain Hawkins."

Her gaze locks onto me and I swear I can hear the wheels in her head squeak as she struggles to place my face.

"You look like you're on the mend."

"What can I say? It's good to be home. Now. Is there something that I can help you with, Captain?"

"It's just a friendly call. Mind if I come in and have a chat?"

Maybelline sucks in a long breath. "Do I have a choice?"

I cock my head with a silent, *What do you think?*

"Just what I thought." She shuffles toward the front door. "C'mon in."

We wait a few seconds while she digs for the key and unlocks the door. However, she doesn't immediately go inside.

"Is there a problem?" I ask.

"No. It's . . . the first time I've been in here since . . ."

"Oh." I chastise myself for the insensitivity.

Maybelline shakes it off and steps inside, but she inches slowly into the place as if she expects something or someone to jump out and attack. She isn't the kind of woman who would admit that her cage has been rattled. Whatever her sister did to her in that basement is going to haunt her for a long time.

"So what can I help you with now, Captain?"

"First thing first: have you heard from your nephew Terrell?"

"Not that shit again," she says. "He's dead."

"Missing," I correct, shifting my attention to Diesel. "Mr. Carver. Nice to see you again."

"It's nice to be seen."

We share a cynical smile. "What about you? Has your cousin reached out to you yet?"

"I own a smartphone, not a Ouija board."

"Funny."

"I was aiming for charming."

"You missed."

Unfazed, he winks at me. My bullshit detector is going crazy. I keep my gaze leveled on him, but there's a steel wall behind his pretty-boy eyes. "What about your other nephew?" I ask, turning my attention back to Maybelline. "Mason. When was the last time you heard from him?"

The question throws the older woman off her game because her poker face slips and she takes a seat in one of her armchairs.

"I haven't seen my nephew since he was six months old. I'm sure you know that."

I move on. "In your statement, you said that night of your escape was the first time you met Barbara Lewis."

"That's right."

"So you had no idea that she was Captain Melvin Johnson's sister-in-law?"

"How would I if I never knew the bitch? Sorry, Lord."

I frown. "I'm sorry. What?"

"I wasn't talking to you," she says, sighing. "Is that all?"

"And what's your relationship to the deceased Captain Johnson?"

"He was usually my arresting officer," she answers, irritated.

"That's it? He never gave you money or tried to help you out?"

She laughs. "And why in the hell would he do that?"

"Because he was Terrell's father, for one thing. Surely he contributed somehow. After all, you raised his son."

"What? Child, what the hell are you talking about?"

Her confusion and outrage is real. "You didn't know, did you?"

"Know what? Terrell's father's was some lowlife name Jerome something or another. I met him years ago."

"I don't know who you met, but according to the DNA tests, Captain Johnson was indeed Terrell Carver's father. And funny thing, Barbara's son, Mason Lewis, is a maternal match to Alice Carver. So I'm sure that you can connect the dots."

The room goes quiet.

"You have nothing to say to that?"

"I—I . . ."

Diesel squats down and throws a supportive arm around his aunt's shoulders. "This is an awful lot of information that you are dumping on her right now. Are you guys sure about all this?"

"Ninety-nine-point-nine percent, according to the tests." I cock my head at their performance. "So you never knew that your missing nephew was indeed the Vice Lord gangster known as Fat Ace?"

"Of course not," Maybelline snaps.

"Uh-huh. Anybody that's been in Memphis more than ten minutes knows that Fat Ace and Python have been beefing for years and here it turns out that they're brothers—and you mean to tell me that *no one* knew? I find that hard to believe."

"I don't care what you believe," Maybelline says. "Besides, all I have is your damn word anyway. A lie ain't nothing for a cop to tell."

Diesel stands. "You need to leave now."

"Humph." I turn away and glance around the house. "Nice place you have here." My gaze skids off knickknacks, candle holders, and picture frames. "I guess it doesn't matter anyway," I return to the subject at hand. "This past August, Mason Lewis was killed in a car crash." I turn and face her again. "The same crash that your *other* nephew, Terrell, supposedly died in. Are you starting to see the problem I'm having with all of this?"

"Leave," Maybelline says.

I ignore the request and then spot another picture sitting on an end table. I walk over and pick it up.

"What? Are you now going to start harassing me about my husband, too?" she complains.

I study the picture.

"Captain?" Diesel jars me back to the moment.

"He's in jail now, isn't he?" I ask.

"Why don't you tell me?" Maybelline says. "You know everything today."

"Getting out soon, right?"

"And?" Her impatience grows.

I sit the picture down and glance at Lieutenant Fowler. He's waiting for me to get to the point too. "At any rate. You can rest assured that all your weird family connections with the former captain will remain locked in the closet. The city isn't interested in digging through all the graves."

"Little girl, you came all the way to the wrong side of the tracks to tell me that? What? Is it a slow day at the office?"

"No. Something else brought me out here."

Maybelline huffs out a long breath as her patience thins.

"I can't believe I'm going to say this, but . . ." I suck in a deep breath. "It's regarding your *great* nephew . . . Christopher. He needs a home."

Treachery

51

Momma Peaches

"Lord Jesus, what am I gonna do with another baby?"

The question spins around in my mind like a damn tornado. It's brought me down to the Power of Prayer Baptist Church. Frankly, I'm a little nervous to stroll in here. As I walk toward the door, I keep glancing up at the sky, waiting for a bolt of lightning to strike my ass down for even thinking about stepping into the Lord's house.

Not only did I surprise myself by getting up at the booty-ass crack of dawn to get my first praise on, I shocked the shit out of all these pastel-wearing good Christians, too. The old biddies, with their tight lips and ginormous hats, are all clutching their pearls and fluttering their fans as if the devil has paid them a visit.

I even spot Josie's wide-as-a-brick-building ass huddled up with Pastor Rowlin Hayes. One would mistake her for the First Lady of the church, she so hugged up on him. I don't know who told her ass that yellow was her color, but they must've had cataracts 'cause the old trick looks like Big Bird after guzzling down six cases of Crisco. But at least her wig is on straight and her taco-meat edges are hidden.

I'm rocking an old throwback color: white. I want to show these bitches that I'm as pure as the fresh, driven snow in the

Lord. My curves may be a smaller since my abduction, but the body is still banging. Ms. Anna down at Fabdivas Hair Salon has hooked my shit up so that my split ends are gone, the gray is back to a 1B except for a small strip in my feathered bangs, and the face is beat with MAC's new winter line. If I rolled up in a club right now, I'd snatch every bitch's boyfriend and send them back home as men.

But that would be the old me.

Pastor Hayes extracts himself from Josie's tight clutch to walk over and welcome me. Josie's wrinkled face twists off and hits the pavement.

"Maybelline Carver," he exclaims, smiling. "Is it really you or are my old eyes deceiving me?"

"Hello, Ol' Ruff Dog. It's good to see you again." He takes my hand and brushes a welcoming kiss against my right cheek.

At the mention of his old street name, he looks up and then around. "Aww. C'mon. You know better than that. It's *Pastor* Hayes now—or Rowlin."

"Okay, Pastor. But I know what I know." Like a certain drive-by that took the Vice Lords' Dough Man out of the game back in the day. He and his crew did the hit right in front of the old G's daughter. Now *she* is the meanest bitch terrorizing the streets.

" 'When I was a child, I spoke like a child, I thought like a child, I reasoned like a child. When I became a man, I gave up childish ways.' First Corinthians three-eleven." His eyes twinkle. "Something tells me that the same is happening for you."

My spine stiffens. But he's right. He's *not* the same boy I used to know. There's not a trace of his past haunting his eyes or weighing down his shoulders. This is a man who is at peace with himself.

And bless my poor soul, I'm jealous.

"Welcome," he says. "I hope that you'll consider us to be your permanent church home." He kisses my other cheek and then strolls off to the next cluster of women who are tittering and batting their eyes.

I give the pastor another look. Ruff Dog aged pretty damn good. He's no longer the skinny and scrappy young buck who was so desperate to get on and prove himself to the "homies." His six-foot-two frame has filled out with the right ratio of muscles. His skin is as smooth as milk chocolate and his neatly groomed beard actually works for him.

"Don't even think about it," Josie hisses from behind me.

I turn to meet this bitch's narrowed gaze head-on. "You again."

She ignores my comment. "He is *waaay* too good for you."

"First of all, there's no such thing. Second, don't step to me like I won't chin-check your ass right here for the whole world."

"Humph. That's what I thought. This whole Christian thing is an act."

"Bitch, please." I wave her off. "I'd rather beat your ass and then ask for forgiveness than to pray daily for restraint. Now get out of my face with your bullshit. You're mad that you can't get a man unless you fall and sit on his ass—ain't nobody interested in mountain climbing every time they want to get a nut."

Josie's hands clinch at her sides.

I laugh in her face. "Girl, bye. You ain't about to do nothing." With that, I stroll off without a backwards glance. Looking around, I'll admit it's a nice church. It's larger than it looks from the outside: stained-glass windows, a ten-foot cross on a stone wall, mahogany pews, and ruby-red carpeting. A ninety-year-old usher hands me a program and then escorts me at a snail's pace to the front.

I still catch a lot of weird stares and hear the buzzing all around me, but I'm determined to ignore these bitches' foolishness. The men are a lot friendlier. From them, I get nods and smiling dentures—even a few winks. Poor Deacon James got smacked over the back of his head when his wife caught him grinning.

Chuckling, I suspect that church might be more fun than I thought. As service time draws near, the pews fill up. The choir kicks things off. The place sounds and feels like we're in the middle of a gospel concert. Cleo Blackmon steps forward and performs a solo.

At her song's powerful crescendo, there are tears rolling down her face. It comes to my memory that the girl lost her younger sister not too long ago. The pain of that loss is so evident on her face and in her voice that she has brought everyone to tears. I've heard on the streets that she is pursuing a music career, but I have never personally heard her sing before. The girl is a powerhouse—a ball of talent that makes me wonder how come she hasn't made it out of the hood yet.

"Amen. Amen," everyone praises as Cleo takes her place back with the rest of the choir.

The deacons breeze through the devotion and then Pastor Hayes takes his place at the lectern.

"Today, the Lord has laid it on my heart to read from Psalms eighty-two, three to four: 'Defend the poor and fatherless; do justice to the afflicted and needy. Rescue the weak and needy; deliver them from the hand of the wicked.' "

Christopher races to the front of my mind again.

Pastor Hayes flips through his Bible again. "Daniel four, twenty to twenty-two."

I try to keep up with the pages, but I have no idea where one book is to the next. I end up closing my new Bible and just sitting back and listening. I need a word from the man upstairs—*any* word. I'm tired and, God help me, I'm starting to feel my age seep into my bones. Raise another child? Do I even have it in me? *But Christopher has nowhere else to go.*

When Pastor calls those in need of prayer to meet him down at the altar, I spring up and rush to the front of the line.

"Just tell me what to do, Lord." My braided hands are weaved so tight that my knuckles turn white. If I'm honest with myself, I'll have to admit that I didn't do such a good job with Terrell. His ascendance to being Memphis's most wanted isn't exactly bumper sticker worthy.

Maybe it's a second chance.

I like the thought of that—a lot.

Pastor Hayes hallelujahs his way down the line of pitiful souls. A few before me get slapped on the forehead with oil and they pop up and take off running through the aisle before falling the fuck out. I'm more than a little freaked and wonder if it's too late for my ass to sneak back to my seat.

The pastor stops in front of me, and I can feel every eye in the place staring.

"The Lord sent us a special guest today. We should all thank Him for helping Sister Maybelline find her way here. We welcome you and pray that this will be the beginning of your spiritual journey."

A few flat "*amens*" chorus after his words.

The pastor looks me in the eyes, and for the first time in my life, I feel as if he sees me—through the bullshit, the regrets and mistakes—past the hard shell, the street smarts, the gutter instincts, and the legions of men that have been in and out of my bed.

"Sister Maybelline, the Lord is telling me that he hears your prayers and he wants you to know that all your toils have not been in vain. He knows your heart and that you are more than equipped to handle the new challenges ahead of you. You have a charge to keep—as we all do as steward of the Lord. Does this make sense to you?"

I nod as tears spill over my eyes.

He reaches for the oil. "Sister Maybelline, by the authority of the Lord Jesus Christ, I lay my hands upon your head, seal and confirm the anointing, and hereby pronounce a blessing upon your life, that your new charge is a blessing given by the Father, son, and Holy Spirit. Amen." His palm slaps my forehead and a bright light knocks me back.

When I come to, people are helping me back to my seat.

Embarrassed, I pull it together, but there's no doubt that my shoulders, my heart, and my burdens are considerably lighter. I know what I have to do now. I have to bring Christopher home.

For the rest of the service, I clap and sing along with the rest of the congregation. As I leave the church, the pastor hollers. out for me again.

"Sister Maybelline, I sure hope that you enjoyed the service this morning," he says, grinning.

"I sure did," I assure him.

"Does that mean that we'll see you again?"

"You just might."

"Glad to hear it." He pats me on my hand and then drifts off to talk to the other church members.

I turn away, but before I can take another step, I feel someone burning a hole into the side of my head. When I look to the right, my gaze crashes into Josie's big yellow ass. "I can't do nothing with that bitch," I mumble under my breath.

I remain in a good mood for the rest of the ride home, but shit quickly falls apart when I spot the white woman sitting on my porch. "Dribbles."

52

Shariffa

Tupelo

Lynch is safe. I'm thankful for that shit, but I'm going out of my muthafuckin' mind stashed out here in East Bumble-Fuck Egypt. Ain't shit to do but sit and wait, but I'm not sure what the hell I'm waiting for. It can't possibly be for Lucifer to calm the fuck down and forget this damn vendetta shit— 'cause that's never gonna happen.

The shit is fuckin' with me. I haven't been able to sleep since I walked into Shacardi's crib and saw her and Brika's heads spinning around like party favors. If Lynch were any kind of man, he would have handled this shit by now—but *nooo*. I had to lock down the weakest nigga in the game. Instead of fighting, Lynch stashes me and Trigger out here—until further notice.

I'm biding my time and biting my tongue. These two sneaky muthafuckas still don't know I got their fucking number. I'll play that card when the time is right.

Meanwhile, Trigger ain't said more than a couple of sentences since we got here. You'd think that I were sneaking around and fucking *her* husband. Clearly she's still pissed and blames me for this situation, but I ain't got time to be dealing with this bitch lost in her feelings.

This morning, I'm up before the sunrise. I can't shut my mind off in thinking of ways to get outta this mess, but all roads lead to one conclusion: kill Lucifer. How in the fuck am I going to get close enough to touch that bitch?

There's got to be some kind of way.

To make shit worse, I'm missing my babies. Lynch refuses to bring them out here and I know that his momma is talking mad shit in his ear and dancing on the ceiling now that my ass is out of the house. It's crazy how everything has flipped in such a short time. A month ago, the world was at my feet.

Now it's gone.

Again.

I want it back. *If I can't be boss, then I'd rather not even be in the game.*

A few hours later, the sun catches up with me and I shuffle out to the kitchen. Trigger is already there, pouring a bowl of cereal.

"Morning."

Trigger cuts me a "drop dead, bitch" look.

I cross my arms and square my shoulders. "Problem?"

"Oh. I gotta problem, all right: you." Trigger jerks toward me with her hands on her hips. "How about you, *for once,* shut the fuck up?"

I rake my gaze over this bitch. "Hold the fuck up. Who are you tryna check?"

"I'm looking at you, ain't I?"

"You fuckin' raggedy-ass ho!" I chest-bump this bum-bitch. "You don't want to start shit with me today. Please trust and believe."

"Why? Whatchu gonna do?" She bumps me back.

"Bitch!" I shove her, wishing I had my gat on me.

"I hate the day I ever met your ass," Trigger sneers. "Your fake-flagging ass has wrecked our set like a nuclear bomb. *I* was the one to convince the girls to give you a chance. *I* got them mixed up in your bullshit, and now they're all fuckin' dead."

"I don't remember holding a gun to your head and I certainly don't remember your ass fucking Bishop in that backroom like a twenty-dollar trick-ho as being part of the plan either. You do remember that it was *you* who texted the go signal? You could've squashed that hit at any fuckin' time. Don't lay all this shit on me. That hit wasn't your first rodeo ride. You know bodies can drop on any given hit. So fuck you, you self-righteous, chinky-bitch!" I sock her in the mouth, catching her off guard.

Blood explodes from her nose and mouth.

Trigger springs and screams like a banshee as she launches forward and fills both fists with my hair.

"Aaaagh!" My hands go wild while she struggles to snatch my ass bald-headed. I get two good grips of her hair as well and yank her shit with all my might. We spin around into the living room and then flip over the back of the sofa and crash onto the glass coffee table. Still, even among a bed of glass, neither of us releases our hold.

Pain pierces every inch of my body as glass stabs and digs, but I hang on to this bitch with my life. Losing this fight is not a fuckin' option. Plugs of Trigger's hair come loose in my hand.

"You fuckin', bitch!" Trigger renews her efforts, and when a clump of my shit is snatched out, I punch this heifer again.

Crack!

Her jaw shatters as her head rocks to the left. My satisfaction over my small victory only lasts for a few seconds until Trigger delivers a right hook that sends me flying. I hit an end table and knock over a lamp that misses bashing my head by a single inch.

Trigger kicks me in the gut. My breath rushes from my lungs, which then have a hard time filling back up.

"You crabby-ass bitch! Nobody wants you," Trigger hisses, rearing her foot back to deliver another blow.

I roll over and catch her foot in midair, and then twist that shit so hard that it knocks her on her ass. I launch to pin her ass down, but the bitch is fast. She rolls toward an old fireplace. I chase after her, grab one of the iron pokers, and swing that muthafucka like Tiger Woods's ex-wife until it whacks Trigger's head.

Clunk!

The bitch drops—and then a large pool of blood seeps out of the side of her head.

"Oh shit!" I drop the poker. "What the fuck did I just do?"

53

Momma Peaches

"The devil is a liar!" I wave my hand in the air, hoping I have a little bit of juice to call on Jesus to have this blue-eyed devil on my porch rebuked. But when I open my eyes this bitch is still there, twitching and looking around.

"Ms. Maybelline, I need to talk to you," Dribbles says.

"Unless you got my nephew here with you, then we ain't got shit to talk about."

"So you know?"

"Girl, bye." I march past her to go up the stairs.

Hardheaded, Dribbles does a U-turn to follow me. "Look. I know that you're angry—"

"You goddamn right, I'm angry with your child-kidnapping, lying ass. I don't know what the fuck you're doing here, but I know your ass best get ghost by the time I get in this damn door. I ain't been saved long enough to resist the temptation of committing a homicide—even on the Lord's day." I jam my key into the lock and rush inside the house. I attempt to slam the door, but Dribbles slips her foot inside to block it.

"Goddamn it, bitch. What the hell is it going to take for you to get a muthafuckin' clue?" I glance up and down Shotgun Row. "This whole neighborhood is going to hell if I can't even be safe from a white bitch harassing the fuck out of me."

Chantal's curious voice floats over from the next-door porch. "Momma Peaches, is everything all right?"

I open my mouth, but Dribbles answers instead.

"Everything is fine. Mind your own damn business," she snaps.

"Oh, no, your ass didn't," Chantal shouts. "Who in the fuck do you think your pale, pasty ass is?"

"Bitch, get yo life." Dribbles gives her the middle finger and then swivels her neck like a black girl.

Surprised by the white girl's balls, I settle a fist on my left hip and cock my neck to three o'clock. Under different circumstances, I might've liked her style.

"Oh, really?" Chantal challenges. "You wait your ass right there, you fake-ass wigga! I got something for you."

Strapping on my invisible Captain Save-a-Ho cape, I grab Dribbles by the wrist and snatch her inside. "Girl, get your ass in here before you get white-chalked on my porch."

Dribbles's face splits with a triumphant smile.

I slam the door. "I don't know what the hell you're smiling for. Just because I don't want a dead bitch at my front door doesn't mean that a damn thing has changed between us."

"I'm hoping what I got to say *will* change things between us."

"Uh-huh." I plop my Bible down on the dining room table and then make a beeline toward the kitchen for some fresh squeezed lemonade—without the Grey Goose. *Lord, I miss my Grey Goose.* "I'm waiting," I tell her, pulling the pitcher out from the fridge. "I ain't got all day and you ain't welcome here past two more minutes."

She nods. "First: I didn't lie to you. We all thought Mason was dead. We even had a funeral for him."

"Uh-huh."

"Honestly. The day Raymond drove me home from the

hospital, we learned the truth. I've been trying to reach you, but once you left the hospital I didn't know how. And now, I gotta right this whole horrible mess somehow. It's too late with Alice, but . . . maybe I set things right with you. That is if you'd let me."

My heart skips a beat. "You mean . . . he wants to meet me?"

"I . . . haven't asked him yet. It might take some time to work on him, but I'm sure that I can make it happen."

God really is the king of second chances. Overwhelmed, I throw my arms around this woman. It takes me a while to re-alize that my ass is bawling like a newborn baby.

Me.

I'm embarrassed, but I've prayed and waited for so long for this moment. I've always wanted to believe that he was out there and I've gone from thinking he was dead to now know-ing who he is and him being alive—to this: meeting him.

To her credit, Dribbles lets me hang on to her neck until I'm good and damn ready to let go. When I get control of my-self, I step back. "Sorry. I'm so . . ."

"You have nothing to be sorry for. This is *loooong* overdue."

She takes my hands. "We need to set a time and place."

I nod along and then remember someone else. "Wait." I keep a tight hold on her hands. "What about Terrell?"

She tenses.

"Terrell is alive?"

I nod. "He'll want to meet him. He now knows who he is and he's dying to reach out."

Dribbles hesitates. After all, it's not every day one plans to get two rival gang leaders to meet in private—but this is a unique situation. "I don't know if—"

"You don't understand. Terrell's been torn up for years over the loss of his baby brother—and all this time, he never knew who he was—of course, none of us did." When she shakes her head, I persist. "If we can get these two together, not only can we heal this family, but we can put an end to a long, bloody war between the gangs."

Dribbles fidgets. "The thing is, I don't think I can get him to come if he knows Terrell will be there," she says.

I let that shit hang in the air for a minute while I think on it. "Well, then, don't tell him. It'll be a surprise."

54

Sharitta

This bitch can't be dead. I can't be having that kind of bad luck.

Hot and panting like a muthafucka, I inch closer to Trigger's motionless body. "Girl, get up." I nudge her with my toe. She doesn't move.

Holy fucking shit. "Why the fuck did you have to fucking *push* me?" I shout. "All I wanted was for you bitches to accept me. I did *everything.* I had y'all's back. I put money in your pocket. If y'all had listened and played your fucking positions, none of this shit would've happened. We could be running *all* this shit instead of sitting on the sidelines, waiting and watching for the Gangster Disciples and the Vice Lords to regroup, recruit, and rearm." An embarrassing sob wrenches from my throat.

Storming away, I stomp barefoot across broken glass to a bottle of Hennessy XO. I twist off the top and take it to the head. The shit kicks back and burns my throat, but I guzzle down half the bottle without losing a drop and coming up for air. I lean one hand against the wall and wait for the alcohol to hit my bloodstream.

Think. Think. Think.

I look at Trigger again and my anger simmers. The right thing to do is to call Lynch and tell him that I've screwed up—

again. But how is he going to take my killing his side bitch—when I'm not sure if *I'm* the side bitch?

I hit the bottle again. My new fuckin' life is a lie. The Grape Street Crips ain't got no love for me. Never have and never will—unless I do something that will put me back on top. Something so that no nigga could spit out of the side of their neck to deny my place as a boss bitch.

The Hennessy kicks in and gives me a great idea.

I head into the kitchen and grab a butcher knife. Fuck. How hard can it be to chop a bitch up? Lucifer does this shit all day every day.

Knife in hand, I march back to Trigger's body and tower over her. I suck in several deep breaths to get my nerve up, but beads of sweat pop out along my hairline. I don't know where to start this shit, and images of the bloody scene at Crunk's Ink and Shacardi's crib flashes in my head.

"All right. I can do this," I give myself a pep talk. Using my foot, I roll the bitch over.

Suddenly, Trigger springs up and grabs my foot.

Stunned, I scream as I fall forward. In the next nano-second, I don't think. I react. Swinging the butcher's knife like a baseball bat, I slice Trigger's throat so deep that blood sprays from her shit like a water hydrant.

Her eyes widen as she clutches her throat to plug the slit.

I roll and then scoot across broken glass to get away.

Trigger makes a horrible gurgling noise and falls back among the shards of glass. Her body rattles around as death steals over her. She twitches for forever until her hands fall away and she stares sightlessly up at the ceiling.

I sit and watch the bitch for about an hour with a death grip on the butcher knife and sober as a muthafucka. Realizing I needed to light a fire under my ass if I'm going to pull this shit off, I gather the courage to stand back up. When I approach her ass this time, it's as slow as a fuckin' snail. I ain't down for another clip of *Friday the 13th*. If the bitch is dead, I prefer that her ass stay that way.

After double and triple checking the shit, I relax. "All right, bitch. Let's do this shit again." I get down on my knees and raise the knife. I hesitate another second and then bring the knife down as hard as I can.

Whack!

But the shit ain't enough and I have to keep whacking on her neck until her head finally detaches.

After that shit, I'm hit with a surge of bloodlust that is stronger than any high I've ever been on. It takes a while to hack up the rest, but during the whole time, I don't see Trigger. I see my next target: Lucifer.

55

Ta'Shara

*P*OW! *POW! POW! POW!*

Fingers numb, I peel open my eyes to see that I've missed all four can targets seven yards away. "Shit."

Profit chuckles as he comes up behind me. "Baby, I hate to say it, but that was pretty damn pathetic."

Sighing, I lower the .45. LeShelle remains a threat and I need to prepare for any and everything. Judging by today's target practice, I have a long way to go.

"Here. Let's go again." Profit wraps his arms around mine to help my aim. "Wait. Wait. Not so tight. Now settle the pistol between the web of your thumb and your forefinger like this." He repositions the gun. "Now get your hand as high as possible. This is going to give you more control. Got it?"

"Got it."

"In order to have a neutral stance, you'll need to rotate your weak hand's wrist forward over your strong hand. This will help your aim, handle the recoil and prevent your fingers from going numb."

"I wish you would've told me that twenty minutes ago," I complain.

"Well. Sometimes, you have to learn things the hard way."

When he chuckles, his chest rumbles against my back and I smile.

"You're not concentrating."

"Sorry." I wipe the smile off my face. "What do I do next?" I ask.

"When you're about to shoot, I want you to lean your body forward. Dominant elbow up." He pushes it higher. "And your support or weak elbow down." He drops his hands from around me. "Take aim of your first target and fire when you're ready."

POW!

The tin can jumps and flips into the air.

"I did it," I gasp and then look back over my shoulder.

His grin spreads from ear to ear. "Again."

I grip the slider and discard a cartridge, replay all Profit's tips in my head, take aim, and *POW!*

Another tin can jumps and flips even higher into the air.

I click the safety on and then let out a loud whoop and fist pump.

"By George, I think she got it." Profit laughs.

We stay at it out here in this big ass empty field in the middle of nowhere for the next five hours. We cover shooting on the move, moving targets, and reloads. By the time we finish, I'm tired, but thrilled.

"I never knew that shooting could be so much fun."

"That's because nobody is shooting back." Profit laughs. "Trust me. That shit ain't no fun."

The obvious truth of his words shaves a couple of inches off of my smile, especially since LeShelle has a few more years of practice.

We climb back into Profit's ride and he reads me like an open book. "Don't worry about it." He leans over and hugs me. "I'm going to make sure that you can handle yourself on these streets like a boss."

"Like Lucifer?"

He pauses. "No offense, but there ain't nobody like Lucifer's sick ass."

"That's probably true."

"No. It *is* true." He starts the car and drives us home.

Before we reach the front step, another car pulls in behind
Profit's.

"Who the fuck are these muthafuckas?" Profit mumbles
under his breath.

"Hell. If you don't know then I don't know," I tell him.

Two seconds later, we have our answer as Mackenzie and
Romil climb out of their vehicle *Dukes of Hazzard* style.

"Yo, Ta'Shara," Mackenzie shouts. "What's up, girl?"

"Mack?" I ask incredulous, stepping from Profit's side.
"What are you doing here?"

Still grinning like fools with beer bottles in their hands,
Mack and Romil approach me.

"What do you mean what are we doing here?" Mackenzie
says. "As soon as we got out, we knew that we *had* to come and
check up on our new girl." She reaches me and swings one of
her long arms around my neck for an awkward hug. "It's time
for you to be officially welcomed into the Flower family."

On cue, a tailgate of music-blaring cars rolls down Ruby
Cove and then pulls up into our driveway. The black-and-
gold-dressed divas spill out of their cars and are equally as
rowdy and . . . drunk as Mack and Romil.

I don't know what to make of what's unfolding, but I'm
touched—so much so that tears burn the backs of my eyes.

"All right! Let's get this party started," shouts one girl, who
is helping to roll a keg of beer toward the house.

"YEAH!" a unified shout goes up.

I twist my neck around in Mackenzie's awkward embrace
to see Profit's stunned expression.

Minutes later, the house is wall-to-wall with Flowers.

Music pours from the Bose speakers while chicks fill and raid the refrigerator.

Profit isn't given a chance to crash the party. The Flowers simply direct him out of his own house.

"Sorry," they sing. "But this is a Flowers-*only* party."

My baby tosses me a look. I nod and smile to let him know that I'm okay with being alone with my new friends, or rather . . . family.

He tosses up deuces a second before the door is slammed in his face. Stunned, he then pops over to the side glass panes, but the girls unknot the thin, black curtains and block his view.

I laugh.

"I don't think your boo trusts us," Mackenzie says, plopping onto the couch. "I hope he doesn't think that we're a bad influence."

"Maybe I should have at least introduced you to him before y'all threw him out."

"Pshaw!" She waves that off. "We know that nigga. It's *you* that everyone wants to get to know." She pulls out a baggie of pre-rolled blunts. "You smoke?"

Shrugging, I figure a lie is needed. "Yeah."

"Oh yeah?" Mackenzie smirks.

Romil shakes her head. "Guess I lost that bet. I had you pegged as an all-around good girl."

Embarrassed, my face heats. "You were wrong."

"Don't let the wide-eyed deer-in-headlights looks fool you," a pretty plus-size girl says crossing her arms. "You are the one that sliced up my girl Qiana, right?"

The air chokes off in my lungs as a cluster of women that are within earshot rubber-necks to see if something is going to jump-off.

"Holy shit," Mackenzie laughs. "That shit was *you?*"

Tension rises as everyone waits for my answer. "Hey, the

bitch came at me sideways and I did what I had to do," I say matter-of-factly, bracing for a fight. I'm new to the gang life, but I know that you never let muthafuckas see you sweat.

Romil giggles.

Mackenzie laughs.

The big-boned chick stares me down, evaluating.

"Yeah," another bitch steps up. "A bitch got to do what a bitch gotta do, right?"

The surrounding Flowers crackle with laughter.

The tension disappears.

"Yo, the name is Dime." She thrusts out her hand.

"Ta'Shara," I say, accepting the handshake.

"Welcome to the family," she says and then turns to introduce me to her two shadows.

"I'm Emerald," one says, flashing me with one of her gold-capped teeth.

"Nisha," the other says. Her whole body looks like a tapestry of cartoonish tattoos.

The big girl is still mean-mugging.

"Ah, fuck, GG. Loosen up," Mackenzie says, flicking on a lighter. "You know that Qiana prances around this bitch like her shit don't stink—she rides on her brother's rep and abuses the privilege. She needed someone to take her ass down a couple of notches." She tokes on the blunt and then passes it over to me.

I hesitate, but then take the burning blunt from her fingers and put it to my lips. I didn't *completely* lie. Essence got me to try it once, but the episode ended with me turning every shade of green in a crayon box while I coughed up a lung.

Instead of going full hog, I sip this shit into my lungs slow and steady, hold it, and then offer it to GG as a peace offering.

She eyeballs me like she's trying to decipher my DNA, but then reaches for the joint as I let the smoke stream through my lips.

"That's my girl." Mackenzie pounds my back. "I knew that you'd be a cool-ass bitch."

I smile, but it feels like I'm doing it in slow motion. My thoughts sound like Charlie Brown's teacher. *Off one puff? What the hell is in this shit?*

"Oh, you feeling that shit, ain't cha?" I think Mackenzie says.

To me, she sounds like a garbled mess, too.

Mack looks to GG "Girl, fix your face. The only reason that you're even being cool with Qiana is because you're still trying to get Tombstone to put a ring on it—and that shit ain't *never* gonna happen."

GG has had enough and stalks right out of the door.

"Aww." I poke out my bottom lip. "She's mad."

Mackenzie waves it off. "Then she needs to scratch her ass and get glad. Some bitches can't handle the truth."

The blunt is passed back to me and I hit it again. No shit . . . my brain cells melt, but I'm also tingling all over. It's that *good* kind of tingle.

More Flowers cram into the house. Their names flow in one ear and out of the other, but I keep smiling, laughing, and even dancing until the day melts into night.

"We're out of beer," Dime shouts, jarring me awake. *When in the hell did I pass out?* I'm plastered on the sofa and it takes everything I have to peel myself off.

Bitches are still partying, laughing, and having a good time.

"Who wants to ride out and get some more beer?" Dime asks, jiggling her keys.

"I'll go," I say. "Let me splash some water on my face first." My foot hits the edge of the coffee table and I almost face-plant into the carpet. I laugh at my own clumsiness.

"Girl, hurry up if you're coming."

"Two minutes." I rush to the bathroom and quickly douse my face. When I look into the mirror, I grin at my reflection. "You're *soooo* fucked up right now."

BANG! BANG! BANG!

"Damn, girl. You coming?" Dime shouts.

"Yeah." I turn off the water and then notice one of my pill bottles on the counter. I know these bitches ain't going through my shit. Opening the bottle, there's only two pills left. *Muthafuckas!*

I pop the last pills, scoop a handful of water, and roll out.

"It's about damn time," Dime complains, smiling and looping an arm around my neck.

Her girls Emerald and Nisha fall in line behind us.

"Yo, T, where are you going?" Mack asks, wiping powder from her nostrils.

"She's going with us on a beer run. We'll be back before you miss her."

I wave bye and then climb into the backseat of Dime's black Toyota. As she pulls out, I glance across the street to see Qiana glaring at me in a fucking dress, all dolled up. Laughing, I flash her a bird as Dime peels off.

56

Qiana

*F*ucking bitch.

I'm caught out here looking thirsty as that Gangster Disciple trash speeds off with Dime and her girls. What the fuck is going on? Did I wake up today in the Twilight Zone?

GG told me about the party a few hours ago, but I didn't believe—couldn't believe it. What the hell did Ta'Shara do to get her spot to blow up with the Flowers? Why is this bitch still a thorn in my side?

Her ass has got to go.

A pair of headlights jars me out of my revenge fantasy.

Diesel pulls up in a sweet silver Mercedes that has me forgiving his ass before he even gets out of the car.

"You look good," he says, exiting his ride with a single yellow rose. As usual, he's GQ fine in all white and exuding a swagger that's out of control.

"I should tell you to go to hell." I cross my arms. "You're more than an hour late."

"You could," he agrees, approaching. "But you won't."

"Oh?" *Cocky son of a bitch.* "And why is that?"

He extends the rose so that its soft floral scent wafts under my nose. "Because you know that by the end of the night you'll be in my bed."

Our eyes lock and my pussy thumps. "You're lucky I still like your pretty ass," I sass, accepting the rose while still throwing him some shade.

A wide smile breaks across his face. "Shall we?" He offers me his arm.

I've never had a nigga treat me like a lady before. I return his big Kool-Aid smile with one of my own and loop my arm through his. Once I'm settled into my seat, Diesel closes the door and then rushes around. "I love your new ride," I tell him, while melting into the leather.

"When you're with me—expect nothing but the best." He winks and starts up the car. "I was hoping to see your brother again."

"Why?"

He shrugs. "We got off on the wrong foot."

"Since you're not from around here, there's no other foot you're gonna start on."

"Humph. Too bad. He seems like a good nigga to know given what you've told me about him—and the chick he works for."

"Ha! Lucifer? I don't think so."

"Why is that?"

"Charlie is tough, but Lucifer is on a whole 'nother level. That bitch don't trust nobody other than Fat Ace and her brother—but her brother is dead so . . ." I shrug.

"Well, I'm looking to make new friends and I can be pretty charming."

I scoff. "You'd have better luck tryna charm a black mamba.

Diesel laughs. "She sounds intriguing. You gotta tell me more about her."

I slice a look at him. "Why?"

"I don't know. I keep hearing her name floating around town. It ain't too often when you hear about a woman that scares most niggas."

"And you're not?"
He meets my gaze. "I'm never scared."
I have no problem believing that.
"Are you scared?" he asks.
"Damn straight. I'm not crazy."

57

Ta'Shara

I'm high as hell.

As I ride in the backseat of Dime's car with the windows down, the night's air feels incredible against my face and hair. I needed this night. I'm so tired of the bullshit that is my life.

"You look fucked up," Dime says, staring at me through the rearview mirror.

"That's because I am."

The girls laugh. A few minutes later, we arrive at Hemp's Liquor Store and we file out the car, giggling and laughing about some dumb shit that I barely understand. However, I am aware when we step into the store that the whole vibe changes. I don't know why, but when I glance around, an Arab man behind the counter is glaring at us like we just did something to his momma.

"Why the fuck are you staring so hard?" I ask, irritated.

My girls snicker.

The dude's inky-black eyes glare back.

"Whatever." I walk off, but Dime is bothered by the man's silence.

"Yo, man. Didn't my girl just ask you a question?" She stalks toward him, face rude as hell.

"Hey. I don't want no trouble." He inches to the left. "Either buy something or get out."

Emerald and Nisha come away from the cooler with their hands filled to the max with cases of beer.

"What's going on?" Nisha asks.

Dime ignores them and goes in on the clerk. "Nah. Nah. You need to apologize to my girl. She didn't do shit to you, man."

"Fuck you, black bitch." He reaches for something.

Dime rush forward, but Muhammad jerks up a shotgun that puts a pause in all of our asses.

"You black, nigga bitches get the fuck out of my store."

"Say what?" Emerald and Nisha dropped their cases and as they crash to the floor, dude cocks his shit and fires at Nisha and Emerald.

BOOM! Click. Click. BOOM!

My gun is in my hand before my brain understands what I'm doing.

POW! First bullet hits his right shoulder.

POW! Second bullet blasts a hole in his throat.

POW! Third bullet splatters his brains all over the cartons of cigarettes behind him seconds before his body crashes to the floor.

"Holy shit!" Dime finally comes up with her weapon, but the shit is over. "Goddamn, T! Fuck!" She turns around and. races over to her girls. "*Fuuuccck!*"

Emerald and Nisha's wide, dead eyes stare up into nothing. There's blood everywhere.

"We gotta get the fuck out of here," she says, shaking her head and now backing away from them.

I'm too stunned to move.

"Did you hear me, bitch? C'mon." Dime grabs me by the arm and jerks me toward the door.

My feet move, but my head is fucked up, replaying everything that just happened in slow motion. "I killed him. I'm a murderer."

"No shit. Get in the fuckin' car!"

58

Qiana

When we pull up to Club Diesel, there's a line wrapped around the building. This isn't the run-of-the-mill hood joint with strippers sliding down poles. The spot is smack dab in the middle of Beale Street and it's clear that Diesel has struck gold.

"You fancy, huh?" I ask when he opens my door.

"Classy," he corrects. "I told you. Nothing but the best with me."

"I see that." I'm glad I chose the snake-print Michael Kors dress instead of that gold Dereon that Li'l Bit almost talked me into. Inside, my jaw hits the floor at the multi-level club that's packed wall-to-wall with moneyed hustlers and glittering bougie bitches. Every two steps, some nigga calls out or latches onto Diesel for face time.

I'm out of place and struggling not to show it. I cling tightly to Diesel's arm and mean-mug every bitch who comes near him.

When we make it to VIP, there's a bottle service waiting and a small army of niggas hugged up in a booth.

"D, my nigga." A man cheeses, standing to slap palms and bump shoulders. "We were just wondering when you were gonna show up, man." His eyes shift to me.

"Yo, man. Let me introduce you to my lady, Qiana. Qiana,

these here are my road dawgs, Madd, Beast, Bullet, and Matrix."

"Hey." I smile and then shift my attention to the gold diggers draped on their arms. They all look at me like I'm something caught on the bottom of their shoes. Then I recognize the Amazon bitch who showed up at Diesel's place the morning after our first hookup. Her ass was so hugged up on him that I chased her out of the house, shooting. There's no love lost between us.

Everybody nods one by one while assessing me. I put on a brave face.

"Have a seat," Diesel instructs.

Once nestled into the leather booth, I glance around like a kid on Christmas morning. "You're a real muthafuckin' boss, aren't you?"

"I thought you knew that shit." He laughs, reaching for two glasses. "What'll you have?"

"The XO."

His brows jump before he reaches for the Henney. "My baby don't play, huh?"

I smile. "I thought *you* knew that shit."

Someone taps Madd on the shoulder and then whispers in his ear. A few seconds later, Madd whispers into Beast's ear. The whispering game circles around the table until Matrix whispers to Diesel.

My nosey ass gets self-conscious, but then I follow the track of Diesel's gaze to the lower level to see who has captured his attention.

Captain Hydeya Hawkins.

"Fuck." I shrink into my seat.

Diesel looks at me. "You know her?"

"We've met." *Did she follow me here? Is she on to me? Does she know where I stashed Jayson?* My heart pounds a mile a minute, but all I can do is watch her. She actually cleans up well. Her short black dress shows off curves and a long pair of legs that I hadn't previously noticed. Her iron-straight hair isn't snatched back into a ponytail either. Instead, it hangs comfortably past her shoulders. She's pretty—and the hot Italian nigga who's whispering in her ear is fine, too. *Husband?*

"Keep an eye on them," Diesel tells Bullet.

"You got it, boss." Bullet leaves the table. However, his side bitch stays put and it makes me wonder who the women at the table are really here for.

"How are you liking everything?" Diesel asks, handing me my drink.

"I'm impressed."

"So you think that you can roll with your man a little while longer?"

The plastic bougie bitches all give me the stink face.

I smile and take a sip of my drink. "I roll anywhere you want me to," I say. *Fuck Profit. His ass ain't got Ta'Shara caked up like this.*

The club lights flicker as the MC steps onto the main stage.

"Ladies and gentlemen, welcome to Club Diesel."

A raucous cheer goes up.

"I want everyone to take a moment to give a hand to the big man himself opening the doors here tonight. Everybody put your hands together for DIESEL!"

Diesel stands and the club erupts into applause.

Beaming, I join in. *I wish my girls could see me now.*

"We got a good show for you tonight. Coming to the stage is a beautiful songstress who hails from right here in Memphis. Please put your hands together for the lovely and talented, Miss Cleo Blackmon!"

Another round of applause ensues as the house lights dim and the spotlight tracks a tall, willowy, and graceful beauty as she steps onto the stage. Immediately, male catcalls go out with a few whistles and cheers.

Diesel turns away from my ear and stares at the beauty on the stage—hard.

The music starts.

> *I lost the use of my heart*
> *but I'm still alive*

Diesel's whole vibe changes. He's in a trance.

Jealousy uncoils in the pit of my gut as my gaze shifts to the soulful beauty crooning Sade. She's an exquisite black Barbie who could have any man she wanted in this whole joint and she's letting every trick in here know it. *Bitch.*

My gaze zooms back to Diesel. He's wide open and doesn't even know it.

Waving Madd to his side, Diesel then turns and whispers something into his ear.

Madd nods and then disappears.

It doesn't take a genius to know what their brief convo was about. I inch closer in an attempt to draw *my man's* attention back to me, but the shit doesn't work. He pulls away—not far, but enough for me to notice.

Simmering, I shoot my gaze back to Miss Cleo. *This bitch has got to go.*

59

Cleo

At the end of my forty-five-minute set, I have the crowd in the palm of my hand. I'm coasting on an incredible high that only a good performance can give. I exit the stage still bowing and blowing kisses to the crowd.

"You did it, baby. You were wonderful," Kalief shouts, sweeping me up into his arms and swinging me around.

"They loved you."

Laughing, I wrap my arms around him and enjoy the moment. It's rare that a performance goes off without a hitch—at least for me. Microphone problems, lighting issues, band screw-ups, I have experienced it all. But not tonight.

"Ms. Blackmon?" A big brick building of a man approaches as Kalief sets me back down.

"Yes?"

"The boss man would like to see you."

"The boss—Diesel?" I ask.

He nods.

Giddy, I clutch Kalief's hand. "This is it," I squeal.

"I told you, baby, that he was going to love you. C'mon."

The brick building throws up a hand and blocks Kalief. "He only wants the singer."

"But I'm her manager, Madd. How is he *not* going to see me?"

"Orders are orders."

"Orders?" I rock my neck to the side and park my hands on my hips. "Well, you can tell Mr. Boss man that I don't take orders. He got me confused."

Madd's brows jump.

"Baby." Kalief pulls me to the side.

"Nah. Don't 'baby' me. Did you hear what he just said?"

"I know. I know. It's cool. Calm down." He takes a breath and flashes a smile at Madd. "Just give us a second."

Madd shrugs and turns his back.

"You need to go with him."

"What? He just disrespected—"

"That shit don't matter right now. We came here to get Diesel's attention. You did that—now let's not go ego trippin' and ruin this shit for us. My man Diesel is a powerful cat and he can get the moves we need done. You hear me?"

"Your man? If y'all so damn tight then why can't you come with me to talk to him?"

"See? You're worried about the wrong muthafuckin' thing. We need this."

"He ain't the only muthafucka with power. Fuck him."

"Fuck him?" Kalief blinks and then snatches my arm so hard that it's a miracle my shit doesn't break off.

"Ow. You're hurting me."

"Good. That means that I got your fuckin' attention. Now kill the damn attitude. I told you how important this shit is. We don't have a line of muthafuckas banging down our door right now. We got to make moves and this is the nigga that's gonna make it happen."

"But—"

"Nah. There ain't no fuckin' 'buts.' You need to do this.

And you need to make a good impression with my man. Got it?" He twists my arm, and I bite back a second protest.

"Got it?" Kalief presses.

"What aren't you telling me," I ask through clenched teeth.

He glares and drives us a few more inches toward World War III. At long last, he releases my arm. "Fuck, Cleo. Just do this shit for me. Why does it always got to be a fight with you?"

"Why can't you just be straight and tell me what's really up with you and this nigga?"

"I done told you. This is about getting you on. We're close. I know it. I can feel it."

He's lying.

"Just do this—okay?"

I cross my arms.

"Please? For me." He steps closer and gently brushes a kiss against my lips.

Sighing, I give in. "All right. I'll do it."

"Good." His smile explodes back across his lips. "I'll wait for you in your dressing room. I'm gonna need to know the blow-by-blow. All right?"

"Yeah. All right." I suck in a deep breath and then glance over at Madd, who's pacing around.

"I'll go."

Madd turns and gives me a simple nod like that shit was already a forgone conclusion. "After you."

May as well get this shit over with. I huff.

"Go on." Kalief pushes me forward.

I swallow my pride and march forward.

"Hey, girl. You tore it up," a woman praises as I thread through the crowd.

"Thank you."

More people agree and slow me up to take pics and shake my hand. By the time I make it to VIP, I feel like a full-fledged star and my anger at this Diesel character has evaporated—a little.

Madd makes the introductions. "Diesel, Miss Cleo. Miss Cleo, Diesel."

I nod at a honey-colored devil with piercing green eyes. The way that he's smiling, he clearly thinks that he's making an impression on me. He's not. I don't like—or trust light-skinned pretty boys. Give me a dark brother like Idris Elba or a Morris Chestnut—and then we can talk.

He stands and towers above me by four inches. "Evening, Cleo. Won't you join us?"

Us? I look around and notice the other people crowded around the table. The bitch next to Diesel with weird patches on the side of her face glares like she's ready to jump my ass. Bitch, please. Ain't nobody want your man.

"I don't want to interrupt—"

"Nonsense. Please." He gestures to a vacant spot across from him. "Sit."

I stiffen. "Is that another order?"

Diesel laughs and two dimples wink at me. "It's just a request."

"In that case." I sit. But his chick—or pit bull—is almost growling at me.

"Loved your set," Diesel says reaching for a new glass. "How long have you been performing in the local circuit?"

"A few years."

"What would you like?" he asks, referring to the open liquor bottles on the table.

"I'll pass."

"It's on the house."

"I don't drink."

That causes snickering to ensue around the table while surprise colors Diesel's face.

"Is that right?"

I flash him a thin smile, hoping this will help him just get to the point of why he asked me up here. If there's a deal to be made, then let's do it.

"All right then." He settles back in his chair. "Let's talk business. Have you had any labels come calling?"

I hesitate. I don't know what he knows or what lie Kalief has told. "A couple."

"And what happened?"

Kalief happened. "Let's just say that things didn't work out."

"Maybe if you got yourself a *real* manager?"

I hit pause. "I thought you were just interested in producing?"

"You're a producer?" his young side chick asks.

Diesel appears annoyed. "Scar, why don't you go powder your nose while me and Cleo talk business?"

She flinches, but clearly she knows her position because she falls back. As *Scar* climbs out of her seat, she gives me another blast of her icy glare.

Diesel watches her, too, as if he's not sure whether she's going to try to whip my ass or not. Not too comforting.

"I'll be back," she says.

Girl, bye. I give her a look. She better not let this fucking dress fool her. I can scrap with the best of the hood rats.

Scar moves away from the table, instantly changing the mood at the table.

Diesel glances at the rest of his crew. "Leave us."

They spring up and scatter away like roaches.

"Good. *Now* we can talk." He smiles.

"About what? I'm not looking for a manager."

"You haven't heard what I can offer you."

"I'm sure it's the world."

"Maybe I'll even toss in the moon, too."

"Funny."

"I'm serious." He sets his drink down and leans forward.

"Tell me what you want and I'll make damn sure that it happens."

"Is that right?" I want to call bullshit, but something tells me that this man is serious.

"I know a star when I see one. I want to be the one that makes all your dreams come true."

"You look like you want to fuck me."

"That, too."

There's a heat *and* a coldness emanating from him that scares me. "I'm not interested."

"Has your bootleg manager-slash-boyfriend ever told you that you're gorgeous when you lie—even more than when you're singing?"

"I should go." I stand up.

Diesel does, too. "I'm not giving up."

"Look, Mr. . . . . ?"

"Just call me Diesel."

"All right. Diesel, there's clearly been some type of misunderstanding. My manager told me that you were looking for new artists and he thought that my performing here would be the best way to get your attention."

"Mission accomplished. And now that you got it, what do you want to do with it?"

"Look. I'm just looking to make a deal—a *professional* deal. Nothing else. I have a man—and I'm faithful."

His cocksure grin grows. "Good to know."

I shake my head. "Have a nice night, Mr. Carver."

He blocks my path. "You know. I don't take no for an answer and I always get what I want. And right now"—his lustful gaze devours me—"you're at the top of my Christmas list."

60

Qiana

Heaven is hanging upside down, sucking on your nigga's monster-size cock while he eats your pussy like an all you can eat buffet. Club Diesel was a major success. Once Cleo kept out of my sight, I was able to enjoy myself. Diesel is a boss on the come-up here in Memphis and I want to be his ride or die. Right now, he has my pussy tuned up the way I like it.

Before this session is over, I'm twisted in all kinds of ways. I've long lost count of the number of nuts I done busted, but I must've passed out, 'cause I wake feeling drugged and the space next to me is empty. I bolt up to find Diesel sitting calmly across the room in a leather chaise, petting a large Doberman pinscher.

"Sleep well?"

Something about the way his eyes rake over me gives me pause. But then he smiles and my pussy thumps all over again. "What can I say? Your dick is a monster."

"You got some good pussy." His lips inch wider. "Maybe you should come work for me. Stack some paper."

"*Work?*" My neck rocks to the side. "Nigga, I ain't no fuckin' hooker."

"No. You're gonna need some tips and more practice before you work *up* to that level—but you got potential."

"Potent—muthafucka!" I spring out of the bed.

The Doberman growls, barks, and then leaps from his master.

I reel back. "Nigga, do something about your damn dog!"

"Solomon, sit," Diesel commands.

The dog sits.

I eye both the dog and its master. "What the fuck?"

Diesel laughs. "Calm down. As long as I'm around, he's harmless."

"And when you're *not* around?"

Solomon growls again, and his white, fanged teeth glisten with thick slob.

Diesel's smile expands. "I hardly see a reason for that shit to ever happen—but if it does, my advice is to bend over and kiss your ass good-bye." He snaps his fingers and Solomon returns to his side.

I reach for the top sheet to cover up.

"No. Don't do that," he says. "I was enjoying the view."

Stuck between being turned on and pissed off, I weigh whether I'm going to follow his order.

"Please," he adds, easing the tension between us.

Giving in, I lower the sheet.

"Lay back and spread your legs."

My heart trips around in my chest as I ease back against the pillows and open my legs.

"Open your pussy."

Biting my lower lip, I glide my hands between my legs and peel open my juicy lips so that my pink clit pokes out to say hi.

"Nice." Diesel whips his cock out of his black briefs. "Play with it."

I smile, liking where this is headed. I dip my hands low and ease two fingers into my slick pussy. After a few deep strokes, I press two more fingers inside and get a good rhythm going.

High off the wet, slopping sounds my pussy makes, Diesel

pumps his fat cock to my rhythm. We're both caught up watching each other.

The pressure in the base of my clit builds, and my breathing thins and becomes choppy.

Diesel stands and walks toward the bed, his hand still pumping his fat cock. "Don't stop," he tells me while pre-come drips like clear, maple syrup over my titties. The shit is so pretty that it sends me over the edge.

"Aaaaaaahhhhhh."

Growling, Diesel's head rocks back as warm come spray-paints my body.

Once I catch my breath, Diesel sits next to me on the bed and pulls out some goodies from the top nightstand drawer.

"You down?" he asks, chopping lines in some blue candy. Hell. I bet if he turned off the lights the shit would glow.

"What's that?"

"Something that will fuckin' blow your mind. Best shit that you'll ever taste. Believe me."

My curiosity is piqued. "For real?" I look at the pretty lines again.

"Wanna hit?"

"Sure. Why not?"

He smiles and hands over a small crystal tube. "Ladies first."

I put the shit to my nose and attempt to snort up a fat line. I don't get but a few crystals up my nose before I jump back with my nostrils on fire.

"FUCK!" I squeeze, rub, and try to wipe it out of my nose. "What the hell is that shit?"

"Easy. Easy." He presses a hand against my chest. "Ride the wave, baby girl. Ride the wave."

I try to relax, but my heart races while I twitch and bounce in place.

"That's it," he soothes.

In the next second, the world melts away and my head feels like its floating off my shoulders.

"You like that, Scar?"

"*Fuuuuuck yeah*," I croak.

"Good. Good." He sets the mirror aside and slides next to me. *Did he do a line, too?* I don't know or at least, I'm not sure.

"I want you to feel real good," he says.

Mission accomplished. Whatever this shit is, it's better than sex. Every cell in my body is having an orgasm.

"Scar, can you hear me?" Diesel asks.

"Mmmm-hmmm."

"Good." He presses his hand in between my thighs to play with my sensitive clit. "I wanna ask you a few questions—and I want you to tell me the truth. You think you can do that?"

"Mmm-hmm."

"Good. Now tell me how you know my cousin's wife, LeShelle Murphy?"

61

Ta'Shara

I bolt through my front door with Dime close on my heels.

"Ta'Shara. Ta'Shara," she keeps hissing behind me.

Go away and leave me alone. I thread my way through the crowd, but bounce around like a pinball as I bump into one chick after another.

"Hey! Where's the beer?" Mack shouts. She's on the couch, holding court.

When I blaze past her without answering, she shouts, "Hey, T! Where are you going?"

I ignore her again.

Mack shifts her focus. "Dime!"

"Later," Dime snaps, remaining hot on my trail. I reach the hall bathroom and attempt to slam the door shut, but Dime isn't having any of that.

I don't have time to argue since I go straight to the toilet bowl and retch.

"Jesus," Dime says, closing the door behind her.

Fuck her. I heave until my stomach muscles seize up.

"Are you going to be all right?"

"I don't understand what the fuck just happened."

"You blasted that shotgun-toting jihadist's head off. You

had to. He was about to murk our asses. We'd be lying on that liquor store floor next to my girls Nisha and Emerald. Thank God you're a quick shot. Where in the hell did you learn how to shoot like that?"

"Are you kidding me? It was fuckin' luck! I just learned how to shoot today."

"Humph. Well, you're a natural. You saved our asses. Now we just gotta get our story straight and everything is going to be cool."

My stomach knots and I retch for another five minutes. *Some boss diva I am.*

BANG! BANG! BANG!

The bathroom door rattles.

"Ta'Shara?" Mack yells. "Are you all right in there?"

"She's fine," Dime shouts back.

Mack opens the door and pokes her head inside. "What the fuck? Why can't she answer for herself?"

Dime turns to challenge her. "Do you mind? We're having a private conversation."

"That would mean something to me *if* I was talking to you."

"Bitch—"

"OUT!" I shout, swiping the spittle from my mouth. "GET OUT."

Dime flashes Mack a smug smile.

"Both of you," I clarify. "NOW!"

Dime spins her wide eyes toward me and I ignore her to tell Mack, "Get her out of here."

Mack returns the smug smile as she holds open the door. "You heard her."

"Fine. Whatever," Dime addresses me again. "We'll talk later." She storms out.

Mack lingers. "Are you all right?"

"Just go," I plea.

"All right. I'm going." She exits the bathroom and closes the door behind her.

I jam my hand into my pants pocket and scoop out my cell phone to call Profit—but the call goes straight to voice mail.

"Noooo." I disconnect the call and dial again.

Voice mail.

"Damn it, Profit. Where in the fuck are you?"

62

Qiana

I feel so fucking good. I'm riding a star across the sky and I don't give a shit if my ass never comes back to Earth. I'm tied down, spread eagle, Diesel's fat tongue lapping my pussy like he's a starved man.

"Look at your nasty ass." Diesel's voice floats to me.

At the praise, my body convulses in the nest of tangled, silk sheets. My mind zooms to another galaxy. Whatever that shit was I snorted, it got me twisted up real good.

"More . . . more . . . more," I repeat like a scratched CD.

Diesel's deep, rumbling laugh surrounds me. In the back of my head, I'm aware there's a few sinister notes in there too, but I can't get myself to give a damn.

"Lick it all up, boy. That's it. She loves that shit."

One solitary warning bell goes off in my head, but I'm still stuck on one word. "More. More. More."

Woof! Woof! Woof!

Another warning bell.

Somehow I find the strength to peel open my eyes. Everything is blurry and spinning around. I blink a few times, but I'm confused to how Diesel is sitting beside me while there's a steady lapping against my clit.

I blink again. "More?"

"Whatever makes you happy, you dirty bitch." There's no smile on his lips when he say this. He dips his fingers into a jar and pulls out what looks like globs of honey. My eyes track his fingers as he then smears the honey into my pussy.

"Lick it up, boy."

I look down between my legs just as his *dog,* Solomon, bows his head and licks up the honey.

"More . . . more . . . more." *Shit. I'm about to come.* I grab hold of my bondages and inch up the bed away from the dog's tongue, but this orgasm is coming whether I want it to or not.

"More . . . more . . . moooooorrrrreeee!" Another mind-shattering explosion detonates and my mind warps and the next time that I open my eyes it must be hours later because the silk ties from my hands and legs are gone and the bedroom is once again empty.

"What the fuck?" I sit up and throw my legs over the side of the bed. When I attempt to stand up, a low growl come from somewhere across the room.

Solomon.

I know this muthafucka hasn't left me alone with this crazy ass dog. I sniff the air and catch the sweet smell of honey. A memory surfaces and my stomach pitches around until I have to make a mad dash toward the adjoining bathroom.

Woof! Woof! Woof!

The dog takes off after me, but I reach the bathroom first and slam the door.

Bam!

The dog crashes into the door. I drop in front the toilet and empty my guts. It goes on and on until I'm dry heaving and cramping. What seems like a lifetime later, I collapse to the floor, sweating profusely.

What the fuck is happening to me? I keep asking that question until my eyes grow heavy and my mind numbs against the cool marble floor.

In a blink, iced-cold water hits my face and I jolt up.

"Welcome back," Diesel says, laughing.

Blinking and sputtering, I glance around. I'm still in the bathroom, but in the shower.

"You gave me a little scare there," he says. His eyes say otherwise. I get the impression that he wouldn't think twice about burying my ass in the backyard if I overdosed.

The idea chills me more than the shower's cold water.

"Are you all right?" he asks.

I nod while searching my memory to what happened. There's a lot of missing pieces and some pieces I worry whether they're real or not. How in the fuck do I ask whether or not he had his damn dog eat me out while I was drugged?

"Here. Let me warm this water up and get you some tow-els so you can clean yourself up. It'll probably make you feel better." He turns on the hot water and then leaves.

Feeling that I have my bearings, I reach for his bottle of liquid soap and wash my body with my hands. While I wash, I review my choppy memory again. I'm not sure about much of it, but I remember throwing up, the dog, the honey, orgasms, the drugs—the questioning. I stop. He asked a lot of questions.

What did he ask?

What did I say?

I don't know, but I have a sickening feeling that I fucked up. I rack my brain for twenty minutes before shutting off the shower. When I step out, fresh towels are sitting on the vanity. I wrap the largest one around me and then creep back into the bedroom.

Diesel is getting dressed.

Stunned, I blink. "Going somewhere?"

"I have some business I have to tend to," he says, shrug-ging. "I called you a cab."

"What?"

"I would take you back home myself . . . but it's out of my way."

He's so cold, my feelings trip up. I look around the room. "Where's Solomon?"

"Miss him, do you?"

Heat blazes up my face. "I'm having some problems remembering some shit. What the hell happened?"

"Only what you asked for." He laughs.

More. More. More.

"What the fuck does that mean?"

He glances over his shoulder. "It means get your shit so I can roll the hell up out of here." A muscle twitches along his temple. "Get. Dressed."

"You sick muthafucka!" I launch toward him with fists flying. I get two good hits in before this nigga backhands me so hard that I fly across the room. Before I can peel myself up, Diesel is on top of me, unleashing holy hell with his closed fist. "Bitch, you got me fucked up." He growls.

With each punch of his fist, the pain multiplies.

"STOP!"

"Nah, bitch. I've done warned you about getting turned up with me."

BAM! BAM!

"STOP!"

"You're fuckin' with the wrong nigga with this shit."

BAM! BAM!

"STOP. STOP. Please stop!"

His fists are unrelenting. He keeps punching until he's either tired or bored. When he finally climbs off of me, I can't see. I can't yell. I can't breathe.

"You're going to learn. I'm going to train your ass if it's the last muthafuckin' thing I do," he vows, hovered above me. To make his point, he kicks the fuck out of me and then stalks off. Coughing and choking on my own blood, I struggle to sit up.

HONK! HONK!

"Your fucking cab is here," he says, pressing his clothes back in place in front of the mirror. "Get your shit and get out."

Despite feeling like shit on a stick, I scramble for my clothes.

HONK! HONK!

"You better not miss that muthafucka," he threatens.

Scared, I stumble out of the bedroom, still dressing as I go. Tears blur my vision as I hop into the backseat of the cab and give the driver my address.

The old man takes one look at my fucked-up face and flinches.

"Go!"

"Yes, ma'am." He shifts the car into drive.

After a final look at the house, I swipe my tears. "Fuck you, nigga."

Diesel's deep baritone floats around my head *"How do you know my cousin's wife LeShelle Murphy?"*

"I killed a bitch for her."

Fuck.

BANG! A car sideswipes the cab.

The taxi careens and swerves over the road before the driver pulls over and hits the brakes.

I'm tossed around and I bang my head on the window.

"Are you all right?" he asks.

"Yeah. What the fuck happened?"

"I'm about to find out," he says, opening his door. But the minute he hops out a single gunshot sends him crashing back into the car.

"What the fuck?"

The back door jerks open, and then the one chick I least expect pops inside with a gun aimed at my head.

"Surprise, bitch. Remember me?"

LeShelle.

63

LeShelle

"Get out. We're going to take a drive."

Qiana's eyes bulge in her busted face. "No."

I click off the safety. "You can try me if you like," I tell her. "But you know that I won't hesitate to splatter your brains all over this muthafucka. GET OUT!"

Qiana snaps out of her shock and then slowly climbs out of the cab.

I direct her to the Escalade, where Avonte is waiting behind the wheel.

Qiana keeps her chin up, but I still see the telltale signs of fear.

"This gotta feel like déjà vu for you," I say snidely. "Isn't this how you and your girls got the drop on Yolanda?"

"You know it is."

"Drive," I tell Avonte.

When we peel off, I return my attention to Qiana. "I do recall us discussing a plan for that night, *but* I don't remember anything in those plans about you performing a C-section and taking her baby."

"You never said anything about that bitch even being pregnant."

"Because the shit was irrelevant. I wanted her *and* that bastard dead. Imagine my surprise when I get out of the hospital and see all over the news that you didn't fulfill your end of our arrangement." I press the gun harder against her skull. "Do I look like the kind of bitch that you can fuckin' renege on?"

Her Adam's apple bobs again, but at least she doesn't bother to spit out no bullshit that's going to cause me to discharge a bullet into her skull.

"Where's the fuckin' kid?"

The apple bobs.

"Think twice before lying to me."

She takes the warning to heart. "He's safe."

"Do you have him?"

"No."

She says the shit so quick and so smooth that my bullshit meter doesn't go off, but that's not enough for me to say that I believe her. "I want the kid," I tell her.

"What? Why? So you can kill him?"

"Why the fuck do you give a shit? He's not yours." I cock my head and study her. "Don't tell me that you've grown attached to that lil muthafucka?" I'm unable to contain my laughter. "What the *fuck* does your ass want with a miscellaneous bitch's baby?"

Her Adam's apple bobs again while the bitch doesn't bother to put up a single argument. I get the sense that there's something that I'm missing here. Every bitch is always on the come-up and working some damn angle. I know because I'm the same fuckin' way. *Why the hell would she hang on to this baby?*

My eyes narrow on her. "You were going to try to fuck me, weren't you?" I hit on something because her eyes bulge again. I can't help but laugh because I'm going to fuck her, too. Doesn't matter. The situation will be rectified, but first I need to find out how bad the damage is.

"What did Diesel ask you?"

"What?"

"The nigga you spent all night fuckin'. I know that his ass grilled you. What did you tell him?"

"I don't know what you're talking about. He didn't ask me anything."

"Bitch." I remove the gun from her head to aim and shoot out the side window.

POW!

Qiana screams.

Avonte jumps and swerves out of her lane into oncoming traffic.

A horn blares and she quickly jerks the wheel so that she can get back in her lane.

Once everyone finishes panicking, I press my gun back against Qiana's temple. "Don't make me ask the fuckin' question again."

"I don't remember," she shouts, her eyes wetting up. "We did a few lines and . . . I don't remember a large chunk of what happened."

"Then what happened to your face?"

"He, we, uh . . . I fell."

Even Avonte laughs at that.

"Bitch, you really must think I'm stupid." But drugging the bitch sounds like some dirty bullshit that grimy ATL nigga would pull. "Did he ask you about me?"

She shakes her head too fast for me to believe her. "I thought you said that you didn't remember shit?" I challenge.

"Well, why would he ask me about you?" she asks. "Why would he even think we know each other?"

I laugh. "Maybe you'll enjoy this one, but you've been sleeping with the enemy, bitch. Diesel is a Gangster Disciple— by way of Atlanta—and my nigga's cousin."

The color drains from Qiana's face.

"Don't you even bother to find out who the fuck it is you've opened your legs for, trick? Or do you Flowers jump on every dick that's in front of you?"

Silence.

"You're a stupid muthafucka, I swear. You shouldn't be playin' in a game that you don't know the name *or* the fuckin' rules." I look up to see where we are. "Pull over in that parking lot," I tell Avonte.

Qiana tenses and shakes her head.

"Don't worry. You've bought yourself a little time."

Qiana swallows and relaxes.

I smile while enjoying the surge of power I have over the moment. I could blow her brains all over this backseat and be done with it, but I can't shake that that shit would be a mistake. I need to take care of the baby first before clipping this last loose string.

Taking a deep breath, I remove the gun from Qiana's head and soften my tone. "Look. You gotta see this shit from my point of view. We agreed to do a job together and then I see that you didn't go through with your end of the deal. You can see why I might be a little . . . *confused*, don't you?"

She doesn't answer.

"Now, I'm going to give you a second chance to fulfill your end of the bargain. Bring me the kid and then everything can go back to being normal. You don't know me and I don't know you and never shall our paths cross again. Got it?"

Silence.

"This is the part where you nod or say that you understand."

"I understand—but I'm going to need some time . . . to get him and bring him back."

"How much time?" I growl.

"A week."

Is she fuckin' with me? "You have forty-eight hours. We'll meet in Hacks Cross in Winchester across from the golf course—ten o'clock. Now get out."

Swearing under her breath, Qiana quickly climbs out of the car. I lock the door and climb into the front seat. "Forty-eight hours. Don't be late—and don't have me come looking for you again. You won't like what happens if I do." I tap Avonte on the shoulder and we peel out of the parking lot, laughing at the busted bitch the whole way.

64

Lucifer

My ass is so sprung. I love how Mason can't stop touching, kissing, and talking to my stomach. These intimate moments are showing a side of him that I've never seen before. Our situation is officially on display. A few in the Vice Lord family have been bold enough to tell me it's about time that I found myself a steady lay and they hope it'll do some good in mellowing my ass out. Those conversations end with me threatening to cut their dicks off. Since they can't tell when I'm joking, they fall the fuck back and play their positions.

In the quiet times, I can't help but be aware of how my pregnancy is changing the dynamics and my position within the set. The shit is fuckin' with me. I've worked so hard to get these niggas to forget that my ass even has a pussy. Now my growing belly erases all that shit.

Fuck. I still have a couple of Crippettes I have to take care of before I kick my heels up and take it easy. "Lynch stashed those other bitches somewhere," I tell Mason, while curled in a comfortable nook under his arm.

"If he's smart," Mason says, kissing the top of my head. "We are talking about his wife."

Hurt, I lean back at his casualness. "What—you ain't still heated over what they did to Bishop?"

"What the fuck do you think?"

I relax. "Good. I want to make sure that we're on the same page."

"I got you—and I'm on that and that Angels of Mercy bullshit, too. You know we're gonna get some heat for that shit."

"Fuck those muthafuckas."

"Humph. We can only fight so many wars at one time, baby."

"What are you saying?"

"That we don't want to overextend ourselves—but, for right now, your man is always two steps ahead on those mutha-fuckas."

My man. "Always, huh? That shit is news to me."

"Smart ass." Mason chuckles and nuzzles my neck. "I promise you, I'm on this shit," he says. "You ain't gotta do a damn thing, but take care of my son." He caresses my stomach again.

"Son?" I smile. "What makes you think that it won't be a girl?"

He puffs out his chest. " 'Cause my swimmers paddle with three legs, you feel me?"

I punch his shoulder. "Boy, stop."

"What?" He laughs. "You asked."

"Well, *I* think that it's gonna be a girl—and she's gonna be a boss bitch, like her mother."

Still chuckling, Mason inches closer. "You got me on that shit. You *are* a bad bitch—and I won't be mad if you spit out a mini-Willow this time around, but *next time. . . .*"

Grinning, I shoot back. "Next time? Who said that there's gonna be a next time?"

"*I* did," he answers, matter-of-fact. He lifts my chin so that he can meet my gaze head-on. "Now that you're officially my lady, I plan on pumping that belly with a whole lot of babies." He leans over me and reaches underneath my pillow.

"What are you doing?"

"Getting ready to have a serious discussion." He pulls out a velvet black box and sets it on my belly.

My heart skips several beats. "What's that?"

"What do you think it is?"

I blink like an epileptic to keep my eyes dry. I don't trust myself to even hazard a guess as to what's in the box.

Now chuckling at my speechlessness, Mason plucks up the box to open it and then sets it back down.

I gasp at the sight of a platinum and diamond ring.

"So what do you say? Do you want to officially be my lady—for life?"

Stunned, I can't stop staring.

"Well?" Mason prompts. "Has a cat got your tongue?"

"I'm thinking. I'm thinking." I smirk, removing the ring from the box and examining it.

"Stop frontin'." He laughs with a nervous note.

He takes the ring from my hand and slides the rock into place on the right finger. "There. Now don't ever take that muthafucka off."

I cock my head, thinking.

Sweat pops out along his forehead. "Willow," he barks, impatient.

After torturing him long enough, a smile breaks across my face. "Of course, I'll marry you. What took you so long?"

Excited, Mason whoops and then kisses me senseless. It's the happiest moment of my life.

65

Hydeya

"I had a nice time last night, *Mrs. Hawkins,*" Drake says, peppering the side of my neck with kisses as I rush through my morning ritual in front of the bathroom vanity.

"I had a nice time, too. It was good to get out and be among the living."

He chuckles in my ear. "I wasn't talking about the club. I was talking about what came after." He squeezes my ass.

I smile remembering last night's four mind-blowing orgasms. "Yeah. That was really nice, too."

"Yeah? I brought out my best moves."

"I noticed. I almost broke out my scorecards. Perfect ten."

Drake brushes his shoulders off and I can't help but press a kiss to his adorable face. But this day is no different from the others. By the time I'm sitting down for breakfast-slash-lunch, my mind is back on the job.

"So that's it? Case closed?" Drake says, correctly guessing where my mind is.

"I'm afraid so," I say, disappointed. "The chief and mayor couldn't have made their position any clearer. They aren't interested in Captain Johnson's dirty secrets. They're convinced that important, innocent political bystanders will be dragged down in the mud with his name."

"Important, innocent political bystanders? Wow. Those are four words that aren't usually in the same sentence." He cracks open a couple of pistachio nuts and tosses them into his mouth.

"All I know is that my hands are tied," I tell him and then sulk with my cooling cup of coffee.

Clearly deciding to ease off the guilt trip, Drake abandons his snack to give me a peck on the forehead. "All you can do is the best that you can do."

"Yeah. I know."

"Well . . . at least now you can dedicate some more time to that double homicide you guys discovered out in the woods."

"Yeah. Yippee." My mind zooms to Qiana and the secrets she's holding to close to the chest. Fortunately, the girl isn't the sharpest tool in the toolbox. It's a matter of time before she or one of her friends crack.

Drake waves. "Hello? Anybody there?"

I blink. "I'm sorry. What?"

He taps the refrigerator calendar. "I was reminding you not to forget what day it is."

My eyes follow to the day circled in red. "Oh. Fuck."

"Yeah. Oh. Fuck." He flashes me a sympathetic smile.

"Can my life get any shittier?" I exit the kitchen and head straight to the bar to top off my cold coffee.

"Better make it a double shot," Drake says.

"I would if I could."

"Hey." Drake eases behind me. "You don't have to go if you don't want. You don't owe him anything."

"He's my father."

"So? It's not like he raised you or anything. Your stepfather did that shit. Frankly, he's the one that turned your life around and put you on the straight and narrow."

"You're Dyson's cheerleader now?" I ask, surprised.

"What? Just because he doesn't like me doesn't mean that I can't give him credit when credit is due. Back in the day, you were just like all these gangbangers you're chas-ing now."

"True. But shit has gotten much worse. These streets chew people up and then spit them out. They rip apart families and destroy hope." I shake my head, thinking of the volume of violence I deal with day after day. "I became a cop because I thought I could make a difference—but I'm just a cog in a system that's been broken for a long time. No one is interested in justice. No one is interested in changing things." Hopelessness weighs down my shoulders as I recall images of Tyneshia Gibson, Yolanda Terry, Melvin and Victoria Johnson—and the entire slaughter at the Royal Knights motorcycle club. "It's all just bullshit."

"You can't believe that," Drake says, rubbing my back.

"Sadly, I do." Caught up in my feelings, my eyes burn with restrained tears.

My husband cloaks me in his arms. Silent, he holds me while I feed off his strength. He's always been good at this. Honestly, I don't know what I'd do without him.

After a good five minutes, I sigh and withdraw. "I better go."

"Are you sure?"

"Yeah. The sooner, I get this shit over with the better." I down the rest of my coffee and then grab my shit before heading toward the door.

The ride out to the Federal Correctional Institute isn't a long one, but it feels like it. I'm a jumble of nerves as I park outside of the facility's release gates and kill the engine.

I don't know how long this shit is going to take. The people inside operate on their own timetable and everybody else has to deal with it. *Drake is right. I can back out.*

I eyeball the keys dangling from the car's ignition, but I don't turn the muthafucka over.

What is it about little girls and their damn daddies? Even the ones who don't stick around.

The morning drifts into the afternoon and at some point, my eyes grow heavy with sleep.

TAP! TAP! TAP!

I bolt up from behind the wheel with my heart in my throat. When I cut my gaze toward the half-open window, it crashes into a pair of eyes that look like mine.

"Hey, princess!"

I can't believe that he still calls me that. "Hello, Isaac."

66

Lucifer

Riiiinnnng. Riiiinnng. Riiinnnng.

Mason moans and rolls away from our tight cocoon, and I miss his warmth immediately. "I betcha it's your mom again," he sighs.

I groan. "Shit." I don't want to deal with her right now. I can't go through another crying session on how much she misses Uncle Skeet's crooked ass. I don't give a fuck how much of a bad daughter that makes me.

Riiiinnnng. Riiiinnng. Riiiinnnng.

"Maybe you should go over and see about her," Mason suggests. "I mean—if she's still having a hard time."

"You preaching? How about you? Your momma has been tryna get you to talk for a solid week. When are you going to talk to her?"

"I know," he mumbles. "But I know what she wants to talk about and I ain't interested in hearing it."

I wait, but Mason changes the subject. "I know you couldn't stand Uncle Skeet, but I gotta say that I miss the old G. Without him keeping the Gangster Disciples in check, our fuckin' workload has tripled."

"Especially since your brother survived that crash, too." *Shit.* I can't believe I said that.

Mason's good eye narrows as his jaw hardens. "What the fuck did you say?"

Fuck it. It's out now. I hit this shit head-on. "Look, Mason. I know the family secret, okay? Dribbles stole you from your *real* mom."

"That's not true!" His face purples as he leaps from the bed. "She *saved* me from my biological piece of shit." He paces around. "Did she tell you that Smokestack pulled me out of an oven? A goddamn oven! If the bitch was a *little* higher that day she might've even turned the muthafucka on," he rages. "Blood or no blood. I don't owe those muthafuckas nothing. I don't know them and I'm not interested in getting to know them."

The shootout at the Rivergate Industrial Park swarms to my mind. The way Python hollered for Mason was with raw emotion. "Look. It's none of my business—"

"You're right. It's none of your business," he snaps.

My look tells him to check his tone.

"Sorry," he growls and resumes pacing. "But you don't know how angry I am even thinking about that shit."

"And you feel *nothing* now that you know that your real mom, Alice, is dead?"

"You goddamn right!"

"Liar."

His face twists, but I can read him better than anybody.

"You'll never get a chance to ask for her side of the story—and there's always three sides. Yours, theirs, and the truth. The way I see it, your biological mom had to feel some kind of way about how shit went down. Alice kidnapped her own sister and tortured her for months, thinking that she had something to do with *your* disappearance. Then she massacred Uncle Skeet and his wife and then snatched Dribbles on her way out. *That* doesn't sound like a mom that didn't love you—that didn't want you."

Mason's pacing slows while emotions race across his burned and disfigured face.

"You made up your mind about how shit went down for a long time and now you're refusing to consider that your version of events might not be true."

Before Mason has a chance to answer, his cell phone goes off.

"I bet *you* it's Dribbles," I tell him.

Mason walks over to the nightstand and reads the name on the screen. His shoulders collapse with dread.

"Talk to her," I urge. "You need to get to the bottom of this or it's always going to fuck with you."

"What am I going to say if she insists that I meet that *woman?*"

"You mean your aunt?"

He flinches, but then nods.

"I can't believe I'm about to say this, but maybe you should. For closure. We ain't got to tell nobody about it. Go and speak your mind."

Mason sighs and picks up his phone.

"I'll give you some privacy." I climb out of bed and reach for my robe. "I'll go down and make you some breakfast."

"Yeah?" His lips curl. "You cooking for me now?"

"This *one* time," I joke.

Mason stops me when I reach the bedroom door. "Babe?"

"Yeah?" I look up.

He hesitates for a moment and then says, "Thanks."

"You're welcome." I head out of the bedroom and then down the stairs. In the living room, Profit is sprawled on my couch. I tighten the belt on my robe as I note the many bullet keloids across his shirtless chest. As I walk past him, he pops up, startled.

"Morning," I greet.

When he sees me, his initial confusion clears and he grunts in reply.

Whatever. With Mason's ring on my finger, I'm not about to let Profit's constantly pissy attitude ruin my day.

"What time is it?" he asks.

"Do I look like a clock to you?" I say and keep it moving. Profit's weighty gaze follows me.

Once I get the coffee brewing, Profit pops up at the kitchen door. "You mind if I make myself a cup?"

I shrug. "Help yourself."

He moves into the kitchen, takes his time searching and slamming the cabinet doors.

Before I know it, he's in my way, bumping and backing into me while I try to get this pancake batter going.

"Second cabinet next to the sink," I snap.

Profit cuts me a sharp look.

"That's it." I plop my batter onto the counter. Before my tirade gets started, Mason races into the kitchen.

"Willow, I got to run out," he says and then looks to his brother. "Morning, bro." He gives him a brief one-shoulder hug and then smacks him on the back. "Did she show you?"

Profit frowns and then glances back to me. "Show me what?"

Mason's chest swells proudly as he tells me, "Show him the ring."

Still chomping on my anger, I hesitate, but then finally hold up my hand to flash Profit my ring.

Something flashes across Profit's face, but it's too quick for me to identify.

"Congratulations," he says, without warmth.

"Now you know that you're gonna be my best man, right?" Mason gives him another hard whack on the back.

"Sure, man. You know I got you," Profit responds, finally trying to fake an emotion.

"Good. Good." Mason returns his attention to me. "I'm gonna have to take a rain check on breakfast. I'm gonna head out and go see Dribbles about . . . that thing we discussed upstairs."

"Really?" I ask, surprised. "Good. You want me to go with you?"

"Nah. Nah. This is something I need to go on and get out of the way."

Profit frowns. "Is something wrong?"

Mason waves him off. "Nah. Everything is cool." He walks over to me, pulls me into his arms for a playful kiss. "No banging today. I want you to start to take it easy." He rubs my belly. "You feel me?"

For once I'm going to bask in his protectiveness—even though we both know that I'm not the kind of chick who's gonna sit on the sidelines.

He gives my ass a firm squeeze and then hurries out of the house.

After the front door slams, Profit resumes glaring at me.

"What?" I bark, jamming my hands on my hips.

"Did I say something?"

"Know what? You need to roll up out of here and go back to your own crib. The party is over by now. Get your chick to make your ass some coffee. I'm not in the mood to put up with your moody ass. Get out!" I storm out of the kitchen to escort him out of my house.

"What the hell is wrong with you?" Profit asks, stalking behind me.

"Ain't shit wrong with me." I grab his shirt from off the couch and toss it over my shoulder at him without breaking my stride. "I'm tired of the bullshit. Clearly, you got a problem with me—and as far as I'm concerned you can roll that shit up and smoke it. I ain't got no more time for it."

"Who said that I had a problem with you?"

Incredulous, I spin around and confront him. "You've got to be shitting me, right? You have done nothing but give me attitude for months. I don't know what the hell I did to you, but I don't give a shit anymore. If memory serves me correct, I was the one that got your ass to the hospital after your girl-friend's sister used your chest for target practice. I'm the one that hunted and carved up the niggas that held you down while you took that ass beating. I'm the one that called *you* up and took you on that drive-by to get at that chick—and *still* I get nothing but attitude. What the fuck is your problem?"

For five seconds, Profit glares at me and then, without warning, snatches me into his arms and kisses me.

67

Ta'Shara

The house is a wreck, but at least the last few Flowers have finally stumbled out of the house. I haven't slept a wink. I'm wired and pacing back and forth waiting for Profit. I've lost count of how many times I've paged and texted him—so on top of freaking out about my own homicide situation, I'm worried whether things are cool with him.

"C'mon, Profit. Where are you?" I pace around the house with my heart in my throat and my nerves twisted in knots. Every other minute those three gunshots sound off in my head. *POW! POW! POW!*

A bullet to the chest.

A bullet to the throat.

A bullet to the head.

"Fuck!" I slap a hand around my mouth and then race off to the bathroom, where I dry heave until my stomach cramps and I'm begging God for mercy—but why should he care? Why would he listen? I'm a murderer—and I'm going to hell, or most certainly jail.

"This can't be happening to me. This can't be my life." I lay my head on the toilet bowl and dissolve into tears. "Profit where are you?"

THUMP!

My head springs up. "Profit?"

No answer, but someone is walking around in the house. I climb off the floor and scamper back to the front. Mack and Romil are in the kitchen, trying to figure out how to work the coffeemaker. "What are you two still doing here?"

"What does it look like?" Mack asks, scooping out coffee grounds for the filter.

"Nah. I mean. I thought that everybody had already left."

"Well, clearly you didn't check the backyard. And don't ask me how we got out there, but I woke up in y'all hammock." She yawns without covering her mouth.

"Oh." I look toward the front door, wishing Profit would return already.

"You want coffee?" she asks.

"No. I'm good." I grab my cell phone from off the sofa and check for missed messages. "Where in the fuck is he?"

Romil props her head up to reveal her bloodshot eyes. "Problem?"

I wince. "You look like hell."

"Clearly, you didn't look in the mirror while you were in the bathroom," she sasses back. "You don't look so hot yourself."

While the coffee brews, Mack shuffles to the table and plops down next to her girl. "So when are you going to tell us what in the hell happened with you and Dime last night?"

My heart jumps into my throat. "Happened? What do you mean? Nothing happened."

They share matching frowns.

"Yeah. That was convincing," Mack deadpans and then crosses her arms to wait me out.

"Something had to happen," Romil eggs on. "Four of you left and only two returned—"

"And without beer," Mack added.

"I don't know what you're talking about." I glance back at my phone. *C'mon, Profit.*

"Humph. If you're looking for your man, he crashed at Lucifer's last night."

"What? How do you know that?"

Mack shrugs. "He came back home last night while you were supposedly at the liquor store and told me to tell you that was where he was going to be."

"Then why didn't you tell me?"

Another shrug. "Forgot."

Relieved, I bolt for the door and race to Lucifer's house two doors down, but just when I lift my hand to knock, a scene through the window catches my attention.

It's Profit and Lucifer . . . kissing.

68

Momma Peaches

"Back again?" Pastor Hayes asks, joining me at the front pew. "The revival isn't until later tonight."

"I know. I, uh, guess I just needed some more prayer. I hope you don't mind."

A smile blooms across his face. "Not at all. All are welcomed here."

I nod and then wait for him to leave, but he lingers, grinning. "I have to tell you, Peaches. It really warms my heart to see that the Lord has brought you here. I know you've been out in the street game for a long time and I've heard about your family troubles in the news." He reaches for my hand. "I want you to know that God brought you through all that for a reason. It's good that you're opening your heart now. It's never too late."

"Thanks. I needed to hear that, Rowlin—I mean, Pastor."

"Rowlin," he corrects, patting my hand.

We sit through a warm silence and then he finally stands.

"I'll leave you to your prayers," he says. "I do need to make a trip out to the hospital to pray for a few of our members, but you can stay as long as you need to."

"Thank you." I watch him walk off and then suck in a deep breath. This meeting may go better than I'd expected. I chose to meet Mason here because it was the only neutral place I could think of. That, of course, is only if Dribbles is able to fulfill her promise. I still don't know what I'm going to say or what I'm going to do when he walks through that door.

What is he going to do?

I don't know. Maybe I should pray about this. Quickly, I fold my hands together and bow my head. "Dear Lord, I know me and you'd come to an understanding and I'm down here struggling and doing the best I can. I said that I was never going to ask you for another thing if you got me out that basement, but I'm going to need you to forgive me because I'm going to have to go back on that promise." I tighten my prayer hands together. "It's too late for Alice to reunite with her sons, but if Dribbles and I—and of course, you—can pull this off and reunite Terrell and Mason, maybe it can be the first step in healing and bringing some peace to this family.

"Lord, I've been in the game a long time and you've seen me do my dirt, but I'm trying to change my ways. If I could just take Mason into my arms and welcome him back. *The Carvers* are his flesh and blood. He belongs with *us*. This time we're going to do right by him. I just ask that you open his heart and mind so that he will give us a chance. I pray these things in Jesus's name. Amen."

Clap! Clap! Clap!

Mason?

I open my eyes and turn with my heart leaping, only for my hope to dash at the sight of Josephine's big ass blocking the church's door. "What the hell are you doing here?"

She stops clapping and settles one hand on her hip. "*I* am where I'm supposed to be," she snaps. "This is *my* church. You're trespassing on my shit now with your fake-ass holy-roller routine. Nobody is buying that '*I'm saved*' shit. Not after all the hell you done raised, the niggas you done fucked, and my *grandson* you done killed." Josie lifts a gun.

The hackles rise on the back of my neck. I stand and inch

out into the aisle. "So what do you think that you came here to do, Josie? Huh? What—you a gangster bitch now?"

Her smile flickers. "I came to finish what Alice promised me she'd do when Arzell and I helped her escape that hospital: send your ass straight back to hell."

POW!

I drop like a stone against the church's blood-red carpet. Oxygen disappears and I choke on my own tongue. However, I remain alert, even if I can't call or scream out.

The bitch shot me! I can't believe it!

Josie's big ass shakes the floor as she runs out of the building. I can smell and taste my own blood—but there's no pain. In fact, I'm numb—all over—and weak. I need to rest my eyes—just for a minute. I'll get up later and go after that bitch. Yeah. That's it. I'll get her later.

I close my eyes, but then hear a door open somewhere and the floor shakes again, before a deep, roaring voice booms, "WHAT THE HELL?"

"Peaches," Dribbles's unmistakable voice shouts.

I open my eyes again to a pair of black Timberlands rushing toward me. In the next second, I'm being turned over and my upper body lifted into a pair of strong arms.

"She's been shot," an authoritative baritone says.

"Should you be moving her?" Dribbles asks.

"We got to get her to a hospital."

My vision blurs and I squint at the faces staring down at me. The man holding me is big, and his face is badly burned. I reach out to touch him, but end up painting him with my blood. "Mason, is that you?"

He hesitates and then comes clean. "Yeah. It's me."

Finally. He's here. Joy puts me on a high that I've never been on before. I can only hope that it's reflected in my face, but I know that I'm crying because he becomes all blurry again.

"I don't understand," Dribbles say in a near panic.

"What happened?" Mason asks me.

That fat bitch shot me!

"Can you tell me who did this?" he asks again.

Hell. I thought I spoke out loud, but maybe I didn't. Damn. I need some water and why is it so cold in here?

I hear the doors again and I roll my head to the left and immediately recognize the two men entering: *Terrell and Diesel.*

"Oh shit," Mason says. "Yo, man. This ain't what it looks like!" He lowers me back onto floor. When he stands, he's completely covered in my blood.

"WHAT IN THE FUCK DID YOU DO TO MY AUNT?" Python roars, but instead of waiting for an answer, he goes for his gun.

Mason goes for his.

In the next second, the Power of Prayer Baptist Church is filled with the sounds of gunfire.

BOSS DIVAS

De'nesha Diamond

ABOUT THIS GUIDE

The questions that follow are included to enhance
your group's reading of this book.

Discussion Questions

1. Lucifer was on a murderous rampage to avenge the death of her brother. Do you think that she took things too far?

2. Do you think Captain Hydeya Hawkins was promoted because she was qualified for the job or that the city believed that she would be easy to manipulate?

3. Qiana is clearly in over her head. Do you think that it was a wise idea to have kept the baby? Why do you think she really kept the child?

4. Python's mysterious cousin, Diesel, seems to be slinking around the edges and even frightens his Aunt Peaches. Do you think he has a hidden agenda or do you believe he really has Python's back?

5. Do you think Shariffa's actions are more about taking over the street game or a vendetta against the Gangster Disciples?

6. Mason has returned from the dead. Had he not, do you think that Lucifer would have been able to maintain her position? Do you think that Profit would've challenged her for the throne?

7. Ta'Shara's safe world has been turned upside down. Now that she's been accepted into the Flowers, do you think that she'll find the courage to get out or succumb to the gang life?

8. Do you think that LeShelle's attraction to Diesel is because of his power, or is it sexual?

9. Momma Peaches tried to turn her life around, but she doesn't seem to be able to catch a break. Do you think that she did the right thing in trying to bring the brothers together?

A sneak peek . . .

King Divas

Coming soon from Dafina Books

Lucifer

My eyes pop open in the semi-darkness and I catch the gleam of a steel blade as it makes a sweeping arch down onto the bed. Instinct kicks in. I roll to the other side of the bed instead of reaching for the gun tucked underneath the pillow.

The knife slices into the pillow-top mattress with a muted *thump!* And *RIP!*

I keep rolling and crash over the left side of the bed. The gravitational pull is cruel and I hit the hardwood floor at an alarming speed and belly first. Pain shoots through every limb of my body. I struggle to block it out as my hand flails to the piece tucked into the nightstand, but my movements aren't as quick as normal.

"Grrrrrrrrrrgh!" My attacker leaps over the bed and grabs a fistful of my hair before trying to yank it out of my scalp.

Another bolt of pain rips through me while cartoon stars spin behind my eyes. Before I can get that shit to stop, my head is mashed into the wall. I make a big dent into that muthafucka because I taste bits of plaster. Balling my fist, I strike out and sock this bitch dead in her pussy—my first clue that my attacker is indeed a woman.

She grunts, but the punch has less effect than if my attacker had been the opposite sex. It's enough for her to release her hold on my head for a millisecond, and I'm able to sweep my arm out and hit those knees.

She drops like a stone.

I spring up on this bitch, but I lose a millisecond when something warm rushes down my inner thigh. A punch squares across my jaw and knocks my ass to the left, where I trip over the foot of the bed.

More cartoon stars. *This bitch is pissing me off.*

My attacker launches toward me again. I block her first two blows, keeping my elbows together, like Bishop taught me. When I come out from behind an arm shield, I wail on this bitch like a heavyweight champion. In no time, I pin her to the floor, my fist as bloody as my thighs.

She whimpers.

While I got this bitch under the moonlight spilling through the window, I snatch the wool mask from her head. When her hair stops tumbling out, I'm shocked. *Shariffa?*

This bitch ain't this muthafuckin' bold. But there's not a damn thing wrong with my eyes.

Enraged, I wrap my hands around Shariffa's neck and squeeze with everything I got. "You stupid bitch!" My arms tremble as my grip tightens.

"ACK. GACK." She chokes, clawing at my hands.

"That's right. Let me hear death rattle around in your chest. When you're gone, I'm going to take my fucking time peeling and slicing your ass from your head to your toe."

"ACK. GAAACK."

"There's not going to be anything left of your treacherous ass. I'm going to make damn sure of that shit."

"ACK. GAAAACK!"

This bitch is seconds away from passing from this world to the other when an ungodly pain shots up from abdomen and straight to my brain.

"Aaaaaargh!" The scream is out of my throat before I have

a chance to stop it. Then it happens again and I pitch over and hit the floor, gripping my belly.

I'm only mildly aware of Shariffa coughing and wheezing in air next to me.

Pull it together. Pull it together. But I can't. *The baby!*

Shariffa scrambles for the knife.

Somehow I swing out an arm and grab her ankle. She trips with a loud *thump!*

Desperate, Shariffa kicks me with her free leg. My head. My neck—and then a firm kick straight to my belly.

"Aaaaaaargh!" *This dirty bitch.* But she's going to win this battle. The knife glistens in the moonlight before it makes its second swinging arch straight toward my baby.

From *Fistful of Benjamins*
By Kiki Swinson & De'nesha Diamond
Available October 2014 wherever books and eBooks are sold.

Prologue

"Oh my God, Eduardo. What do you think they will do to us? I don't want to die . . . I can't leave my son," I cried, barely able to get my words out between sobbing and the fact that my teeth were chattering together so badly.

The warehouse type of room we were being held captive in was freezing. I mean freezing like we were sitting inside of a meat locker type of freezing. I could even see puffs of frosty air with each breath that I took. I knew it was summertime outside, so the conditions inside where we were being held told me we were purposely being made to freeze. The smell of sawdust and industrial chemicals were also so strong that the combination was making my stomach churn. Eduardo flexed his back against mine and turned his head as much as the ropes that bound us together allowed. He was trembling from the subzero conditions as well.

"Gabby, just keep your mouth shut. If we gon' die right now, at least we are together. I know I ain't say it a lot, but I love you. I love you for everything you did and put up with from me. I am sorry I ever let you get into this bullshit from the jump. It wasn't no place for you from day one, baby girl," Eduardo whispered calmly through his battered lips. With everything that had happened, I didn't know how he was staying so calm. It was like he had no emotion behind what was happening or like he had already resigned himself to the fact that we were dead. In my opinion, his ass should've been crying, fighting, and yelling for the scary men to let me go. Something. Eduardo was the drug dealer, not me, so maybe he had prepared himself to die many times. I hadn't ever prepared myself to die, or to be tied up like an animal, beaten, and waiting to possibly get my head blown off. This was not how I saw my life ending up. All I had ever wanted was a good man, a happy family, a nice place to live, and just a good life.

"I don't care about being together when we die, Eduardo! You forget I have a son? Who is going to take care of him if I'm dead over something I didn't do?" I replied sharply. A pain shot through my skull like someone had shot me in the head. I was ready to lose it. My shoulders began quaking as I broke down in another round of sobs. I couldn't even feel the pain that had previously permeated my body from the beating I had taken. I was numb in comparison to the pain I was feeling in my heart behind leaving my son. I kept thinking about my son and my mother, who were probably both sitting in a strange place wondering how I had let this happen to them. That was the hard part, knowing that they were going to be innocent casualties of my stupid fucking actions. I should've stuck to carrying mail instead of stepping into the shit that had me in this predicament. I was the dummy in this situation. I was so busy looking for love in all the wrong places. I had done all of this to myself.

"Shhh. Don't cry. We just have to pray that Luca will have mercy on us. I will try to make him believe that it wasn't us. I'll tell him we didn't do it. We weren't responsible for everything that happened," Eduardo whispered to me.

"But he's the one who got us out so fast. I keep thinking that he only did that because he thought we might start talking. He got us out just so he could kill us, don't you see that? We are finished. Done. Dead," I said harshly. The tears were still coming. It was like Eduardo couldn't get what I was saying. We were both facing death and I wasn't ready to die!

"You don't know everything. Maybe it was something else. Let me handle—" Eduardo started to tell me, but his words were clipped short when we both heard the sound of footsteps moving towards us. The footsteps sounded off like gunshots against the icy cold concrete floors. My heart felt like it would explode through the bones in my chest and suddenly it felt like my bladder was filled to capacity. The footsteps stopped. I think I stopped breathing too. Suddenly, I wasn't cold anymore. Maybe it was the adrenaline coursing fiercely through my veins, but suddenly I was burning up hot.

"Eduardo Santos," a man's voice boomed. "Look at you now. All caught up in your own web." The man had a thick accent, the kind my older uncles from Puerto Rico had when they tried really hard to speak English.

"Luca . . . I . . . I . . . can . . ." Eduardo stuttered, his body trembling so hard it was making mine move. Now I could sense fear and anguish in Eduardo's voice. That was the first time Eduardo had sounded like he understood the seriousness of our situation.

"Shut up!" the man screamed. "You are a rat and in Mexico rats are killed and burned so that the dirty spirit does not corrupt anything around it," the man called Luca screamed. I squeezed my eyes shut, but I couldn't keep the tears from bursting from the sides.

I was too afraid to even look at him. I kept my head down, but I had seen there were at least four more pairs of feet standing around. Eduardo and I had been working for this man and had never met him. I knew he was some big drug kingpin inside the Calixte Mexican drug cartel that operated out of Miami, but when I was making the money, I never thought of meeting him, especially not under these circumstances. I was helping this bastard get rich and couldn't even pick him out of a police lineup if my life depended on it.

"Please, Luca. I'm telling you I wasn't the rat. Maybe it was Lance . . . I mean, I just worked for him. He was the one responsible to you. He was the one that kept increasing everything. I did everything I could to keep this from happening," Eduardo pleaded his case, the words rushing out of his mouth.

"Oh, now you blame another man? Another cowardly move. Eduardo, I have people inside of the DEA who work for me. I know everything. If I didn't pay off the judge to set bail so I could get you and your little girlfriend out of there, you were prepared to sign a deal. You were prepared to tell everything. Like the fucking cock-sucking rat that you are. You know nothing about death before dishonor. You would've sold out your own mother to get out of there. You failed the fucking test, you piece of shit," Luca spat, sucking his teeth. "Get him up," Luca said calmly, apparently unmoved by Eduardo's pleas.

"Luca! Luca! Give me another chance, please!" Eduardo begged, his voice coming out as a shrill scream. His words exploded like bombs in my ears. Another chance? Did that mean that Eduardo had snitched? Did that mean he put me in danger when I was only doing everything he ever told me to do? Did Eduardo sign my death sentence without even telling me what the fuck he was going to do? I immediately thought about my family again. These people obviously knew where I lived and where they could find my mother and my son even after they went back home. A wave of cramps trampled through my guts. Before I could control it, vomit spewed from my lips like lava from a volcano.

"What did you do to me, Eduardo?" I coughed and screamed through tears and vomit. I couldn't help it. I didn't care anymore. They were going to kill me anyway, right? "You fucking snitch! What did you do?" I gurgled. I had exercised more loyalty than Eduardo had. The men that were there to kill us said nothing and neither did Eduardo. I felt like someone had kicked me in the chest and the head right then. My heart was broken.

Two of Luca's goons cut the ropes that had kept Eduardo and I bound together. It was like they had cut the strings to my heart too. Eduardo didn't even look at me as they dragged him away screaming. I fell over onto my side, too weak to sit up on my own. Eduardo had betrayed me in the worse way. I was just a pawn in a much, much bigger game. And all for what? A few extra dollars a week that I didn't have anything to show for now except maybe some expensive pocketbooks, a few watches, some shoes and an apartment I was surely never going to see again. Yes, I had been living ghetto fabulous, shopping for expensive things that I could've never imagined in my wildest dreams, but I had lost every dollar that I had ever stashed away for my son as "just in case" money. I had done all of this for him and in the end I had left him nothing.

"Please. Please don't kill me," I begged through a waterfall of tears as I curled my body into a fetal position. With renewed spirit to see my son, I begged and pleaded for my life. I told them I wasn't a snitch and that I had no idea what Eduardo had done. I got nothing in response. There was a lot of Spanish being spoken, but I could only understand a fraction of it; so much for listening to my mother when she tried speaking Spanish to me all of my life.

"I promise I didn't speak to any DEA agents or the police. Please tell Luca that it wasn't me," I cried some more, pleading with the men that were left there to guard me. None of the remaining men acted like they could hear me. In my assessment, this was it. I was staring down a true death sentence. I immediately began praying. If my mother, a devout Catholic, had taught me nothing else, she had definitely taught me how to pray.

"Hail Mary full of Grace . . ." I mumbled, closing my eyes and preparing for my impending death. As soon as I closed my eyes, I was thrust backwards in my mind, reviewing how I'd ever let the gorgeous, smooth talking Eduardo Santos get my gullible ass into this mess.